"'Lisabeth."
he w...

Another roll of thu... ...stable. Cain pressed ... ...d. "'Tis over now," he ... ...passed."

The hard knot of tears in her throat began to dissipate as she allowed herself to be soothed by the softness of this man's voice, by the gentleness of his hands.

"Your hair smells of strawberries," he whispered close to her ear. She felt the feather touch of his breath skim along the curve of her ear, causing her to shiver with untold sensation. A touch of hair, and then his cheek was pressed lightly to hers, warm flesh to cold, joined by the wetness of her tears. His mouth lingered at her temple. Her breathing grew shallow. Her mouth ached to trace that shape with her lips. That she could expect greater kindness from a hired killer than from her own betrothed caused a flag of warning to spring up in her...

Cain tipped her head back. Her cheeks were dry now, but he could still taste the faint salt taste of her tears as he gave her a light, grazing kiss in the center of her mouth. Then he was angling her head to the side and slanting his mouth hard across hers, branding her with a thief-taker's passion...

The White Raven

Also by Mary Mayer Holmes

The Irish Bride

Published by
POPULAR LIBRARY

The White Raven

Mary Mayer Holmes

POPULAR LIBRARY

An Imprint of Warner Books, Inc.

A Warner Communications Company

POPULAR LIBRARY EDITION

Popular Library® and the fanciful P design are registered
trademarks of Warner Books, Inc.

Cover illustration by Morgan Kane

Popular Library books are published by
Warner Books, Inc.
666 Fifth Avenue
New York, N.Y. 10103

 A Warner Communications Company

Printed in the United States of America

First Printing: August, 1988

10   9   8   7   6   5   4   3   2   1

To Susan Hubbard—wife, mother, daughter, friend, neighbor, and the best marketing person in the city of Madison, maybe in the entire universe.

To Rosemary Ferris—for listening, laughing, commiserating, and always knowing the right questions to get my brain in gear.

To Brian—of all the wonderful things that have happened in my life, you're by far the best.

With Love—
M. M. H.

acknowledgments

With special thanks to Dr. Jonathan Dohnalek for sparing the time to consult with me on my infinite questions about eighteenth-century medicine.

In England, before the establishment of a formal police force, criminals were often captured and brought to justice by ordinary citizens who received small rewards for their services. During the reign of William and Mary, the system of rewards was given a firm legal basis by an act that offered forty pounds for the conviction of a highwayman. The informer to whom the reward was given also received the highwayman's horse, weapons, and money. This act established a new kind of private policeman or bounty hunter—the thief-taker.

chapter
one

In the southwest of England, three days' saddle ride from the clamor of London and a day's ride from the Cornish coast, a weathered granite plateau scars the smoothness of Devon. The land is a vast open space of crags and mists, of wind-tortured brush and stark isolation. It is a region of moor dominated by swift-running streams and towering granite tors that the wary claim are not so much eroded shafts of rock as fingers raised in warning.

The land is known as Dartmoor. It is a bleak place, a godless place, and on the night of 27 April 1752, it was a meeting place.

It was called Hound Tor and it rose from the loins of the virgin granite like a great spiny reptile that had escaped extinction. From the encroaching peat bog it strained upward, arching against the sky, its animal's back skinned of flesh so that only its granite vertebrae could be seen radiat-

1

ing outward. No footpath led to its summit. Low-lying mists obscured hazardous tracts of turf and bracken along its base. It was a treacherous, windswept place where loose boulders could crush a man and where wild dogs prowled among the outcropping of stone. Viewed in daylight Hound Tor was a rugged tower of rock whose vast scattering of crags, of fractured ledges and scored bedrock bore testimony to almost inconceivable antiquity. At night, looming out of the mist with the moon lighting its crouched shoulders, Hound Tor seemed to breathe with the pulse of an ancient beast, suddenly alive and, despite its sheer mass, on the move.

A dog howled.

Miles Loveland groped for a handhold along the granite scarp. His heel slipped on the rock beneath him, sending a shower of loose stone down the slope and a stab of fear through his vitals. Scrambling for solid footing and finding it, he paused and looked upward. Through the blue black mist of night he spied the pinnacle of the tor ten feet above him and he exhaled a relieved breath.

Another whining howl. Closer still.

Removing a rumpled handkerchief from his coat, Loveland mopped the sweat from his face. Damn but the sound of those dogs rasped at his nerves. He shoved the handkerchief back in his pocket and felt beneath his fingers the butt of his pistol—loaded with shot and ready to blast the snout off one of those bastards.

The brow of Hound Tor terminated in a crown of sawtoothed spires. Behind these spires the rock sloped like the steps of an amphitheater to form a shallow crater. Miles Loveland leaned panting against one of these spires. The wind battered his body, its cold intensity making his ears ache. He peered down into the black pit of the crater and cursed the clouds that absorbed the moonlight, yet from what little he could observe, nothing was afoot. With his heart beating at twice its normal rate and a band of perspiration prickling his neck, he descended.

He took no more than three paces before his attacker was upon him. Loveland struggled with the gloved hand that clamped itself across his mouth, but when he felt the point of a dagger at the soft flesh below his ear, he stopped his thrashing to become a docile prisoner.

"'Tis better," his attacker breathed, and recognizing the voice, Miles rolled his eyes and brandished his fist in the air. With a rumble of laughter the man released him.

"Holy Mother of Christ, I wish you'd stop doing that!" Miles turned to face his attacker. He fingered his mouth for bruises and worked his jaw back and forth. "I swear that one of these nights you're going to scare me so badly that my heart is going to stop beating. And then where will you be? London agents for the kind of work we're involved in are not easily found."

"A man cannot afford to take unnecessary chances, agent, especially in the kind of work we're involved in." The man jumped down onto the next level, his cloak flapping out behind him. "Come along. We have much to discuss."

An outcropping of boulders protected the floor of the crater from the thundering gusts of wind that ravaged the summit. To the lee of one boulder the man built a peat fire within a circle of stones. He handed a cloth sack to Loveland in exchange for a parchment scroll, and while Loveland dumped the contents of the sack onto the bedrock, the man paced before the fire, skimming the words that his superior in London, Gellicoe Lint, had penned. Grit and sand crunched beneath the heels of his heavy jackboots. As he walked, the star-shaped rowels that rotated on the ends of his spurs rattled and spun and glinted in the firelight.

"He doesn't sound pleased."

"Indeed he's not," said Loveland. "He doesn't know why the masquerade in Bridestone Barrow, but he trusts you know what you're doing, so he'll go along with you for a time. He says the old marquess is above reproach and can't understand what you can possibly gain by snooping about the estate. Is this all the money?" He ruffled the bank notes in his hand. "We'll never get rich at this rate."

"For you, agent, 'tis never enough." The man hunkered on one knee. He crossed his arms atop his bent leg, and while he studied the substance of the parchment, Loveland studied him.

His eyes were a pale blue that seemed to burn with a memory he longed to avenge. Across his chest he wore a bandoleer of knives. From his hip there hung a rapier whose lethal point knew well the feel of flesh and the taste of blood. On his right hand he wore an open-fingered glove that Loveland had never seen him remove, but no man dared ask what secrets lay beneath the black wool. He had no past; he had many pasts. Some said he looked foreign —that his ancestors might have been ancient seafarers washed upon Cornish beaches, or black-haired sailors who survived the defeat of the Armada. The fishermen in St. Ives claimed he had sailed with them to catch pilchard. The tinners in West Penwith swore he had mined ore with them in their underground shafts. Everyone knew how he acquired the break that left the hook in his nose. "From blocks and tackles," said the fishermen. "From shovels and picks," said the tinners. Whatever his past, he always looked to be smoldering beneath the surface, a bed of dry tinder, ever ready to ignite.

When the blue-eyed man had committed the information on the parchment to memory, he rolled the document up and fed it to the fire. The edges curled and blackened like a soul burning in hell. "Tell me of the girl."

Loveland stuffed the money into the sack then removed a leather snuffbox from his coat. He held it close to the fire. "I should first tell you of the marquess. Quintus St. Mary is his name and he's outlived six wives, two sons, and most of the livestock in Bridestone Barrow. His granddaughter's name is Elisabeth. She appears to be his only living relative. Sad thing about the St. Marys. They breed exquisite bloodstock, but they seem incapable of breeding sufficient offspring to continue the line." Unlatching the box, he took a pinch of the powdered tobacco between his thumb and forefinger and inhaled deeply. "Ahh. Excellent stuff. Excellent. Would you care for a pinch?"

The man loosed his rapier and with a sportive thrust trained its flashing point at the corpulent mound of Loveland's stomach. "What I would like, agent, is for you to finish supplying me with the information I requested."

Loveland sucked in his breath. His ruddy coloring deepened. "People are supposed to mellow with age. You only grow more impatient."

"With due cause, agent. With due cause." He sheathed his blade. "Finish what you began."

Red faced and wheezing, Loveland fumbled for his handkerchief and swabbed his face once again. "I tell you, I can no longer tell when you jest and when you're serious. Now where was I? Oh, yes, the girl. She's betrothed to a

Cornish gent by the name of Penmarck. Thomas Penmarck, Earl of Moreleigh. Due to be married in a bit less than a month. This Penmarck is an old friend of the family's. Bought some bloodstock from the marquess when the girl was a child, so he's been in a position to watch her grow to womanhood. The match will be a profitable one for Penmarck. He's marrying himself a fortune. His heirs will inherit the wealth of both the St. Marys and the Penmarcks, and his firstborn son will become one of the most powerful men in England."

"What of the girl's parents?"

"Dead. Both of them. Happened some time ago. There was an uncle too. Quite a scandalous affair I'm told, but he's gone too."

A hint of a smile touched the man's lips. "Gone? Or dead?"

Loveland snapped shut the lid of his snuffbox and returned it to his pocket. "The estate will be entailed to the girl's firstborn son. Gone. Dead. What does it matter?"

"It matters," said the man in a low voice. "It matters a great deal."

Loveland could not fathom the fellow's mood this eve. In all the years he had dealt with him, he had never known him to be so unsettled. "They'll be expecting you at Maidenstowe. Tell them you have a writ from Henry Fielding."

"And the thief?"

Loveland rolled his eyes. "The bogus thief who has been plaguing the village of Bridestone Barrow, at your behest, has filched his last chicken. He's returned to London unmolested. Good thing, that. I can see the look on Lint's face should one of his finest accidentally have his neck stretched by the hangman's hemp. The stage has been properly set for your arrival. Lint says he'll be willing to wait a solitary month for you to finish your business. Four weeks, no longer."

"Four weeks." The man's laughter escaped in an ugly, distorted sound. "He would wait four weeks. I have waited a lifetime. There is treasure at Maidenstowe, agent. And I will have it. All of it."

He rose, unbending his long, booted legs, and tossed the front panel of his cloak over one shoulder. The agent looked up. Where moonlight bathed the granite turrets above and behind the man's silhouette, a dark shape stirred, and the agent sucked in a cold, dreaded breath.

"Sweet Christ. Behind you."

From the eastern crown of the tor the aberrant form grew into life. Its eyes glowed with an evil iridescence. Its paws skittered and scratched along the surface of the bedrock. Wolflike, its squat head was slunk low on its neck and its flews were drawn back, exposing pinkened gums and fanged teeth that frothed with saliva. A steady, malignant growl rumbled from its chest and rolled down into the crater, paralyzing Miles Loveland whose sudden fear scented the night wind. Like an aphrodisiac it summoned the hound who, sniffing it, was drawn downward.

Loveland sprang to his feet, his face moist with fat beads of sweat. "The creature is probably blooded and looking for a plump morsel to sink his chops into." He smoothed the vast bulge of his stomach with an unconscious gesture then snatched his pistol from his pocket. "By God, he'll find no feast here tonight."

The blue-eyed man smothered the muzzle of the pistol in his fist. "Put the gun away." With steady eyes he watched the hound descend. It was a foul, skulking thing, a re-

minder of the primal decadence that still roamed the earth.
"Give me your neckcloth." He unsheathed his rapier.

"Why don't you just shoot—"

"Your neckcloth!" he hissed.

The agent's numbed fingers flew to his throat. He unraveled the muslin cloth and handed it to the man who wrapped it around his sword blade and flamed it in the dying embers of the fire.

The hound had reached the floor of the crater by now, but seeing the flaming skewer sear the night he retreated back up the broken incline, hunkering there, panting, biding his time.

The man held the improvised torch high in the air. With his eyes stalking the hound, he motioned Loveland for his saber then struck out toward the eastern slope.

The hound sniffed again and the wind brought to his nostrils the scent of this other human. And on him, he could smell no fear. Confused, the animal retreated again, loping farther up the craggy terrain. Halfway up he turned.

The cloaked being still pursued him. His heavy boots tramped over rocks that should have been impossible to scale and from his body there emanated an odor that the mongrel had never smelled in a human before—an odor that was clear and strong and signaled his intent. The animal's senses plunged into discord as the scent intensified. With a wildness of spirit he bounded to the lip of the tor and there awaited his prey.

The man climbed. The burning muslin threw off curls of black smoke. His breath steamed through his lips. His spur rowels spun their deadly points on their axes again, and again, and again. Ten feet below the summit he could feel the animal's insane growl as if it were vibrating within his own skull. He vaulted onto the granite ridge. The salivating hound crouched, eyes gleaming, teeth bared. The crosswinds that bludgeoned the summit licked the torch, splitting the flame into many tongues. The man thrust the flaming blade close to the mongrel's face, baiting him, enraging him, so that when the wind snuffed out the last burning thread of muslin, the hound sprang forward, leaping for the man's throat.

The saber rose and with a ferocious whoosh sliced downward, severing the mongrel's neck.

The man resheathed his rapier, content that he had just provided a source of undefiled pleasure for the carrion birds who would greet the dawn.

They called him Cain.

He was the thief-taker.

The village of Bridestone Barrow was located on the northeastern fringe of Dartmoor, where the bleakness of moorland gave way to gentler hues and billowing patchwork fields. A league west of the village, on a high bluff that commanded a spectacular view of distant tors and flattened hills, sat the great house of the parish, Maidenstowe.

Fenced by high stone walls and skirted by flagstone terraces that boasted stone benches, statuary, and circular fountains, the manse boasted an acre of roof over three stories of finely dressed stone whose pigment was wrought in soft, buttery tones. A great, sweeping U-shaped fortress, it seemed impervious to wind and weather. So it sat solid and austere, as it had for well over three centuries, anchored to the underlying bedrock, secure as a Norman keep.

On the morning of 28 April, Thomas Penmarck sat in

Maidenstowe's east drawing room, contemplating how thoroughly he despised the decor. The walls screamed out at him in red Genoese velvet. The marble fireplace was sculpted into a frieze of ravening lions. And the arms and back of every chair was an intricate carving that combined grotesque snake-tailed birds and falcons' beaks in a harsh twist of ebony.

Having been skewered in the back by the pointed bill of one avian atrocity five minutes earlier, Thomas sat straight-spined on the edge of a chair that might have been conceived in a medieval torture chamber. He vowed that after Elisabeth became his wife, the first thing he would do would be to refurbish the halls of Maidenstowe with something more dignified than screaming red velvet.

His eyes drifted over the hanging portraits of three centuries of St. Mary earls, viscounts, and barons. The second thing he would do would be to banish Elisabeth's forebears to a chamber where he wouldn't have to look at them. He thought it a miracle of nature that a family whose members bore striking resemblances to monkeys and bovines could produce a creature as lovely as Elisabeth. The dark hair and dark eyes that had stamped themselves on each St. Mary visage for centuries had diluted themselves in the year of Elisabeth's birth. Her hair was a pale white blond, her eyes a clear, brilliant blue, and her bones were not mean and squat like her father's, but lithe and delicate.

He perused the faces of Quintus St. Mary's two deceased sons before he came to the portrait of Elisabeth at sixteen. His eyes lingered there with a hotness that filled his chest with its warmth. She was prettier now than she had been at sixteen. Her face had lost its baby's roundness and her smile was more self-assured. He gazed lower, his pulse thrumming when he considered how well she had filled out her woman's shape. With an unconscious gesture he rubbed his palm in anticipation of the day when he could lay bare her flesh, when he could slide his tongue across—

"Thomas? You should have sent word you were coming."

He stood as Elisabeth made hesitant passage into the room. She was dressed in a pale yellow wrapping gown, her eyes still soft with sleep, and when he saw the ribbon tie that secured her gown at the waist, he stretched his hand and knew that stripping the wall cover at Maidenstowe would not be the first thing he would do after he was married. Nay. It would not be the first thing at all.

"Elisabeth." He kissed her hands in greeting. "I thought to surprise you."

"Indeed you have, m'lord. 'Tis so infrequently you deign to grace us with your presence that I questioned the truth of Frith's announcement."

Thomas Penmarck was the catch of the season—titled, monied, intelligent, free of disease, and exceedingly well formed for a man twenty-three years Elisabeth's senior. He had been born with one leg shorter than the other, but the heel of his boots had been built up to compensate for his infirmity, so few people knew of his imperfection. He was a man of ordinary height with the square, stocky build of a peasant, but his raiment proclaimed his lordly status. His white damask coat was embroidered with a wealth of silver and gold threads. His breeches were white damask; his waistcoat a dazzling silver brocade that shone like mica. Conforming to the trend in recent fashion his face was painted with a thin application of white lead and his cheekbones were bright with carmine smudges. He wore a powdered wig that was brushed high over a pad and waved over his temples in stylish pigeon's wings. His appearance was impeccable, but it was not his appearance that caused Elisabeth's disquiet in his presence.

"Your palms are so hot, Thomas. Have you been warming them over the fire?"

He laughed at her question as he escorted her to the nearest love seat. A lace pinner cap hid the hair she had hastily knotted atop her head. Double lappets of crepe streamed down the back of her cap to her waist, and as she sat, one lappet fluttered over her shoulder, draping itself across her bodice. Thomas fingered the end of that streamer and smoothed it down the angle of her cheek. "Should I apologize for arriving unannounced?" His voice was a seductive undertone, but Elisabeth, uncomfortable with his nearness, pulled away from his hand and scratched her cheek, leaving his hand suspended stupidly in the air.

"You have no need to explain any of your actions to me, m'lord." Throughout the years she had learned that he expected to answer to no man, much less any woman, so she knew her comment would please him, even if her gesture did not.

Coughing to clear his throat, he curled his fingers into his palm and withdrew his hand, seeming to accept her coolness as he always had. He graced her with a stiff smile as he lowered his hand to his lap.

"Have you no curiosity how I spent my time these past weeks, Elisabeth? I've been preparing a place for you, and a more splendid place you will never find. I've refurbished the suite of rooms that my brother and his wife occupied when they were alive. The ones on the west front of the house, overlooking the ocean. I'd thought never to change those rooms, to keep them as a shrine to Cicely and Justin's memory, but you've made me rethink all that. When a man takes a bride, he should concern himself with the future, not the past. I think if Cicely and Justin were alive today, they would applaud my change of attitude. So I've exorcised twenty-four years of memories from those rooms and they now await your arrival."

"That's kind of you, Thomas." She offered him a wan smile, but she could not muster the enthusiasm that she knew he expected.

Thomas shook his bewigged head. He searched her face with eyes that were black as ebony inlay. "Why is it that every time I mention Cornwall, you look as if I have sentenced you to Newgate?"

Elisabeth fidgeted with the end of her lappet. "I don't look as if—"

"Yes, you do!" Slapping his thighs he heaved himself to his feet and began pacing before her. He thrust his hand out for emphasis, prompting layers of white lace to cascade downward from his wrist. "Quintus has done me a great disservice by rearing you the way he has. Never allowing you outside the bounds of the parish. Caging you within the walls of this house like some nightingale."

"That's not so, Thomas."

"It *is* so."

"I leave every week," she defended. "Quintus accompanies me to the workhouse every Wednesday."

"Indeed! You visit the one place where no sane being should ever set foot. When I think of the vermin and pestilence—" Spinning around, he stabbed a bejeweled finger at her. "There will be no visiting workhouses after we are

married, Elisabeth. You'll not carry the foulness of those
wretches into Thirlstane with you."

The words he mouthed seemed blasphemy to Elisabeth.
"'Tis the responsibility of every gentlewoman to aid those
less fortunate than herself, Thomas. My grandmother performed such duties. My mother performed such duties.
Now 'tis my responsibility to—"

"—obey the dictates of your husband! I will not have
you jeopardizing your well-being. Once in Cornwall you
will cease all activity with workhouses. You will obey me
in this. Do you understand?"

She stared at him, the brilliant blue of her eyes clouding
with emotion. She wanted to grab his elegant powdered
wig and yank it down over his nose. Resisting the urge,
she merely sat and stared at him, saying nothing.

This was the Thomas Penmarck who caused her disquiet, for he was a man vastly different from herself, quick
to anger, slow to admit a wrong. He needed to be right on
every point of order and demanded that his opinion be the
collective opinion of everyone in the room. He was a
mirthless man. A dour man. She was not an argumentative
person, but she discovered she could argue with Thomas
on any topic he cared to discuss. She had known him all
her life, but after all these years she still did not feel as if
she knew him. And what she did know of him, she did not
like. She would marry Thomas Penmarck because it was
her duty to wed the man whose estates and titles her grandfather had decided would most benefit her future offspring.
But, in truth, she abided her grandfather's choice not from
a sense of duty.

She abided it from a sense of fear.

Thomas lifted his brows at her lack of response. "Elisabeth?"

"I have a gift," she said, refusing to bend to his dictates in the matter. "It . . . I have a talent. For growing herbs. For prescribing their use. Emma calls it a gift."

"Emma." Thomas spat the word out like a grape seed. He resumed his pacing. "Emma is an addlepated crone who—"

From the front of the house there came the echoing clank of brass on brass. Thomas stopped midstride and looked toward the corridor. "Are you expecting visitors?"

"Frith will see to it."

"Indeed." He shook his head. "You will find when we travel to London that polite society pays their respects in the afternoon, not at ten o'clock in the morning. You live among peasants, Elisabeth. I would venture I am marrying you not a moment too soon to rescue you from bucolic obscurity. Now, what was I saying?"

Elisabeth felt her skin straining across her cheekbones. "You were saying how you thought the woman who has played the role of mother to me since my youth is an addlepated crone."

Thomas looked over his shoulder at her, frowning at the way his words sounded on her lips. Bowing his head, he walked back to the love seat. "I misspoke, Elisabeth. Forgive me. But it galls me that you risk life and limb for people you don't even know. I want no ill befalling you." He seated himself and brought her hand to his mouth, brushing her knuckles with his lips. "You are very precious to me."

She allowed the display of affection with reluctance, wondering if Thomas would have agreed to marry her had she not been endowed with a fortune. The man was no fool. He was not blind to her lack of affection for him. No doubt he considered the wealth she would bring to the marriage ample substitute for her shortcomings.

"I'm relived you're not angry," said Thomas. He reached into the pocket of his waistcoat. "A less tolerant woman might have had me thrown out of the manse for saying much less. You shame me into realizing what a fortunate man I am." He removed his hand from his pocket. "I have something for you." And before Elisabeth could tell what it was, he was looping it over her head and straightening it around her neck.

She looked down at a pink velvet ribbon from which hung a slender, six-inch cylinder of enameled porcelain. Puzzling over the cylinder, she lifted it into her hand, noting the spheres of glass embedded in each end. She touched the artist's markings and felt beneath the tip of her forefinger the ridges of pink and green enamel painted onto the glaze. "'Tis lovely, Thomas. But . . . what is it?"

"You don't know? Perhaps this will help." Grabbing either end of the cylinder, he elongated it to twice its size. "Do you know now?"

And now, she did. "A ship's long-glass, isn't it? But 'tis so delicate. I can't imagine a ship's master daring to use it." She held it to her eye and aimed it at the floor. The Turkish carpet floated before her vision in a blur of red and black.

"No ship's master ever used it. My brother had it specially made for Cicely so she could maintain a lookout for his ship from her bedchamber window. You can adjust the focus by sliding the second cylinder up and down."

Elisabeth shortened the shaft. The swirls and arabesques

of the carpet swam into focus. She extended her arm and tested the air with her fingers. "The floor looks so close. I thought I could touch it." She swung the glass upward and lengthened the cylinder, spying at the opposite end the magnificently jeweled and padded codpiece of the first Baron of Drewsteignton. Her eyes grew wide. The baron's considerable endowment, reproduced in oil, had never looked so considerable. She shifted the glass.

"What do you think of it?"

"Fascinating, Thomas. Truly. Thank you."

"The painters discovered it when they were mucking about Cicely's chambers. I thought perhaps you could use it over the next month to peer across Dartmoor and accustom yourself to the idea of living in Cornwall."

"Yes," she said quietly, knowing she could not escape marriage to this man. "Perhaps I shall." She continued moving the glass—over the tear-shaped pearl that studded the ear of the third Viscount of Upton Pyne, over the leather gauntlet and steel arm guard of the second Earl of Newton Abbot. She found a crack in the pink marble of the fireplace, then swung the glass toward the corridor, squinting at the object within her scope.

It was blue, and not sky blue or robin's egg blue. This blue was pale and translucent, like aquamarine. But it wasn't a soft blue. It looked hard, and cold, and—

It blinked.

She caught her breath and snatched the glass from her eye.

Long faced and liveried, Frith stood at the threshold. "A caller to see Sir Quintus, my lady. Says he's a thief-taker."

Elisabeth riveted her attention on the dark-cloaked man who stood beside the St. Mary steward. He was tall and straight, like a gallows tree, and his eyes were a hard, pale blue, like aquamarine. His presence in the doorway—the way he stood, the way he held his head—marked him an indestructible man, as indestructible as the granite tors that darkened the moorland. His eyes were cold, yet calm, and they stared at her in the same way she imagined he might stare across the moorland, through the blackness of night, waiting for victims. The bend of her knees went limp with that look. "Forgive me, sir." She forced the words out in a breathy whisper as she shortened the long-glass.

The man acknowledged her with a single nod of his head. Frith motioned him into the room.

"Shall I inform his lordship of the gentleman's arrival, m'lady?"

"Please. He's been anxious about the man's where-abouts."

"Very good, mum." The steward sketched an elegant bow and left the room, the thin braid of his pigtail wig swinging above the flared skirt of his coat. Elisabeth motioned the thief-taker to a chair.

"I assume Henry Fielding informed you of our di-lemma?" She eyed him as he strode to the nearest chair. His boots were not the boots of a gentleman. They were heavy, square-toed jackboots that were formed with slightly spreading funnel tops above the knees. The leather was so stiff and black with tar that Elisabeth puzzled how the man could lift his feet with such apparent ease. The hem of his cloak brushed his boot tops, and as he sat, he swung the front panels of the garment behind shoulders that looked heavy as a bull's. Elisabeth heeded the leather bandoleer that crossed his chest. It was slung from his right shoulder to his left hip and protruding from it were the carved hilts of a brace of daggers. She swallowed slowly.

"I know of your dilemma." His voice was deep, with a richness like warmed cream. His nose was finely shaped save for a knuckle of misshapen bone that distorted the bridge. It appeared to have been broken at one time. She wondered how. His skin was sun baked and windburned, his cheeks long and lean and hollow. His hair was black as the seeds of a poppy and tied back in a queue, but the strands were so uneven that Elisabeth guessed he used one of the blades in his bandoleer to randomly hack them off. Given his profession she wondered what else he had hacked off with those blades. A chill passed through her.

"Well, I don't know of your dilemma," objected Thomas. "What's the meaning of this, Elisabeth? Henry Fielding? Thief-takers?"

His curiosity amused her. "If you visited Maidenstowe more than once every six months, m'lord, you would find it less mystifying. The village has been plagued by a thief for some weeks now. Quintus wrote to Henry Fielding requesting the service of a thief-taker." She gestured to their guest.

Thomas bristled at her explanation. "You might have apprised me of the situation, Elisabeth. I might have lent some personal assistance. After all, I was a highly decorated member of my regiment. I brought more deserters to task than any officer in the regiment's history."

"I'm aware of that, Thomas. But I would guess you have matters of greater import to attend to than the capture of Bridestone Barrow's thief."

He made no comment to this, but threw a long look at the thief-taker. "There was no need for you to come, but since you're already here, you might as well try your hand at bagging the wretch."

The thief-taker's brows were long and thin and he arched them over those pale blue eyes of his. "'Tis generous of the marquess to allow you to speak with such authority in his absence."

Elisabeth saw Thomas's body grow rigid at the comment. Hoping to diffuse the sudden tension, she addressed the thief-taker. "I forget my manners, sir. Allow me to introduce my intended to you. Sir Thomas Penmarck, Earl of Moreleigh."

The thief-taker nodded once again, but Elisabeth sensed it was more a gesture to indicate he had heard her than a gesture of respect.

"I suppose you've done this sort of thing before," continued Thomas. "Or has Henry Fielding sent an apprentice to do the work of the master?"

Elisabeth bowed her head with embarrassment that Thomas was being so ill-humored. The thief-taker pondered the question before answering. "I have bagged one or two wretches, m'lord. But no doubt my meager successes would pale in comparison to your superior talents."

His comment was laced with such obvious sarcasm that Thomas's face became a florid knot of twitching muscle. His hand flew to the sword at his hip while Elisabeth's flew to his arm, pulling back on his elbow. She shot an exasperated look across the room, and though the thief-taker's expression was impassive, she could detect amusement in his eyes. He looked more thief than thief-maker. Behind those pale blue eyes she guessed there existed a man who had cultivated a great capacity for hatred. He seemed ill disposed to be sitting in this room, ill disposed to have made their acquaintance, ill disposed to be here at Maidenstowe. She hoped he would catch his thief quickly and be gone, for with his ruggedness and his knives and the steely set of his eyes, he was a frightening figure to behold.

Frith's voice sounded from the doorway. "Excuse me, m'lady, but the marquess is still abed. Would you have me serve chocolate and rusks to your guests?"

Elisabeth exhaled a quick breath of relief. "Thank you, no, but perhaps you would be good enough to show—" Her lips remained parted for a moment, then closed. Mortified, she looked into the thief-taker's face. "My apologies, sir. I did not ask your name."

"Cain," he said, holding her gaze to his own, daring her to look away. And to her wonderment, she could not.

"Cain," she repeated, finally wrenching her gaze from him. "Frith, would you show Mr. Cain to his quarters in the east wing?"

"Very good, mum."

The man stood. "Cain, my lady. 'Tis simply Cain." He bowed his head then struck out across the floor, his spur rowels rattling like the halfpennies in a beggar's cup. Elisabeth turned toward Thomas. He was staring after the thief-taker, seemingly in a daze.

"Thomas?"

"He should have told us his name before he stepped inside the room. Cain. Do you know who the man is?"

Elisabeth's eyebrows dipped in confusion. "He's a thief-taker."

"He's not just any thief-taker. He's the most redoubtable thief-taker in the realm. Over two hundred brigands have swung from Tyburn because of him." He touched his sword hilt as he dwelled on that thought. "He's fortunate you were here to stay my sword arm. I doubt Henry Fielding would have appreciated my maiming the man."

"Indeed," said Elisabeth, wondering who would have maimed whom.

"What I don't understand is why Fielding would send so reputed a man as Cain to apprehend one tawdry thief. It's akin to using a cannon to kill a fly. Perhaps the name Quintus St. Mary carries more weight than one would suspect."

As he continued to talk, Elisabeth found her attention drawn to the loose flesh at his throat. Unbidden she lit on an image of the thief-taker's throat, recalling how firm and tight it was. Surprised that she'd been so bold to notice such a thing, she blinked away the image.

"Actually, it would have been better for your grandfather had Fielding sent a lesser thrall. The man is insulting. I don't like him."

"You don't have to like him, Thomas. He will capture our thief and then he will be gone. You will never have to exchange another word with him." Grabbing his elbow she stood up, dragging him with her. "You have yet to see the wedding gifts in the gallery. Lord and Lady Helmsley sent a life-size marble statue of a naked wood nymph. Emma keeps wreathing flowers around it to guard the young woman's privacy and Quintus keeps plucking the petals and scolding Emma for obstructing his view."

But Thomas wasn't listening. He was studying the dozens of portraits that hung from the room's crown molding. "He looks vaguely familiar."

"'Tis not a he, Thomas. 'Tis a she. If it were a he, I'm sure Emma would be less than generous with her flowers."

"No, no. Cain. He looks familiar. Look at the faces in

those portraits, Elisabeth. Don't you think he bears a slight resemblance to the fifth viscount . . . or the sixth?"

Elisabeth hurried him to the door, dismissing not only his observation, but the fifth and sixth viscounts as well. "He resembles no one I have ever seen, in person or in oil."

But Thomas, whose curiosity was not as easily sated as Elisabeth's, was not so sure.

In the green salon, on the second floor of Maidenstowe's east wing, Cain sank into a walnut chair that seemed to be smothering beneath its own ponderous weight. Wincing, he peeled the glove off his right hand and began to massage the milk white scar that flawed his palm. After all these years it still pained him, but he had learned to wield his blades despite the pain. Necessity had dictated it, just as necessity had dictated that the memories live on in his mind, causing him pain he would never be able to ignore.

He leaned his head against the back of the chair, closing his eyes to the room and his mind to the image of the girl he had left downstairs.

She would never have allowed him beyond the threshold if she'd thought him someone other than Fielding's man. He suspected when she discovered who he really was and what he intended, she would rue the day she ever heard the name Cain.

"Soon, my lady," he whispered into the silence of the room. "Very soon." And this time, he had fooled even Lint.

chapter
two

———

Later that afternoon, while Thomas absented himself to peruse the most recent additions to the St. Mary bloodstock, Elisabeth, unbeknownst to her intended, paid her weekly visit to the parish workhouse. The building was located in the village of Bridestone Barrow, a short distance from the vicarage, beyond a gated flint wall that was too high to see over. It was set back in a field of stone, a rectangular house of mud and lath whose walls seemed scarcely able to bear the weight of the shabbily thatched roof. In many places the mud had fallen away, exposing the crooked spaces that separated the underlying wood. With the hem of her gown soaked from the profusion of rank vegetation that choked the landscape, Elisabeth pushed open the door and stepped inside.

"My lady!" The overseer of the poor at Holy Trinity Church also held the office of churchwarden and, as such, was responsible not only for the distribution of alms to the poor, but also the disposition of the parish workhouse. His name was Treacle, and upon seeing Elisabeth, he hastened toward her, his leather pumps scattering rushes as if they were goose feathers. "I was thinking yer coach might 'ave broken an axle or the marquess taken with an ague. I hope yer delay wasn't due to some misfortune, mum."

It was indeed a misfortune, thought Elisabeth, but not of the kind Treacle suggested. She shook her head as she set her basket of medicines on a nearby table. "My delay was due to Sir Thomas. An unexpected visit."

Treacle helped her remove her pug hood and mantelet. "You shouldn't 'ave come then, mum. 'Is lordship don't make the trip to Maidenstowe that often. 'E couldn't 'ave been pleased about yer leaving 'is side to spend time 'ere at the workhouse."

Elisabeth draped her outer garments across the table before hooking her forearm beneath the handle of her basket. She flashed Treacle a conspiratorial smile. "I doubt he would be pleased . . . if he knew. Unfortunately, when last Thomas saw me, I was on my way to my chambers suffering from a severe case of female megrims. I left instructions that I was not to be disturbed. In fact, Mr. Treacle, I believe I am still there. Now, what do you have for me today?"

Treacle nodded his approval as he led her across the floor.

The house was but a single large room over which hung a grid of naked rafters that supported the sagging thatch. The mud floor was hard packed and cold and befouled with rushes that emitted fumes so noxious that Elisabeth preferred not to think about the origin of the smell. The long east and west walls were lined with flock beds that were scattered about like nests, and on one of these flocks lay a child who remained motionless even as Churchwarden Treacle stopped beside him.

"The Lady Elisabeth is 'ere to see you, Ned," said Treacle, but the child continued to lie curled on his side, his hand cupped over his ear, saying nothing. Treacle shook his head. 'E's been like this for two days, mum. Won't eat. Can't sleep. Won't get up."

Elisabeth knelt beside the boy then tilted her head to peek at his face. His eyes were round as cow's eyes and so filled with pain that she guessed he might burst into tears at any moment. "Can you tell me where you hurt?" she asked gently, but all he could do was contort his brow and moan something incomprehensible. She touched the fingers he had clamped to his ear, but when he stiffened at the contact, she drew her hand back and frowned. "'Tis your ear that pains you then?"

He moaned again, but by this time, Elisabeth already had her answer. Reaching into her basket, she withdrew a small glass phial.

"Will 'e be all right, mum?"

"A few drops of oil of sweet almonds and I wager he'll be picking stones and gathering wild nuts better than anyone." She unstoppered the phial and lowered it so the boy could eye the contents. "It won't sting. You have my word." And her voice was so soft and indulgent that after a few moments' hesitation the child balled his hand into a fist and dragged it away from his ear. Elisabeth smiled up at the churchwarden who shrugged in response.

"I've spent two days tryin' to get 'im to do that very thing, mum. Must be in the tone of voice."

She treated Ned's ear with four drops of oil and while she waited for the cure to take effect, she ministered to the other occupants of the workhouse who had ailments that required tending. For Amelia Spicer, who was suffering from a hoarseness in the throat, she took pennyroyal, seethed it in water, and made a decoction that she instructed the girl to drink with a little sugar before going to bed. For old Will Bolton's heartburn she mixed salts of tartar with water and stood eagle-eyed beside him until he drank every drop she'd prepared. She presented Lucinda Strump a phial of verjuice with which to wash the canker in her mouth and made a plaster of boiled ale for the canker on Hannah Hawkin's nose. And as she was searching her basket for a phial of fleabane juice, she felt a tug on the ruffled flounce at her elbow. She turned her head to find Ned standing bashfully one-legged beside her.

"Ear's better, m'lady."

She smiled at the sudden calmness in his eyes and gave the hair on his dark head a good-natured ruffling. "Your ear is better and your stomach"—she bent her head close to his midriff, listening intently—"is growling. I suspect more medicine may be in order."

He curled his lips in distaste of what evil brew would be forced down his throat. "More medicine, m'lady? Like the tonic you give me the day I had the heat in my stomach?"

"Worse," she confided, suppressing a grin at the horror that had crept into the boy's eyes. "This medicine can only be found in the vicarage kitchen. I want you to knock at the back door and inform Reverend Fincham's cook that Lady Elisabeth requests two ginger cookies be placed in your very hand so you might eat them immediately. For medicinal purposes, of course. Do you suppose you feel well enough to do that?"

The look on his face mutated from abject horror to elation. "Ginger cookies, m'lady? Two of them? I can do that, m'lady. I can do that right now!" And before she could utter another word he was out the door, leaving Elisabeth to shake her head comically behind him.

Twenty minutes later, her ministrations complete, she stood at the door with Churchwarden Treacle who looked more forlorn than any of the six people she had treated that afternoon. "If I didn't know you to be a man of robust health, Mr. Treacle, I would suspect you were suffering from some dark and troubling malady."

"That I am, mum. 'Tis called heartache. I don't know wot we're going to do when you leave us is the problem. It worries me wot's to become of us. But I know 'tis a selfish thought. You deserve every happiness that the Earl of Moreleigh will rain upon you as 'is wife."

Happiness? thought Elisabeth. She had never coupled the word happiness with anything having to do with Thomas, least of all with their marriage. When she became his wife, it would be her duty to yield control of her goods, her will, and her person to her husband, and her main purpose in life would become that of producing heirs. *Happiness?* She would be living with a stranger. Breeding with a stranger.

Her throat closed at the thought of his hands on her.

"I've no cause to complain," Treacle continued as he threw open the portal for her. Elisabeth stepped into the open air and breathed deeply, chasing away her momentary panic. "The marquess 'as always done well by us, mum. We probably 'ave less scurvy than any workhouse in Devon. And we're not oft bothered by thieves, but when we are, the marquess's ready to reimburse 'is tenants for their losses. A good man is your grandfather."

Elisabeth hiked up her gown as she picked her way through the field in Treacle's wake. "Have there been anymore thefts of late?"

Treacle shook his head. "Three nights ago, mum. John Hooke was robbed of four pence on the high road. Be glad when that thief-taker arrives."

"He's here," said Elisabeth, nearly colliding with the churchwarden when he whirled round to face her. "He rode into Maidenstowe this morning."

"High time!" Treacle postured. "These magistrates are deuced slow when it comes to dealing with matters outside London. Did the fellow say wot took 'im so long to get 'ere?"

Elisabeth shrugged as she lit on an image of the man with the black hair and pale blue eyes. "He didn't say much of anything actually, other than the fact that he's called Cain."

"Cain? God's bones, mum, 'Enry Fielding sent Cain to catch Bridestone Barrow's thief?" With a booming guffaw Treacle turned round and resumed walking. Elisabeth hurried to keep pace.

"Why do you laugh?"

"Because our thief isn't long for this world if 'tis Cain who's been sent to catch 'im. 'E's caught thieves aplenty throughout the realm, mum. As far north as 'Adrian's Wall and as far south as the Romney marshes. 'E can probably tell you where every rock, road, and gibbet are in Mother England 'cause 'e's no doubt seen 'em all. Some say 'e's invincible, mum. I say our thief is doomed with such a one on 'is trail."

Elisabeth slowed her steps as Treacle hurried ahead to open the gate in the flint wall. *Some say he's invincible.*

The words echoed in her head, but it was not the idea of the thief-taker's invincibility that caused a wave of jealousy to swell within her. She glanced back over her shoulder at the crumbling wall of the workhouse. The thief-taker heeded no boundaries. He roved from Scotland, to Cornwall, to the Channel without fear or impediment. But her boundaries were as clearly defined as the lines on her palm.

In her twenty-two years she had been no farther east than the parish workhouse nor farther west than the walls of Maidenstowe. She lived in a world that measured a solitary league in length and a few miserly acres in width—an orderly world whose boundaries she had never dared test. So she envied the thief-taker his travels and his freedom and his courage. She envied him the experiences he'd had in the years she'd been traveling between Maidenstowe and Bridestone Barrow, in the same coach with her grandfather, dwelling on the terrible sin of her youth—the sin that had resulted in her benevolent captivity, the sin she hoped she could expiate by marrying Thomas Penmarck. Perhaps then she could look at her grandfather without feeling shame, or guilt. Thomas would take her to Cornwall, to London. He would introduce her to the world the thief-taker knew. But as she passed through the gate in the flint wall, she wondered, *at what price?*

Quintus St. Mary was a diminutive man with stooped shoulders and gangly arms that lent him the appearance of an organ grinder's monkey. His powdered periwig was of the full-bottomed style that had been fashionable fifty years earlier, and his head seemed to have shrunken with age so that without his wig he looked much like a very old potato.

Having remained in the coach the two hours Elisabeth had spent in the workhouse, Quintus St. Mary was feeling cramped and arthritic and was in no mood for pleasantries on the jolting ride back to Maidenstowe.

"The roof on the workhouse needs to be rethatched before it caves in," Elisabeth advised in a vibrato loud enough to be heard over the squeak of their coach wheels.

"New roof? Hah! I'm already a pauper because of that fool thief who's running amok. The old roof stays."

"And they're in desperate need of new flocks. The present ones are all louse infested." As if attesting to that fact, she scratched a sudden itch at the back of her neck.

Quintus eyed her with suspicion. "If you're playing host to an infestation of vermin, stay away from me. I bathed a short nine months ago and have no intention of repeating the process anytime soon. You seem to forget that overexposure to soap and water can kill a man, young woman. Look at Sir Edmund. Agreed to a bath last year and dropped dead afterward. So kindly keep your vermin on your side of the coach."

Elisabeth sighed. They had discussed this time and again. "Sir Edmund slipped on a cake of soap and broke his neck."

"Still dead, isn't he? A bath, a purge, and a bloodletting in the spring, I say. Sufficient for any man."

"If you provided new flocks for the workhouse, you'd be less likely to be contaminated by vermin." She rubbed her left wrist, then began scratching in earnest.

"Impertinent," snapped Quintus. "Damned impertinent. My fourth wife was impertinent." In the next instant they skidded into a rut so deep that the coach seesawed violently from starboard to port, propelling Quintus's eighty-four-

year-old body into the side of the vehicle. "Fool!" he bellowed at the coachman. They lurched sideways again. The
leather shades on both windows shot up. Boosting himself
upright, he assaulted the roof of the coach with his walking
stick. "Slower! We're not running the third race at Ascot!"

Elisabeth leaned forward in her seat to lend her assistance in straightening her grandfather's waistcoat, but he
shooed her away with an impatient hand. "I don't need
your help, young woman. It's the bloody coachman who
needs help. Cocky whelp."

She leaned back again, not at all surprised that Quintus
had refused her assistance, but she was too accustomed to
his rejection to feel disappointment. He had been like this
for years now, ever since the death of her parents. He'd
been devastated by the two deaths sixteen years ago, but he
had borne the weight of his sorrow silently, never speaking
to her of the incident, never casting blame. But Elisabeth,
six years of age at the time, had cast her blame immediately and had lived with her guilt since then. For it was she
who had caused her parents' death on that spring day in
1736. It was her fault that the nursery at Maidenstowe was
filled with cobwebs and dust rather than the squalls of
newborns. When Quintus St. Mary died, so too would a
lineage that had survived for three hundred years.

And it was all because of her.

She and Quintus had deftly avoided the subject for a
decade and a half, but she knew he had to blame her for the
tragedy. It was the reason he never touched her unless he
was forced to. It was the reason he could not bring himself
to call her anything more endearing than "young woman."
So when he told her last year that he had decided to betroth
her to Sir Thomas Penmarck, she could not object. If she

defied Quintus, he might call her ungrateful. Anger might cause him to give vent to the emotions he'd suppressed for sixteen years. He might grow incensed enough to blame her aloud for her parents' deaths, and she could not bear that. To know he blamed her was one thing, but to hear him say it would be something else entirely.

It was, indeed, her worst fear. The skin on the back of her neck prickled at the thought of living with such condemnation.

Through the window of the coach she spied the stone cross that marked the place where the road forked. The right byway followed the slope of the bluff upward toward Maidenstowe. The left byway angled downward, toward the moorland. As they lurched and swayed along the cliff road, Elisabeth slanted a look at the green gray monotone that was Dartmoor.

She had never ventured down the moorland road. Indeed, Dartmoor was a place through which the sage man hurried during the day and through which only the foolhardy dared venture after night had fallen. She knew that the great stumps of rock she saw silhouetted against the horizon flaunted names such as King Tor and Hound Tor, but they were not real to her. Dartmoor was not an orderly part of her universe, so she avoided it. It was unsafe. And considering how many unsafe places cluttered her life already, she was unwilling to contend with another.

Besides, Quintus had forbidden it, and she could not afford to disobey Quintus.

She startled as he thumped his walking stick on the floor. "If this thief-taker person is anywhere near up to snuff, he should make short work of capturing our brigand. By God, I think I'll have a new gibbet erected right outside the church so that bloody thief can see where his pagan bones will rot when we catch him."

"Everyone is so certain of the man's skill," said Elisabeth. "Perhaps we should reserve judgment until the felon is in hand." His comment prompted her, however, to consider the certainties in her own life.

There were but four: One could survive on tolerance rather than love and still reach one's twenty-second year.

Seeds planted in good soil and watered frequently yielded healthy plants and flowers of great beauty.

The thief-taker would no doubt catch his thief, and she would marry Sir Thomas Penmarck, for better, or worse.

"God's nightrail, young woman, you look positively peaked. If you're going to swoon, kindly do so on your side of the coach."

"Will you be visiting again on your way back from London?" Elisabeth asked early the next morning.

Thomas shook his head as they walked the path to the stables. "I'll make the return trip by water. I've wasted enough time stumbling about on these cursed cart roads. If the crown doesn't appropriate funds for turnpikes soon, the southwest of England will be sucked into the depths of its own peat bogs."

The stables where the famous St. Mary Blood horses were bred formed a square around an inner courtyard and paddock. Located east of the house, behind a wild woodland of lime and whitebeam, it was a structure as elaborate as the manse itself, constructed of golden stone over which creeping vines and English ivy drifted in leafy waves.

Elisabeth shivered as she strolled the stable path, for it tunneled beneath a dense canopy of twining wood. She had left her mantelet in her bedchamber this morn because the sunshine had looked deceptively warm, but she now regretted her decision for a spring chill still cooled the air. Hugging her arms about herself, she maintained what she considered a safe distance from Thomas. She feared if he saw her shiver he would volunteer his services to warm her, and that was something she would rather avoid.

"I trust your groomsboy will have my horse saddled and ready for my departure?"

"Have we ever failed in our duty to serve you, Thomas?"

He cocked his head, giving her question thoughtful consideration. "There was that one time. Two or three years ago. I waited an unconscionable amount of time for that lazy whelp to tighten my girth satisfactorily. I hope you got rid of him, Elisabeth. I would never allow such incompetence where my bloodstock is concerned."

Elisabeth slowed her pace to hide her expression. It was so like him to dwell on the one time when their efficiency had been lacking. He probably remembered every unkind deed that had ever been visited upon him, every slight, every injury.

"In addition to being absent from supper last night, your friend never slept in his bed," Thomas remarked as he slowed to accommodate Elisabeth's lagging pace.

Elisabeth stopped midstride. "Friend?"

"Your thief-taker friend." He straightened the ruffles at his wrist as they resumed walking. "His manners are deplorable."

"He is not my friend, Thomas. He is a man in my grandfather's employ. And what business had you prowling about his bedchamber?"

"I care little for your tone, lady. You sound as if you're defending the man's ill-grace."

"I am defending nothing but his right to privacy in our home."

"A thief-taker has the rights of a sow, which is to say, he has none."

Elisabeth's breath soughed through her nostrils in an irritated rush. Taken aback, Thomas stared at her. "Why am I sometimes given to believe you disapprove of me, Elisabeth?"

" 'Tis not you I disapprove of, sir. 'Tis your pedantic posturing."

"My what?"

She marched ahead of him. Cutting diagonally across the courtyard, she hastened into the main entrance of the stable block. Stanchions lined the north wall from tack room at one end of the building to feed room on the other, and before one of these stanchions stood the groomsboy with Thomas's horse. Elisabeth crossed to the boy, snatched the reins from his hands, and dismissed him abruptly. She heard Thomas laughing behind her.

"You amuse me with your startling insights, Elisabeth. I told you the man looked familiar. How can I confirm my suspicions if I don't question him?"

She turned to him. "Your horse, m'lord. I trust it meets with your approval that the beast is saddled and anxiously awaiting your departure."

"As are you, my lady?"

Ignoring his mockery, she extended the reins to him, but he did not accept them. He fixed his tricorne atop his head then eyed her from her pinner cap to the ribbon tie of her wrapping gown. "You have the look of a buttercup about you, all dressed in yellow. You would do well to observe that flower, Elisabeth—how submissive it is to the dictates of the wind. Such a flower requires little taming."

"Whereas a wife demands a great deal? If that prospect disturbs you, m'lord, mayhap you should consider planting a garden rather than taking a bride." She thrust the reins toward his hand unaware that beneath the ceruse on his face his skin grew hot. He threw his shoulders back, making himself appear suddenly taller, more formidable. He took a step toward her.

"For a year now you have discouraged my affections, Elisabeth, but even the patience of an earl has its limitations. Have you no kind words of farewell for me? No wifely caresses to send me on my way?"

In a moment of unease she scanned the length of the stable block. Save for herself and Thomas, the building was empty. "Good-bye, Thomas," she said without emotion, taking an involuntary step backward.

"Come, Elisabeth. Surely you can summon some small measure of ardor for the man whose bed you'll be sharing in little more than a fortnight."

Within the mask of white cosmetic on his face she saw his eyes blaze with frustration, with craving. Thinking to run, she let go the reins, but before she could put one foot in front of the other he grabbed her arm and pulled her against him. She winced at the press of his waistcoat buttons against her breast. "Stop it, Thomas."

"'Tis not unseemly, lady." His mouth was hot against her throat. "Let me lesson you in the appetites of your lord husband."

She turned her face to the side trying to escape his lips, but he caught her chin in his right hand and wrenched her face around to meet his, smothering her scream with his mouth. She clawed at his fingers, pushed at his arm. He thrust his tongue deep into her mouth. And in that instant, feeling violated in that part of her being that was private and dignified, she knew that Thomas viewed her in the same light that he viewed sows and thief-takers. She had no rights, and when she married, she would have even fewer for he would rob her of whatever privacy and dignity she now called her own.

Clenching her fists she pushed against his shoulders, trying to escape the pressure of his mouth. He crushed her lips against her teeth, distending her flesh, chafing the soft interior of her mouth with his tongue. She could taste the grit of his cosmetic. She smelled the fatty dressing and rice powder of his wig and thought she would suffocate. The muscles in her arms strained. She pushed harder.

She dug her fingers into his cheekbones, caking his face paint beneath her nails. He stiffened. In his throat she heard a sound resembling the growl of a rabid animal. Of a sudden he was more madman than lord. His hands could not get their fill of her. He raked his fingers through the knot atop her head, tearing her pinner cap from where she had anchored it. Hair needles jabbed into her head. Pain coursed through her upper lip with such sudden intensity that tears sprang to her eyes, and on her tongue she tasted the warm, metallic taste of her own blood.

He yanked on the ribbon tie at her waist and threw open her bodice. Her fingers became talons. She knocked his tricorne off his head. She tore at his ruffled cuffs as he shaped his palm around the breast that was hidden beneath her chemise. She warred with his hand, scratching and clawing his fingers. Another pain in her lip. She felt a tingling sensation begin to spin in her head and a thickness in her ears.

Breathe. She couldn't breathe.

"My lady appears rather distraught," came a voice from the edge of her consciousness. "Release her, m'lord. Slowly."

Air flooded her lungs as Thomas wrenched his mouth from hers. Her chest heaved with the effort of breathing anew. The spinning in her head diminished. She opened her eyes to find they were no longer alone, but had been joined by a horseman whose gleaming rapier was poised at Thomas's throat.

"This is not your affair, thief-taker." Thomas held his head motionless as he eyed the long length of Cain's rapier.

The sword blade turned a quarter inch to tilt with Thomas's windpipe. "Do I look a patient man, m'lord? Release her."

With back stiff and head cocked at an impossible angle, Thomas eased his grip, and when she felt his fingers slacken, she broke away from him, running toward a nearby stall. Cain leaned forward in his saddle. He gave the underside of Thomas's chin a playful slap with the flat of his blade. "I would hope that apologies are forthcoming, m'lord."

Thomas's voice was strained. "Apologize all you like, thief-taker, but I'm not likely to forget this outrage."

Cain's laughter reverberated through the empty stable block. Thinking him distracted, Thomas shot his hand to the frog at his hip to release his sword. The laughter stopped abruptly. Thomas looked down at his right hand to find Cain's rapier leveled at his wrist.

"If you wish your hand to remain attached to your wrist, I would be less foolhardy, m'lord."

"Bastard."

"An accurate assessment of both my ancestry and my character. But there is still the matter of the apology. Loudly, now, so my lady can hear."

His face implacable, Thomas jutted his chin in the air. Cain's lips slid into a wicked smile.

"Does it content you to know that a swineherd effects better manners than you, m'lord?" He heeded the claw marks on the man's cheek. Then with teeth clenched, voice low and frightening, "I can run you through faster than you can blink, Penmarck. So I urge you to speak the words, for there is a depraved part of me that would rather skewer you to that horse stall than allow you to ride from here unscathed. Speak, damn you."

Thomas sidled a look at the thief-taker. What he saw in the cold blue depths of his eyes forced the words from his mouth. "I'm sorry, Elisabeth," he said without remorse, voice hushed and eyes unwavering.

Cain thrust the point of his sword beneath the angle of Thomas's jaw, coaxing his chin upward. "Louder."

"I'm sorry, Elisabeth!"

"Better. Much better." Satisfied, Cain withdrew his blade then leaned sideways in his saddle and speared Thomas's fallen tricorne. With a quick flex of his wrist he rainbowed it through the air off the tip of his blade. "You dropped something." Thomas juggled the tricorne for several moments before gaining control of it. "Now get out of my sight before I remember how truly foul a thief-taker's manners can become."

"I should call you out for this," spat Thomas. Not waiting to place the hat on his head, he gathered up his horse's reins, braced his foot in the stirrup iron, and hoisted himself into the saddle. He glowered at Cain. "You'll pay dearly for this insult, thief-taker," he vowed, then spurred his horse forward.

"In hell, m'lord," Cain yelled at his retreating back. "But no doubt you will be there to greet me!"

Silence flooded the building. Cain sheathed his sword then gazed the length of the sable block. Elisabeth stood four stanchions away, angled against the support of a stall gate, her back facing him, head bent. Her pinner cap was missing, but its absence intrigued Cain for where the lappets usually hung there now flowed an unbound wealth of white blond hair, and he regarded it in awe.

Ladies of fashion coiffed their hair high off the forehead in loose waves or over pads, with side curls and back curls, and twisted whatever remained in an ornate bun. The entire creation was then dressed with a heavy application of sticky pomatum and white powder and festooned with flowers and plumes, ribboned topknots, jeweled pompons, lace, and tinsel. A London fish market did not boast so much colorful activity as might be found idling atop a lady's head. So Cain stared at this hair that was so long, so pale, so unfettered, for never before had he seen so wondrous a sight. When he'd had his fill, he dismounted and looped his stallion's reins around a support beam.

Elisabeth heard the rustle of wheat straw as footsteps approached. "He has gone, m'lady," came the thief-taker's voice behind her.

She knuckled tears from the corners of her eyes. "I regret subjecting you to so vile a scene, sir," she said in a whisper of breath. She turned around to face him. "The morning has turned so cold. I . . . I can't seem to stop shaking." She held her gown tight against her bodice, her fingers too unsteady to retie the ribbons at her waist. Her eyes were veined red with recent tears and her mouth and chin were smeared with blood.

Giving the ties at his throat a savage jerk, Cain swung his cloak off his shoulders and draped it around her. She disappeared within its voluminous folds.

"If you would allow me, my lady." Without waiting for her permission he eased her hands from her bodice, realigned the folds of her gown over her chemise, and tied the ribbons at her waist in an artful bow. He did this without pomp, without embarrassment, as if he were as seasoned a dresser of women as he was a taker of thieves. "A skewering would have benefited the man immensely," he spat as he removed a handkerchief from the pocket of his jackboot. Straightening, he cupped her chin in his hand and applied the linen to the blood staining her face. She clenched her teeth in an effort to stop shivering. "There is a small gouge on your upper lip, my lady. So much blood from so small a cut."

She nodded silently as he held the linen to her mouth.

"If I might rinse the cloth in the trough outside, a dousing with cool water might prove a welcome balm."

As he strode to the door, she followed him with her eyes—the bandoleer crossing his wide back, the sway of his scabbard against his leg, the flex of muscle in his thighs and buttocks. She wadded his cloak beneath her chin. She could feel the heat from his body still locked within the folds of wool, and she willed her bones to absorb that warmth. Closing her eyes she rubbed her cheek against the cowl of wool circling her neck. It smelled of horse and . . .

and sweat—healthy male sweat undisguised by cologne, a smell infinitely more masculine than Thomas's rice powder and rouge.

At that thought she opened her eyes and for an unspeakable moment stared at the fingers she had curled around the black wool. Her fingertips were smudged with cosmetic and beneath her nails she saw clots of ceruse, and rouge, and flesh. Thomas's flesh.

An anguished knot began to vibrate in her throat. She stiffened her arm and held her hand away from her as if it were diseased. *I will not scream,* she told herself, trying to close her mind to Thomas's violation. *I will not give him the satisfaction of screaming.*

Eyes wild, she searched the doorway for Cain, anxious for his return.

The entrance remained empty.

The ground seemed to seesaw beneath her feet. She looked down, and it was then that sanity returned. Snatching up a piece of straw, she plied it beneath each of her nails, ridding herself of the last vestiges of Thomas. She never wanted to look at him again. Never wanted to feel his touch. Never. So she scraped, and scratched, and peeled, and when her skin was free from his taint, she opened her palms and rubbed them hard against her over-petticoat.

Cain reappeared. Halfway across the room he hesitated, then hunkered down on one knee. Elisabeth saw him pluck something from the straw.

"Have you lost something, sir?" She was amazed how deceptively strong her voice sounded.

"Not I, m'lady. You." Bracing the object between his left thumb and forefinger, he held it up for her perusal while with his right hand he continued to sift through the surrounding straw. The object was thin as the stem of a windflower, long as her baby finger, and wrought in silver encrusted with brilliants. Her hand flew to the crown of her head.

"My hair needles."

Cain found a second one and then a third. "Have you an idea how many are missing?"

She walked slowly in his direction, and as she did so, she freed her hair from the tent of his cloak and combed her fingers through the loose strands. "Five, I think. Mayhap six."

She stopped a short distance from where he knelt and scanned the floor. She saw no telltale glimmers buried within the straw, but Cain's eyesight was obviously keener than hers, for he found a fourth hair needle in the exact spot where she had been looking.

"'Tis not necessary that you find all six, sir." Her voice was apologetic. "You've misspent enough of your time with me." But his pursuit seemed relentless. Sorting. Sifting. Separating. For a moment she considered what Thomas might have done in similar circumstances. He certainly wouldn't do the searching himself. He would balk at sullying his clothes, or begriming his hands. So he would summon the groomsboy and assign *him* the task. Thomas would care little about the servants' clothes or hands.

She studied Cain's hands as they sifted through the straw. His fingers were long, his palms broad. They looked to be hands more powerful than those of the parish blacksmith's, swifter and more agile. She wondered why he wore an open-fingered glove on his right hand and none on his left. Why would a man wear only one glove?

Her gaze traveled higher, to his bent head. Despite its unruly cut, his hair was clean and wonderfully free of pomatum and rice powder. The strands curled of their own accord, looking as soft and black as sheared wool. She wondered at the feel of those curls beneath her hand, at the feel of his cheeks, for his flesh was incredibly smooth and unblemished. His visage seemed a contradiction in terms —hard yet soft, fierce yet gentle. Yesterday she had thought him frightening. Today the only word she could think to describe him was spectacular.

Hoping to aid with the search, Elisabeth made a half turn and immediately spied her pinner cap lying in the straw. She bent down to pick it up. The lappets were hanging by a solitary thread and the crisp circlet of lace was finger-marked with blood. She crumpled it in her fist. When she returned to the manse, she would have it burned.

Turning round to Cain again, she startled when she found him on his feet and towering before her. She hadn't even heard him move.

"Five," he said, holding the last hair needle in the air like a rushlight. "If there is another, my lady, it remains as elusive as Bridestone Barrow's thief." He placed the needles in her palm and folded her fingers around them. The touch of his flesh was warm against her own, warm . . . and unhurried, as gentle as Thomas's had been rough. And she wondered how it could be that a common thief-taker would visit more kindness upon her than her own betrothed. It seemed a paradox that a man who wore steel across his chest would act more the gentleman than a man who wore silk. It seemed grossly illogical that a man who boasted neither land nor title displayed attributes of finer quality than those of his betters. She could not understand the reason for Cain's actions. She meant nothing to the man, but she would not press him for his motive. Questions might breed familiarity. Familiarity might breed friendship. And friendship with a thief-taker could prove more dangerous than a midnight ride through Dartmoor. People from two such different worlds shared no common bond, save for a furtive touch of fingertips in a chilly stable block.

"Lift your chin," whispered Cain.

She did as he instructed. He lifted the wet handkerchief and as he pressed it to her mouth, she concluded that he'd been right. Cool water was a welcome balm.

Checking the cut again, he nodded. "You heal quickly, my lady. The bleeding has stopped." Their glances crossed as he stepped back, blue eyes piercing blue. The intensity of that look made Elisabeth suddenly self-conscious. Discomfited, she averted her eyes and nodded toward Cain's stallion.

"There are brushes and stable rubbers by the tack room, sir. I trust you'll want to make use of them."

"Do you hear that, Scylla?" Cain said in a loud voice. "Lady Elisabeth is concerned with your well-being."

In response the stallion stiffened his left foreleg, bent his right knee, dipped his head forward, and effected as pretty a bow as Elisabeth had ever seen. Her lips parted in amazement.

"However did you teach him to do that?" St. Mary equines were the finest Blood horses in all England and the fastest in the world. But not one of them could bow.

"I taught him with patience, my lady." Making his way to the animal, Cain smoothed his hand down the length of his muzzle. The stallion stood over eighteen hands high, big barreled and black, with long legs and heavily muscled quarters. So great was his size that Elisabeth guessed his veins ran thick with the blood of medieval war-horses. "A gentle hand, a spate of soft words, and patience, my lady. With such a combination a man can tame many things."

Elisabeth wondered if he were speaking of horses, or women. But she smiled, thinking his philosophy more to her liking than Thomas's. "You indicated to Thomas that you were a man of little patience, sir."

Cain scratched the space between the stallion's ears. "I have no patience for stupidity, my lady. But there are other things that promise great rewards if a man can bide his time. For those things I have cultivated much patience, and I suspect the rewards will surpass even my grandest expectations."

Looking suddenly irritated that he had allowed himself to say so much, he bent down and began to strip layers of cloth from Scylla's hooves—cloth that muffled the sound of the animal's iron shoes on their nocturnal sojourns.

"You caught no thief last night?" Elisabeth asked.

He shook his head. "Perhaps tonight."

Bemused by his sudden change of mood, Elisabeth eyed him for a lingering moment. He was an enigma, this one-gloved man who could speak so eloquently of patience while toting an array of deadly steel across his chest. He seemed something more than a thief-taker, but she didn't know what. Who was this man known only as Cain?

Walking toward him, she reached up to remove the cloak from her shoulders. "Your cloak, sir."

"'Tis a cold morning," he said without looking up. "You need the protection more than I."

And because her bones still felt cold as porcelain, she

snugged the wool about herself and nodded her assent.
"Thank you."

He made no reply. He tossed one set of rags to the side
and continued with his labors. And as she watched him
work, she remembered those same hands sifting through
straw to find her hair needles, and she felt obligated to
repay his kindness.

"Henry Fielding would think ill of us if we starved his
most illustrious thief-taker," she said quietly. "Since
you've taken no sustenance since your arrival, would you
honor us with your presence at the dinner table today?
Emma's culinary abilities are quite remarkable."

Cain was silent as he smoothed the feathering on
Scylla's leg. When he finally looked up at Elisabeth, his
eyes were unreadable. "Very well, lady. Even luminaries
must eat."

"The withdrawing room at a quarter 'til three then."

He bowed his head in compliance.

Elisabeth left the stable block then, unsure about con-
sorting with the thief-taker, but, as a great lady, too gra-
cious to allow his actions to go unrewarded.

A flagstone terrace with carved balusters and circular
fountains bordered the northern facade of Maidenstowe,
and below this were the formal gardens, the likes of which
Cain has never seen, not even in Cornwall.

From his second-story bedchamber window he eyed the
miniature box hedges in all their precise formations—the
spirals and circles and wedges, the taller yew hedges
shaped like cones and balls and fans. There was little in
bloom save a hedged triangle filled with petal upon petal of

yellow daffodils. The brightness of the flowers reminded
Cain of the gown Elisabeth had worn that morning and he
brushed his thumb across the tips of his fingers, remembering the feel of the gown, the texture of her chemise.

He shook his head, breaking the flow of his thoughts.
"Fool," he cursed, resuming his surveyance. In contrast to
the sturdy bulk of the manse the garden seemed a place of
great fragility, and Cain wondered if Elisabeth was responsible for its design, for it bore details of almost painful
delicacy—delicate as she was delicate, elegant as she was
elegant. *And still you think of her?* he berated himself.

Beyond the formal gardens he spied a bowling alley,
banked high on two sides with shrubs and willowy foliage.
Beyond that lay another garden, not formal. A kitchen garden perhaps, or an herb garden. He was about to turn away
when he caught sight of a figure in that garden, and even
from this distance he could tell that the figure was that of a
woman and that her hair was pale as the sands of a Cornish
beach.

Elisabeth.

He had stood behind her this morning, aching to touch a
naked finger to those unbound strands, but he had denied
himself the pleasure, as he must.

"Damn you," he rasped. Pushing away from the window
he set a restless pace about the room. Why had he interfered? His plans for the wench were no kinder than Penmarck's treatment had been. So why had he acted with
such chivalry?

He forced himself into a chair and laced his fingers behind his neck.

He knew why he had interfered. Because he was still

haunted by that other time. Even now, when he closed his eyes, he could see the woman's face, hear her screams. She had died twisted and broken, and he had watched, unable to help. Sometimes, at night, he would relive that moment and would awaken with his heart racing and moisture wetting his cheeks.

He had vowed long ago to avenge that death. *An eye for an eye.* Those words were seared on his soul as indelibly as the mark was seared on his flesh. Lowering his arms he touched a finger to the palm of his gloved hand, remembering. "'. . . and I shall be a fugitive and a vagabond in the earth,'" he recited in a whisper. "'. . . And the Lord set a mark upon Cain, lest any finding him should kill him.'" And so it had come to pass that he had lived the life of a fugitive and a vagabond, but to avoid being slain, he had become the slayer.

He flexed his fingers then bunched them into a fist. He had spoken too freely this morning. Did he want to alert the girl to his ruse? Heaving himself to his feet he walked back to the window.

She was still there. His eyes clung to her of their own volition. His course was inalterable, but the undertaking had seemed easier when the girl had been a faceless entity. He hadn't anticipated her comeliness. He hadn't expected her to be trusting, and kind, and . . . and sensible. It would have gone better for him if she'd been a fish-faced hag with the tongue of a harlot. But she wasn't. She was spare and lovely, and her hair was . . . extraordinary.

"You grow soft, my friend," he said to himself. "Soft, and distracted." He flattened his right hand against his chest, massaging it with his left. There was no room in his plan for distractions. There was only room for revenge, and death. So he would remember his hatred; he would suppress his lusty urges; and one day soon, when he had lulled them like babes, he would spring his trap. On that day, Quintus St. Mary would discover they had all disappeared—the thief, the thief-taker, and Elisabeth St. Mary.

chapter
three

"My father was fond of saying that if Quintus had boasted any more wives, we would have been forced to hang their portraits in the grand ballroom rather than the withdrawing room."

Cain turned at the sound of Elisabeth's voice. It was a quarter 'til the hour of three o'clock, and he had removed his bandoleer and sword in preparation to dine. He wore a plain muslin shirt with full bishop's sleeves and a front closure that tied at his throat, and where the bandoleer had pressed for endless months against him, his shirt was stained a faint reddish brown. Elisabeth wondered if he felt naked without his knives, and when she lowered her gaze to the place where his shirt snugged into his breeches, she imagined a vision of nakedness so splendid that she quickly looked away.

Cain nodded toward the full-length portraits that graced the north and west walls of the small saloon. "Your grandfather had seven wives?"

"At last count he had only six." Hoping the bend of her

thoughts was not apparent in her eyes, she walked farther into the room and stopped before the last portrait on the north wall. "This is my mother's portrait."

Afternoon light entered the room through two French doors that opened onto the east terrace. The thirty-foot ceiling swallowed most of the light and veiled the faces of the St. Mary women in shadow, but Elisabeth knew her mother's face as she knew her own, so she did not need to reacquaint herself with the fine strokes of the artist's brush.

The painting was an eight-foot masterpiece rendered in oil. It highlighted Gillian St. Mary's light brown hair and blue eyes and captured with uncanny preciseness the indulgent smile with which she had always favored her daughter. She had displayed that same smile on the day that Elisabeth had sent her to her death. She had been wearing the same gown.

Suffering a coldness that had little to do with the temperature, Elisabeth inhaled a quick breath and turned her back on the portrait. Cain had not moved, but he was regarding her with such curiosity that she guessed her unease was obvious. Forcing a smile, she elevated her forearm to indicate the length of black wool that was draped over it. "Your cloak, sir. Thank you for allowing me its use." As she walked the dozen paces toward him, she smoothed idle fingers across the wool, remembering how his body heat had lingered in its folds that morning—how his warmth had soothed her chilled bones.

"I-uh, I took the liberty of having Frith brush it off for you. And I found a small rent in your hood, so I fashioned a few stitches to repair it." She hung it over his forearm, treating the garment with the same respect she would give a monarch's robe. Her knuckles brushed his shirtsleeve in the transfer, an innocent touch of flesh to fabric, but the hardness she felt beneath that shirtsleeve made her think that the muscles in his arm and the blades of his knives were cast from the same steel.

He bowed his head in thanks. "I must confess a marked ineptitude where needle and sewing silk are concerned, my lady. My proficiency lies more in the realm of creating the rents than in repairing them."

"They tell me 'tis one of the benefits of marriage, sir. Having a wife to repair the damage you wreak upon yourself." She knew she should have stopped there, but suddenly she could not help herself. "Given your chosen profession I would wager you've kept a wife sufficiently busy for years now."

He studied her for a long moment with those pale blue eyes of his—a cold-blooded look that made her regret the intrusiveness of her last comment. "Had I taken a wife, my lady, I would have indeed kept her sufficiently busy, but not in the manner you suggest."

His eyes made a lazy sweep of her, touching her in a raw, primitive kind of way—in a way that no lord would ever look at his lady. She imagined that a generation of women had blushed beneath that same gaze; that a generation of women had responded to the promise of danger and passion that smoldered in the depths of his eyes; that a generation of women had fed this man's hunger with the softness of their bodies. And she had no doubt that his hunger was incessant.

Her neckline was low, her open bodice fashioned in blue brocade and filled in by a stomacher worked in silver tissue. She wore no jewelry. Her only adornment was a ruffled collarette that circled her throat like a choker. She fussed with that silver ruffle now in the hopes that her forearm would hide the swell of her bosom from his probing eyes. She had never thought her stomacher indecently low, until now. She had never thought it possible to feel naked while draped in yards of blue brocade and silver tissue, until now. Wishing she had brought a fan with which she could cool her scalding cheeks, she sidled a look at the doorway. "Quintus should be here presently," she said, rushing the words so that they all seemed to run together. "He's usually quite punctual."

"An admirable quality," Cain admitted as he slung his cloak over his shoulder. "More enduring than beauty; less entertaining than virginity." With that, he released her from his perusal and wandered from her side to stand before one of the mammoth portraits on the wall. As he walked, the heels of his jackboots clicked against the waxed hardwood floor—a sound that seemed to echo his authority, as if he owned Maidenstowe and all its possessions.

"Your grandfather demonstrated a rather singular taste in women," he observed.

Elisabeth eyed the six portraits. "Quintus has always preferred fleshy to thin."

"A definite understatement, my lady."

"He maintains that he looked for the same qualities in a wife that he looked for in horseflesh—good teeth and enough padding on their flanks to insure a comfortable ride. My father contended that this room contained the most offensive display of womanflesh in the southwest of England."

Cain shot her a curious look over his shoulder, but she merely shrugged. "My father possessed a most irreverent sense of humor." She gazed at the portrait that had captured Cain's attention. "That was Quintus's fifth wife, the Lady Fiona. I'm told she had a large wart on her face that the artist was kind enough to omit from the painting. My father contended it would have been far kinder to paint the wart and omit the face. And that's the Lady Hortense." She nodded toward the gargantuan female in the next portrait. "My grandmother. She purportedly brought with her the largest dowry of all Quintus's wives. We often wondered how she transported so many valuables to Maidenstowe without being robbed. My father theorized she probably ate them."

Pivoting round, she pointed to the St. Mary brides in order of succession, from west wall to north. "The Ladies Agatha, Margaret, Minerva, Winifred, Fiona, and Hortense. Or as Father called them, Aggie, Maggie, Minnie, Winnie, Fanny, and Mother."

"And whose portrait hung there?" Cain nodded toward the space that divided Hortense from Elisabeth's mother. Filling the space was a rectangle of wallcovering that was a brighter hue than the faded yellow surrounding it.

"That was Aunt Constance. My father had an older brother James. Constance was Uncle James's wife. Some years ago she was discovered in one of the walled yew gardens, sprawled between the climbing peas and the weeping pears, engaging in some rather creative contortions with the stable master. Quintus was understandably outraged. He banished Constance from the house and provided her with enough coin to buy passage to France, then he ordered her portrait removed from its place of honor and destroyed. Uncle James had been in India for six months, so when he returned to discover what had happened, he set out across the moors after her, but he was accosted by thieves outside Postbridge and died of his wounds. The family learned some weeks later that the ship Constance had boarded lost its mast in foul weather and sank off the coast of Calais. There were no survivors."

"How convenient for you."

Bemused, she looked up at him. "Sir?"

He pondered the vacant space on the wall. "If there was no issue from your aunt and uncle's union, your father would face no impediment in claiming his right to the next marquessate. But if there had been a child, a male child, your father's ascendancy would have been ruined and you, my lady, would be no more than a tenant on these lands rather than a vessel through whom their ownership will pass."

"*If* there had been a child. But my aunt died without issue. Why ever would you think otherwise?"

He did not answer immediately. He crossed the short space to stand before Elisabeth's mother's portrait and stared up at it as if it reminded him of something he had long ago forgotten. His profile showed no softness as he stood locked in embittered silence. Indeed, Elisabeth thought, one might think his face cut from stone—hard, angry stone.

"Why would I think otherwise, my lady? Mayhap because I know that men can sometimes cheat the Reaper. They can be miraculously resurrected, even those thought long dead. Do you know what became of the stable master?"

"I . . ." She thought back, then frowned. "I imagine he was dismissed, but I don't recall ever hearing the man's fate discussed. The incident happened years before I was born, sir."

"Did you find the man's fate unworthy of your contemplation? He was, after all, a mere stable master."

A spark of irritation crept into Elisabeth's voice. "I told you I do not *recall* hearing the man discussed. That does not mean my grandfather did not bemoan his loss. I can only hope his fortunes were less ill fated than those of my aunt and uncle."

"You defend a whoremonger?"

Elisabeth's cheeks burned at his casual use of the word. "I do not defend him, sir. I merely think that death is an extreme punishment to pay for passion."

"Indeed, lady? What then would you deem a fair price to pay for unavowed passion?"

That he would ask so inappropriate a question took her aback. "You seem to derive great pleasure from playing devil's advocate, sir. I pray you are less swift to judge with your knives than you are to judge with your tongue. And I tell you this. My grandfather is the last in the line of noble lords. When he dies, so too will the name St. Mary. There are no ghosts walking the halls of Maidenstowe—no spirits waiting to become the fifth Marquess of Stoke Gabriel."

He turned slowly and peered down at her, his eyes betraying nothing. "As you will, my lady." But there was something in his tone that piqued her curiosity.

"Sir, if you are privy to information concerning—"

"Your mother was quite lovely," he interrupted her, returning his attention to the portrait. "You have her eyes. How long has it been since her passing?"

Elisabeth grew suddenly quiet. She cast an unwilling glance at the portrait. "It will be seventeen years next month."

"Seventeen years," he reflected. "Seventeen years must seem a lifetime to one so young."

"A woman of twenty-two years is hardly young, sir."

"How did she die?"

The words filled the room with their ugliness. She willed the thirty-foot ceiling to swallow the hideous sounds, but the echoes would not be silenced. No one ever spoke of the circumstances surrounding her parents' death. *Never.* But this man with his knives and his riddles dared speak the unspeakable, and she despised him for it. He was a stranger. He had no right to ask such a question. But he *had* asked, and the words hung in the air between them, mocking her, reminding her of the tragedy she had wrought. Her ruffled collarette felt suddenly tight, as if it were choking her, and in the place where her hairline curved against her forehead, she felt her flesh prickle with spikes of dampness, as if it were shrinking against her skull. She shot another look at the doorway in the hopes that Quintus would miraculously appear, but the hall remained empty, dooming her to remain alone in this room, with this man, surrounded by the horror of his words.

"She . . ." Her mouth went dry. Her tongue seemed to swell in her head, forcing her to struggle with the words. "She . . . both my parents drowned." She stared into nothingness, her eye sockets feeling as if someone had set them aflame. "A boating accident. On the ornamental pond." And then she could say no more, for she felt as if the words had become tangible things, heavy as millstones, dragging her into the depths of a bog from which there was no chance of escape. Her eyes fanned the room in a desperate attempt for diversion, and in the southwest corner of the room, on a high marble pedestal, she found the one object that could save her.

"You have yet to see Maidenstowe's grandest possesion, sir. Quintus says 'tis a treasure of inestimable worth." In a flurry of blue brocade and silver tissue she spun away from him. As she hastened across the floor, she used the tips of her fingers to sponge moisture from her cheeks and brow, and when she stopped before the pedestal, she touched a hand to its solidity to steady herself. She enjoyed only a few moments respite before she heard the click of his boot heels in her wake.

The pedestal stood five feet high. Atop its plinth, hooded in black velvet and crowned with a gold tassel, sat an object whose shape resembled that of a small domed birdcage. Elisabeth pulled upward on the tassel revealing, beneath the slow glide of velvet, a dome of glass that encased the figure of a dragon. She set the hood on a nearby chair then wondered what was going through Cain's mind as he stood a foot away from the pedestal, eyes riveted on Maidenstowe's grandest treasure.

"A Chinese empress presented the dragon as a gift to the Jesuit priest who converted her to Christianity. No one knows how it came into the St. Marys' possession, but Quintus hypothesizes it might have happened during the reign of Philip and Mary, when gifts passed between Spanish and English lands."

The dragon was a fierce, sinuous length of solid gold. It glared at the world through blood-red rubies on either side of its head. Encrusted in its long belly were no fewer than a hundred diamonds, each one as large as a pea. Its tail coiled around a treasure chest that was carved in black jade, and within the opened chest a wealth of gemstones pooled their colors to dazzle the human eye and stir human greed. Cain lifted his eyes from the spectacle to gaze at Elisabeth.

"I have seen no ornamental pond on the estate. Where did the accident take place?"

She could feel the blood draining from her face, bleaching her lips to a color she knew would rival her cheeks for paleness.

"Forgive me, m'lady," Frith announced from the doorway, "but the marquess awaits your presence in the small dining room."

Elisabeth gestured her thanks to the steward then fixed Cain with a look that, in another age, might have turned him into a pillar of salt. "Maidenstowe once boasted on ornamental pond, sir. After the accident, Quintus ordered it drained. It was his one small revenge."

As if in dismissal, she motioned him to the chair where she had set the velvet hood. "There is little need for you to bring your cloak to the dining table. I suggest you leave it here and retrieve it after you dine." But she would not be accompanying him. Nor would she ever invite him to dine with them again. He trespassed beyond the limits of good taste and imperiled the secrecy of those things she wished to keep private.

She knew now who this man was. He was a man who could not be trusted.

The small dining room at Maidenstowe was ninety feet long and lit by great branches of candles that stood tall as a man. Walking across the threshold, Cain felt he had taken up trident and net and stepped into the arena, for the room was a vast mural depicting Rome's Colosseum. As he walked the length of the dining table, paralleling Elisabeth's progress on its opposite side, he scanned the faces of the hundreds of spectators who crowded the walls, and for a brief moment thought he spied movement among the cheering hordes. A head bending toward another. A pointed finger. Almost as if someone had recognized his face and was spreading a warning throughout the room.

He slanted a look across the way at Elisabeth. She had coiffed her hair this afternoon into long curls and looping braids intertwined with silver ribbon, but he found the creation too busy for his tastes. He preferred her hair as he had seen it that morning, long and unbound and heavy with its own weight. Her skin seemed translucent in the candle flame, its soft angles and rises as luminous as the glaze on a china plate. She looked to be made of honey and cream. It had been long years since he had conjoined flesh with anyone as lush as Elisabeth St. Mary, and when he imagined the glide and stroke of that rhythm, he sustained a wrenching in his genitals that nearly lifted him off his feet.

Quintus St. Mary occupied a high-back chair at the head of the table. As Cain neared the far end of the room, he locked his attention on the marquess. The old man's head was sagging against his chest. He was slumped low in his chair and his body was still as death. Frowning, Cain slowed his steps. The old man was obviously unwell. In fact, he looked to be more than just unwell.

Pausing behind his assigned chair, he waited for Elisabeth's reaction, but she seemed oblivious to the marquess's condition. When Frith pulled a chair out for her, she seated herself without the least concern.

"My lady?"

She glanced across the table at him, her look uncertain. "Are you waiting for something, sir?"

He canted his head in Quintus's direction. "If it has escaped your attention, my lady, the marquess appears disenchanted with the idea of eating. If I might be allowed a further observation, I would say the marquess appears somewhat disenchanted with the entire idea of breathing."

Elisabeth followed his gaze. "He does look rather waxen, doesn't he?" Removing her table linen from its ring, she spread it over her lap. "Tell me, sir, do you prefer stout or port with your meal? We have an excellent selection of each."

"You ask me if I prefer stout or port while your grandfather molders in his chair?" His breath steamed through his nostrils like fire through some hellish inferno. "It does not sit well with me to play the underwit in your foolery, lady. You will tell me what game you play, and you will tell me now."

Elisabeth blanched at the unspoken threat in his words, at the barely leashed fury in his eyes. "He has feigned death for seventeen years now, sir. 'Tis his game, not mine. I merely deal with his episodes by ignoring them. Frith can attest that I speak truth. Frith?"

"Quite so, madam."

"Seat yourself, sir. Please." Her voice was breathy. "The dressing on ladies' wigs has turned rancid while waiting for Quintus to tire of his charade."

"Poppycock!" Levering himself on the arms of his chair, Quintus boosted himself upright. "You're impertinent, young woman. Damned impertinent. My third wife was impertinent and look what happened to her." As he straightened the fall of his peruke, his eyes went suddenly blank. "Or was it my second wife?"

"First wife, m'lord," came the toneless reply from the steward who placed a golden crusted pie before Elisabeth.

"I knew it was my first wife." Quintus scoffed under his breath. "You didn't have to remind me."

Cain sat down slowly and heavily, spearing the marquess with a look that was not at all pleasant. "If you are so anxious to join the dead, m'lord, I know several men who would be willing to oblige you for the price of a meal."

"Does that include you, young man?"

Cain steepled his fingers and fanned them wide. His mouth slid into a cool, controlled smile that showed the animal whiteness of his teeth. "Do you not worry that the Fates might one day grant your wish?"

"Wish? It's not a wish, young man. It's reality. How do you think you're going to leave this world? I'll tell you how. You're going to leave it the same way *I'm* going to leave it. You're going to die. We're *all* going to die! And when it's *my* turn, I'll not abide any sniffling and slobbering over the event. I've been preparing the girl for my eventual demise for years now. And you saw the result. Was she weepy? No, she wasn't weepy. She was impertinent! Damned impertinent. Cut the pie, young woman. Emma calls it *Beignets de Grenouilles*. And you, thief-taker, I've ordered a new gibbet constructed outside the parish church and I expect one tinny thief to be in your possession by the time the last nail is driven into the cross-piece."

"And when might that be?"

"Noon tomorrow."

Cain bellowed his laughter. "You expect little of me, sir." Elisabeth cut a wedge in the pie.

"Little? Young man, for what I'm intending to pay you for your services, I expect you to put a swift end to this thievery business."

As Elisabeth coaxed the wedge out of the pie, the crust suddenly erupted like water through a burst pipe. She shrieked as unidentifiable bits of meat splattered onto the table linen then threw her forearm before her face as a dark, bulging shape leaped far across the table. Alive and quivering, it landed at the base of a gilded candelabrum.

Cain's arm shot out like a cracking whip. The plateware rattled. The flatware jumped. There was a *whoosh* and a thud, and when the deed was done, he threw a long look at Quintus whose eyes were glazed with such shock that they seemed frozen in his head. "You did say the pie was called *Beignet de Grenouilles*. Did I just have the pleasure of killing the *Beignet* or the *Grenouilles?*"

Elisabeth leaned back slowly in her chair, heart racing and breath shallow. She blinked at the grotesque tableau, then blinked again, but her eyes were not deceiving her. Cain's right fist was secured around the hilt of a long, thin blade. Its sharpness had pierced the heart of the thing that had leaped from the pie, and skewered it to the table.

"What was in the pie, Quintus?" she asked, bile rising in her throat.

Silence.

"Frith?"

"Emma calls it 'Frogs Legs in Pie,' m'lady."

Elisabeth's stomach executed a slow roll as she realized what it was that Cain had just speared. "I won't ask whose idea it was to serve up the whole frog. That was a most unkind thing to do, Quintus. To our guest *and* to the poor frog."

"Blabbermouth," Quintus shot over his shoulder at the steward.

Cain wrenched his blade out of the table and wiped it clean on his napkin. "Are you planning more festivities for the second course, m'lord?" He turned the blade once in the candlelight, in silent inspection of the gleaming steel, then tested the point against the tip of his forefinger.

"More? Frith, am I planning more?"

"No, m'lord."

"I'm not planning more," he relayed to Cain. "And young man, if you can dispatch our brigand as effectively as you dispatched our web-footed friend, I'll see that a bonus of fifty pounds finds its way into your hands. Frith! Remove the creature's carcass from the table, and you, young woman, can finish dishing out the pie."

Elisabeth gave her grandfather an adamant shake of her head. "We'll start with the second course, and I warn you, Quintus. If I stick my fork into anything else that attempts to leap, spit, or hiss at me, I shall eat my remaining meals at Maidenstowe by myself . . . and so will you."

"Impertinent," Quintis snipped. "Damned impertinent. My first wife was impertinent."

While Quintus orchestrated the disposal of the frog, Cain shoved his shirtsleeve to his elbow to restrap his blade to his forearm. In the light thrown out by a dozen tallow candles, the girl watched the man's movements. From the inner crease of his elbow to his wrist his flesh was pale as her own. He secured his blade within its leather bindings, then, as if by habit, bunched his fingers together in a fist.

She saw his skin lift with that movement. She saw his

long, hard sinews flex against the strapping that braced his arm, and she felt a sudden aching that caused her to stroke the knuckles that had brushed that forearm only a short time before.

The man rotated his arm, checking his bindings for tightness, and the girl saw that unlike the inside of his arm, the outside was matted with hair that was as coarse and black as the hair on his head. But it was not a bestial display. It seemed more a subtle testament to manly strength and inconceivable power.

Cain drew his sleeve down to his wrist, concealing his blade beneath the flowing muslin of his shirt. Elisabeth wondered if there was a matching blade on the other arm. She had thought he'd come to the table weaponless. She realized now that ruthless men did not allow themselves the luxury of laying down their weapons. And this man, whose reflexes were honed to such lethal quickness, would no doubt part company with his soul before he would part company with his knives. His knives were more a part of his being than the air he breathed.

He *was* his knife. His eyes bore the coldness of metal; his limbs bore the hardness of steel. And as she picked her way through mutton with caper sauce and rabbit smothered in onions, she relived, in her mind's eye, the movement when Cain's arm had shot out. She could hear the stillness shatter. She could imagine the blade plunging as deeply into her flesh as it had plunged into that of its prey, penetrating straight and true.

A moist contraction sluiced through her loins, snatching her breath away. She knotted her fist in the pit of her stomach to quell the spasm, but it would not be quelled. Like an aching tooth it tormented her with its rhythmic throbbing and caused something deep within her to tear, to weep.

But these tears were not the salty tears of joy or sorrow. They were the slick, viscous tears that bespoke a man's allure and a woman's desire. She felt the core of her womanhood flood with those tears and drench her body with unspeakable sensation. She warred with her emotions, schooling herself to reason. She was betrothed to another. She could not succumb to this man's appeal as Constance had done with the stable master. She could not condemn herself to the same fate her aunt had suffered. The thief-taker's face marked him as a savage killer. He was not a man to be trusted. He would vanish from her life in a matter of days. But despite all this, she felt drawn to him in a way she had never felt drawn to another man. Thomas Penmarck repelled her with his touch, but her body had proved to her, of its own accord, that she would respond differently to the touch of a man who was hard, and quick, and smoldering beneath the surface.

She would not be repelled. She would not be repelled at all.

Halfway through the fillet of veal, Frith received a message from the kitchen that he delivered to Elisabeth immediately. "There is word from the stable master that your mare seems ready to foal, m'lady. You did indicate that you wanted to be apprised of the situation?"

At the mention of the stable master Elisabeth's face burned crimson. Folding her table linen onto the table, she prayed her forehead was not as red as it felt. "Thank you, Frith. I'll change my gown and leave immediately."

Quintus shook his head as she stood up. "I don't see

why you're bothering, young woman. 'Tis the creature's second foaling. You'll only be in the way."

Cain was on his feet by now, acting the part of the gentleman. Elisabeth made reply to Quintus's comment while exchanging a furtive glance with the thief-taker. "If it were my second time, I should still want someone with me." She dipped her head at Cain. "Sir," she said, then made her way down the long expanse of floor. As she walked, she scanned the faces of the hundreds of spectators who crowded the walls, and for a brief moment thought she spied movement among the cheering hordes. A head bending toward another. A pointed finger. Almost as if someone had divined her inner turmoil and was spreading the tidings throughout the room.

It was nearing five o'clock when Cain returned to the withdrawing room. He retrieved his cloak from the chair where he'd left it, and as he tossed it over his arm, he marked the view through the French doors. It would be dark soon—time for him to mount Scylla and scour the byways for the felon who was no felon, for the thief who was not there.

Stopping before the marble pedestal, he touched a fingertip to the glass dome. The gleam of the dragon filled his eyes so that his pupils seemed overlaid with gold. Elisabeth had called it a treasure of inestimable worth. Inestimable indeed. He knew men who would sell their wives and children to own such a treasure. An enigmatic smile played across the hard line of his mouth.

He knew men who would kill to possess something of such great worth.

*   *   *

The winds of April spawned rain in the southwest of England, and the rain reduced the umbilical cord of road that stretched between Bridestone Barrow and Maiden-stowe to a flowing river of mud. As Cain made his way back to Maidenstowe that night, he could hear little except the suction and squish of Scylla's cloth-bound hooves. The driving rain sliced into his face and eyes. The wind whipped his hood off his head. His hair plastered itself to his skull and hugged the curve of his neck like great, black feelers. He cursed the wind and damned the rain and some-time before midnight decided that the weather was too foul to continue his charade. He would postpone his bogus thief-taking until tomorrow when the conditions would, he hoped, be more favorable.

As he passed the fork in the road that was marked by the stone cross, he sloughed rain from his face with both hands. He was so cold that he could feel ice beginning to glaze the tips of his ears and nose; so cold that he could think of nothing except a warm fire, a dry bed, and . . .

Strawberries.

For some unknown reason he had been smelling straw-berries all evening. Why his nostrils should be teased by so unlikely a smell in April, in the middle of nowhere, was beyond him, but the smell lingered, even as the stink of mud threatened to overpower it. *Strawberries,* he thought, shaking his head at the absurdity of it.

In a short forty-five minutes he had Scylla rubbed down and stabled for the night. Before he left the stable block he paused at the entrance. He narrowed his eyes against the rain and shadows and peered into the same blackness he had spent a lifetime peering into. But this blackness was not total. Beyond the paddock, in a block of stalls directly opposite him, a soft glow interrupted the night, and he wondered at the reason.

His curiosity pricked, he circled the paddock to the opposite stable. As he drew near, he heard a long, straining grunt of pain. He ran the rest of the way and when he looked over the half door of the stall, he saw the reason for those grunts of pain and felt his insides twist in response.

"Help me," Elisabeth pleaded. "Please help me."

.

chapter four

Elisabeth had been in the stable for hours. In that time the mare had shown every sign of a normal labor, so Elisabeth had dismissed the stable hands for the night. But within the last half hour the mare's contractions had become long and agonizing and her moans punctuated her inability to expel her fetus. Elisabeth now regretted her hasty decision to dismiss everyone. She needed help and she needed it now, but she was reluctant to leave the animal even for the amount of time it would take her to fetch assistance.

The foal was presenting itself backward, feet and tail first, and between the mare's contractions Elisabeth was reaching into the birth canal, trying to straighten out the limbs she knew must be tangled. But her hand lacked the strength to twist the foal's limbs, so the mare continued to wheeze her pain while Elisabeth knelt on the fresh bedding, her arm buried shoulder deep in the mare's birth canal, her face misshapen with the strain—until she saw Cain standing on the other side of the door.

"Help me," she urged in desperation. "Please help me."

Cain stepped inside the stall and shed his wet cloak in one motion. With the next, he was kneeling beside her, his knees parted wide as he thrust his shirtsleeve up his arm. Another painful contraction ripped through the mare as Elisabeth withdrew her arm.

"Your presence might prove more beneficial at the other end, my lady." He removed the leather brace and dagger from his forearm. He lifted his bandoleer over his head then positioned himself in the spot Elisabeth vacated. Nine inches of the foal's hind legs were protruding from the mare in a sac of bluish white membrane.

"I fear the foal might drown in her mother's fluid." Elisabeth whispered the words as she toweled her arm dry. She stood behind Cain for a moment, and when the contraction ended, she watched him plunge his hand deep into the mare. His shoulders twisted mightily as he used his upper body strength to free the limbs that Elisabeth had been unable to maneuver. His breathing quickened with his efforts. He shifted his body to lever himself and she could see the cords in his neck swell and his lips draw back over his teeth in a savage grimace.

"Stop twisting on me, dammit," he swore at the foal's unseen forelegs.

Impelled to action, Elisabeth struggled through the deep layering of straw to kneel beside the mare's neck. "There, beauty," she soothed as she massaged the animal's flesh with her fingertips. "Shhh. Cain will make everything fine. Just fine." The mare lifted her elegant head and, with nostrils distended, emitted a piercing sound that sent darts of cold shooting up Elisabeth's spine. Elisabeth threw Cain an imploring look, but his attention was focused elsewhere as the mare shuddered with the force of another contraction.

"Come on, pretty," he coaxed in a gravelly voice. Seizing the foal's hind legs firmly above the fetlocks, Cain pulled gently, guiding them outward.

The contraction ended. Elisabeth stretched upward to see over the mare's flanks, but what she saw tugged at her heartstrings, for the foal's head was still buried within the birth canal, deprived of oxygen. "Cain?" Hopelessness mingled with the anxiety in her voice. She looked him full in the face then, and when he returned her gaze, she thought she perceived a crack in his veneer of indestructability—a softness around his mouth, a thread of anguish in his eyes, as if he too realized it might already be too late to save the foal.

The mare bellowed her pain. Cain grasped the foal's legs once again, and with a final effort drew it from the mother's body. It lay wet and inert on the straw as he wiped the membrane from its face and cleared mucus from its nostrils, yet the glossy flesh did not quiver with new life. The eyes did not open. Elisabeth stared at the perfectly formed newborn, poignantly aware of the loss of life. Cain, however, seemed reluctant to admit defeat. Taking care not to sever the umbilical cord, he lifted the foal into his arms and angled its head downward. "Come on, pretty. I'll not let you go now."

He shook the animal gently to clear any fluid that might be blocking its passages. The liverlike substance that prevents fluid from entering the foal's lungs while in the womb spilled from its mouth, but still the foal did not breathe. More anxious now, Cain set the animal back down on the straw and began to massage it with vigorous strokes.

Elisabeth watched him toil, his big hands raising the nap of the foal's hair into long wet ridges. "Breathe, damn you," he rasped. He repeated the process again and again, bending forward and back, forward and back, until Elisabeth thought his spine would surely break. She beheld the foal's spindly legs and the fringe of soft horn that covered its feet, nature's way of protecting the mother's bag of waters from being pierced by a sharp hoof before birth. With time, the fringe of horn usually wore off, but it seemed to Elisabeth that this foal would not have the chance to wear it off.

Cain sat back on his haunches. He dragged his right forearm across his brow in apparent exhaustion then reached for the towel that Elisabeth had discarded on the straw. "I'm sorry," he said, heaving himself to his feet, and because he could find within himself no words of consolation other than the ones he had already spoken, he walked away, leaving Elisabeth to grieve in silence.

In the corner of the stall he found a bucket of water. With his back facing Elisabeth he squatted down, removed his glove, and rinsed it in the water. After wringing it out, he draped it over the side of the bucket then dunked his left arm in the liquid, scrubbing residue from his flesh with his bare right hand. His flesh squeaked as he stroked his palm down the length of his arm, and that sound made him aware of other sounds—rain battering the roof, water dripping off the overhang and splatting to the ground, thunder in the distance. He listened for the sound of Elisabeth's tears, but he heard nothing save for the soft whickering of the mare and the rustle of straw. He hung his head for a moment, surrendering to his own grief, then just as quickly looked up again. He could remember only one other time when he'd felt so physically drained. The exhaustion made him wary, for a tired man neglected caution, and that was a luxury he could ill afford.

He thrust his hand back into his glove, and as he stood he interlocked his two hands, forcing the wet wool into the vees between his fingers. A solitary lantern hanging from a peg on the wall bathed the room with drab yellow light. When he turned, he blinked to readjust his eyes to the brightness, then puzzled over the sight that greeted him.

Elisabeth's white blond head was bent close to the foal's face. Her hand covered one of the animal's nostrils, and into the other nostril she was . . .

Thinking his eyes were playing him false, he stepped closer. She was *breathing* into the other nostril, as if she thought herself capable of imparting life to the tiny creature. "My lady." He went down on one knee. "The foal is dead." But this pronouncement did not stop her, for she continued to blow deeply into the curve of the newborn's nostrils. He reached out a hand to draw her away, but as he did so he caught sight of movement beneath him, and he looked down.

A foreleg twitched.

"Jesus."

Elisabeth lifted her head and when she saw the reason for Cain's epithet, she began to blow great draughts of air into the foal's lungs.

Hind legs kicked out. The foal snorted, a joyous sound as it filled the stall. Cain sat back, watching as the newborn shook its head, opened its eyes, and blew a continuous stream of air through its nostrils, accustoming itself to life. He had thought there was little in life anymore to merit his wonder, but this girl who stood no taller than his shoulder had just proven him wrong. She had done the impossible. She had imparted life to the dead, a feat so unnatural that the thought of it caused the skin on his forearm to tingle with odd sensation.

He watched her as she leaned forward to peek at the foal's underside. She moved with suppleness and grace, reminding him of a willow wand bending against the wind. But in her spareness there was strength. Of that he was sure. A weaker female would still be weeping over the incident with Thomas Penmarck. This female was different—different from other women; different from himself. Indeed. It was her greatest pleasure to restore life; it had become his to take it away. A deep, abiding shame washed over him at the disparity in their natures, and he ground his teeth together in irritation that she continued to make him languish in self-recrimination.

He saw a smile break across her face as she determined the sex of the foal. He watched her hasten around the animal to stand before him. Eyes bright and face aglow, she grabbed his right hand in both of hers. "Congratulations, sir." She pumped his hand up and down in exhilaration. "'Tis a boy."

But Cain was unable to share her exuberance. Her virtue made him feel vile, unclean. Her touch was trusting and kind, but he did not want her to be trusting. He did not want her to be kind. *Damn you,* he cursed as he glared at her hands. *You don't know who I am. You don't know why I am here.*

He stilled the motion of her hands abruptly, then seized her wrist with fingers whose grip would not be broken. On the day he exacted his vengeance, he would see that she wept a virgin's tears and bled a virgin's blood. On that day she would be no different from any other woman he had used to slake his lust. No different except in one respect—the other women, at least, had been willing. He looked up, locking eyes with her.

Elisabeth felt her breath catch at the sudden change in him, for he was staring at her with eyes that looked to be hovering on the brink of insanity—feral eyes. Savage eyes. And his hand—She tried to wrest her hand from its imprisonment, but she was solidly trapped.

"What do you want from me?"

"Want? 'Tis not what I want." He rose to his knees, then his feet. He tightened his grip around her wrist so that her blood seemed to thicken in her hand, settling like lead. "'Tis what I will. And what I will, lady, has little to do with patience or virtue. I grow bored with virtue." He drew back on his arm, drawing her closer to his chest. And then in a voice that crackled with hoarseness, "I tire of patience."

His tone sent fear coursing through her veins. His intensity convinced her that what she had suffered at the hands of Thomas Penmarck would be child's play in comparison to what *he* was capable of meting out. She felt the pull of muscle in his arm as she tried to lean away from him and in his eyes she saw the hunger that she had only guessed at earlier. His was the all-consuming hunger of a predator. Her heart hammered a rapid tattoo against her ribs as she realized she was the prey.

"Nay!" she cried out.

In that moment a burst of white light made daylight of darkness. The interior of the stall seemed to quiver with motion as the lightning flamed and receded, flamed and receded. Elisabeth turned her face into her shoulder, blinding her eyes to the brightness, but she could not close her mind to the dreaded memories that the lightning roused. She pinched her eyes shut. The image of the ornamental pond seared into her consciousness, and with it fragments of the scene whose horror still stalked her. The glide of the dinghy. The pristine whiteness of her father's wig. The sway of her mother's hand directing him to left, to right— directing him toward the wooden sailboat that had foundered in the middle of the pond and was spinning in slow circles on the breath of the wind.

In her mind's eye she saw the dark-bellied clouds that hung low in the sky on that day seventeen years ago. She saw the cat's-paws that ruffled the water, and to the accompaniment of her mother's laughter she saw her father lean over the side of the dingy and—

A great boom of thunder shook the walls of Maidenstowe, crippling Elisabeth with the images it froze in time and memory. She curled her fist against her ear trying to blot out the din, and when she could not she let out a high, puling sound like that of an animal snared in the jaws of a steel trap. The sound cooled the hotness in Cain's blood. He slackened his grip on her wrist. She responded by tearing her hand from his grasp and clapping it over her other ear.

Another burst of lightning streaked across the room. Head bent and eyelids clamped shut, Elisabeth staggered backward, flattening herself against the wall. Her chest heaved with fright. She steadied her hands over her ears. Her features bunched painfully together as a second roll of thunder crashed above them, causing her to press the back of her hand to her nostrils as if the sound had released something fetid into the air.

"Ohhh God!" she choked.

Cain took a cautious step toward her. Her face was profiled to him as she cowered against the wall. "The storm will do you little harm if you remain inside," he reassured her as another deafening burst of thunder broke around them.

"The smell," she whispered, short of breath. "Can you not smell it?"

He took another step, inhaling deeply as he did so. Straw. Horse. Rain. These things mingled their scents on the night wind. "I smell nothing foul."

"The air. It . . . it reeks of it."

"Reeks of what?"

A flash of lightning. A roll of thunder. Elisabeth shielded her face in the crook of her elbow while images fixed themselves on the backs of her eyelids. "The pond. They were on the pond because I wouldn't return to the manse without my birthday gift."

Cain advanced toward her, stopping when he was but a foot away. "Gift?"

"A boat. A . . . a grand sailing vessel that Quintus gave me for—" The wall trembled with the storm's violence. Elisabeth swallowed her words and gasped for breath. Cain reached out his hand to her, then, feeling suddenly awkward, withdrew it.

"Quintus gave you a boat," he said in a calming voice.

She nodded once. Twice.

"He gave it to you on your birthday."

She nodded. "My sixth birthday." She drew the words out on a long breath behind the protection of her forearm.

"Your sixth birthday." Only then did he make the connection. If she was twenty-two years of age, and her parents had died seventeen years ago next month, she would have been either five or six when the mishap occurred. Jesus, had her parents drowned on her sixth birthday? Had there been a lightning storm that day too? Is that why she was so terrified?

"Quintus gave you a grand sailing vessel on your sixth birthday," Cain repeated. "You must have launched it on its maiden voyage right away."

She lowered her arm until it was yoked around her throat. Her eyes were dazed and distant. "It had canvas sails," she said. "But when it reached the middle of the pond the sails collapsed and it began spinning round and round. They wanted me to leave it there. They wanted to hurry me back to the house because the sky was dark with storm clouds."

"But you wouldn't return without your boat."

"I . . . I screamed when they tried to take me away. I cried so horribly that they had to indulge me. I knew they would fetch it if I cried. I was their only child and . . . and they loved me."

The room quivered with light again. Elisabeth gritted her teeth and breathed through her nose as if this would render her agony more tolerable. The thunder was directly overhead now and it exploded around them like battle fire. Cain shouted to be heard above the roar.

"Your parents gave in to your tears. What did they do?"

Elisabeth shook her head. "I can't."

"Was there a pier that extended into the pond?"

She shook her head more vigorously.

"A boat? Did they row out to fetch your toy for you?"

"Stop it!" Her voice was high, shrill.

"Did the boat capsize? Is that how they drowned?"

"No!" A blaze of lightning ignited the darkness, paralyzing Elisabeth. Eyes transfixed, she stared into the light, seeing again the trident of fire as it had streaked to earth, hissing toward the dinghy. "The lightning!" she cried. She blinked in rapid succession, trying to erase the images. "It came from nowhere and it hit them! It . . . it lifted them into the air and when I looked they"—her voice grew eerily quiet—"they weren't there anymore. Gone. They were gone. And the smell. Sweet Jesus, the smell!" She clawed at her nose as if by stripping it from her face she would escape the smell. Cain grabbed her hands before she could do herself harm, but she fought him with a strength he had not imagined she possessed.

"You're . . . hurting . . . me," she cried, struggling against his restraint.

"You hurt yourself."

"I kill people!" she screamed. "Did I not make that clear? Did you fail to understand what I did to my parents?"

He held her firmly as she twisted her limbs left and right. "You did not summon the lightning!"

"I killed them!" She drilled him with a look of such naked guilt that he felt as if he were being crucified. "The lightning bolt did not kill them. The water did not kill them. *I* killed them! With my selfishness. With my disobedience." She sounded as if the words were choking her, then softly, she said, "I killed them."

He had thought her incapable of weeping, but when she spoke those final words, he saw that her vulnerable side was indeed close to the surface. Her brow constricted, pulling the tight flesh awry. The gentle dip at the root of her nose crimped like the segments of a fan. Her eyebrows puckered over the bone. He saw her eyes glaze with tears and then he saw those tears float onto her cheeks, scalding flesh whose texture looked to be smooth as warm custard. She compressed her lips to still their quivering and when her tears drifted into her mouth, she hung her head, unable to fight him any longer.

"Does it please you to witness my shame?" Her shoulders trembled with her sobs, but her voice was quiet, her emotion spent. Cain let go her arms. She crossed them over her abdomen and hugged her hands to her waist, and as she stood there with her back braced against the unyielding support of the stable wall, he saw her tears gather along the contour of her chin and spill like raindrops onto her yellow wrapping gown.

Look at her, an inner voice commanded. *You wanted to see her weep.* But he had not realized it would be so painful a thing to watch, and this circumstance confounded him. He had seen over ten score necks stretched at Tyburn tree. He had seen grandmothers disemboweled and young men drawn and quartered. He had watched these things without emotion. Why then would this girl's tears touch a part of him that had remained immune to the obscenities he had lived with for over two decades?

He lifted his right hand close to his chest and in a gesture so unconscious that he no longer realized he did it, he stroked his gloved palm with the thumb of his left hand. He knew why the girl's tears ate away at him. He knew, because there had once lived a child whose nostrils had likewise burned with the stink of scorched flesh. He knew, because that child had once spoken in the same pleading voice as Elisabeth St. Mary and had been ignored. Cain imagined the horror of a six-year-old child seeing her par-

ents obliterated before her eyes. He imagined the nightmares, the fear, the emptiness . . . the tears. He had wept
similar tears long ago, in a dark room, without benefit of a
kind word or a comforting hand. He wondered who had
comforted Elisabeth when she had wept. He wondered if
anyone had. Had the child she had once been cried in the
same darkness and solitude? Had she reached out, as he
had, to find only emptiness?

And despite who she was and what he had vowed, he
could not watch her cry without remembering that time in
his life before he had become the man known only as Cain.
He could not forget how precious a gift comfort would
have been.

" 'Lisabeth," he whispered. Reaching out, he shaped his
hands around the back of her head and drew her gently
against the solid bulk of his chest. His fingers touched
curls and looping braids and when he bent his lips to her
hair, he closed his eyes and breathed in deeply, smiling of a
sudden, for her hair was sweet with the very fragrance that
had tantalized his senses all eventide. Her hair smelled of
strawberries—wild, fresh strawberries, summer ripened
and waiting to be picked. How had his cloak . . .

And then it struck him. He had wrapped his cloak
around her earlier that day. In the short space that she had
worn it, the cloak had absorbed the scent that clung to her
hair, almost as if the wool thirsted to disguise the smell of
horse and sweat with something of a sweeter nature.
Thirsted, he admitted, as he thirsted.

He felt her stiffen as another roll of thunder rumbled
above them, but the intensity was diminishing as the storm
moved steadily eastward. Cain pressed his cheek to the

crown of her head. "'Tis over now," he calmed her. "'Tis passed."

Not knowing what to do with her hands Elisabeth curled them into fists and angled them against Cain's waist. He felt the light pressure against the waistband of his breeches and judged that this was probably the closest she had ever come to hugging a man. He tilted her head back slightly, balancing its weight in the long hollows of his palms; thinking not of what must eventually come, but of the here, the now.

"'Lisabeth," he whispered again, in a voice so thick with desire that it seemed to wrap itself around her in the same protective way his cloak had. The hard knot of tears in her throat began to dissipate as she allowed herself to be soothed by the softness of this man's voice, by the gentleness of his hands. Unlocking her fists she opened her hands and touched them shyly to the same place where she had angled her fists. Beneath her palms she felt the unyielding contour of flesh that was lean and hard, and she warmed to his earthly appeal.

"Your hair smells of strawberries," he whispered close to her ear. She felt the feather touch of his breath skim along the curve of her ear, causing her to shiver with untold sensation. In response she flattened her hands at his waist and clung tightly, for she could no longer feel her feet.

He touched his mouth to the top of her ear, and when he felt her shiver, he lifted his head slightly, looking rather than touching. He had never given much heed to this part of the female anatomy. When he took a woman, his need was usually so immediate that he did not care one whit if the wench even possessed ears.

Elisabeth's ears were fine and delicate, like seashells.

The scroll of flesh at the top was so thinly skinned that it looked fragile as the handle of a porcelain posset pot. He saw pockets of shadow hidden within the intricate recesses of her ear and he wondered if that darkness had a taste, a texture. Her lobe was detached from her ear and hung full and soft. *As full and soft as a woman's breast,* he thought, feeling his loins tighten with his desire.

In the glow of lantern light he saw the film of fine, pale down that glazed that lobe, and with the flat of his thumb he touched it, amazed at its incredible softness. He stroked slowly upward, then down, tracing the outer curve of the sac to the place where it attached to her head. The lobe, with its rounded fullness, reminded him of other shapes. Fleshy shapes. Malleable shapes. Shapes that had provided bawdy sport for his hands . . . and his mouth. Lazing his thumb along the sweet angle of her jawline, he touched his thumbnail to the underside of her earlobe and with a gentle motion lifted it upward to meet his waiting mouth.

She felt the warm touch of his tongue as it played over her lobe, coiling around it in a slow, slithering movement. His mouth was a place of moist heat and slickness, and as he continued to ply her flesh, she felt her ear begin to throb with heat and her loins begin to throb with moisture. His breath quickened against her ear, sheathing it in a caress of warm air that flowed downward over her neck and prickled the flesh at her hairline. His own hair was damp and tangled and she felt wispy strands of it tease the corner of her eye as he shifted her head gently in his hands. A touch of hair, and then his cheek was pressed lightly to hers, warm flesh to cold, joined by the wetness of her tears.

"Sweet," she heard him whisper against her temple. Male to female, hollow to rise, their cheeks conformed one to the other, and her tears, flattened and skewed between them, evaporated as quietly as morning dew. His mouth lingered at her temple. His lips were firm and dry and touched her with a softness that made Thomas's earlier brutality seem all the more abhorrent.

Her breathing grew shallow as she reacted physically to the touches of his mouth—slow touches that whispered along the bone of her cheek to the inside corner of her eye. She felt his lips part against her closed eyelid and, echoing the gesture, she unconsciously parted her own. His mouth tarried over the web of fine blue veins that patterned her lid and with the tip of his tongue he memorized each tiny stroke, as if he found each one a rare and precious treasure.

He tipped her head back. Her cheeks were dry now, but he could still taste the faint salt taste of her tears as he worked his mouth over the rise of her cheekbone to her lips. She held her breath as he gave her a light, grazing kiss in the center of her mouth. She felt the cool touch of his nose against her own and then he was angling her head to the side and slanting his mouth hard across hers, branding her with a thief-taker's passion.

He slid his hands down the back of her head to her neck, then crossed his forearms behind her, enfolding her from shoulder to shoulder within his solid embrace. He surrounded her with his body, smothered her with his mouth, his warmth. She felt the tip of his tongue glide along the evenness of her teeth then slide upward to stroke the sleek underside of her lip.

The rush of his breath filled her mouth. Her fingertips went numb with sensation. Her breasts seemed to swell against the hardness of his body. She held her lips very still as Cain probed the soft, wet places of her mouth, but when she felt the hotness of his tongue pressing against her own, she recoiled at the intimacy and careened headlong back into reality.

An image of her aunt and the stable master blazed into her consciousness—limbs and flesh intertwined in a secret garden, but secreted from no one. Had they once coupled in this very stall? There were eyes everywhere and loose tongues aplenty. Just as a servant had found her Aunt Constance, a stable hand could find her . . . and Cain. Would she be banished from the estate for cuckolding Thomas? Or would Quintus express his displeasure in the one way she feared the most?

Her insides withered as she imagined his censure. Stricken, she flattened her palms against Cain's chest and stiff-armed herself away from him, bolting out of his embrace before he found the presence of mind to stop her.

"Elisabeth!" He spun around and reached out a hand for her, but she held up her palm to ward him off as she backed toward the door. Her eyes looked suddenly haunted.

"This . . . this did not happen. This *can*not happen. 'Tis madness. *Madness.*" She flung open the stall door and raced into the night. Cain made to give chase, stopping himself before he had taken two steps.

No woman had ever run away from him. It galled him that this one had, but he swallowed the insult as he regarded the stall door. "Run while you're able," he whispered after her, for he knew that in the end there would be no escape from him.

chapter
five

"Something wrong with your 'ead, mum? You've been rubbin' it 'alf the mornin'."

Elisabeth stilled the hand with which she was massaging her temple and returned it quickly to her embroidery frame. "A bit of a headache is all." She jabbed her needle into the satin canvas and bent over her work with exaggerated concentration.

"Drafts," counseled Emma, bobbing her head. Emma Pigeon's face was round as a full moon, her cheeks red as polished apples, and from beneath the ruffle of her mobcap her graying hair stuck straight out in little corkscrew curls that floated around her head like the moons of Jupiter. She stood at one end of the trestle table that dominated Maidenstowe's kitchen, a long, homely piece whose surface was pockmarked with deep gouges and stained with the juice of summer berries. Flour from her apron sprinkled the air as she buried her fists deep in a bowl of dough that billowed halfway up her arms.

"Drafts," she repeated. "If you'd be closin' the drapes

'round your bed, mum, the bad vapors in the night air would be less apt to get inside your 'ead and cause it to ache."

Splotches of heat warmed Elisabeth's cheeks as she dwelled on the reasons for the pain in her head. Anxiety over her behavior with the thief-taker and fear of discovery could wreak mayhem on the calmest of minds. "I shall be sure to close the drapes, Emma."

"You be doin' that, mum. Good and tight. Imagine that draft settlin' in like that and you not even in your bed 'alf the night."

Elisabeth held her needle suspended above her embroidery, guilt rampant in her downcast eyes.

"Frith said, 'e 'eard you come in in the wee hours of the morn, mum. You must 'ave 'ad a long night of it with yer mare. But I 'ear she delivered a fine colt, and that, despite that 'orrible storm. Better 'er than me, mum, and that's a fact."

Relieved that her evening's tryst with Cain hadn't been discovered, Elisabeth poked her needle once again into the satin, but her hand was not as steady as it might have been. "Why do you say better her than you?"

Emma covered the bowl with a cloth then moved on to the next bowl, driving her fist into the center of the dough that swelled above the rim. "I've been through that four times, I 'ave, and I'm not rememberin' any of it kindly. My 'Enry got four babes on me. All four of the little angels born dead, they were. No, mum. I'm thankin' the Good Lord I don't 'ave to be sufferin' like that again." Realizing what she'd just said, she threw an apologetic look across the table at Elisabeth. "The Lord cut my tongue out for a fool. 'Ere I am blatherin' 'bout things that a new bride 'as no need to 'ear. I wasn't meanin' to say that I wouldn't do the same thing all over again, mum. It's a woman's lot and she don't fret about the pain when she's thick with the bairn of the man she loves."

Elisabeth stared at her embroidery. Within the year she could be thick with the bairn of a man she despised. How jealous she was of the love Emma had shared with her Henry. How grand it would be to wed a man who cared naught for her dower lands. A man who tasted of strong soap rather than rice powder. A man whose kiss could make her feet feel detached from her ankles.

She thought of Cain, then quickly dismissed him. It was dangerous to think about him; dangerous to think what might have happened had she not run from him last night. But she could not deny there was a part of her that hadn't wanted to run, for within the circle of his arms, for a fleeting moment, she had felt all the affection she'd been denied since her parents' death, and she had wanted it to last unto eternity.

Lacking the enthusiasm to continue with her stitchery, she set her needle down on the recessed edge of the embroidery frame and folded her hands in her lap. "What's it like to be in love, Emma? Does it happen all at once? Does it happen gradually? Can you remember how you felt?"

Emma crinkled her nose as if that might help stimulate her memory. "Gory, mum, my 'Enry and me said our 'I do's' when I was fifteen, we did. That was some"—she ticked years off on her fingers—"some fifty odd years ago. Don't remember whether it 'appened slow or gradual anymore. More than likely we both 'ad itches what needed scratchin', so we marched ourselves to the parson to make it all legal like."

Elisabeth looked mildly disappointed. "'Tis all you re-member?"

Wiping her hands on her apron, Emma sat down heavily on the deal bench that flanked the table and propped her dimpled elbows up before her. "Give me a space to think, mum. It might come back. I do know these noble gents might be thinkin' that marriage 'as everything to do with land and politics and nothin' to do with love, but they're wrong, they are. For a woman, marriage 'as everything to do with the way she feels 'bout a man. Take your Sir Thomas. 'E's not an easy one to warm up to, 'e's not, wot with 'is bein' so stiff and serious. I spoke to your grandfather more than once tellin' 'im that 'e wasn't doin' right by you, but I suppose I was speakin' out of turn."

Elisabeth forced a smile, but it came out frail at best. "I don't imagine your Henry was anything like Thomas."

Emma laughed at that, a great toothless grin splitting her face. "My 'Enry wasn't nobility, mum, but 'e could make me feel a besotted fool when 'e'd a mind to. Made me feel safe and good, 'e did. And there be days when 'e could look at me and make the 'airs on my arm stand on end. 'Ad a knack for making me feel miserable and wonderful all at the same time. It 'urt to be near 'im and it 'urt *not* to be near 'im. Some days I'd be so taken with 'im that I couldn't feel my 'ead, my feet, or the ground I was walkin' on, like someone cleaned out my insides and stuffed me full o' eider yarn. My 'Enry 'ad 'is faults, but there's none could make my 'eart smile like 'im." She sucked on her toothless gums for a moment before nodding decisively. "That's when you know, mum. When a man makes your 'eart smile."

Elisabeth pondered the shelves of Chinese porcelain and

delftware that lined the walls, and as she did, her lips shaped themselves into a tight compress. Thomas had never made her *mouth* smile much less her heart. In fact she thought him incapable of such a feat. But Cain . . .

The muscles in her face underwent a series of changes, embodying every sentiment from awe to delight. She had felt a besotted fool when he'd kissed her last night. He had made her feel safe and good, but to attach any lasting sentiment to what had transpired between them would be to invite disaster.

Emma scratched her cheek with fingertips that striped her face with ribbons of white. "Could be when 'is lordship makes you 'is bride, 'e'll add a bit o' grease to 'is joints to loosen 'imself up. Though it wouldn't be surprisin' me if he come to you with 'is breeches still buttoned and that white lead all over 'is face."

The image made Elisabeth feel as if the air were being squeezed from her lungs, but Emma, seeing the unease flicker in the girl's eyes, bobbed her head with sage understanding.

"You needn't be shy with Emma," the old woman clucked. "I know wot be worryin' you, I do. I fretted about the same thing myself. Every bride frets about it, mum." She threw a cautious look over each shoulder before lowering her voice. "It don't 'urt as much as some would 'ave you believe."

Elisabeth trained a queer look on the woman. "It?"

"It," Emma repeated, a conspiratorial gleam in her eye. "Course, the pain might 'ave something to do with the man. I 'ave it on good authority that they're not all the same size"—she dropped her gaze to her lap—"down there."

Enlightened at last as to what they were discussing, Elisabeth lent the woman her undivided attention. Such conversations were rare in her experience, but she was naturally curious about men, and "it." Emma was bound to know more about these matters than Elisabeth, whose knowledge of carnal matters was derived mostly from common sense and observing the St. Mary bloodstock mate. "I had never given much thought to the idea of pain," Elisabeth admitted. But she remembered the incredible length that a stallion flaunted prior to mounting a mare, and she wondered how there could be anything *but* pain. Her tongue suddenly felt like a lump of dry clay in her mouth. Despite the unease she felt at discussing such delicate matters aloud, she forced herself to ask, "How big do your authorities claim a man can get... down there?"

"Well, mum, the way I 'ears it, there's blokes walkin' around who are long as broad axes and thick as my ankle. Surprises me 'ow some of them can walk without trippin' over the things. Then there's the poor unfortunates like my 'enry. Hung like a polebean, 'e was. Not the same color as yer ordinary garden variety bean, mind you, though the thing might 'ave been a sight easier to find if the Lord 'ad thought to slap a bit of color on it."

Elisabeth recalled the endowment of the first Baron of Drewsteignton as seen through the scope of Thomas's longglass. The man in the portrait had an inordinately smug look on his face. Was his size the reason? Were men proud of such physical attributes? She didn't dare ask Emma why size would constitute a source of pride, but neither could she allow the subject to fade when she was learning things that might be vitally important to her as a married woman.

Suppressing her embarrassment, she ventured another question. "How can you tell . . . well . . . how big it is without actually seeing it?" The thought of broad axes and pain was suddenly making her nervous.

Emma waggled her right thumb in the air. "You look at the bloke's 'ands, mum. Now, when 'is clapper is just 'anging there, chances are it'll be the same size as 'is thumb."

"His thumb?" Elisabeth studied the length of her own thumb and frowned. "Have you taken actual measurements?"

"No need for that. A woman simply knows these things, mum. A wee thumb means a scrawny clapper. But if a man's thumb is almost of a height with 'is other fingers, then we be talking broad axes, because 'is thing can grow to *four times* its length when it's of a mind to. Four times its length and 'ard as 'orn. Next time you're in the drawing room, mum, you be givin' the portrait of yer relative the first baron a good looking over. 'E's got the second biggest thumbs I've ever seen, 'e does."

Elisabeth smiled that Emma had lent her observation to such things. "And who claims the honor for having the biggest?"

"Why, the stable master that yer Aunt Constance lured 'tween her thighs, mum. 'E 'ad 'ands big as anvils, 'e did."

No one had mentioned her aunt's name for years, but here, in the space of two days, Elisabeth found herself drawn into two separate conversations about her. It almost seemed a warning. "Why do you say she lured him?"

Emma favored her with a wry look that said "A woman simply knows these things." "Well, mum, if the truth be known, yer Aunt Constance was one of those Mediterranean types. Not like us, they're not. Tend to think with wot's between their legs 'stead of wot's between their ears. And that 'andsome swain that come to work in yer grandfather's stables got a fever brewin' in 'er blood that drove 'er to madness. She'd 'ave to be mad to do wot she did with 'im."

Mad, thought Elizabeth. As mad as she had nearly been last night. But no matter the appeal of Cain's mysterious seduction, she could not succumb to him as Constance had succumbed to that other stranger, in that other time. Constance's mistake served as a timely reminder to her. Great ladies who fell into disfavor ended up disgraced, or dead.

"What do you remember about the stable master, Emma?"

The old woman worried the hairs on her chin with the back of her hand. "'Ard to remember anything about 'im, mum, me bein' in one place and 'im another. 'Ad a funny name, 'e did. Escapes me now. But 'e was a tall one, 'e was. 'Ad black 'air. Black as the bottom of my kettle. And a fair 'and with your grandfather's bloodstock. Would 'ave lasted a long time if he'd known enough to keep 'is clapper out of places it 'ad no business bein'."

Tall and black haired. *Like Cain*, Elisabeth thought. And for some reason, that bothered her. "Do you know where he was from? Or where he went after Quintus dismissed him?"

Emma gave her head a thoughtful tilt. "Don't know wot 'appened to 'im, mum, but seems to me 'e 'ailed from somewhere in Cornwall. 'Ad that dark Cornish 'air, you know. And I'm rememberin' that 'e was quite the storyteller. They 'ave the gift for spinning yarns, the Cornish do."

Was the thief-taker Cornish? Elisabeth wondered. Improbable as it seemed, was there some connection between Cain and the stable master? Yesterday, in the withdrawing room, Cain had seemed uncommonly interested in the fate of the man. Why?

He can't be Cornish, an inner voice reassured her. *How can a man who rarely speaks slip into the role of a Cornish bard?* Impossible. And yet... "Thomas is Cornish, Emma. I've never heard him spin a yarn or tell a tale."

"'E's no doubt savin' them to tell yer children, mum."

At the thought of bearing Thomas's children, something cold and dreadful surrounded her heart. She thought of the pain and indignity she had suffered at Thomas's hands. Touching a finger to her top lip, she remembered the harshness of his violation and the taste of her own blood filling her mouth. She imagined herself on all fours and Thomas playing the part of the stallion. He would be all brawn and trumpeting virility, and she would be at his mercy. "'Let me lesson you in the appetites of your lord husband,'" he had said. For a moment nightmare images swirled in her head—images of broad axes and pain and blood. Images that might have become reality had Cain not interfered.

"Coo, mum, yer white as my bread dough. Doin' a poor job of putting yer mind at ease, I am. A sip of cordial water's wot you need." Flattening her palms on the tabletop, Emma boosted herself to her feet. "And I'll 'ave one with you, I will." The ring of keys at her side jingled as she crossed the floor.

Elisabeth bowed her head, staring at the cloth that was

stretched between the wood of her embroidery frame. The
piece was worked entirely in white and depicted a solitary
raven whose head was cocked to the side as if eavesdropping on the secrets of ages past. She thought it a fair rendi-
tion of the raven with which Thomas stamped his
correspondence. She had seen the actual signet ring with
the Penmarck family crest only once, for with all the thievery on the moors, Thomas rarely wore it on his travels.
But she had been working the piece for five months now
and hoped to finish it so she could present it to Thomas
before the wedding.

She wondered if he would care she had spent five
months plying feather stitches and French knots for him.

She wondered if he would ever look upon her with kindness.

She wondered how she would fare living with a man
who would never make her heart smile.

The warm breath of summer whispered through the
moorland that afternoon, erasing all vestiges of the storm
the night before. Kneeling at the edge of her garden, Elisabeth ranged an eye over the greening lawns of Maidenstowe. The greenness bore a fragrance as fresh as winter's
first snow, a subtler smell than that given off by the rectangle of rain-soaked earth before her.

Her garden occupied an area as large as the stable yard,
a vast area for one person to oversee, but she had accepted
the challenge and smiled now to think that it had thrived so
well under her care. She had arranged the garden into a
patchwork quilt design, like that of the distant fields, and
had delineated each separate section with crushed stone.
Within the sections she used twine to plot where her seeds

should be planted to produce an overall symmetry that, during the summer, would blossom into diamond shapes and circles, ovals, triangles, and spades.

As she marked her handiwork, she realized she had stamped the same order upon her garden as Quintus had stamped upon her life, assigning boundaries and limits, and it took her aback to think how easily she could impose the same dictates she sometimes ached to rebel against. At some point during the past seventeen years she had no doubt learned there was safety in order, reward in order. Greater reward than she had ever anticipated. For she had never nurtured a plant that did not repay the kindness in some way—with its beauty, with its curative powers. And when she used the plant as a curative, she reaped more reward, for to see a man healed or a child made well brought infinite satisfaction.

The smile on a child's face could seduce her into thinking herself loved. So perhaps she nurtured her garden for selfish reasons. Looking back now she could see how tending it had softened the realities of her life, for by tending this plot of earth and worrying over its progress, she had not allowed herself time to pine for the love Quintus withheld from her. She had transferred the affection she sought to her garden, and so she had survived.

The sun lingered on her back, warming the fabric of her gown so thoroughly that she could feel the hot press of her corset lacings against her spine. The heat put her in a mood for the days of summer, but thoughts of summer suddenly led to thoughts of Cornwall, and she didn't want to think about that now—not while the sun was warm against her spine and the air was sweet with the smells of new grass and moist earth.

She leaned back on her heels and bowed her head forward, turning it to one side then the other, with a motion as unhurried as the swing of a pendulum. A frilled white lawn cap, fitting close to her head, hid the blond of her hair, and atop this she wore a flat, broad-trimmed hat of leghorn straw that was lined with cherry silk and tied below her chin with velvet ribbons. As she bent her head forward, she bared the pale flesh of her neck to the sun's warmth, and she closed her eyes for a space, thinking a forbidden thought, for the sensation was no less warm than Cain's breath had been as he'd whispered her name against her ear the night before.

"You left in great haste last night, lady. Why?"

Elisabeth's eyes flew open. Against the dark soil of the garden she saw a taller shadow superimposed on hers—a shadow that obscured the shape of her own and cast a sudden coolness upon her back. She swiveled her head round. Cain stepped into her line of vision. He stopped by the edge of the garden, standing with his feet braced apart and his hands clasped behind his back. He did not look at her as he studied the expanse of brown earth before him.

Wary of this man whose presence could only spell doom for the ordered nature of her life, she held her head high and answered him crisply, in a tone that belied her discomposure. "Your boldness last night was inappropriate, sir. You forget both yourself and the fact that I am betrothed to another."

"To a man who bloodies your lip with his affection." He snapped his head round and impaled her with a look so frightening that she could not identify him as the same man who had welcomed her into his embrace hours earlier. "'Tis the brand of affection you prefer, lady?"

" 'Tis not the brand of—"

"Have you sampled the affections of a wide array of suitors? I would guess from your response last night that you had never before been kissed, or held, or touched."

Warm blood dyed her cheeks, but her eyes did not waver from his face. "I do not think inexperience is something for which a lady need be ashamed. I simply tell you, sir, that what happened last night must never happen again."

A muscle worked in his cheek as he contemplated her words. "I kissed you last night, lady. Nothing more. I take my pleasure with women with the same frequency that some men piss, so do not expect me to act the part of the lovesick swain or to feel compelled to repeat our encounter. It meant as much to me as a toss with a London tart, which is to say, it meant nothing at all."

Feeling as though she had just fallen through a gallows door, Elisabeth looked away from him, humiliated. She had somehow thought him cast from finer thread than other men. She saw now that her assumption had been a gross error in judgment. He was a commoner with common manners. But more to the point, it hurt to think that even a commoner found her unacceptable.

Anxious to be away from him, she gathered up the small pouches of seeds that were scattered around her and dumped them into her arm basket, then boosted herself from her knees to her feet.

"Your garden has the look of you about it," said Cain, breaking the silence that had lengthened between them. "The perfect rows of stone. The precise formations of plants. You could not simply throw everything together. It had to be exact. Perfect."

Elisabeth swept her hand across the back of her over-petticoat, brushing grass and twigs from the fabric. "My regrets that you find order so offensive."

"We do not speak order. We speak a haunting obsession for correctness, for perfection. Observing what you have done here, I would say you carry the concept to the extreme."

His words pricked her skin like the pointal of a hound's tongue seed, adding fire to her words. "Without order there is chaos. If you knew anything of gardens, you'd realize that the only things to thrive in chaos are weeds. And furthermore, sir, should you ever require an herbal decoction to restore your health, I pray the person preparing the decoction will know the difference between parsley and hemlock. *I* know the difference, but should I send someone to fetch herbage for me, I have no assurance *they* will know the difference. Does it not seem provident to you then to plant herbs in specific configurations so that they may be identified by their design rather than by their leaves or flowers? 'Tis easy to recognize hemlock when it grows in concentric circles or spirals. 'Tis more difficult to recognize it when 'tis growing in a neat row next to the parsley. So I disagree with your assessment. I do not have an obsession for perfection. I have an obsession for life and its preservation."

"A veritable St. Elisabeth. How commendable."

Elisabeth stabbed her tongue into the side of her cheek and shot him a withering look. "I trust you slept soundly enough last night, sir. You obviously did not sleep long enough." She snatched her basket from the ground and looped it over her forearm. Cain tossed his hand in the direction of the garden.

"I have little knowledge of herbs, lady, but even I can

identify some of the herbage that is sprouting hither and yon without benefit of its growing in circles, or diamonds, or squares."

"My compliments. When your thief-taking days are over, perhaps you can apprentice to a London apothecary whose knowledge is less extensive than yours. I'm sure a man whose qualifications include the ability to identify *some* herbage will find himself in great demand. Good day to you, sir." And as she made to return to the manse, she bristled that he had not even had the courtesy to wish her the time of day before throwing himself into such glowing criticism of her gardening techniques. She did not see his eyes roving the dips and rises of earth as she walked away from him, eyes that roved curiously at first, then with stark understanding.

"It happened here, didn't it?" he called out. "The pond. Your garden occupies the area where the ornamental pond once sat."

His words stopped her midstride. Exhaling a cold breath, she turned round, slowly and silently. She observed the place in the center of the garden where, in a month's time, purple-headed lavender would show its many heads —to the place where, seventeen years ago, they had found the remains of Richard and Gillian St. Mary.

Statue-still, she gazed at the small patch of earth with its tidy trail of greenery. "'Tis why the plants grow in such profusion," she said, her voice small and distant. "After Quintus drained the pond, he refilled it with cartload upon cartload of soil from his tenants' gardens. He summarily buried the past beneath tons of rich, dark earth." She paused to stare. "I sowed lavender in the place where they found my parents. My mother always wore lavender. I remember how it clung to her clothes and scented the air when she walked."

Cain regarded her full in the face. "And it was after your mother's death that your fear of storms began. Why has your grandfather done nothing to allay your fear? Why has he allowed it to continue for so long?"

Elisabeth lowered her gaze to her arm basket. With her right hand she fingered the bright embroidered script on one of the linen pouches. "He does not know of my fear."

"He doesn't know? Storms are common as crows on the moorland. How could he not know?"

"Because, sir, I did not *wish* him to know. The manse boasts many rooms. 'Tis not difficult to hide oneself in the corner of a vacant salon where one can endure one's fears in solitude. 'Tis not difficult to feign a malady of the head or stomach when one hears the first rumblings of thunder."

Cain shook his head. "So you become the perfect child who fears nothing and is kind to everyone."

"I am not perfect! Why do you throw that in my face as if it were soiled linen? Do you know why he does not know of my fear? Because if he knew, we would have to discuss my parents' death. And should that happen, if Quintus was reminded of my part in the event, there would be nothing to prevent him from condemning me."

"No man would condemn a child for the thing you accuse yourself of doing."

"You are mistaken, sir." Her eyes looked suddenly bruised, wounded. "Do you know he has not spoken my name since my parents died? He has called me child, young lady, young woman. He has not deigned to use my Christian name for seventeen years. He has not so much as hugged me or patted my hand as other grandfathers might do with their grandchildren. Condemn me? He finds me so loathsome he cannot bear to speak my name lest his tongue rot in his head!"

She tilted her head so that the brim of her hat might shield her face from his probing eyes, but Cain was relentless. "You do not call him Grandfather."

"He does not wish it. He advised me when I reached the age of six that his name was Quintus and I should address him as such. One only uses the term grandfather when there is an exchange of affection between family members, or are you as untutored in family politics as you are in gardening?"

He continued talking as if she had not spoken. "Your perception of your grandfather could be incorrect. You should confront him, lady."

"So that I may be branded a killer for the rest of my life? Do you offer advice on how I am to live with such condemnation?"

"Is the quality of your life any the better for not knowing?"

"Can you not understand the meaning of fear?" Her voice cracked with emotion. "Why should I expect you to understand? How could a thief-taker know anything of fear? How could a man who finds comfort in the cold steel he wears strapped to his chest ever have suffered a moment's trepidation?"

"My knives do not protect me from fear, lady. I have known fear. I know it can wrap itself around a man's soul and suck the life from him. I know it can weigh down a man's spirit until it destroys him. I also know that if a man confronts it, his fear can become his strength."

"Nobly put, but 'tis not you who must live with the consequences."

He executed a slow half turn, his body rigid, his hands resting on the hilt of his sword. "Mayhap you savor your fear. Perhaps it allows you an excuse for self-pity."

She did not answer him. She lifted a pouch from her basket and, deep in abstraction, lingered on the script that marked the linen, staring at it as if she had never seen it before. "Sundew," she said, lifting her eyes to the square of earth where she usually sowed the plant. "I remember drying the seeds last year, but when I opened the pouch today, it was empty. Have you ever seen sundew, sir? There are tiny hairs on the leaves that retain moisture, so the leaves are always moist, even on the hottest days. 'Tis as if the plant is constantly weeping. Perhaps I should find a cheerier plant to replace it."

"I have seen sundew growing at the base of Bowerman's Nose. If the plant is so essential, why not dig a small number up in the moorland and transplant them here?"

She laughed an odd, humorless laugh. "How optimistic of you to think that Quintus would ever condone my venturing into the moorland. Did you forget that my Uncle James was killed on the moorland, sir? That my father was struck by a bolt of lightning right here on the very fringes of the moorland? Do you expect my grandfather would permit me freedom of movement in light of those circumstances? I am his sole surviving relative, sir. The last conduit through whom his wealth and property might pass. Were it not for my weekly visits to the parish workhouse, I would see nothing outside the walls of Maidenstowe. Quintus may find it difficult to love me, but he has little difficulty in protecting his property. And what am I if not another piece of property?"

Cain regarded her strangely. "It confounds me whether your blind obedience deserves my admiration or my pity. You have so convinced yourself that your childhood disobedience caused your parents' deaths that you have become a bastion of obedience in atonement. You have followed your grandfather's edicts no matter how ridiculous or constraining simply because you believe that any disagreement will gain you Quintus's disfavor. I find it incomprehensible that you have never ventured into the moors, nor seen the Thames, nor tasted sea spray on your lips. Your obedience has worked to your detriment, lady. 'Tis sad you have done yourself so great a disservice."

His criticism of her was so reminiscent of Thomas's that she bristled visibly. "So far this afternoon, sir, you have found fault with my gardening, my character, and my judgment. I had thought this penchant for criticism to be a trait peculiar to Thomas, but you apparently share more traits with him than I imagined."

"You know nothing of me," he seethed. There was anger in his voice, but she could not guess whether the anger was directed at her or himself. Whatever the case, be she gently bred or not, she tired of being civil to this man who could do little this afternoon but insult her.

"I know nothing of you, sir. And if the truth be known, there is nothing I care to know." She left him then, feeling as vindicated as she imagined a lady might be allowed to feel.

"We visit the parish workhouse on Wednesdays, young woman. When I awoke this morning it was Saturday. That being the case, would you be so good as to tell me what the blazes we're doing in this coach, headed for the parish workhouse?"

Elisabeth reached into her basket of medicines and removed a phial of liquid that she held up for Quintus's perusal. "Oil of sweet almonds."

He gave his mouth a perverse twitch. "Is that supposed to mean something?"

"If you had been awake this morning when Churchwarden Treacle called, you'd know what it meant." She tucked the phial back into the basket. "Ned's ears have worsened since Wednesday, so Mr. Treacle thought he should apprise me of the situation. A few drops of the oil will alleviate the pain. It worked quite well two days ago."

"You couldn't have given the phial to Treacle? Could have spared me a trip if you'd thought of that, young woman."

Still stinging from Cain's evaluation of her yesterday, Elisabeth came to her own defense in rather uncharacteristic manner. "'Tis not as if we squander our days roaming aimlessly about the countryside. We make so few trips outside Maidenstowe it surprises me you even consent to own a coach."

He sniffed his indignation. "My third wife wanted a coach to one-up my second wife." He screwed up his eyes in thought. "Or was it my fourth wife wanted to one-up my third?"

"I can't see how our venturing on two outings in a single week will cause any harm," Elisabeth continued. "We're probably guilty of being involved in too few outings in our day anyway, Quintus. Perhaps we've deprived ourselves irreparably by staying so close to home. I mean, I've never seen the River Thames, nor ventured into the moorland, nor tasted sea spray on my lips." She had dwelled on those words since Cain had spoken them. She had been reasonably content with the passive mood of her life until he had stirred the waters. What she saw as quiet isolation he saw as privation, and that irritated her.

"By God, it *was* my fourth wife," Quintus stated emphatically, then changing his expression, he said, "I think. Dammit, young woman, if Frith were here he'd know. Frith knows everything. And furthermore I think it a capital idea that we're going to the workhouse. Gives me a chance to see the new gibbet. Not that we're going to need it any time soon. What with the way this thief-taker is dragging his feet, I could be moldering in my grave before he ever bags the lout who's supposed to swing from it."

"He has been here only three days, Quintus."

"Doesn't matter. A man of his reputation should have snared that miserable footpad on his first night out! Don't know what's taking him so long, unless he's cooling his heels at Maidenstowe to take advantage of some free food and lodging. But that doesn't wash, does it? He hasn't sat a meal with us since . . . since he gelded that frog on the dining table. The man's table manners are appalling. Simply appalling."

"Two days ago you implied that his dexterity be applauded."

"Did I?" He fluffed his periwig. "Impertinent of you to remind me, young woman. Damn impertinent. My sixth wife was impertinent."

As the iron-hooped wheels of the St. Mary coach clattered over the granite viaduct that spanned the River Teign, Elisabeth found she could not keep silent. What if what

Cain suggested yesterday were true? What if her perception of Quintus were incorrect? Was she needlessly committing herself to a loveless marriage? She had to gauge how ill-disposed Quintus would be should she voice reservations about the betrothal he worked so hard to arrange. "Quintus," she asked as she fiddled with the phials and pouches in her basket, "what would happen if, for some reason, Thomas and I . . . well . . . if we never married?"

"Never married?" He bent forward and gave his walking stick an angry thump on the floor. "Thomas Penmarck had better entertain no thoughts of crying off on this marriage. I've spent too much time laboring over details to have him back out now. No marriage? I'm expecting you to produce at least one healthy, squalling heir before I die, young woman, and I don't have much time left, so this marriage had *better* take place. I can't waste more time arranging another betrothal for you. I'll be dead in my crypt and worm-eaten before the papers can ever be signed. No marriage?" He thwacked his cane on the floor again. "It'll be *his* bones hanging from the new gibbet if he dares approach me about canceling this wedding. Damn the man anyway!"

Elisabeth's stomach tightened into wrenching little knots. She had guessed that Quintus's ire would know no bounds if his affairs were tampered with. Unfortunately, she had guessed correctly.

"You're looking absolutely peaked, young woman."

Elisabeth sighed. "If I swoon, I'll remember to do so on my side of the coach."

"See that you do." As they neared the village of Brides-tone Barrow, the coach slowed for a flock of black-faced sheep that were wandering in the road ahead. Elisabeth peered out the opposite side of the coach, marking a thatched stone cottage that sat far back from the road, wishing she could marry simply, like Quintus's tenants; wishing she could choose a mate without having to consider land, or wealth, or power.

"Did you love any of your wives, Quintus?"

He prefaced his answer with a snort. "Never."

"Did any of your wives fall in love with you?"

"Love, young woman, is an unnatural emotion that exists solely in the minds of poets. Emotional tripe is what it is. Has no more substance than air."

"But without air, a person dies."

Quintus's thorny brows beetled over his nose. "Impertinent," he sniffed. "Damned impertinent."

Her spirits dampened, Elisabeth retreated once more into silence. She wondered if Cain's opinion of love was consistent with Quintus's. *Emotional tripe. No more substance than air.* Perhaps love was emotional tripe. And perhaps the warmth of emotion she had felt in his arms two nights ago had no more substance than air. But the fact was that it hurt to be near him and it hurt not to be near him and ever since he had kissed her she had felt as if someone had cleaned out her insides and stuffed her full of eider yarn.

And none of this made her heart want to smile.

Late that same night two men sat at a table in a dim corner of the Horn on the Hoop tavern in London. The common room was smoke filled and stank of rancid mutton fat, and every time the door opened there drifted into the tavern not only another customer, but the stench of putrefying offal flung into the streets from second-story windows.

Thomas Penmarck trickled an ample measure of vinegar

onto his pocket handkerchief, restoppered the cruet, and held the vinegar-soaked linen to his nose. "A man sometimes forgets the vile odors that lurk in the streets of London."

"I'll be wagerin' that's the only thing in your life you ever let yourself forget," grated the man across the table from him. "Never known you to be one given to forgetfulness." The man brushed his knuckles along his stubbled jaw then reached up to finger the misshapen knob of flesh where his left ear had once sat. "And I s'pose you're sitting there hard as bone just thinkin' 'bout what you'd like to've done to your blond bride on your recent visit. She'll be in for a treat when she gets you 'tween her legs, won't she, mate?"

Thomas drilled a malignant look at the man. "Should I ever hear you utter Elisabeth's name again, Skagg, I'll cut your filthy tongue out of your head. You're not fit to carry her name around in your head."

The man named Skagg grinned savagely as he raised a mug of stout to his lips. Thomas wadded his pocket handkerchief in his hand.

"What do you know of a thief-taker who goes by the name of Cain?"

Skagg wiped his mouth on his shirtsleeve. "He kills people. And when he doesn't kill 'em hisself, he hauls 'em back to Newgate and lets someone else do it for 'em. He catches cutthroats and scum. Like me . . . and you."

Thomas ignored him. "He's taken up residence at Maidenstowe. The old man hired him to catch the thief who has been hounding the village. I don't trust the wretch. There's something about him that bothers me. He looks familiar, but I can't place him."

"You want me to see what I can dig up on him?"

"No." Thomas rubbed the place on his neck that had withstood the thrust of Cain's rapier. His face burned once again with the insult. "I want you to kill him. I don't care who he is. I just want him dead."

chapter
six

On Sunday morning a missive arrived from Churchwarden Treacle. Frith delivered it to the kitchen where Elisabeth was watching Emma begin preparations for Sunday supper. Breaking the seal, the girl unfolded the parchment and read aloud: "'Fiona lent her bonnet out yesterday and worked the field all day bareheaded. The sun played havoc on her freckles, my lady. She woke up this morning with her head aching, her eyes aching, and her face red as a rough-headed poppy.'" Elisabeth smiled at the image before continuing. "'Dizzy too. She couldn't stand up this morning without falling on her—'" Elisabeth squinted at the word. "I can't make this last word out."

"Head," supplied Emma.

Elisabeth frowned. "'Tis a longer word."

"Arse."

"I think the word is . . . pallet. 'She couldn't stand up this morning without falling on her pallet.'"

Emma nodded. "If a body's got to fall, a pallet's as good a place as any."

Elisabeth cocked her head as she thought aloud. "Cyanus juice might soothe the ache in her eyes. But it sounds as if the sun has already wreaked its damage on her complexion. There's little I can do to prevent her skin from blistering, but if I decoct a pot of ointment or salve, it might relieve the burning." She sighed. "'Tis a trifle early in the season for sunburn. I fear Fiona has caught me rather ill-prepared." The most effective treatment for sunburn, she'd discovered, was a mixture of sundew leaf juice and milk. But she had no fresh sundew in her garden.

Confounded, she walked to a side table in the corner of the room. Pouches of her compounds and simples crowded the top of the table, and on several wall shelves sat clusters of stone pots, earthen pots, glazed pots, gallipots, and glass jars—containers wherein were stored the specific preparations with which she treated the sundry complaints that plagued the occupants of the parish workhouse.

For ten minutes she perused clarified juices, syrups, decoctions, electuaries, distilled waters, and oils—remedies to treat anything from the ague to black jaundice. With her dried herbs and roots and bark she could prepare a julep for purging the body or a poultice for cooling inflammations, but she could do nothing for Fiona's sunburn without sundew, the plant that Cain had seen growing at the base of Bowerman's Nose. There was nothing to prevent her from sending someone into the moorland to fetch the plant for her. That would be the logical thing to do. The safe thing. The obedient thing.

The word stuck in her craw as she strode the length of the room to where Emma was de-legging pigeon. It weighed heavily upon her that both Cain and Thomas would deride her for what Cain had termed her "blind obe-

dience." She had always considered this her grandest virtue, but they had blithely dubbed it her greatest weakness,
and their criticism made her angry, at them and at herself.
It embarrassed her that this obedience had prevented her
from sampling even a minimum of what others of her sta-
tion had experienced. By submitting to her fears she had
allowed herself to become smothered, trapped, and it net-
tled her. She might be mistress of Maidenstowe, but she
was more a mistress to the restrictions of her captivity. She
was angry that she had become so devoted a slave to her
fear, and today she felt just angry enough to allow a rare
streak of defiance to rear its head. If there was sundew to
be found near Bowerman's, she would not send someone
else to fetch it.

She would fetch it herself.

"Have you ever seen Bowerman's Nose, Emma?" She
ran her fingertips along the edge of the table and batted
away the dismembered leg that came flying across the table
at her off the tip of Emma's knife.

"Once, mum. When I was a girl. Due south of 'ere I
think it is. Beyond the River Bovey. You ever seen the
Bowerman, mum?"

Elisabeth shook her head. "Nay, but I'm not so interested in the Bowerman as I am in sundew."

Emma bobbed her head in confusion. "Is that a fact?"
She returned to her cutting. "The Bowerman's a fair distance from 'ere, mum."

Elisabeth compressed her lips. Emma was probably
about to tell her that it was too far away for her to travel.
She would probably threaten to tell Quintus. She would ask
why, after all these years, Elisabeth was about to venture
into the moorland when she could very well send someone

else to do her bidding. She squared her shoulders and braced herself for the woman's objections.

"Lots of scrub and brush 'tween 'ere and the Bowerman, mum. You suppose, since you're 'eaded in that direction anyway, you might keep an eye peeled for juniper berries? I'm needin' six crushed ones for my compote, I am, and there's none to be 'ad around 'ere."

Elisabeth felt the tension in her spine slacken. She smiled. "Six juniper berries. I'll be sure to remember."

"The pigeons will taste better for the berries, they will. And funny you should mention the Bowerman. Did you know, mum, that legend 'as it that the Bowerman was named after a man who lived on the slopes of 'ound Tor, among the crags? Pity the bloke if 'e looked anything like the pile o' rocks 'e's named for. Would 'ave been easier on the eyes lookin' at a boiled pigeon carcass, it would. The man must 'ave been ugly as a bald-'eaded baby."

But Elisabeth was listening with only one ear as she plotted how she would further her escape. Today was Sunday. Many of the stable hands worked only part of the day on the Sabbath. She would find a groomsboy to saddle a mount for her, a boy who would never dare question his mistress's intentions. But if he did . . . she smiled at her own deviousness. She would tell him she had acquired an interest in the flora and fauna south of the Bovey, and she could not remain at Maidenstowe while they beckoned her attention.

Would a boy accept that?

Much to her surprise, he did.

She approached the Bowerman from the west, traveling across the scrubby heath on a little cob mare. The area of Dartmoor formed a plateau that was shaped like a blunted arrowhead. She found her way south along the plateau, across a wasteland of narrow lanes and open cart roads, and around granite trackways that the bog had sucked into its depths like overturned gravestones. As she rode, she eyed this terrain that not even a late summer's misting of heather would cheer. She eyed it warily at first, then with greater confidence. The moorland was treeless, without meadow or hedgerow to soften its harshness, but it belonged to her for there was no other horseman about. She was alone, and free, and she sucked in a lungful of air with almost manly vigor. It seemed she had donned wings rather than riding jacket and hat, and those wings could transport her anywhere. So she narrowed her eyes and tightened her grip on the reins and smiled broadly as she roamed amid the rocks and bracken of this forbidding place. But it was no longer forbidden to her for Elisabeth St. Mary, mistress of Maidenstowe, had deemed it so.

She found Emma's juniper berries in a heath south of the Bovey and a bounty of sundew in the same place. She dropped a handful of berries into an empty seed pouch, then wrapped the sundew in moist muslin and tucked both items into her saddle pouches. She might have returned home then, but the sight of what she assumed was Bowerman's Nose in the distance roused her curiosity, so she traveled a mile farther over the rough turf, and at the base of a rise that sloped gently upward for two hundred yards, she tethered the mare, located a footpath, and made a careful ascent to the summit.

The Bowerman stood twenty feet high and was, in essence, a tower of stone blocks that rested atop each other in precise balance, from the smallest stone at the top to the largest at the bottom, sitting upon a base whose plane was dead level. To Elisabeth it seemed that the formation was an oblique rendering of a man's profile, with a single block shaping his body, another forming his head, and another constituting what could be either the peak of his cap, or as the name implied, his nose. Unlike the other tors of Dartmoor that were little more than weathered stumps of rock, the Bowerman seemed to be the work of human hands, for there was something premeditated in its composition, something that was too accurately constructed to be the result of random erosion.

She pondered what the sculptor's model had looked like, for the twenty-foot shaft of stone had a prehistoric aura about it, as if the man called Bowerman had existed in a guise more primitive than that of modern man—squatter, hairier, apelike. Elisabeth traced a finger along the vertical crack that split the largest block then sat down on the plinth and looked out over the moorland.

She felt brave sitting atop this mysterious outcropping of antiquity. Brave, and immensely proud of herself. She had found her way into the moorland, accomplished what she had set out to do, and nothing had befallen her. Her bold disobedience had resulted in her being neither struck by lightning nor beset by thieves. She smiled an exhilarated smile, a smile of freedom, of fearlessness. At this moment, with the moorland stretching out before her, she felt as if she could do anything. Bending forward she rubbed the ankles of her boots and could almost hear the sound of her imaginary shackles dropping away. "Pity me, will you, thief-taker?" she said aloud. And musings about the thief-taker prompted other thoughts of the man.

Four nights had passed and he had yet to catch his thief. An odd happenstance considering his reputation, but he seemed to have been struck both deaf and blind. Thomas would likely gloat over Cain's failure. Cain would no doubt guffaw that Thomas thought he bore a resemblance to the fifth or sixth viscounts of Upton Pyne. Thomas had been quite insistent on the matter, she remembered, but in truth, she had seen no similarities between Cain and her two ancestors, not in coloring, bone structure, or disposition. But Cain reminded Thomas of someone. Who? She knew of no one as tall and black haired as Cain. The only other person who even vaguely fit that description, if Emma could be trusted, was Aunt Constance's Cornish stable master.

This last thought seared through her consciousness. Was it possible that Thomas had known the stable master in Cornwall? Or if not in Cornwall, then here at Maidenstowe? Thomas had been conducting business with her grandfather for long years now. Surely his path had crossed that of the stable master. Perhaps Cain, being tall and black haired, inspired images of the stable master in Thomas's mind. Possibly. But what if the resemblance between the two men was based on something other than supposition? What if it was based on fact? Could stable master and thief-taker be related?

A trill of excitement fluttered in her chest. It made perfect sense! Thomas recognized Cain because Cain and the stable master shared a family resemblance. And Cain's main objective for being at Maidenstowe was not to catch a thief, but to avenge that long ago insult to the relative who had been caught with the mistress of the house and been banished for the indiscretion. That would explain his grilling her on the fate of the stable master. It would explain his talk of dead men, and resurrection, and his desire for secrecy. It would explain his surliness in the garden, for if his heart was locked on revenge he would certainly not want to admit that he had derived pleasure from the kiss they had shared, especially if she were the enemy. But how would he exact his revenge? What was his intent?

She would find out. She would confront him this evening in the stable, as he readied Scylla for their nightly sojourn. She would find out who she was and why he was here. *And then what?* an inner voice asked.

And then, she did not know. But she felt smug and wondrously courageous that she would dare such a thing. "'Tis you who is to be pitied, thief-taker, imagining your deception would go undetected." She said it in a loud voice that echoed over the moor, and when the reverberations stopped, she touched her hand to her lips, remembering the shape of his mouth.

There was such gentleness in him. He hid it well beneath harsh words and secrecy, but it was there. She had felt it. And despite who he was and what he professed, he had touched her heart in a way that no other ever had, and try as she might, she could not forget it.

Thomas's long-glass hung around her neck. Straightening she lifted the cylinder to her eye and extended the scope. The land was dark and angry, its granite ribs sneering up at her like a mouth full of teeth. To the west, the peaks of three granite tors pierced the soft bellies of clouds that hung low in the sky, while southeast of the Bowerman, a half mile in the distance, there rose another tor. It was pockmarked with crags of barren rock, and a host of carrion birds soared above the saw-toothed spires of its summit.

Her attention lingered on the spired tor and she wondered if, along its slopes, there grew a wealth of plants and herbs whose use might be of benefit to her.

Of course there might be, she decided, shortening the long-glass. But she realized she was merely confecting an excuse for herself. The truth was she was reluctant to surrender her freedom so quickly.

The northwest wind, suckling on the moist breast of the upper Atlantic and growing fat on the excess, freshened during the afternoon. Elisabeth stamped her hand on the crown of her three-cornered hat to prevent it from flying off her head as she maneuvered her mare across the half mile expanse of marsh that separated the Bowerman from the spired tor. It looked like a rotting corpse with its collars of black earth and elbows of rock impaling the dark swelling of its skin. Elisabeth dismounted and looped the cob's reins around a tall spike of granite that stuck upward from the ground like a bony finger.

There was no footpath upward, a circumstance that should have alerted her to the tor's isolation and prodded her to ask why the tramp of human feet did not mar the soil here, but she was too excited to worry, so she left the cob behind and forged her own path.

The ground where the tor began its rise from the moorland was thick with undergrowth and brush. Elisabeth made her way around the northern base of the tor, and at the foot of the eastern slope found that the dense growth of vegetation was sparser here, allowing entry to higher ground. She waded through the thigh-high tangle, pulling the petticoat of her riding habit along behind her for its heavy folds of velvet kept catching on the prickly brambles. As she wrestled her way out of the undergrowth, the full hang of her petticoat dragged across a clump of yellow gorse, and she was suddenly imprisoned. The spiny little shrub shot into the velvet like a porcupine throwing its quills.

An impatient yank on her hem did not free her. She let go of her hat to tug again with both hands. This, too, did not free her.

But when her hand left her hat, the wind swept beneath the brim of her tricorne and blew it off her head, carrying it high on a current of air toward the upper elevation of the tor.

With her mouth hanging open as if to call it back, and her hand stretching outward as if to catch it, Elisabeth watched her hat tumble and twist in the breeze and then disappear behind an outcropping of moorstone halfway up the scarp. "Don't you dare move," she muttered. "Stay there. Right there." Bending over the spiny bush, she grabbed a fistful of the petticoat with both hands and gave a stubborn yank backward. Half the bush broke away from its roots and attached itself to the underside of her petticoat as she made her escape, but she shook it off, kicked it away, and with a determined breath started upward.

Beyond the dense undergrowth that wreathed the lower slopes, the land widened into a band of greenish black turf. Stepping onto this tawny sweep of earth, Elisabeth windmilled her arms to balance herself as her tall leather riding boots sank past their heels into the spongy sod. She lifted her petticoat high to prevent the hem from becoming any more soiled than it already was. With more guarded steps now, she plodded through the soft yielding moss, her footfalls making squishy sounds and leaving slight depressions in the earth behind her.

Reaching higher, firmer ground, she stopped to catch her

breath. Above her, a ledge of granite bowed outward from the tor like a giant saucer. To the right of this, between two boulders that dwarfed the surrounding crags of stone, a narrow way tunneled upward to the next elevation. The opening was just wide enough to allow her to squeeze through it sideways, allowing about two inches leeway between the tip of her nose and the opposite wall. With her palms pressed flat against the opposing surface, she guided herself upward. Her fingers curled into the lichen-encrusted stone as she inched her way along, her boots crunching on the scree of pebbles and gravel that formed a loose mosaic beneath her feet.

The terrain was no gentler on this higher elevation. It was crowded with gray rock—a wild cemetery of moor-stone crypts and tombs that were jammed together in angry configurations, funneling the wind through fissures that cut the stone to its marrow and sent it whistling back down the slope in a ghoulish howl. She covered her ears as strong surges of wind battered her head, and through slatted eyes she scoured the crags that rose above her, blinking away the sting of tears that the wind drove in horizontal streaks across her cheeks. Seeing no trace of her hat, she continued upward, weaving her way around the knots of granite on what meager bits of solid ground she could find. When the summit loomed only twenty feet above her, she circled around to where a low ring of rocks formed a protective cul-de-sac and peered back down over the face of the tor, her feet tingling with the height.

It was then that she spied her tricorne. It was thirty feet to her left, where a wide shelf of level rock fronted a sheer vertical wall, angled into the ell where two massive boulders abutted. She smiled her satisfaction as she clambered over the rocks to retrieve it.

One of its three corners was bent, and the blackcock plume was missing, but it was only three years old and she was relieved to have it back. She held it firmly as she stood for a moment pondering how she would get back down again, all thoughts of further exploration forgotten.

The bedrock on which she stood was deeply scored with fracture lines over which a crust of dark lichen and creeping juniper had grown. With hat in hand she wended her way back across the flat dish of bedrock. Where she stepped, the rock was water smooth, worn slick from run-off. The wind gathered behind her, driving her before it, and she rushed her steps as it blew her, placing the weight of her foot on the froth of vegetation that crowded up between a narrow cleft.

The lichen gave way like loose thatching, skittering down into the black depths of the fissure as it tore away from the rock. As it disintegrated, Elisabeth's boot disappeared between the gaunt lips of stone. She cried out, losing her balance as her left knee buckled beneath her. She threw her body to the left, trying to break her fall, but in doing so the foot that was wedged between the rock twisted around at an unnatural angle, jamming itself between two jagged protrusions. She felt something snap as she fell forward onto the heels of her palms. A searing stab of pain knifed upward through her right leg, and she held a long agonizing breath as the shock waves radiated through her body. When the pain became tolerable, she eased backward on her skinned palms, wriggling her way above where her foot was caught so she could gauge just how badly she was stuck.

The dead air that stagnated in the jaws of the chasm wafted up to her, chilling her with its moist, rank breath. Her foot was caught between two knobs of rock that formed a vise above her ankle, but this was less troubling to her than the feel of this lifeless air creeping from its pit and crawling about her flesh.

She reached into the fissure. Pinching the boot above where it was caught, she relaxed the muscles in her foot and began working the boot back and forth, gently, see-sawing it up and down, scraping and gouging the flawless texture of the leather, but slowly working her way out of the vise until she gave a final breathless push downward and was free. Lifting her foot onto solid ground, she scooted away from the fissure.

She rotated her ankle in endless circles as she sat and convinced herself that the snapping she had felt had been in her mind rather than her foot, for the pain had eased, leaving a strange numbness in its place. She shambled to her feet, shifting her weight from right to left as her foot balked at the pressure. From where she stood, she eyed the waiting terrain with a sudden desperate dread, questioning her ability to retrace her steps over the face of the tor. It was a very long way down and longer still around the tor's base to the place where her horse was tethered. She hobbled forward a few steps, then stopped, realizing for the first time that her hands were empty and her hat was—

Her eyes darted about.

—gone.

Exasperated with herself for her clumsiness, she looked

upward and, seeing the brow of the tor only twenty feet above her, began to toy with another alternative. Why not climb up instead of down, cross the summit, then descend the western slope that would lead her directly to her horse? It would be a shorter route than the one she had followed upward, and surely the hazards could be no worse than the ones she had already encountered. And so thinking, she braced her body for pain and hobbled upward.

At the summit of the tor, where the granite spires wreathed the shallow crater, Elisabeth sank down exhausted on a stump of rock. She could go no farther. Bending her knee she drew her leg up closer to her body and held her booted foot in her hands. There was little sense trying to talk herself out of the pain any longer. There was something terribly wrong with her foot and she couldn't walk another step. She was, to her utter horror, stranded on a mountaintop with no safe way to get back down again. Fighting off a wave of panic, she twisted herself around to look down into the crater, but her attention riveted instead on something that lay several paces below her, something whose foulness putrefied the air, and her heart fluttered slightly as she stared at it.

It was an animal, perhaps a dog, whose neatly severed head rested yards away from its neck, and whose carcass had been defiled by carrion birds. That she would find a dog at this great height was baffling enough, but to have it decapitated as well—she shivered at the possibilities, and glancing toward the northwest, saw the outline of Bowerman's Nose in dark relief against the sky. Of a sudden Emma's words echoed again in her head. *Legend has it that the Bowerman was named after a man who lived on*

the slopes of Hound Tor, among the crags. On the slopes of
Hound Tor . . .

In the distance a dog howled.

She stared at the carcass with sudden understanding.

She had found Hound Tor.

chapter seven

Although a slow and painful process, Elisabeth had managed to drag herself into the mouth of the crater where, among the tor's many boulders, she could seek refuge from the wind. Before the last rays of daylight were spent, she had found shelter in a four-foot-long space formed between two adjoining boulders. The interior faces of the rock formed a tent of cover over her. So she sat with her knees tucked under her chin and her arms circled around her legs, listening to the thunderous march of clouds that struck sparks in the sky above her.

She had been disobedient and now she was being punished. With a lame foot. With lightning. She should have expected this. It happened every time there was a disruption in the order of life at Maidenstowe. And now she could not even hide in the corner of a deserted salon to escape the lightning. She bent her forehead against her knees to mute the effects of the brightness. Never again. She had tasted enough freedom today to last a lifetime. Its appeal had worn remarkably thin. And she cringed to think what lay ahead. Quintus was no doubt at this moment pacing the floor with worry, not for her welfare, but for what her welfare meant to the estates. His wrath would be unfathomable. And what that wrath would prompt him to say filled her with a fear more paralyzing than that caused by the lightning that danced above her head. For the pleasure of a day's freedom, she had blithely and at her leisure cut her own throat.

A sheet of lightning illuminated the summit of the tor, then streaked downward to where the cob mare was tethered. The horse whickered and pranced and pulled on the reins that were knotted around the granite marker, but she could not break loose. In the darkness she sensed subtle movement about her, as if the very rocks were slithering across the bog to surround her, and when lightning once again broke across the moor, she saw the dark shapes worming their way in her direction, and their eyes, like fathomless spheres of light boring holes in the darkness.

The mare's terrified whickers filled the night. She strained against her reins, forefeet pawing the darkness. Another blaze of lightning and she could see the spikes of bone that protruded from their gums, long and white and bubbling with froth. She could smell the foulness that spewed out from the deep pit of their stomachs. The mare kicked out as they surrounded her, her whinnies tearing from her throat as the hounds nipped at her fetlocks. She split the skull of one hound as it crawled beneath her flailing hindquarters, yet at the same instant a larger hound attacked the mare's foreleg, laying open flesh to the bone. With jaws wide, a dozen more hounds slunk closer, until suddenly they were upon her.

Elisabeth heard the mare's cries echoing up to her from

the bog. The horror of the sound made her remember the animal she had found. She curled her fingers protectively around her throat, and as she looked outward from her hiding place, she felt the air in her lungs freeze with terror.

The groomsboy at Maidenstowe was not yet thirteen years of age. As he stood before Quintus St. Mary at a quarter to the hour of ten that night, he questioned his chances of ever reaching that milestone.

"You didn't try to stop her?" the marquess bellowed.

The boy paled. "My lady told me that Flora and Fauna beckoned her south of the Bovey, yer lordship, and I wasn't of a mind to stop her if it was visitin' the sick she was about."

"Flora and Fauna?" Quintus shot Frith a suspicious look. "How the devil did she meet these people?"

"I believe they're juniper berries, m'lord."

Quintus's eyes grew very small and very beady. "She rode into the moorland to visit two juniper berries?" He thwacked his walking stick on the floor in anger. "You think me daft?"

Frith's left eyebrow arched high over his socket. "Emma informs me that the Lady Elisabeth ventured into the moorland to pick juniper berries for Emma's compote and sundew for Fiona Ratchet's sunburn. One might refer to these items as flora and fauna, m'lord."

Quintus ground his teeth together. "Do you know the time, Frith? Do you know how long she has been gone? Do you know if anyone **has** been sent to look for her? Why wasn't I informed earlier?"

"You were sleeping most—"

"Dammit, man, I don't want to hear excuses! Find the

thief-taker. With any luck he may be more proficient at finding young women than in apprehending thieves. And dispatch the rest of the stable into the moorland after her."

"Yer lordship." The groomsboy raised a finger. "I mentioned to the thief-taker before he left this evening that should he happen upon her ladyship in his travels, he should encourage her to return home, what with its getting dark and all. He asked me where she'd gone and I told him exactly what I told you, yer lordship, but he didn't say no more about it. I hope—"

"*I* hope no ill befalls that young woman, boy, because if it does, I'll see to it that this is the last night you ever spend on this earth. Now get out of my sight. Both of you!" He thrust his hand toward the door. And when he was alone, he sat his chair and thought of the sons he had sacrificed to Dartmoor. Feeling very old, he bowed his head into the hollow of his ancient palms. "Not you too, young woman. Not you too."

The animal's cries had finally stopped, but the agony of those cries had imbued Elisabeth with a terrible foreboding of the danger that was afoot this night, a danger that eclipsed even her fear of the storm. The air was heavy with moisture. The sky still flamed with branches of white light that gave the tor the appearance of being in motion. Yet despite this, she felt an uneasy stillness settle about her. Her hiding place seemed suddenly unsafe, accessible to whatever was out there. As if to appease her uneasiness, she crawled out of her sanctuary. With her body pressed close to the boulder for support, she peered across the summit then upward, where standing stones parried with lightning bolts.

Darkness shrouded the skittering noises that echoed down to her, but even those faint noises filled her with unspeakable dread. A burst of light splintered the dark. In the fleeting seconds when the mountaintop was drenched with light, she saw the two skulking shapes in blackest silhouette, the tongues that lolled from their mouths still warm with blood, and she saw the malicious gleam in their eyes as they marked her presence.

A howl went up from one, then the other.

In blind terror she hopped one-legged around the boulder. Her hands groped along the rock. She cursed the smoothness that slid beneath her fingertips, making any hope of scaling the boulder an impossibility. The air vibrated with low growls. She heard paws scratching rock as the hounds descended and she moaned as she bumped into a rock that formed a barrier across her path.

She had wandered into a horseshoe-shaped convergence of stone. Two boulders formed the sides of the shoe and a smaller, waist-high rock formed the base. She had bumped into this smaller rock and in a blaze of lightning saw the contours of the boulder that hemmed it in on the left. A spark of hope rose in her breast. The face of the boulder was fractured in a series of horizontal strips that formed a triad of ledges to the top—three natural steps that were long and wide enough for a person to secure his footing and climb to the top. It would be a treacherous climb in the dark, but no hound could possibly follow her up the face of a boulder.

She stepped high onto the crest of the smaller rock and pulled herself to the top. Behind her, she heard the deep nasal sounds of the dogs as they caught her scent. Gathering the folds of her petticoat into her left hand, she felt along the surface of the boulder until her fingers found a nub of rock. She grasped the protrusion, angled her foot onto the first ledge, and pulled herself upward.

She was three feet above the level of the lower rock. She flattened her body against the cold surface of the boulder and thrust the tips of her fingers into two vertical crevices that split the granite. Her breath escaped in short gasps of pain. Her eyes watered at the thought of balancing her weight on her injured foot for even the few seconds it would take to raise her left foot to the next ledge.

Bracing herself to continue, she turned her face toward the sound of paws rasping against the hardness of bedrock. In the shadows that filled the entrance of the horseshoe, she caught movement out of the corner of her eye and a whiff of the putrescence that rolled off the mongrels' bodies. A flash of lightning froze them for all time in her memory, and with a cry of horror she clawed at the rock just above her, locating a protrusion shaped like the tusk of a wild boar. She locked her fingers around it and strained upward, then screamed as a savage growl reverberated below her.

With a powerful lunging leap, one of the hounds sprang onto the lower rock then reared up to paw the ledge where Elisabeth was struggling upward. His neck was strong as a lion's. He tore at her over-petticoat, snaring it on the points of his teeth, shredding the velvetlike tissue. His jaws snapped higher. Elisabeth felt the power of the animal dragging her backward. She found a toehold in a shallow fissure, but fear made her clumsy.

Her boot slipped.

Her foot skidded down the face of the stone.

Her knees banged hard into the rock.

The hound stretched his neck toward her dangling left foot, and as she scrambled for a toehold once again, the animal gripped the heel of her boot in the vise of his jaws, twisting, turning, tearing.

Her scream ricocheted into the night. A cold glaze of sweat coated her fingers as she wrenched her foot back and forth. Her fingers began to slip from around the tusk-shaped rock. The hound's snarls grew louder, more vicious. He moved with Elisabeth's wriggling foot, elongating his thick neck to follow her upward, stretching himself like a snake.

A flash of lightning.

Elisabeth spun her head to look over her shoulder and in that blaze of light saw the tall, fluid shape of a man standing at the mouth of the cul-de-sac. His cloak fluttered in the wind like the petals of a black orchid. His arm moved swiftly and in the batting of an eye the air whooshed with the sound of his speeding dagger.

She heard the pulpy thud of steel into flesh. Another dagger sang through the air. The animal let out a gurgling howl as that second dagger pierced its throat, killing him, Elisabeth's foot still trapped in his death grip.

Lightning leapt around them as the other mongrel bounded toward the specter of the thief-taker. Elisabeth choked out a warning, but even as she did so, she saw a slender gleam of steel rise above Cain's head. The animal lunged. The gleam of steel descended, cleaving the hound from chest to loin.

In a half dozen strides Cain was at Elisabeth's feet. He prized open the jaws of the hound with hands so anxious they shredded sinew and shattered cartilage without effort. Elisabeth's foot came loose. Cain removed his daggers from the hound's flesh, wiped them clean on the carcass, then muscled the animal over the slope of the rock to the floor of the crater. He reached up and circled his hands around the girl's waist then gently coaxed her away from the place to which she clung so desperately. Lifting her down to the first ledge, he turned her around to face him.

"Are you able to walk?"

The pain of standing on two feet made her eyes glassy. She lifted the foot she had injured in her fall, but her knees were so weak with shock that she would have fallen over had Cain not grabbed her by the shoulders to balance her. "Did the hound hurt you?"

She bowed her head against the solidness of his chest and as she did so, he cupped his gloved hand around the back of her skull, holding her tightly, as if reassuring himself that she was safe. His heart raced wildly. She could feel it thudding against her forehead, pounding more wildly than her own. And his hand. He held her so firmly that she knew, if he wished, he could crush her skull like a grape. But he did not. He held her as if she were something precious to be savored, and she nearly drowned in the feeling. It was in that instant, surrounded by the blackness and horror of Hound Tor, that she felt her heart smile.

She shook her head in answer to his question. "I . . . I fell. Earlier. But I think something broke." With that dazed expression still stiffening her features, she peered downward, as if she could see her foot through the darkness. "I'm sorry, but I don't think I can walk."

A droplet of rain splatted onto the rock behind her. Then two drops. Then three. Wordlessly, the thief-taker swooped her into his arms, and as the sky began to pour forth the rain that had thickened the air all evening, he carried her down the western face of the tor, to the great black shire, who, at a whistle, galloped to them at a dead run. Elisabeth bent her head and visored her hands over her brow to shield her eyes from the driving rain. Cain steadied Scylla and was about to swing Elisabeth onto the saddle when she clutched the cloak at his neck.

"Please. My horse."

There was a wildness in her voice that forced him to speak gently. "The hounds have left nothing of the beast that resembles a horse, my lady."

"Oh, God." She bowed her head against his chest, sickened by the memory of those torturous cries and the horror of what had been wrought as she'd listened. "Take me home. Please, take me home."

They struck out across the moor in a northerly direction. The man held the girl close against him. He tented his cloak about her to protect her from the pelting rain, and as she leaned against him, she felt the heat radiating from his big body and was warmed.

A half mile north of Moretonhampstead, with the rain nearly blinding him, Cain turned off the road at the sign of the Saracen's Head and urged Scylla into the shelter of the stable. "See that he's rubbed down and bedded for the night," he instructed the man in charge. Dismounting, he lifted Elisabeth to the ground, swung his wet cloak off his shoulders and bundled it about her from head to calf. Then, before she had time to exert any pressure on her foot, he gathered her again into his arms and headed into the violent fury of the night.

The common room of the Saracen's Head Inn was deserted save for the barkeep who was wiping down tables. As the door of the inn banged open, the man slowed the motion of his hand to see what the storm had blown in. Cain kicked the door shut with the heel of his jackboot then stood cold and dripping as he leveled his pale blue eyes on the aproned hosteler.

"You have a room to let?"

The hosteler eyed him with suspicion. He nodded toward the froth of white petticoat that was visible beneath the cloaked shape in Cain's arms. "Are you sure it's only one room you're needin', mate?"

Cain shifted the girl in his arms, exposing his bandoleer of knives. "One room," he said in a voice that was calm and deadly. "And hot food."

The hosteler caught a single look at the array of knives on Cain's chest before dropping his rag and wiping his hands on his apron front. "One room and hot food. Happy to oblige you, mate. Give you the room at the end of the hall." He headed toward the stairwell, his step hurried and spry. "Best room in the inn. As far away from the stables and the jakes as a body can get."

The room was mean and cold. Within its confines were a narrow bed, a high-backed chair, a low rush stool, and a rickety washstand upon which sat a basin and ewer and a modest stack of clean linen towels. The hosteler lit the fire in the hearth and promised to send someone with food as soon as a tray was prepared. The burgeoning fire dispelled the bone-chilling cold, but the room remained mean. Cain lowered Elisabeth into the room's lone chair then angled it around to face the fire. He drew the hood of his cloak off her head, and as he stood over her, he brushed a damp strand of hair away from her brow and gently stroked his knuckles from her hairline to the crown of her head, lingering there, as if time no longer mattered to him.

"At the risk of being indelicate, my lady, if the fire is to be of any benefit, you should remove your wet clothing." Extending his arm across her chest, he secured his hand beneath her armpit and lifted her high enough off the chair to slide his cloak out from beneath her. He fanned it on the floor before the hearth then proceeded to remove his bandoleer and sword.

Elisabeth crossed her arms over her stomach and hugged her hands to her sides to prevent herself from shaking. The sounds of her mare's howls still rang in her ears. She wondered if this was the cause of her shivering or if she was still reacting to the idea that those howls could have been her own. She glanced toward Cain who had stepped out of his boots and was placing them close by the fire. It seemed he was about to follow his own directive about disrobing.

She turned her face away from him. "Th-thank you, sir, but I should prefer to leave all my clothing on."

"You can contract an ague from wet clothing. Or the consumptive disease. Had you a wish to kill yourself, my lady, you should have remained atop Hound Tor. But since I expended the effort to drag you all the way down here, you might do me the honor of trying to stay alive, at least temporarily." He strode barefoot to the bed, returning with a woolen blanket that he dropped onto her lap. "Indulge me."

What he said about the ague and consumption was true. Having no wish to flirt with death again, Elisabeth nodded her compliance. Cain retreated somewhere behind her to allow her an element of privacy. With nervous fingers she unfastened the front hooks of her riding jacket then poked her head around the wing of the chair. Cain was toweling his hair in the far corner of the room and paying her no heed. She shrugged out of her jacket, dropped it to the floor, then began to fumble with the tabs of her over-petticoat.

"Do the crises of your life always happen in clusters?" he asked from his corner.

She wriggled the petticoat of her riding habit over her head. She deposited it atop her jacket, tented the blanket around her shoulders and hugged it beneath her chin. "Until several days ago I had been the victim of only one other crisis in my life." She still wore her chemise, corset, and four under-petticoats, but she wasn't about to remove another stitch.

"You have doubled your incidence within the past week. I would venture that you are making up for your previous deficiency at an alarming rate. Have you finished disrobing?"

When she indicated she had, he crossed the floor to hang his shirt on a drying peg that was driven into the mantel. He had stripped down to his breeches and a towel draped around his neck, and when he turned to face her, he looked so blatantly naked—from his mane of black hair to the waistband that pressed against the tight sinews of his stomach—that she dropped her gaze to her lap and nearly choked trying to decide whether she should inhale or exhale.

"Are you well?"

She nodded but continued to keep her eyes averted as he hung her riding jacket and velvet petticoat on pegs beside his shirt. Only with difficulty did she find her tongue. "No matter how many crises I have experienced in the past week, sir, no matter how dire the circumstances, you have appeared from nowhere to lend your unflagging assistance.

I not only owe you my gratitude"—she looked up at him, her eyes wide, and blue, and full of worship—"I owe you my life."

He was magnificent in his nakedness, his bearing tall and straight, his aura charged with danger. She was not ignorant of the male anatomy above the waist, for on many occasions she had applied plaisters and poultices to the chests of the infirm, but never had she witnessed a man more exquisitely formed than this man. His shoulders looked to be wide as the mantel and thick as a shank of beef. His arms were hard and shaped with long ropes of muscle that made her fingertips tingle with the desire to touch. She considered the power that must abide within arms that could slay a hound with a single downward stroke, and she grew quick, and warm.

"How . . . how did you find me?"

He thrust the stool toward her with his foot then hung his fists on the loose ends of his towel, pulling the material taut around his neck. "You have your groomsboy to thank for that." Beneath the towel she saw that his chest was dusted with coils of black hair, like the outside of his forearms, and that his flesh was underlaid with whipcord sinew and hard slants of rib. His flesh was as lean and hungry as his eyes. "The boy mentioned your sudden botanical interest in the moorland, but I could not imagine that Hippocrates himself would be wandering about the moors at dusk. You little fool." Faster than she could blink, he released a dagger from the strap on his forearm and slapped it into his palm. "The locals never travel the paths around Hound Tor because they fear the packs of wild dogs that live among the crags. Did you never think to ask of the dangers you should avoid before you left?"

His voice became so steely that she eyed him and his knife with growing fear. "It was only two days ago, sir, that you were berating me for lacking the courage to strike out on my own into the moors. You seemed not at all concerned then with the dangers lurking amid the crags. To hear you talk, one would have thought that none existed!"

"You have never heard the tales surrounding Grimspound, and Wistman's Wood, and Hound Tor?"

"If I had heard them, you can be assured that each of us would be spending this eve much differently! Why is there such anger in your voice? If finding me was going to turn your mood so black, why did you even bother looking for me?"

He speared her with a feral look. He had searched for her because for two decades he had fought to arrive at this juncture, and now he was so close. Just a little while longer and revenge would be his, but he could not secure it without Elisabeth. She was the mortar that united all the pieces of his plan. Without her, there would be no plan, no satisfaction, no revenge. He had searched for her because he needed her, but there was another reason that had impelled him to action, a reason that even now, he could not admit to himself.

He turned the knife in his palm. The gesture dried the spittle in Elisabeth's mouth. Not waiting for him to respond to her question, she nodded toward the blade. "What are you intending to do with that?"

His laughter was grim as he seated himself on the stool before her. "You look as if you're expecting me to carve my initials across your forehead."

"Initial," she corrected in a voice barely audible. "You have shared but one of your names with me."

Her comment triggered something volatile in the pale blue depths of his eyes. "I have only one." Lifting her right foot into his hand, he sliced upward through her leather boot with his knife.

The big toe of her foot was broken, and if the swelling and redness had not advised them of the condition, the fact that she jumped a half foot off her chair when Cain touched it would have. He cut her stocking away to her ankle and shook his head. "You'll not be doing much walking on this for a while. You may be forced to hire a sedan chair to carry you down the aisle to your groom and a lackey to carry you up the great stone steps of Thirlstane."

Elisabeth froze. "You have seen it? You've seen Thirlstane?"

He recovered so quickly that if she hadn't been watching him so intently, she would have missed it. But for a fleeting moment his hands had gone rigid and his features had collapsed, as if he'd just divulged something he had vowed never to divulge. He set her foot atop his knee, his composure returning swiftly. "Anyone who has ever ventured into the claw of Cornwall has seen Thirlstane. I am only one of many."

But she didn't believe his explanation. He didn't want to admit he had seen the estate, and in Elisabeth's mind there could be only one reason for that—because he didn't want her to know he was Cornish. Tall, and black-haired, and Cornish—like the stable master before him. Was it mere coincidence? Perhaps, but she thought not. It was rare that a Cornishman ever left Cornwall. It was uncanny that two Cornishmen would ever happen upon the same estate in faraway Devon, unless of course the two men knew each other, and one had come back to seek retribution for the injustice visited upon the other.

He set her foot on the stool before crossing to the wash-stand for more towels. She watched him slyly as he tore the linen into strips and knotted the ends together, but watching him only increased her desire to ask more questions. Why did he never remove his glove? Where had he learned his skill with knives? What was his last name? How would he seek his retribution? Who was his mother? *His mother . . .*

She recalled something he had said earlier—that if there had been issue from her aunt and uncle's union, a male child specifically, then *she* would be a mere tenant on these lands rather than a vessel through whom their ownership would pass. And in the same breath he had said something about resurrection, that men can sometimes be miraculously resurrected. What was he intimating? Her aunt and uncle had died thirty long years ago.

Or had they?

She stared at the thief-taker, transfixed by what she was thinking. What if the reports of her Aunt Constance's death had been wrong? What if she had survived the shipwreck? What if she had been expecting a child when she had been banished from Maidenstowe? The stable master's child.

Her mind raced with mental calculations. The child would be approximately thirty years of age today—an age that could very well match Cain's own. Was he, then, the one who had sustained the resurrection? Was this man Constance's bastard child come to avenge not the injustice done to his father, but the injustice done to his mother?

She snugged her blanket more tightly about her chin as Cain made his way back to her. What did he want? His mother's dowager share of the estate? He would want the money and land that had been denied him. But Quintus would be reluctant to oblige him.

As Cain began wrapping her foot in the linen, Elisabeth grew aware of a band of wetness clinging to the back of her neck. Slipping her fingers beneath the blanket, she discovered Thomas's long-glass still circled about her neck, so taking the wet ribbon in her hand she worked it over her head then set the long-glass in her lap. Cain continued his ministrations without looking at her.

"How many years have you been thief-taking?" she asked his bent head, wincing as he banded the linen about her toes to stabilize them.

"As many years as you have lived."

"You are not that old."

"You asked. I told you. Believe what you will."

Her eyes lingered on the elegant shape of his fingers as they worked the dressing over her foot. She wondered if the stable master's hands had been so lovely. "I know who you are," she said into the silence. "I know why you've come to Maidenstowe."

He neither looked up nor hesitated in his labors. "Have I acquired an identity other than that of thief-taker? Someone of immense wealth I hope."

"You needn't be secretive, sir. 'Tis not my intention to betray you. On the contrary, I might lend assistance to your cause."

He did look up then. The corner of his mouth slanted into an angle that was somewhere between a sneer and a smile. "My cause, lady?"

Elisabeth nodded. "I know what it is you seek, and though I doubt that Quintus will acquiesce, I promise to do everything in my power to see that you are justly compensated for everything that has been denied you. I have no idea if there is legal precedent for what you try to do, but we have fine solicitors in London who would be most willing to provide counsel, for a modest fee of course." She graced him with a hopeful look that he did not return. "You have no idea what I'm talking about." It was more statement than question.

"None." He found the two loose ends of the linen and tied them together then rested her foot against the angle of his knee.

"I . . . I know of your parents," she said, beginning anew. "'Twas not your fault, so I think 'tis time people stopped punishing you for their sin."

"Their sin," Cain repeated. "Which was . . . ?"

Adulterous fornication popped into her head before she lit on a word she could say aloud. "Infidelity, sir. Infidelity that resulted in the birth of a bastard child. A male child."

Cain nodded his sudden understanding. "I assume I bear the dubious distinction of being that bastard child?"

Elisabeth could not read his face. "You indicated to Thomas only last week, sir, that such was the case."

"Ah yes. When he was demonstrating his affection for you. I remember it well. And who, if I might inquire, have you cast in the role of my illustrious parents?"

She concentrated her attention on the pink and green enamel markings on the long-glass's outer cylinder. "The stable master and . . . and my Aunt Constance." She did not hear him laugh. She didn't even hear him breathe. She sneaked a look at him.

"Pity your grandfather destroyed your aunt's portrait. Imagine the resemblance you might have drawn."

"You admit it?"

"The progeny of a stable master and a lady," he mused. Snatching his dagger from the floor, he poised it at the place above her ankle where her stocking was split into a vee. He flipped her petticoats in the direction of her knee, then with the point of his blade at the base of the vee he began to slice upward through the patterned white silk of the stocking.

Elisabeth gripped the arms of the chair, not daring to breathe as she watched him. The tip of the blade was so near her flesh that she could feel the down on her shin part before its advance. Her eyes grew round. Her heartbeat slowed.

"If I am who you say I am, what reason would I have to return to Maidenstowe?"

"To claim your mother's dowager portion of the estate." The flesh at the nape of her neck tingled with menace. She nipped her bottom lip between her teeth. The blade was at the middle of her shin.

"Which, no doubt, is considerable." He continued slicing upward, his voice low and steady, the blade glimmering in the firelight.

"It could be considerable. Yes."

"And you would help me obtain what has been denied me."

The blade flicked toward the center of her kneecap, whispering over her flesh. Her knuckles tensed to a point where she thought they might crack. The soles of her feet prickled with sensation. "I would do whatever I could on your behalf," she said, her voice breathy.

"Then 'tis regrettable I must decline your offer."

"Decline?"

He palmed his knife then curled his fingers around the garter that rode her leg just above her knee. She felt the warm glide of his fingers as he slid the garter over her kneecap, slowly, patiently, like a high priest preparing a virgin for sacrifice. "My mother was not your Aunt Constance. My father was not the man who seduced her under the weeping pear."

"How do I know you speak truth?" She suffered the brush of his knuckles against the long curve of her leg. Warm flesh on cold. Hard flesh on soft. She felt the scratch of his woolen glove against the side of her calf, then, emboldened, wondered if the hairs matting his chest would feel as coarse when pressed to the skin beneath her chemise—if the hair on his forearms would feel soft pressed to her naked spine.

Cain slid the garter to the middle of her calf. For a moment he cradled her leg in his palms, touching her with wool and flesh and steel—touching her with such intimacy that she felt an electrifying current race through her veins to the center of her womanhood, where pulses mingled with moisture. Of a sudden her legs felt weightless; her breasts felt full and hard and ripe for the caress of a man's mouth.

"How do you know I speak truth?" he asked, aping her. "Because, lady, your stable master's ineptitude precludes any possibility of my being related to the man." He slid the blade of his dagger beneath her garter, pressing it flush against her leg. She startled reflexively at the cold touch of metal, but he held her calf so firmly in his left hand that he prevented her from kicking free. Of a sudden her heartbeat raced, her mouth went dry. A dangerous warmth bathed her toes and spread upward. She tried to pull back on her leg, but he would have none of it. "Do . . . not . . . move," he warned. He lifted up on the knife, stretching the garter away from her leg, then turned the blade so the cutting edge lay crosswise against the frilly circlet.

"If I had decided to seduce the mistress of the manor," he finally said, slashing upward with his blade, "I wouldn't have been caught."

Garter and stocking fell to the floor. Elisabeth cried out as if she had just witnessed one of her limbs falling to the floor rather than her garter. Her muscles screamed at her. Her emotions felt drained. And it took her more than a few seconds to start breathing naturally again.

She eased her grip on the chair. She had lost all circulation in her fingers. They were stiff, cold. She bowed her head, willing sensation back into her neck. Nervous relief washed over her, but following hard upon the relief was an inexplicable rush of disappointment and loss, that he no longer held her, that he might never do so again.

Cain plucked the silk from the floor then nodded toward the ribbon attached to her long-glass. "Your ribbon needs drying." He removed it from her lap, lifted her foot from between the deep vee of his thighs, and backed off the stool.

"Emma tells me the stable master was tall and black haired, like you," she persisted in spite of her exhaustion. "And he was Cornish. Can you deny being Cornish?"

Cain tossed the stocking into the fire. Tongues of flame devoured it. "I owe you no explanations." He set the long-glass behind a candle sconce on the mantel to prevent it from rolling off, then stretched the ribbon out to allow it to dry.

"But don't you see? If you admit your ancestry, it could

change everything. What if . . . what if you were entitled to a large portion of the estate? My dowry could be depleted to quite an ordinary amount. It might reduce me to the ranks of the lesser nobility."

"I have never known anyone to express such delight at the prospect of poverty."

"Thomas could decide not to marry me!" she railed, trying to make him understand. "If the terms of the contract changed considerably, I would no longer be so fine an economic gain to him. He could dissolve the agreement. Please!" Her voice shook with emotion. "I cannot marry him! You cannot save me from the jaws of one vermin to deliver me into the hands of another." Then more softly, "Please."

Cain stroked the damp velvet with the balls of his fingers. The soft nap of the fabric brought to mind the shadowed softness of Elisabeth's inner thigh, and he drew his hand into a tight fist, girding himself against another, more enduring surge of arousal. He had not wanted to slide the garter down her leg. He had wanted to glide his palms over her thigh, higher and higher, until his fingertips found that part of her that Thomas Penmarck waited to claim. But he would not have been satisfied at merely finding. What he found, he would have taken. And he would not have stopped until his hunger was sated again and again.

He wanted her.

The thick, straining flesh between his legs bespoke his need. The crystals of sweat on his brow bespoke his desire.

He wanted her, but he could not have her. If she did not wed Thomas Penmarck, his plan would fail. No marriage, no revenge. 'Twas simple as that. And he would allow nothing to stand in his way, not need, nor want, nor desire.

He glanced at her over his shoulder. "So you have no wish to marry Penmarck. What do you propose to do in lieu of that? Become a spinster? A mother abbess?"

She told him with her eyes what she proposed. She wanted *him* instead of Penmarck. She wanted to exchange wedding vows with Cain, thief-taker, rather than Thomas Penmarck, Earl of Moreleigh.

Cain's eyes became long slits of frigid blue as he raked her up and down. "What you are thinking is sheer folly."

"How do you know what I am thinking?"

"Because you are a fanciful girl who dreams fanciful dreams. A stolen kiss on a storm-filled night and you imagine yourself in love. If a stump-legged beggar had kissed you, I suppose you would have thought yourself in love with him!"

Elisabeth flinched at the cruelty of his barbs. She wanted to scream at him that if he would let her, she could warm the coldness in his eyes. If he would allow her, she could give back to him in kind the cherished moments of affection he had showered upon her in the stables. He had made her feel whole, and good, and loved. He alone had done that. None other. But what she said to him instead was, "You stole more than one kiss."

"You were fortunate 'twas all I stole."

"Why? So I might surrender my maidenhead to a man I despise?"

"Would you rather surrender it to a man whose hands drip with the blood of thieves?"

"Yes." She exchanged a defiant look with him. "I have felt the gentleness flowing within those hands. I know that despite how forbidding you appear, you—"

"You know nothing!" he raged, stabbing a long finger at

her. "You blather about gentleness but *you . . . know . . . nothing*!"

"I know there is an emotion binding us one to the other. It draws us together despite who we are and what we feel. Why do you deny its existence? You *must* feel it. You have to feel it. Why do you push me away!"

She saw within his eyes a battle of warring emotions. She saw his jaw pulsate and a ridge of muscle in his arm flex, and then he was storming at her like a beast from the fires of hell. She threw her arms before her face to shield herself from him, but he was not deterred. He swept her up into his great naked arms, strode the length of the room in a half dozen steps, and dumped her none too gently onto the bed. The feather ticking ballooned around her. She fought her way to her elbows within the tangle of her blanket. He yanked the boot off her other foot and dropped it to the floor. And then he stood tall and rigid at the edge of the bed, his voice raw with emotion.

"You listen to me, girl. I told you once, but you chose not to hear. I want no female baggage cluttering my life. I take my pleasure when I want, with whom I want, and then I leave. Do you understand? No attachments. No whiny females clinging to my waist. A woman can be of service to me in only one way—when she is flat on her back with her knees parted. I do not *want* to hear talk of emotional bindings. I do not *want* what you offer so readily. Hear me well, lady. I do not want you. Is that clear? Did you hear the words? Shall I say them again? I do not—"

A knock at the door silenced him. "Beggin' your pardon, guvna', but I've a tray for you and the lady."

Clenching his fists around the ends of his towel, he stormed to the door and threw it open to admit the tavern maid. "Set it on the washstand," he grated, directing the woman to the only table in the room.

The woman was not unpleasant to look upon. The hair that escaped beneath the ruffle of her mobcap was clean and she appeared to have no teeth missing. She wore a quilted over-petticoat that fanned wide over her hips and a simple muslin bodice that drew attention to the spectacular fullness that undulated beneath the fabric. She set the tray down then returned to the place where Cain stood.

The hotness in his blood turned to fire. He was tired of being noble. He was tired of fighting Elisabeth *and* himself. He had a man's need, and if Elisabeth St. Mary required further proof of his disinterest in her, he would damn well show her.

"That be all, guvna'?"

"Nay. There is one more thing." He banded his arm around the tavern maid's waist, and in clear view of Elisabeth's observation, ground his mouth savagely against her lips. The maid's surprise turned to delight. She flung her arms round Cain's neck, returning his passion with well-practiced ease.

Watching, Elisabeth felt her cheeks sting with humiliation. That he could kiss this serving wench in her presence knowing the extent of her own feelings for him left her cold and empty. She had opened her heart to him, and this was her payment.

She felt embarrassment watching them. She felt self-conscious watching their mouths grind hungrily against each other, and when she saw Cain's hand plunge beneath the woman's muslin bodice to free her huge, brown-nippled breast, she knew pain so exquisite that she could feel the life being wrung from her heart. He cupped his hand around the underside of the woman's breast and crushed it against his naked chest. It was then that she turned her face away, unable to witness any more of his obscenity.

He had made himself clear.

He had made himself perfectly clear.

She heard the groping and panting and breathing for a short space longer, only until the hosteler bellowed a woman's name into the hallway. In a trice the maid was out the door, slamming it behind her. Elisabeth heard Cain's footsteps tread across the floor, and after awhile, a question asked with calm indifference.

"Would you care for a bowl of porridge?"

She didn't answer him.

She never wanted to share another word with him again.

At first light, with the rain ended, Cain escorted a somberly silent Elisabeth back to Maidenstowe. At the Saracen's Head Inn, in the room at the far end of the hall, Thomas Penmarck's long-glass lay behind the candle sconce on the mantel, its velvet ribbon dry, but utterly forgotten.

chapter eight

It took the physician from Dunsford a half day to arrive at Maidenstowe and an hour to treat Elisabeth. By the time he left, he'd swaddled her foot in enough bandages to style a creation that rivaled the size of her head. He also provided her with a dose of laudanum that alleviated her pain by making her sleep for twenty-four hours.

On the second day after the incident on Hound Tor, as she lay abed, she heard a tap at her door through the dreamy haze of the physician's drug. Yet she could not force her lips apart to bid the caller enter for her muscles were still heavy with sleep. The tap sounded again, followed by a creak of hinges. Elisabeth struggled to lift her eyelids. She heard the thud of booted feet and the jangle of spur rowels, and through the thickness of her lashes she saw a perverted image of the man as he advanced toward the bed.

Cain.

Instinctively her mouth began to curve upward, until something in her subconscious balked at the motion, causing her to remember what she had forgotten in her sleep—that this man did not want her. Her brow creased at the memory. She felt a vibration in her throat that threatened to choke her, but she refused to humiliate herself further in his presence. She was an aristocrat. She could be dignified even in the face of his rejection.

She cracked her right eye, then her left, forcing her lids to remain open as she regarded Cain. Her mouth felt as if it were full of cotton wool. "Is there some additional point you wished to make clear, sir? Some point you failed to demonstrate at the inn?" She moistened her lips with the tip of her tongue. "I am extremely tired. Please say what you have to say, then be kind enough to leave."

"I would guess you would feel refreshed after sleeping an entire day away."

She did not answer him.

"Your blithesome mood seems to have evaporated, my lady."

"It will improve when you leave, sir."

He paused before continuing. "I'm sorry you find my presence so offensive."

Silence.

He cleared his throat. "It occurred to me this morning that I had neglected to remove your long-glass from the mantel at the Saracen's Head. Am I correct, or did you retrieve it without my knowledge?"

While you were kissing your tart? she thought, her eyes growing hot at his remembered insult. "If you failed to remove it, 'tis still there."

"As I thought. If you can abide its absence for a space, I promise to return to the inn to reclaim it within the week."

"I have no wish to be the recipient of any more of your

favors, sir, so you needn't waste your time. The long-glass may remain where it is."

"I feel responsible."

"Truly? It surprises me that you think yourself capable of feeling anything." She saw a shadow of pain flit across his face.

"I will return it to you within the week, my lady."

She shook her head. It was incongruous to her that a man who could crush her heart without a whim of conscience would bother worrying about the return of a trinket. "Do as you wish, sir. It matters naught to me."

He bowed his head and turned to leave, then suddenly turned back to face her. "There has been little activity from your thief in the past few days. I begin to suspect he might have been frightened away. If all remains quiet for the next week, I shall consider my endeavor here at an end."

"With not a single drop of blood shed," Elisabeth added. *Except my own.*

"The thief was not a true cutthroat. He did little harm."

Which was more than Elisabeth could say for the thief-taker. She wished he had never been sent. She wished she had never heard the name Cain. She wished he would go so she could feel wretched in solitude. "Is that all, sir?" she said in a dismissive tone.

Cain bent his head toward her foot. "Did the physician predict how long you would be abed?"

"The toe should mend in a fortnight or less." *He made no mention how long it would take my heart to mend.*

"I should be gone before you're up and about then."

Elisabeth stared at her bandaged foot. Why was he doing this to her? Did he enjoy watching abject misery parade across her face? Did he enjoy condemning her to a life with a man she detested? Was she so mean a creature that no man could find within himself the ability to love her? First Quintus and now Cain. What was wrong with her? Dear God, why couldn't anyone love her?

"Should I not see you again before I leave," he continued, "I would hope that if you have occasion to think of me in the future, you will be able to do so with kindness."

In her mind Elisabeth heard the thunderous pound of waves against the rocks of Thirlstane. On her lips she tasted the powdered grit of Thomas's cosmetic. She blinked moisture from her eyes as she answered in an even voice, "I doubt I will ever have occasion to think of you again, sir. Good day."

He hesitated for a moment as if he would say something more, but then he turned and crossed the room to the portal, closing the door behind him.

Elisabeth refused to look at the door. She rubbed her eyes with the heel of her palm, but when she finished rubbing, her eyes were more blurred with tears than they had been before. She stared at the fire in the hearth, trying not to think of the words Cain had spoken, but they kept echoing in her head, reminding her of his rejection. *I do not want you. Is that clear? Did you hear the words?*

"I *heard* the words!" she sobbed, pressing her fingertips to her lips, remembering how he had once kissed her. "Why did you rescue me from Hound Tor? Why couldn't you just leave me to die?"

She pinched her eyelids shut, and in her anguish and desolation, she wept.

Quintus, accompanied by Frith, paid her a visit later that same day. "I thought you had a broken toe?" he quipped, noting the bulbous lump that her right foot had become. "Did the physician decide you had gout as well?"

Elisabeth sidled him a listless look. "Perhaps you could send Emma up to help me remove some of these bandages. I think the physician's treatment was a bit excessive."

"And Frith tells me you're refusing to take your laudanum. Has your foot stopped hurting?"

She nodded. "It mustn't be a very bad break." Which wasn't true, for even now she felt sharp stabs of pain knifing up her leg, but she welcomed the pain. It made the fact of her undesirability seem less acute. It made her forthcoming marriage seem more palatable.

"Capital. If you're up to walking, I've just the thing to lift your spirits. A change of scenery is what you need, young woman." He tossed her a rayle for her shoulders.

"Quintus, I . . ."

"My decision is made. Dissenting opinions are unacceptable." He waved the head of his walking stick at her to prod her along. "You've just received a wedding gift from the Cookworthys. I've had it placed in the drawing room."

"Really, Quintus, I'm not in the mood for . . ."

"Piffle." He threw the rayle over her shoulders himself and motioned Frith for assistance coaxing her to her feet. "It's hidden beneath linen sheeting, but it has the shape of a cannon. I've always wanted a cannon. A finely tooled bronze thing with eight-pound balls. My fourth wife had a fondness for eight-pound balls."

And knowing there was no help for it, Elisabeth fastened the rayle at her throat and allowed herself to be escorted slowly and painfully through corridors, down stairs and through more corridors to the first floor drawing room.

"A hip bath?" crowed Quintus when she had removed

the linen sheeting. "They have the unmitigated gall to present you with a receptacle for bathing? See that it finds its way to the garden, Frith. We'll use it as a planter."

Gritting her teeth with the pain, Elisabeth seated herself on a nearby settee and listened to Frith's counsel as he propped her foot up on a stack of pillows. "One needs to exercise caution with hip baths, m'lady. Look at poor Sir Edmund. He took a bath last year and dropped dead afterward."

"He slipped on a cake of soap and broke his neck," Elisabeth replied dully.

"Indeed, m'lady, but the gentleman is still dead."

"Actually," said Quintus, "if this were anything but a hip bath, it might be a rather stunning piece."

Not at all interested in any item sent in celebration of her forthcoming marriage, Elisabeth nonetheless canted her head to the side to get a different perspective of the thing. "Whose head is that on the front?"

Quintus stabbed his walking stick at the bestial head in question. "That, young woman, is a winged goat. Quite a good likeness. You see how much extension the sculptor put into the horns? And feel the points on the end. Sharp as a dirk."

Elisabeth was beginning to think her grandfather's first suggestion not at all unfitting. Perhaps they *could* set it in the garden and use it as a planter. "And what are *those* things?" She indicated the profusion of images that grinned up at her from either side of the bath, their decadent smiles captured in heavy polished brass.

Quintus bent down for a closer look. "Snake-tailed birds, a fern frond coiling around a serpent's head, a small gargoyle, and . . . good God." He straightened up so fast that she heard his joints pop. "This one looks like my first wife. She's come back as a bathtub."

But Elisabeth couldn't laugh. She couldn't even smile, and seeing that, Quintus dismissed the steward and sat down next to her on the settee. He trained his rheumy old eyes on her. "You're brooding."

She shook her head in denial.

"I can see it for myself, young woman. My fifth wife was well versed in the art of brooding, so I'm acquainted with the symptoms, all of which you seem to be manifesting with great relish."

Elisabeth traced the cracks in the ceiling with her eyes. "What did your fifth wife brood about?"

"Everything. Nothing." He shrugged. "I think her stays were perpetually laced too tight."

"I'm not wearing stays."

"Which leaves me no clue whatsoever as to why you're brooding. Unless, of course, you've suddenly become lovesick."

Elisabeth's eyebrow slanted upward at the comment. She turned to regard her grandfather. "Why do you say that?"

"I recognize the symptoms. Loss of appetite. Despondent. Dullness about the eyes."

"Your fifth wife, I suppose."

"No. That old mastiff we used to keep. He acted the same way when your grandmother died."

She looked away from him again. "Thank you for that lovely comparison."

"Well, you're certainly not acting like yourself! Nothing has died on the estate in recent history—nothing except that damn frog and I rather doubt you'd have cause to brood about that. So you leave me with no recourse but to conclude that you're moping about someone's absence. I must admit, I never realized you were quite so fond of Thomas. Makes me a little smug to realize I effected a match so much to your liking."

His reference to Thomas made her feel as if every living organ within her had been sucked out of her body. She felt as empty as the inside of a dried burr, hollow, unfulfilled. Her skin felt old and desiccated. She was afraid if she rubbed her fingers across her arm, her flesh would crumble like an autumn leaf. And when all her flesh disintegrated, there would be nothing left of her. She would disappear quietly, just as she had lived, and no one would remember that she had even walked the earth.

There was no cause for hope in her life. What she wanted, she could not have, but she no longer knew if she could settle for the alternative. Cain had made her feel loved, wondrous. Having sampled the wonderment that could exist between a man and a woman, she had no wish to submit to Thomas's mauling. She had lived most of her life in fear of her grandfather's condemnation, but that fear suddenly paled in comparison to the thought of Thomas's hands on her, and what those hands might do. Her grandfather's weapon would be his words. Thomas's would be his hands, his mouth, his—

Her stomach lurched. Oh, God! She couldn't go through with it. She seemed doomed to a living hell one way or the other, but she couldn't condemn herself to the hell that Thomas offered. In a moment of stunning perception she realized that sometimes, there were things in life that could be far worse than the fear of condemnation. Giving up her will to Thomas was one of those things.

"You think me fond of Thomas?" she asked, her voice quiet.

"Of course you're fond of him. You've been acting like a ninny ever since he left last week. How else would you explain your behavior?"

"I'm not fond of Thomas. I would rather be manacled to the floor of the condemned hold in Newgate than recite vows as Thomas's wife. He . . . I find him dour and mirthless and . . . and old. He enjoys belittling people. He always has to be right. No matter what the topic, Thomas must always have the last word. I can see him as neither husband nor father. His heart remains closed to me, Quintus, and when he touches me he . . ." She closed her eyes and doubled her fists. ". . . he makes my flesh crawl!"

Quintus opened and closed his mouth. He squirmed from side to side on the settee, scratched beneath his periwig, and finally pinched his face into an impossible contortion. "Thomas? Old? The man is only twice your age. *I* am old, young woman. Not Thomas. As for your other postulations, I quite agree. He *is* rather a prig, isn't he? Never liked the man much myself."

Elisabeth's eyes grew wide as gold sovereigns. "*You* never liked him? If you didn't like him, why did you choose him as a husband for me?"

"Money, young woman. Land. Power. He might be emotionally constipated, but he's still the best damn catch in England." He nodded, then cocked his head. "If you never liked him, why did you agree to the betrothal?"

She bowed her head. "I was afraid."

"Afraid? Of what?"

She was hovering on the brink of a place she had avoided for seventeen years. She could retreat, or she could lunge forward, and only God Himself knew which would be the worse evil. But either way, it didn't seem to matter anymore. Nothing seemed to matter anymore. She searched the old man's face. "I was afraid what you might say if I crossed you."

"As well you might. I would have been damned angry." And then his expression changed. His voice became soft, inquisitive, as if he had reservations about asking his next question, as if he too were standing on some kind of brink. "Was there anything specifically you were afraid I might say?"

Elisabeth gave him a silent nod. She rubbed her nose and held her gaze downcast. Her voice trembled. "I was afraid you might tell me I was an ungrateful wretch. I was afraid my opposition would rankle you so much, you would tell me that anyone who had done what I'd done deserved no special favors."

"And just what is it you think you have done?"

The stinging began in her eyes again. She tried to blink it away, but the sensation became moisture, then tears. "I killed them," she choked out, her words echoing through the emptiness within her. "I was disobedient. I wouldn't return to the house without my s-ship. If it hadn't been for me, they never would have ventured into the m-middle of the pond. If it hadn't been for me, they would still be alive." Her fingers shook as she blotted tears from her cheeks. "I know you blame me. 'Tis why you could n-never bring yourself to love me. 'Tis why you could never even bring yourself to s-say my name."

She wiped her face with the back of her hand, with the heel of her palm, with her wrist, and when her eyes were dry enough to focus again, she looked at Quintus, then stared, for he no longer looked like her grandfather. He looked shriveled, and bent, and incredibly sad. "Quintus?" She heard his breath rattle in his lungs, and she suddenly realized how fragile he was.

"I've lived eighty-four years, young woman. Never let anyone tell you that long life is a blessing. It's not. The only thing long life enables you to do is to watch everything around you die. Six wives. Two sons. Two daughters-in-law. I stay awake at night wondering how many of them might still be alive if I'd had more foresight—if I hadn't been so close-minded. I killed your Aunt Constance, you know. Couldn't wait for your Uncle James to return from India to deal with her. She was like a bad tooth that needed pulling, so I had to get rid of her myself. If I hadn't sent her away, your uncle wouldn't have had to run after her. They might both be alive. Just like your parents."

He grew quiet and pensive, as if bolstering himself to say something he had never wanted to say. "What happened to them wasn't your fault, young woman. It wasn't your fault at all. I'm the one who killed them, just like I killed everyone else."

Elisabeth swiped her hand across her eyes again, clearing her vision. Of all the things Quintus might have said, she never expected him to say this. She shook her head. "But you weren't even there that day. How can you blame yourself?"

"I gave you the boat, didn't I? I couldn't give you a doll or a hobby horse. No. I had to give you a boat with real canvas sails that could founder in the middle of the ornamental pond. If I'd given you a doll, none of this would have happened. I had no foresight. None whatsoever."

"*I* was the one who made my parents step into the boat and row out after it, Quintus. Not you."

"A five-year-old child doesn't *make* her parents do anything, young woman. A five-year-old child is responsible for nothing except being five years old. Your parents chose to retrieve your boat. You didn't make them. But you see, if it hadn't been for me, they couldn't have made that decision. If it hadn't been for me, they would still be alive."

Elisabeth felt suddenly detached from reality. Quintus was telling her he didn't find her blameworthy, but she found it difficult to accept. "You should have told me of your misgivings. I could have put your mind at ease."

He shook his head. "Couldn't."

"Why couldn't you?"

Silence, then, "I was afraid you would tell me you blamed me for the whole affair. Living with my own blame was bad enough, young woman, but if I'd had to live with your blame too—well, that would have been unconscionable."

It struck her then, the irony of what each of them had been living with for the past seventeen years. Fearing the other's blame, they had allowed an insurmountable barrier to rise between them. If only they had feared less, what comfort they might have given the other. "Oh, Quintus."

He fidgeted with the head of his walking stick. "Am I to understand, young woman, that you don't blame me for what happened after all?"

"I blamed myself, Quintus. Never you. Always myself."

"Yes, well, you needn't have. And about that other matter." The room became so quiet that Elisabeth could hear the sound of her own heart beating. He began again. "It was always in my mind, young woman, that if you should become too familiar with me, you might one day feel comfortable enough to ask why your parents had to die. So I had to keep my distance from you. It was imperative that you think me unapproachable, that you think me on the verge of death. I had to shield myself from any questions you might ask, you see. It was the only way I could protect myself.

"My father once told me and his father once told him that the only things of importance in this life are land and wealth and power." He narrowed his eyes at her then, and she could see the rims of his sockets brimming with ancient tears. His voice quivered. "They were wrong. I've learned many a thing in eighty-four years, young woman. Seems as if a man can appreciate simple things more at the end of his life than he can at the beginning. And there's one thing I never understood that became quite clear to me as I watched you grow." His mouth creased oddly, and she realized he was smiling at her. "I know now why we call our children's children grand, because you are that, young woman. You are indeed."

She could no longer see him for the tears that were streaming down her face, but crying had never felt so wonderful. He had not said he loved her, but she suspected it was in his heart. And if it was in his heart, it would eventually find its way to his lips. She could wait. To hear her grandfather speak those words, she could wait forever.

"Now don't go getting teary eyed on me, young woman. There are matters that need my attention. First, I'll pen a missive to Thomas. A cryptic note telling him I need to see him immediately. Then I'll have a bank note drafted to help ease his disappointment. Perhaps two bank notes. His disappointment could be quite prodigious."

Elisabeth had never seen her grandfather so cooperative. "Why are you being so solicitous, Quintus? I've disrupted your plans for me. I'm ruining everything."

"Young woman, were it not for the thief-taker's courage, you would be an undigested lump in the stomach of some rabid hound and I would be an old man who had nothing left to live for. In light of that, you've ruined nothing."

The thief-taker, she thought, remembering one other matter that needed tending. "About the thief-taker, Quintus, I . . . I think his presence has frightened away our brigand, so I see no reason why we should have to accommodate the man any longer. He should be dismissed. Allowing him to remain longer will only serve to increase his fee and decrease your coffers."

The old man studied her for a long, clear-sighted moment. "The man saved your life."

"I made offer of a reward to him," she said, recalling her humiliation at the Saracen's Head, "but he refused to accept it. I have no wish to look upon his face again."

Quintus shrugged. "As you like. I'll have Frith inform the man I wish to speak with him. But it makes little sense to me why this sudden aversion to thief-takers. The fellow doesn't seem bad by half."

Without waiting for her to reply, he popped off the settee. "I'll leave you here with your bath. Right now I must find Frith." He inhaled deeply then let out a long breath. "I haven't felt this good for decades! I might even venture 'tis time to mend my ways. I should start celebrating life rather than anticipating death." He hastened to the door, looking back at her from the threshold. "We'll dine in your bedchamber this evening. By the fire. Just the two of us. Would you like that, Elisabeth?"

"Yes. I'd like that very much."

"Good. I'll see you at nine."

And when he had gone, she frowned. He had said . . . The word floated about the drawing room on butterfly wings, whispering into the corners, fluttering about the ceiling. And she listened, savoring the sound.

Elisabeth. He had called her Elisabeth for the first time in seventeen years.

She reached out a gentle hand as if to capture the word, and thinking it caught within her palm, she pressed it to her heart, and knew peace.

That same night, at a table in the far corner of the common room of the Saracen's Head Inn, Cain lifted a tankard of ale to his lips with one hand, while with the other, he traced the enameling on Elisabeth's long-glass. The brew was strong and bitter, but not strong enough to make him forget the deep hurt he had caused the girl. He had seen it in her eyes. She'd made him feel like the scum on the surface of a stagnant pond. She'd made him feel like filth, and he hated himself for it.

If he had been anyone else, he would have fought the immediate world for the right to make Elisabeth St. Mary his wife. He would have killed to claim the virginity of such a bride.

If he was anyone else.

But he wasn't.

Over the rim of his tankard he eyed the other occupants of the common room. There were three men huddled at a table across the way, and a besotted yeoman passed out on a bench before the hearth. A travel-weary coachman exchanged bawdy laughter with the tavern maid whose acquaintance Cain had made two nights earlier. Seeing her now filled him with self-loathing for the liberties he had taken with her in front of Elisabeth. A throbbing pulse heated his groin as he dwelled on the details of that night, but he was remembering the feel of the silken flesh of Elisabeth's naked thigh, not the woman's bare breast.

He swigged another mouthful of ale as if that might cool his ardor, then wiped his mouth on the back of his hand. The front door to the inn swung open. His gaze traveled to the door as Miles Loveland reentered the common room. They had quaffed six tankards of ale between them, and this was the second time Loveland had had to visit the jakes behind the inn to relieve himself. He was still straightening the falls of his breeches as he staggered to the table.

"Your bladder is the size of a pea," sneered Cain.

"You should follow my example. Ridding your body of its foul humors might improve your mood." Loveland fell into his chair. He leaned forward, elbows propped on the table and head propped on the heels of his palms. "You drink as if you're trying to forget something. You'd better give me your message for Lint before you forget that too."

Cain worked the cylinder of the long-glass up and down, up and down, slowly, relentlessly. He was indeed trying to forget. Trying to forget the years he had spent fashioning his revenge. Trying to forget that despite his vows, despite his resistance, he had fallen in love with the woman he had hoped to use as the instrument of that revenge. Weak. He was weak. Everything had gone awry and it filled him with a mindless rage that festered like a boil.

"Tell Lint my work here is complete. I'll return to London within the week."

"Within the week? He gave you four weeks. You've only used one."

"Your mathematical abilities are truly astonishing, agent." The snores of the yeoman trumpeted through the room. The three men across the way glowered at the disturbance then collectively pushed their chairs back from the table and stood up. Cain lent them a casual glance. They were battle scarred and unsavory looking, the kind of men who roused suspicion in a thief-taker's mind. But not tonight. He had other demons to contend with tonight.

As the men left the inn, the wind blew their hair back from their faces, but Cain had already returned his attention to Loveland and therefore did not see that the last man out the door boasted only one ear.

Cain swilled down the rest of his ale and gestured the barkeep for another. Loveland shook his head while attempting to keep his elbows anchored to one spot on the table, but they kept inching voluntarily in a direction away from his body. "You drink too much," he reiterated as his head followed his elbows across the surface of the table. "Tell me, did you find the treasure you were looking for?"

"I found it."

"Do you have it with you?"

Cain shook his head. "It remains at Maidenstowe."

"So why the ruse? What had you waited your entire life to do that you accomplished in one short week?"

Cain smoothed his fingertips across the velvet ribbon of Elisabeth's long-glass. "It had been my intention to kill a man and rape a woman, but I no longer have the stomach for the rape."

It was an hour later when, heavy eyed and sluggish, Cain left Miles Loveland to head back toward Maidenstowe. A quarter mile from the inn he drew rein to listen, for there were muffled noises in the darkness ahead of him. Though his eyes were bleary he could distinguish movement in the shadows. Horses. More than one. The rattle of stirrups.

His hand went to his sword a moment too late. They surrounded him from every direction. Scylla reared up on his hind legs, his front hooves clawing the air. One of the horsemen screamed as the beast's hoof struck his shin, shattering the bone in his leg.

"Aaaaargh!"

"Shut up!"

"My leg, Skagg. Jesus, my leg!"

Scylla reared again but the motion was too violent for Cain to maintain his balance in his present state of inebriation. His arms flew out. The reins slid through his fingers and in the next instant he was being catapulted into the air. His breath escaped in a painful "Woof" as he hit the ground. With his senses still reeling he staggered to his feet and withdrew his sword, cutting the legs out from beneath the horse of one of his attackers. Man and beast collapsed in a writhing heap. The animal's howls rent the night air as he crushed the man beneath him.

Cain turned at another sound. He raised his sword above his head and sliced downward at the shadow before him. Another scream pierced the night as his blade found purchase in flesh, and something else.

"Pray for your immortal soul if you know how, slime."

Cain pivoted toward the voice. He raised his sword then cursed as it flew from his hand into darkness. He jumped backward. Steel sliced through the place he had just vacated. The man came at him, slicing viciously through the darkness. Cain groped at his bandoleer. His fingertips brushed the wooden hilt of his dagger just as he felt a searing pain slash across his belly.

He sucked in his breath and let fly his dagger. He heard a cry, then silence. He clutched his hand to his stomach. His shirt was ripped. Beneath the muslin a slick wetness oozed onto his fingertips. He squinted into the darkness. There was no movement around him. No sound save for Scylla's labored breath. He searched the ground for his sword. Finding it, he stepped toward the fallen lump of humanity in the road. He stopped, and waited, and listened.

Silence.

He took another step. The man was directly at his feet. He tested the brigand's arm with the toe of his boot. He heard movement. A familiar whoosh of steel, and then he tasted the agony of his mistake as the man's sword plunged deep into the flesh of his upper thigh.

The night grew thick around Cain's head.

And then he heard laughter.

chapter nine

"My lady? My lady."

Elisabeth crimped her eyes against the light that intruded on her sleep, but the brightness persisted, as did Frith's voice.

"We're in rather a spot of bother, m'lady."

Moaning hoarsely, she braced her forearm across her eyes. It had to be the middle of the night. "What . . . time is it?"

"A bit after two, m'lady."

"Unnnhh." She moistened her lips and in a drowsy voice mumbled, "What kind of bother?"

"The thief-taker, m'lady. He's come back in something of a dreadful state. I've helped him to his bedchamber, but from the looks of him, he needs assistance with more than just the removal of his boots."

Elisabeth snatched her forearm from her eyes. She squinted into the candle flame that Frith held close to his face, suddenly more awake than she wanted to be. "What's happened to him?"

"He can hardly walk, m'lady. And he's torn away part of his cloak to wrap around his thigh, but the cloak *and* his breeches are soaked through with his blood."

Elisabeth threw off her covers.

"I thought to enlist Emma's assistance before disturbing you, m'lady, but Mrs. Pigeon is sleeping this eventide with a bottle of Daffy's Elixir cradled in her arm. The bottle is, I fear, half empty."

"Which explains why you're unable to wake her up." Elisabeth propped herself to a sitting position and swung her legs over the side of the bed. "Can you fetch me a petticoat and my rayle?"

"But, your foot, m'lady."

Elisabeth tugged her night-chemise over her knees and elevated the foot that, minus the physician's excessive dressing, looked more like a foot. "The pain isn't so bad. I shouldn't have any problem if you would lend me your arm."

Slap thump, slap thump. Mobcapped, petticoated, and barefoot, she made her way from west wing to east—three hundred and five steps over cold marble and polished wood. *Slap thump, slap thump*. And with each footfall there grew in the pit of her stomach an all-consuming dread of what she would find behind the door of the green salon. Cain had hurt her, but she certainly did not wish him dead.

Frith opened the door to Cain's bedchamber. "I tried to remove the counterpane before he fell onto the bed, m'lady," the steward whispered as he escorted her inside, "but I was regrettably unsuccessful. I fear 'tis ruined."

Elisabeth's gaze flew to the bed—to find it empty. She saw Cain's boots standing toes outward by the head of the bed and with her eyes downcast she noticed something else. The dark wood of the floor was smeared with something that glistened wet and red in the candlelight. Long streaks of blood, as if he had dragged himself across—

She spun round in the opposite direction.

He was propped on his left elbow before the fire and in his right fist there flashed the cold steel of his dagger. He peered at her across the room, and she saw such pain in that look that her stronger instincts for healing overpowered the feelings of animosity she held for him. He was no longer Cain. He was simply a man who needed her help. In the next instant his elbow slid from beneath him and he fell back onto the floor, too weak to hold himself up.

Slapthump slapthump slapthump. She eased herself onto the floor beside him and touched the backs of her fingers to his cheek. His skin felt clammy. His complexion was the color of bleached bone.

"Leave me," he rasped.

She looked up at Frith. "Bring me my basket of medicines from the kitchen. And linen dressings. And I'll need hot water. And brandy. Hurry."

The steward's mules clip-clopped across the floor as he left. Elisabeth slid sideways, to a place where she could better examine Cain's thigh.

"You find my presence so . . . offennnsive, lady." He gasped the words, struggling to form them. "My death should . . . please you."

"There will be no death, sir. Not if I can help it." She eyed the strip of woolen cloak he had secured around his thigh. It was wet with seepage from his wound and she was reminded of the tenant she had once seen fall on a pitchfork. His wound had been in the same area as Cain's, but he had severed something so vital in his thigh that he had bled to death within minutes. She willed herself not to think about that now.

"I don't think I can loose the knot you tied without hurting you."

In response he opened his right fist, baring his dagger to her. "Cut it," he wheezed.

She did not have to be asked a second time. She lifted the dagger from his palm and worked the blade beneath the strip of wool on his outer thigh then carefully sliced upward. "Why did you drag yourself over here?" She cut through the last of the wool and began to peel it slowly from his leg. Frith had been right. The wool was soaked through with his blood.

Cain's face contorted with his pain. "The fire. Thought I could . . . stop the bleeding by . . ." His breath grew ragged. ". . . cauterizing the wound."

Elisabeth lifted the fabric off his thigh. "You were going to do it yourself?"

"No other . . . volunteers."

She leaned over his thigh. Above the wound his breeches were torn open and against his flesh she saw he had pressed a square of fabric, possibly a pocket handkerchief, that had reached its saturation point long ago and would forever be dyed a permanent red. She eased it off his flesh, slowly, gently, fearful of what she would find beneath. "How did this happen?" She removed the compress then choked down a rising wave of nausea at the sight of his mutilation.

"Three men. Couldn't see . . . who they were. One named . . . Skagg."

Her fingers went cold. She could see no flesh, only blood.

"Attacked me." He gulped down a great draught of air and clenched his teeth against the pain.

"How did you escape?" She tried to keep the vibration out of her voice as she probed the wound for flaps of skin that she could sew together.

"Butchered two of . . . the bastards. Wounded one. *Jesus!*" He stiffened at the pressure of her fingers. His breathing quickened.

"You need stitches."

"No time."

"Frith will be coming soon." She threw a desperate look over her shoulder at the door.

"I'll ble*eee*d to death before you . . . thread your needle. The knife. Use the knife."

Elisabeth was well lessoned in the art of stitching wounds, but what he was suggesting she do with his knife horrified her. It was barbaric. She hesitated, indecision clouding her eyes.

"Elisabeth."

"I—"

"Give me the knife then . . . damn you." He tested the floor with his fingers. She snatched the blade into her hand.

"Nay. I'll do it," she whispered, marking the rapid flow of blood from the wound. In a trice she was on her feet.

Slapthumpslapthumpslapthump. She whipped a bolster off the bed for his head. Turning round, she stumbled into his jackboots. They skidded sideways across the floor, spur rowels rattling in the silence. Pain shot through her foot, but she ignored it.

She grabbed clean towels from the dresser, threw them over the bolster, angled a ewer of water against her hip, and hastened back to Cain. He lifted his head then let it drop back to the floor. "Lie still," she cautioned as she set the ewer and linen beside him.

"Dally longer . . . and you'll have little need . . . to voice . . . that directive."

She worked swiftly and methodically. She slid the bolster beneath his head, lit a dozen candles that sat in a gilt girandole, and moved the structure close to Cain to cast steady light on his thigh. Removing the chamber's bed warmer from a hook beneath the mantel, she filled it with hot coals and carried it to Cain's side. She sat down close to his thigh, angling herself so that her legs ran parallel to his arm and her feet were close to his shoulder.

"I'm going to cut away the leg of your breeches," she said as she gently elevated his knee. She sliced through the kneeband and slashed upward along his outer thigh to a place well above the wound. When the fabric was split lengthwise, she made a crosswise slash and cut the breeches around his leg, close to his groin. With that done, she flipped the lid of the bed warmer and drove the knife into the coals.

"When you press the knife . . . to my wound," he rasped, "my leg will jerk. Hold the blade . . . tightly. Use both hands."

She blew a stream of air between her lips as she inched the leg of his breeches away from his wound. She heard him suck in his breath. "I'm sorry."

He shook his head, indicating she should continue. His forehead was wet with perspiration. His lips were chalky. She plucked the final threads of fabric away from his flesh and tossed the material toward the fire. She angled his leg to allow herself a better view of his inner thigh, reached for the ewer, then tipped the spout, irrigating the wound with tepid water.

Briefly cleansed of blood, the wound appeared less jagged than she had originally thought, but it was deep, and long as her middle finger. "'Tis not a pistol wound," she said, relieved that there was no ball left inside to putrefy. Yet she worried what had been severed to cause so great a flow of blood. "Why did they do this to you?"

"A thief-taker's enemies are . . . legion."

She irrigated the wound again, hoping to rid it of any foreign matter, then pressed a clean towel atop it. "Did you allow the man who did this to you to walk away unscathed?"

"Thought I . . . killed him. He was . . . lying in the road. Then did this."

She yanked her rayle off her shoulders and wiped her hands on the pristine white cotton. "How did you flee if the man was still alive?"

"Scylla. He heard the man . . . laugh. Was . . . beside me before I could . . . whistle. Found the . . . stirrup iron and . . . rode away."

As he talked, Elisabeth coiled another towel into a figure eight and knotted the ends together. She placed the twisted linen in his hand. "Bite down on this. It should prevent you from biting through your tongue when we begin." He curled his fingers around it. She mopped her brow with her forearm. "I think we're ready." Nervousness settled like lead in her bones.

She removed the knife from the coals in the bed warmer. The metal was black with carbon. Dipping the fingers of her right hand into the ewer, she flicked water onto the blade to gauge if it was hot enough. The metal hissed and spat the water back at her. It was hot enough.

Cain lifted the linen to his mouth. He reached his left hand behind him to grasp the leg of a heavy walnut chair. He clenched his right hand in a fist close to Elisabeth's leg. Biting down on the linen, he nodded his head for her to begin.

She swabbed her brow again and rubbed her eyes to clear her vision. "On the count of three," she said, voice shaking. "One . . ." She removed the towel from his leg. "Two . . ." She centered the blade over the gash. "Three."

The metal sizzled against his flesh. She held the knife with both hands, but his leg bucked so violently that she wrenched it away for fear of wounding him further. The stench of charred flesh assaulted her nostrils—the same stench that had carried on the wind the day the lightning struck her parents. The smell made her recoil. She pressed the back of her hand to her nostrils. She felt suddenly debilitated, paralyzed. She shot a look at Cain's face. Perspiration streaked his temples and beaded his upper lip. Ridges of veins distended his forehead. His breathing was labored and irregular. His eyes were clamped tight; the sooty hairs of his lashes shiny with moisture. She could feel his pain like a living thing within her, overriding her paralysis. The need to make him well eclipsed her impotence. She swallowed her nausea, leaned her weight against his knee, and transferred the knife to her left hand.

"Try to be still," she pleaded. She centered the blade once more. "I'll hold your leg down as best I can. A few seconds more, Cain. Bear with me."

Down went the knife. His leg jerked, but not so violently as it had initially. She held the knife steady and steeled herself against the noxious odor of hot metal meeting flesh. She ticked off five seconds in her head before lifting the knife, and when she saw that the bleeding had stopped, she exhaled the breath she'd been holding and set the knife down. Only then did she realize that her foot had gone numb. She looked down. Cain had seized her ankle at some point. His fingers were wrapped so tightly around her that he had cut off the circulation to her foot. She placed her hand over his and smoothed her palm over his wrist and forearm. He was rigid as a deal plank. " 'Tis over. Rest now. Rest." She massaged the hand that wore his open-fingered glove and breathed more easily when she felt his fingers slacken around her ankle.

The door opened behind her. Frith entered the room carrying a bucket in one hand and Elisabeth's basket of medicines in the other. "I'm sorry for taking so long, m'lady. I took the liberty of retrieving a nightshirt from my chambers for the thief-taker." He hastened across the floor and set both items down, then peered at Elisabeth's handiwork over the top of her head. The cauterized wound was red, raw, and already beginning to blister. "Will you be able to save the leg, m'lady? Foul-looking thing, isn't it? And the stench. Smells like a charnel house. Should I throw open a window? Charnel house fumes can be quite deadly."

"Fine." She stood up, preparing to fetch a cake of soap from the dresser, but once on her feet, the weight and risk of the actions she had just taken began to immobilize her. The soles of her feet began to tingle. Her ears became thick with the sound of buzzing and the remembered hiss of the blade against his flesh. She touched her hand to her nostrils. The shuffle and scuff of the steward's footsteps faded softly. The sound of her heartbeat mingled with the buzzing in her ears until she could hear naught but her own breathing and the unrelenting sizzle of burning metal. Turning to face the steward, she lifted her hand to her brow.

"Forgive me, Frith, but I think I am going to be quite . . . unwell."

The steward took a calm step forward, catching the girl on a half turn as she passed out in a dead faint. "Quite so, m'lady."

She awoke to find herself occupying one of the room's monstrous chairs. The bed's green satin counterpane was bundled tidily about her. She rubbed a kink in her neck and squinted at Frith who was laying a blanket across the bottom portion of Cain's legs. The groan she elicited caused the steward to turn toward her.

"You're well, m'lady?"

"I fainted," she said, feeling more than a little ridiculous. In all her years of treating the scourges of the infirm, she had never swooned. She nodded toward Cain. "Does he fare well?"

"He appears to be resting quite comfortably. I took it upon myself to wash the area around his wound and remove his clothing. He has a nasty gash across his midsection that I washed and dressed. You might notice that my nightshirt is a trifle small for him, but at least the man is minimally decent now."

Elisabeth smiled at the steward as she straightened in her chair. "Did you also take it upon yourself to put a dressing on his thigh?" She threw off the counterpane and bowed her head, drained and exhausted.

"A loose one, m'lady. Much like the one you placed on my hand when I burned it several months ago."

"You remember how I fashioned your dressing?"

"I remember the pain of the burn, m'lady. The very air touching it was cause for great excruciation. I don't envy the thief-taker's having to endure such travail. His pain would have to be extreme."

Elisabeth hobbled to Frith's side. Yes, she thought, his pain would have to be extreme, yet he hadn't cried out even once.

"Shall I escort you back to your chambers, m'lady?"

"I'd prefer not to absent myself from him tonight. Should he awaken later, he may need me."

The steward's eyebrow shot up. "I could stay with the man, m'lady."

"You've already done more than enough, Frith. Perhaps in the morning one of the footmen would help you carry him to the bed. It might be safer to move him then."

Frith eyed Cain from head to foot. "Mayhap in the morning all the footmen will help me carry him, m'lady." He collected the stained towels, Cain's garments, Elisabeth's blood-stained rayle, and the bucket, and when he had departed, Elisabeth transferred the counterpane from the chair to the floor. She made a fluffy heap of it beside Cain, then lay down beside him, propping herself on her left elbow so she could look at him. Blankets covered his torso and lower legs, leaving his wound uncovered save for the nightshirt. Elisabeth snugged one of the blankets around his face then rested a tentative hand on his pillow. His face was angled toward her. Very gently she touched a lock of hair that had fallen onto his forehead and smoothed it back. The hair at his hairline was still damp with perspiration. His brow was hot as with fever.

"I'm here for you," she whispered, wanting to cradle

him in her arms but afraid she might wake him. She traced the elegant shape of his eyebrow with her fingertip, then boosting herself upward, placed a feathery kiss on the warm flesh of his brow. She was wont to explain why she still bore affection for this man after all he had said and done to her. 'Twas incomprehensible. But the bond existed and there was little she could do to disguise it. Call it what she might, she knew only one fitting word for it. "I love you," she breathed against his hairline, knowing this could well be the only time she would ever voice that sentiment aloud in his presence.

Scooting close to him, she lay her mobcapped head on the edge of his pillow, and with the feel of his breath warming her face, she closed her eyes.

It seemed to Elisabeth that she had only just dozed off when she heard the noise. Sobbing. Whimpering. She lifted her head off the pillow and gazed at Cain. His lips were pinched tightly, his features were skewed into ugly distortion, and down his cheek there crept a solitary bead of moisture. He was sound asleep, yet this man who could kill with the prowess of a leopard, was crying.

His head thrashed from side to side. "Nay!" he cried out in a voice that sounded young and terrified. "Leave her!" His right hand shot upward as if he were lunging for something in his dream. Elisabeth caught his hand and cradled it against the underside of her chin, then with her left hand, pressed gentle fingers to his brow.

"Hush," she crooned, trying to calm him with the serene stroke of her fingers and the softness of her voice. "Shhhh. 'Tis only a dream." She pressed her cheek to the curve of his brow, forcing his head to remain still, and when he indeed had stopped thrashing, she shifted his hand from her neck to her mouth and touched her lips to the length of each finger that was not encased in his glove. He seemed so vulnerable to her at this moment. And this vulnerability triggered in her a corresponding emotion to protect him while he could not protect himself. To nurture him in his weakness. To love him wholly, as a woman loves a man.

"I would take away the pain if I could," she said in an undertone. He moaned in his sleep and sobbed a final sob. Elevating her head slightly, she traced with her eyes the solitary stream of moisture that hugged the contour of his nose and floated onto his lips. Then, leaning over him, she brushed his lips with her own, kissing away the salt of his tears, tasting on her tongue the anguish evoked by his dreams. Her kisses were light and lingering and bespoke a lifetime of affection that she had ached to give and have returned.

He grew more peaceful. His countenance grew calm. Elisabeth eased away from him as her legs were beginning to cramp. She sat upright on the counterpane, and still grasping his forearm to her chest, began to sway with it, as a mother might rock her babe. She smelled the starch and rainwater smells of Frith's nightshirt and as she cupped her palms once more around Cain's hand, she felt the unnatural stiffness of his glove, and she held it away from her to peruse it.

In the glow of the firelight the glove was overlaid with a reddish hue and it took but a moment to realize what had caused the wool to harden. It was caked with blood.

Without hesitation she began to pluck at the wool, coaxing the open fingers over his knuckles. The glove was stubborn, like a pair of too tight breeches, but she wriggled it up and down and managed to work it from the heel of his palm to the base of his thumb. It was then that she lit on the tail end of a scar in the center of his palm. Frowning, she worked the glove higher. When it sat at the base of his fingers, she saw the entire scar as it had been emblazoned on his flesh. In disbelief she stared at it, not moving, barely even breathing.

In the center of his palm, defined by skin of a paler pigment than that surrounding it, he bore the mark of a felon—a "T" burned into his flesh, a mark that proclaimed to the general populace that this man was a criminal who had been caught and punished for his misdeeds. Confused, Elisabeth lowered his hand to her lap, unable to drag her eyes away from his palm. She could not fathom how anyone could have made so incredible a mistake. Cain was thief-*taker,* not thief. Who had done this to him? Why? She smoothed a finger over the scar and realized in that moment that hers had not been the first hand to brand his flesh with hot metal. But there had been justice in her actions. Where was the justice in falsely branding him a thief?

"What did they do to you, my love?" she whispered. She could understand now the reason for the coldness in his eyes, and her heart ached for him. "So many secrets," she said, caressing his hand. "So much pain." But there would be more pain should anyone else see the mark before he had an opportunity to explain himself.

Quickly now, she fit the glove back over his hand, judiciously guarding his secret. In the morning she would learn the truth.

Feeling a secret closeness with him, she tucked his hand back under the blanket, and when she heard him whimper again, she chastened herself for having forgotten the one drug that would alleviate his pain. The physician's phial of laudanum lay on the candle stand in her bedchamber. It would take her long minutes to trek from east wing to west then back again, but the effect the drug would have on Cain would be well worth the walk.

Slap thump, slap thump, slap thump.

She removed the unlit candle sconce from its stand by the head of Cain's bed. In turning round, she spied his upended jackboots on the floor and hobbled a few steps to set them aright. She lifted one boot into her hand and when she bent down to retrieve the other, she noticed that a number of objects had tumbled out of the inside pocket of the boot.

She recognized one item immediately. Her long-glass.

Placing the boot and candle sconce on the floor, she sat down beside the overturned jackboot and lifted the long-glass into her hand. Was this the business that Cain had been about when he'd been accosted? Guilt riffled through her. Had she remembered to remove it from the mantel of the Saracen's Head, none of this would have happened.

She worked the velvet ribbon over her mobcap and straightened it around her neck, then returned her attention to the floor. Several coins had spilled out of a small leather pouch. She gathered the coins together and when she lifted the pouch, she saw that, hiding beneath it, lay a ring of some kind. She emptied the coins into the pouch. She secured the drawstrings then roved her forefinger through the center of the ring and held it toward the light thrown out from the fireplace.

The center stone was a rectangle of milk white chalcedony into which was etched the figure of a . . . She angled the stone in another direction and squinted at it. The light was too dim to make out the etching, but it reminded her of—

Her mouth went dry. *Nay, it cannot be.*

Her fingers tightened around the ring. She heaved herself to her feet and *slap thumped* her way to the girandole of beeswax candles beside Cain, and when the light was flaming about her, she lifted the ring toward its brightness, praying that what she'd imagined was not true.

But it was.

She had seen this ring only once before, but for the past five months she had been working its likeness with feather stitches and French knots. Within the chalcedony was etched the figure of a bird—a solitary white raven whose head was cocked to the side as if eavesdropping on the secrets of ages past. This ring, whose presence Cain had hidden in his jackboot, belonged to Sir Thomas Penmarck, Earl of Moreleigh.

Her eyes flew to Cain. He looked familiar to Thomas not because of his resemblance to the fifth viscount or the stable master. He looked familiar because he had *robbed* Thomas.

The brand on his palm figured more prominently now. He had played his game and duped them all with his daring heroics, she more than anyone. Her nerves wrenched in her stomach. The ring confirmed what she had been unable to see minutes earlier, what she had been unwilling to admit.

The man lying at her feet was not a thief-taker.

Dear God, he was a thief.

chapter

ten

What does he want with us? Why is he here?

Elisabeth asked herself the same questions over and again the following day. Her answer was always the same. *He is a thief come to rob us, just as he robbed Thomas.* The reality of the situation cut her to the quick. He was not noble and heroic. He was a thief. And he was dangerous. Yet he would be more dangerous should he suspect she had learned his secret. And if he saw her face, he would know immediately.

To prevent that from happening she delegated his care to Frith and one of the upstairs maids. As long as Cain was recuperating abed, he would be relatively harmless. But once his wound healed sufficiently enough for him to walk, he would want to finish what he had come here to do.

She felt his deception like a talon piercing her heart. How could she have been so poor a judge of character?

Because the man was kind to you.

But his kindness had been calculated, she reminded herself. He'd had to be kind to win her trust.

He saved your life.

This gave her pause. He had indeed saved her life. But *she* had returned the favor last night. They were even. But still . . . Perhaps she owed him the courtesy of listening to his explanation before she shared his deception with Quintus. She would have to tell Quintus. Together, they needed to decide what measures they should take against him. Knowing Quintus, he would probably demand that Cain be hanged from the gibbet that had been erected to accommodate Bridestone Barrow's thief.

The image of Cain's dead body rotting in an iron cage settled so vividly in her mind that she could not bring herself to seek Quintus's counsel immediately. Despite her knowledge of Cain, she found it difficult to condemn a man she had convinced herself she loved.

For seventeen hours she maintained her silence.

At eight o'clock the following evening, her silence, perforce, came to an end.

"The fact that he has insulted every maidservant who has entered his bedchamber indicates that the man is feeling better," Frith explained as he stood beside Elisabeth's bed. "But his threats do concern me."

"What kind of threats?"

"He has vowed, m'lady, that if the next female who steps across his threshold is not you, he will spear her petticoat to the floor."

"Where is his bandoleer?"

"I set it beneath the candle stand last night, m'lady. This afternoon it was occupying a place beside the thief-taker on the bed."

Elisabeth pursed her lips in self-disgust. "I should have taken his bandoleer and sword last night."

"My lady?"

She shook her head. "Nothing. I was careless, 'tis all. If he has access to arms, I suppose I must go to him."

"The man no doubt wants to extend his gratitude to you for saving his life, m'lady. I suspect he means well, even if his manner is a trifle gruff."

Elisabeth found him looking less than comfortable in his bed in the green salon. A sinister growth of stubble darkened his face. His nightshirt was untied at the throat and exposed a V of naked chest to his breastbone. His eyes seemed to burn in their sockets as he peered at her.

"Your threats seem an inappropriate form of gratitude, sir." She hovered at the foot of his bed, not daring to venture closer. Cain set aside the dagger with which he was toying.

"Why have you foisted the steward and his minions on me? I do not care to have the man pawing beneath my nightshirt to attend my dressing."

" 'Tis his nightshirt, sir."

"But my thigh that must suffer the man's touch."

"No doubt you would suffer less obviously if one of the maidservants consented to do the pawing."

"A female's touch would be preferable, lady, but your maidservants sport little that resembles anything female."

He looked at her then with eyes that told her she had performed a kindness that no other human being would have wasted time performing. There was awe in that look, and gratitude, and some other emotion that sent an unwelcome tremor up her spine.

"Come here, Elisabeth." He flung the sheet off his legs and patted a space beside him on the bed.

She eyed the place he indicated with apprehension. Her feet were anchored to the spot.

"You look fearful of a sudden. What do I look? A wild hound? A brigand?"

Her heart lurched at his comment. He rubbed the growth on his jaw then motioned her forward with the fingers of his upturned palm. "Come."

Hoping to discourage suspicion, she forced one foot ahead of the other and seated herself next to his feet.

Cain frowned. "Would it affront your sensibilities to sit an arm's length closer?" He shifted his torso to make room for her by his hip. "Here."

With some reluctance she did as he bade, but sat perched on the edge of the bed ready to escape should the need arise. She glanced over her shoulder at his feet. "'Tis closer than one arm's length."

"And not nearly close enough." He saw alarm flash in her eyes and seized her arm before she could flee. "What plagues you, Elisabeth? Do you suddenly remember you are betrothed to another?"

"No longer," she breathed. "There will be no marriage. In a sense I have you to thank for that, sir. But I'm sure you have no wish to discuss the change in my marital status. Unwanted pieces of baggage make for painfully dull discourse." She saw an undercurrent of emotion riffle through his eyes as he grasped what she had just revealed to him. She watched despair mingle with hope, anger with joy. She watched them mingle and drain through him, almost as if he had *wanted* her to wed Thomas and now that she wasn't, had no idea how to respond. But he found platitudes quickly enough.

"I hurt you deeply," he whispered. "Forgive me."

You deceived me! she wanted to scream at him, but she was sitting too close to his knives for such honesty. Her eyes darted over the hilts of each of his daggers, for the first time realizing that all the carvings were identical—each one a black serpent with a blood-red tongue. Had he stolen those too?

"How long did you remain with me last night?" he asked, uncurling her fingers so that he could join his palm to hers.

She willed herself to effect a smile that was as cunning as his treachery. "I remained until you were resting comfortably, sir."

He lowered his eyes to stare at the connection of their flesh. "Did I . . . mutter anything in my sleep?"

You cried in your sleep and I kissed your tears away, she remembered, but aloud she said, "You moaned rather effusively. You were in a great deal of pain."

"But I said nothing?" He hazarded a rare smile then, but his delight was painful for her to look upon, for with his lips curved into a yielding line and his eyes soft and tame, he seemed without guile, without artifice. He seemed everything she knew he was not.

"Have others mentioned you are given to prattle in your sleep, sir?" She tried to draw back on her hand, but he flattened it against his chest, cutting short her escape.

"Should I choose to share my bed with another, I do not misuse my time sleeping. I was only asking, lady, because as you say, I was in a great deal of pain. I have known men whose tongues have grown loose when so afflicted."

"Your tongue remained firmly fastened." *Except when you cried out to "leave her." To whom were you speaking? What other secrets are you hiding from me?*

"I owe you much, Elisabeth."

"You owe me nothing."

"You saved my life."

"As you saved mine. A life for a life, sir. 'Tis well met."

"Not well met, my lady. You have given me more than my life." His voice was husky, his eyes hot. "Much more than my life. And I burn to return the favor." He brought her hand to his mouth, and holding her fingers flat, kissed the center of her palm.

Your desire comes too late! she flung at him in silence, even as the touch of his lips sent flutters of warmth dancing up the back of her arm. "Please stop. My hand—"

"—is soft . . . and lovely." He shaped her palm to the side of his neck. Where the curve of her thumb conjoined his flesh, she felt a cadence that beat strong and sure, duplicating the rhythm of his heart. "There are places on a man's body that ache to be touched by—"

"Stop it!" She wrenched backward on her arm. He caught her wrist midair.

"You did not want me to stop at the Saracen's Head!"

"I did not know you then!"

"What did you not know?"

Their eyes ignited sparks. Elisabeth wet her lips, chest heaving. "I am going to check your dressing, sir, and then I am going to leave . . . if you would release my arm."

"Can you not *see* what I feel for you?"

She glared at him, refusing to debase herself by following his gaze.

" 'Tis what a man feels when he wants a woman. And there was a moment at the Saracen's Head, lady . . . there was a moment when your eyes bespoke your willingness to sample the heat from these loins."

"You act the savage!"

"Aye, lady. A savage who would lesson you in things Thomas Penmarck would lack the patience to show you." He pulled her against his chest and vised her head in his hand, but her eyes grew dark with such loathing that he could not kiss her. He could not even look at her.

Making a fearsome sound in his throat, he thrust her away from his face. Elisabeth angled her chin toward her shoulder and eyed the hand that held her in its grasp.

"Are you through, sir?"

He saw suspicion in the eyes that had once looked upon him with calm affection. He saw aberration in the face that glowered at his hand. At his glove.

And then he knew.

"You saw."

Elisabeth nodded.

He released her. She hastened to her feet and backed away from the bed. Cain cradled his hand against his chest. "What do you intend to do?"

She kept limping backward, putting acres of space between them. "'Tis all you have to say by way of explanation? What do I intend to do?"

He trained wary eyes on her. "It would seem you have already supplied your own explanations."

Alone and stranded in the middle of the floor, she hugged her arms to herself for comfort. "Why did you come to Maidenstowe?"

"You know the answer to that."

"I know the stated reason, sir. What is the real reason?" She thought she saw a flicker of indecision cross his face, as if he were weighing the outcome of truth versus more lies, but in the end, silence reigned. He said nothing, which lent confirmation to her suspicions. "It does not surprise me that a man as well practiced in chicanery as yourself finds the truth so unpalatable. Truth is a bitter decoction for those unaccustomed to its taste. But I will do you the courtesy of being more truthful with you than you have been with me, sir. In answer to your question, at first light I shall send someone to fetch the constable in the next parish. He is quite adept at questioning thieves. He will know what to do with you. And when next I see Thomas, I will return the ring you stole from him."

His look of silent resignation dissolved in a heartbeat. His eyes grew crazed, malevolent. He curled his lips back over his teeth with a viciousness more terrifying than that of the hounds who stalked Hound Tor. Elisabeth retreated steadily toward the door as he thrust his arm over the side of the bed and swept his boot into his hand.

"Thomas said you looked familiar, but he could not place you. 'Tis clear now how you could speak so explicitly of Thirlstane. Did you pose as a thief-taker then also? Did you take up residence there as you have here? Or did you pose as a laborer or woodcrafter, working on the very suite of rooms that Thomas was preparing for my arrival? Tell me, Cain. Tell me what kind of blackguard has wormed his way into our lives!"

He upended the boot over his lap, shaking it furiously. The inside pocket was empty. He flung it across the floor and speared her with eyes that dripped blood. "Give me the ring."

"I believed in you. *Trusted* you!"

"The ring, Elisabeth."

She shook her head. Her shoulders bumped against the portal. Reaching behind her, she secured her fingers around the brass door handle. "You will never touch that ring again. Thomas will be thankful for its return."

"Should Thomas Penmarck ever *see* that ring, I will kill you. Do you hear me, girl? I will *kill* you!" He swung his legs over the side of the bed, doubling over with pain before his feet could hit the floor. Elisabeth depressed the tongue of the door handle and snatched the key from the lock-plate. She did not recognize this man's voice; she did not know his face. Heart pounding, she raced into the hallway and slammed the door behind her.

"D*aaaa*mn you!" His voice exploded through the closed door. "Damn you to hell!" She shot the key into the lock and turned it once, breathing more easily with the man imprisoned behind a barrier of thick hardwood. Her hand shook as she slid the key from the lock-plate and smothered it in her fist. Something thudded into the wood on the opposite side of the door. Frith bore down on her from the opposite end of the hall. He raised his eyebrow as another thud echoed out to them. Elisabeth stepped away from the door.

"Keep everyone away from this room, Frith. From the east wing entirely. The thief-taker is not to receive food or drink or any other amenity."

"You will rue this day, Elisabeth! Give me the ring!" A thunderous crash. An echoing clatter. Elisabeth imagined the candle stand skidding across the floor, its contents scattering hither and yon. Frith blinked at the portal.

"Quite so, m'lady."

"And at first light I want you to dispatch a messenger to the constable of Underdown. Tell the constable that we have captured Bridestone Barrow's thief and await his instructions as to how we should proceed. I would appreciate the constable's presence at Maidenstowe to question the thief directly."

"I will kill you!"

Frith blinked at the portal again. "Would you prefer the messenger be dispatched tonight, m'lady?"

Elisabeth shook her head. "First light will be soon enough."

"As my lady wishes. Should I inform the marquess of the situation?"

"I . . ." She clutched her hand to her breast and stared at her fist. Once more she shook her head. "It makes little sense for Quintus to lose sleep over the matter. I will apprise him of the situation tomorrow morning before the constable arrives."

Frith bowed at the waist then presented his arm to his mistress. "Shall I escort you to the dining room for supper, m'lady?"

"I would rather you escort me to my bedchamber. Food seems to have lost its appeal this evening."

"You'll wish you had let me die, Elisabeth! You'll not escape me! I swear it! On my mother's grave I swear it!"

Frith hurried her down the hallway, away from the sound of Cain's threats. "I could prepare a tray for you, m'lady. Eels in green sauce and roast swan."

Elisabeth leaned heavily on the steward's arm. She could not think of eel while Cain's epithets rang in her ears. She could not think of roast swan while her heart was breaking.

One hour and a half later, in the small dining room, Quintus St. Mary, unmindful of Cain's epithets, belched mightily as he polished off a second helping of eel.

In the west wing of the mansion, Elisabeth St. Mary

penned a missive to the constable of Underdown, explaining to him her suspicions about the man locked in the green salon.

In the green salon, save for the hiss of logs on the fire, all was quiet. The door remained closed, but the brass plate mounted over the door's locking mechanism was dangling by a single screw.

After supper that night Quintus retired to the withdrawing room with a stack of documents, his wooden writing box, and a goblet of port. Frith tossed another log on the fire, then, with his scrupulously erect gait, walked to the settee where Quintus had burrowed himself.

"Will there be anything else, m'lord?"

Quintus pondered the legal documents beside him. "I plan to spend the night combing Elisabeth's marriage contract. If there's a graceful way out of this imbroglio, I intend to find it."

"Very good, m'lord."

The old man smiled a private smile. "It will be very good, won't it? No need for you to pace the floor waiting for me to finish, Frith. I'll see myself to bed when I'm done."

The steward's features ran together in awe. "Alone, m'lord?"

"Alone? Of course alone. Why do you sound so astonished?"

"You've never seen yourself to bed alone, m'lord."

"Afraid I'll lose my way? I've slept in the same room for eighty-four years, Frith. The possibility of my getting lost is quite remote. Now go to bed. I've work to do. Leave the doors. I'll latch them when I retire.

And work he did. For twenty minutes he penned words and pored over words . . . until the portraits of his late wives began to crowd in on him. He peered across the length of his right shoulder, sneering at the portrait of Hortense on the north wall. "What are you staring at?"

It was then he heard the whine of hinges, and twisting round, squinted at the shadowed figure who had slipped through the french doors. Making out the face, Quintus hoisted himself upright in the corner of the settee. "What are you doing on the terrace at this time of night? I might have mistaken you for a thief. Why didn't you come through the house? Oh, never mind. 'Tis fortunate you're here. There's something I need to discuss with you."

With a slow, purposeful stride, the man made his way to the marquess. As he walked, the heels of his boots clicked against the waxed hardwood floor—a sound that seemed to echo his authority, as if he owned Maidenstowe and all its possessions.

Elisabeth didn't sleep that night. She imagined she could hear Cain's threats thundering down her chimney flue, so she spent the night propped up in her bed with her eyes locked on her bedchamber door and a poker across her lap. When the first pale glimmers of daylight washed her room, she threw on a wrapping gown, coiled her hair beneath a pinner cap, and delivered her missive to Frith who was standing at the front door, awaiting the arrival of a groomsman.

"Barker will see the constable receives your message, m'lady. He's a good man, Barker is."

Elisabeth rubbed her eyes. They stung from lack of

sleep. "I imagine my grandfather will be abed for hours yet."

"No doubt, m'lady."

She sighed and drew the corner of her lip between her teeth, her rigid stance reflecting both distress and indecision. Frith cleared his throat.

"If you would care to take your ease in the small parlor, m'lady, I could serve you refreshment after I dispatch Barker."

She smiled her gratitude, for indeed, until Quintus awoke or the constable arrived, she had little to do except allow her stomach to churn with worry. "Thank you, Frith. I would appreciate that." And then, before she turned to leave, she said, "Have you heard further clamor from the green salon since last night?"

"None, m'lady. 'Tis quiet as a church. One might wonder if the man were still alive."

But Elisabeth knew Cain was still alive. Men of his ilk did not die that easily.

The small parlor was located off the east terrace, sharing its south wall with the music room and its north wall with the withdrawing room. As she hobbled past the latter, Elisabeth spied a flash of white periwig, and frowning, back-pedaled a step. "Quintus? However did you manage to creep downstairs without Frith's hearing you?"

He was locked in his favorite position—angled into a corner on the settee with his limbs sprawled and his head bowed forward onto his chest, but Elisabeth was in no mood to suffer his buffoonery this morning.

"You vowed to start celebrating life," she chastised him. "If you fancy this a celebration, I would venture you're off to a dreadfully poor start." She limped several paces into the room, and when he made no effort to rouse himself, she continued walking to the French doors.

Daylight slanted across the statuary on the terrace, gilding the figure of a nubile girl who, for two hundred years, had balanced a water jug on one hip while pressing a bit of drapery to her naked breast. She was plump and freckled with lichen and for a moment Elisabeth envied her the ability to regard the world without emotion, through eyes of stone.

"The constable of Underdown will be arriving sometime later this morning, Quintus. I sent for him because of . . . because of Cain." She inhaled a deep breath. "He . . . he's not who he claims to be. He's a thief and a liar and he bears the mark of a felon on his palm." She cradled her right hand in her left, pressing her thumb into the hollow of flesh that, on Cain's hand, blazed with a milk white scar. "He was very clever in his ruse, posing as a thief-taker. He undoubtedly hired some underling to harass the village so he could present himself as our savior. 'Tis baffling how he was privy to the fact that you had written Henry Fielding about a thief-taker, but I trust the constable has methods of gleaning such information from criminal factions."

She bowed her head and with her fingertips traced the cold contours of the door's gilded handle. "'Tis discomfiting how easily he gulled us. But we were not the first to fall prey to his trickery. I thought him related to Aunt Constance's stable master. I thought 'twas the reason Thomas found his face familiar. But I was wrong on all counts. He's nothing more than a common thief. He stole Thomas's signet ring. I cringe to think what else he's stolen. He probably lied his way into Maidenstowe so he could prospect for valuables at his leisure."

She turned round, addressing her words to the motionless pouf of wig that was visible above the back of the settee. "I locked him in his room last night." She slid her hand into the side placket of her gown and curled her fingers around the broad-handled key that lay in the pocket she'd tied around her waist. "I thought myself in love with him," she confessed, choking out the words. "Can you imagine what folly? The man is a thief and a liar. Decent people do not marry thieves and liars." She blinked away the sting in her eyes and stiffened her jaw against the emotion welling in her throat. "Decent people see them hanged."

Quintus remained silent, a circumstance that seemed to undermine the seriousness of the situation. Hurt and betrayed, Elisabeth lashed out at him. "Say something! I may be condemning a man to his death and I don't know if I own that right, but I don't know what else to do. I despise him for his deceit. I despise myself for falling in love with him. It hurts!" she sobbed. "Why does it hurt so much?"

She stared at the settee, and when there was still no movement on the other side, she took a hesitant step forward. "Quintus?"

The silence rasped along her nerve endings, filling her with a sudden, unspeakable dread. She took another step forward. "Please don't do this to me. Quintus?" Two quick steps and then she was running, her mind a blur, her body numb to the grind of bone in her foot.

She stopped at the side of the settee, where his back lay against the armrest, and poised her hand above the white frizz of his periwig. "Quintus," she whispered, unable to touch him. Her palm hovered above his head. Her throat constricted. She lowered her hand then snatched it away, doubling it into a fist that she pressed against her mouth.

She stepped around the side of the settee and made a quarter turn to face him. His periwig hung in horizontal curls to his waist. It hung without movement, as if there was no breath in his lungs to lift his chest. *"Nooo."* She sank to her knees, grappling for the hand that dangled lifelessly above the floor.

His flesh was cold and waxy; his fingers rigid. "Noo!" she cried, and the sound echoed back at her, mimicking her grief as she lifted his hand toward her cheek.

Blood. His palm was dark with it, dried now, like a layer of rust.

She choked out a hideous sound as she swept her hand over the red brocade of his waistcoat sleeve, searching for the source of the blood. She touched his thigh, his hip, then brushed aside the white curls that hung to his waist.

The underside of his wig was tinged with red. The floral tapestry that patterned his coat was overlaid with another design—a design that spread outward in a random pattern above his heart. A design that was as bright a hue as the scarlet of his coat. "Frith!" she screamed, her eyes riveting on the puncture mark slashed in the brocade. *"Friiiiith!"*

Her vision blurred with scalding tears. She sagged against the edge of the settee, bowing her head against Quintus's hip. She shifted her legs beneath her to support her weight, and when she did, her right knee bumped into something that spun away from her and rattled against the floor.

"Frith," she whined softly, unable to cry out his name again. She shaped her hand around her grandfather's knee, clinging desperately. *We're all going to die,* she could hear him say. *And when it's my turn, I'll not abide any sniffling and slobbering over the event.*

"You didn't want tears." She whispered the words as moisture squeezed beneath her eyelids. "I'm sorry." She moved her knee to relieve a cramp in her leg. Whatever had fallen onto the floor thumped into her kneecap again. She thrust her hand beneath the settee. Her fingers skimmed something long and cold and hard . . . like a—

Like a dagger, she thought as she dragged it into the open.

And so it was. A dagger whose six-inch blade was stained with blood. A dagger whose carved hilt bore the image of a black serpent with a blood-red tongue . . . like the other knives in his bandoleer. Cain's bandoleer. Cain's knife.

"Why?" she sobbed, clutching the knife in her fist. "Holy Mother, why?"

As if drawn by instinct, she pivoted her head toward the southwest corner of the room. And then she knew why.

The glass dome atop the marble pedestal was smashed. The golden dragon with its fierce ruby eyes and jeweled belly was gone.

A fireball of rage flamed in her lungs. "A bauble?" she choked. "You killed him for a bauble?"

Struggling to her feet, she touched Quintus's head with a tender hand, then tightening her grip on the knife she limped across the room, her eyes suddenly set and unfocused, her spine rigid, like a sleepwalker in the midst of a nightmare. She passed through hallways, beneath chandeliers, and up stairs, remembering not one step she took, not one thing she saw. Her toe began to throb so violently that by the time she reached the green salon on the second floor, her face was awash with tears of pain, but the pain only served to fuel her fury.

The door to the green salon was closed, but it creaked open on the barest touch of Elisabeth's fingertips, sending the inside lock-plate clattering to the floor.

The bedchamber was empty. Like the gold dragon in the withdrawing room, Cain was gone. His boots, cloak, bandoleer—all gone.

Her knuckles tightened white and angry around the knife hilt. For an agonizing day she had fretted over why he was here, what he wanted with them. And now she knew.

He had come to Maidenstowe to steal a treasure and he had allowed no obstacle to stand in his way. The man whose life she had saved was not only a thief and a liar. He was a murderer—a cold-blooded murderer, without feeling, without conscience. And she would see him hanged from the highest gallows in England.

Her eyes roved the bed, the overturned candle stand, but they were not Elisabeth's eyes. Gone was the soft, brilliant blue of young innocence. In its stead was the hard, pale blue of a woman who was no longer prey, but predator.

Thomas arrived that same evening.

"My conduct when last I saw you was reprehensible, Elisabeth. I spent this entire week in London thinking that unless I made proper apology, your feelings toward me might deteriorate beyond redemption, so I couldn't return to Thirlstane without first settling matters between us." He angled his arm around her shoulders. Elisabeth stared straight ahead, her profile as stony as a flint wall. "I'm thankful now I changed my plans. You needn't worry about

anything, Elisabeth. I'll see to all the arrangements personally."

"I have already seen to all the arrangements."

Thomas patted her hand. "You're very efficient in spite
of your grief over this . . . this atrocity. But I warned you. I
told you the man was not to be trusted."

Elisabeth's throat tightened. "You were right, my lord."
She had assigned to Cain qualities he did not possess and
had fallen in love with an illusion, an image. He was not
real. Thomas was real. Thomas was her future. Yesterday
she might have cried over that happenstance. Today, she
was beyond tears.

"You must pen a letter to Henry Fielding alerting him to
the existence of this impostor. Justice must be served, Elisabeth. You can't allow the man to go unpunished."

With cold eyes she marked the parchment she had set
aside when Thomas arrived. "The letter is written, m'lord.
It merely awaits my signature."

"Good. And perhaps in future you will be more inclined
to listen to me, Elisabeth." He squeezed her hand, a gesture that bespoke a vein of compassion beneath his right-
eous facade.

After a moment, with fingers that had lost all claim to
warmth, she squeezed back.

chapter
eleven

On Monday, sixteen May, a jeering mass of humanity mobbed Oxford Street in London as a procession of prison carts struck out from Newgate. Tyburn Tree awaited.

It was hanging Monday.

Cain sat the windowsill of Gellicoe Lint's office three stories above the mayhem, but even that seemed too close. Gellicoe Lint, whose existence Henry Fielding cloaked in secrecy. Master spy. Purveyor of justice. Defender of the Crown against all her foes. Sworn enemy of felons, thieves, and miscreants. He was a huge man, nearly seven feet tall and solid as a barrel of flour. His face was broad, his nose long and curved, and his head was shaved to accommodate the wig whose use he disdained at all times except when meeting with Henry Fielding. It was impossible to determine his age, for he had looked the same for twenty years, but Cain knew there were buzzards circling Dartmoor whose visages were less frightening than the one Gellicoe Lint displayed to the world. He had a great, deep, booming voice that resonated like a fist against an empty barrel. And at the moment, it was booming at him.

"Harry spent what . . . five, six weeks filching poultry in that damned little Barrow place. And you . . . you've been unavailable since April. And to what end? Do I have some corrupt peer standing before the King's Bench, begging for mercy he doesn't deserve? No. I have a dead nobleman and a price on the head of my best agent! This wasn't the outcome I expected from your recent activities."

Cain turned toward the man. His eyes lengthened to slits. "What did you say?"

"Bears repeating, does it? Which part did you mishear? The part about the nobleman or the price on your head?"

The corner of Cain's mouth quirked upward with humor. "I think you conspire to punish me for my absence with an ill-conceived jest."

"Jest? There's a letter here somewhere." He looked left and right, then heaved himself out of his chair. "It was here only an hour ago."

Cain closed the shutter on the scene below him, locking out the stink of coal fires and gutters. His windpipe burned with the stench. Not even a hard spring rain could cleanse London of its smells. The thought of rain brought to mind other thoughts—of a storm-ridden night at Maidenstowe, of Elisabeth's hair . . . *and strawberries*. Reflexively, he canted his head toward the hooded cowl circling his neck, but he found no lingering trace of strawberries clinging to the wool. What he smelled in its stead was horse and sweat. He swallowed hard while his breath rattled aimlessly in the hollow pit that his chest had become.

"Aha!" Bookshelves, crammed with thick leather binders, lined one wall. At a right angle to this wall stood a slant-front secretary fashioned with a multitude of narrow drawers and cubicles. It was in one of these cubicles, beneath a hunk of crusty cheese, that Gellicoe Lint found the letter he was looking for. He unfolded the parchment and scanned the contents to refresh his memory.

"The missive is addressed to Henry Fielding. It maintains that the man who arrived at Maidenstowe claiming to be a thief-taker was an impostor. On the night of four May, the man known as Cain murdered Quintus St. Mary in cold blood and stole from the premises one gold dragon whose value is beyond estimation. The injured party is offering a reward of one thousand pounds for the capture of said thief and murderer. And the letter is signed, 'The Lady Elisabeth St. Mary.'"

Lint took long strides back to his desk. "You're thigh should mend at about the time your neck is likely to be stretched." His chair creaked as he lowered himself into its depths. Outside, the cries of the mob on Oxford Street began to fade as the prisoners' carts snaked beyond the building. Slapping the parchment onto his desk, Lint bunched his hands into fists. "I'm a calm man, pup. A reasonable man. 'Tis why I intend to sit here and say nothing while you explain to me what in the bloody hell this business is all about."

"I am not a killer of old men," said Cain, but he could see a thread of doubt clouding Lint's eyes and felt jarred by his mistrust. "You don't believe me."

"The girl makes a convincing case in favor of your guilt. Take off your cloak."

"Do you look for a sign attached to my chest that proclaims my guilt? Mayhap I should simply remove my glove if 'tis signs you are looking for."

Lint ignored his comment. He made an abrupt gesture for him to do as he'd bid. Stormy eyed, Cain wrenched on the ties at his throat and swung the cloak off his shoulders. Lint nodded at his bandoleer. "You normally sport ten daggers across your chest. Today you sport only nine."

"I left the tenth buried in the flesh of the man who carved his signature on my thigh."

"According to Lady Elisabeth you left it buried in her grandfather's heart. He was murdered with a dagger, one whose hilt is carved in the shape of a serpent with a scarlet tongue. Like the other nine you wear across your chest."

Cain touched the hilt of one of his blades. "If I had performed the deed, would I have been so witless as to leave my knife buried in the man for all to see?"

"Greed has led more than one man down the path to carelessness."

"Greed? For what? A gaudy dragon on a marble pedestal?"

"Greed for wealth beyond one's imagination. A man of humble means might find himself envying the riches of Maidenstowe."

Cain turned his head and spat on the floor. "I doubt the trinket would have fit in my saddle pouch."

Exasperated, Gellicoe braced his elbows on the desk, leaned forward, and splayed his fingers on the sides of his bald pate. "Is it your claim that the knife does not belong to you?"

"'Tis my claim that it was not my hand that thrust it into the marquess's heart! The knife could very well be mine. Perhaps the man who assaulted me came looking for me at Maidenstowe and found the marquess instead. How am I to know 'til I see the blade itself?"

"And how are you to see the blade with a thousand pounds riding on your head to insure your capture?"

Suffering his own brand of exasperation, Cain pinched the bridge of his nose, sighing. "I regret the old man's death, Lint. But I did not kill him."

"So you say. But while you prowled about Maidenstowe a man was killed and a treasure stolen, and I want to know why."

Cain shook his head. "I can give you no answers."

"Damn you!" The desk shook beneath the force of Lint's fist. "Why did you disappear on the very night that the dragon was stolen and the marquess killed? Why couldn't you wait for the constable? What did you feel you had to hide?"

Cain returned Gellicoe's stare without blinking. *Everything,* he thought. *I have everything to hide.* "If you think me guilty, you know where you can collect your reward."

"Dammit, man, I don't want a reward. I want the truth!"

Cain said nothing. Lint slid back in his chair, and one by one, began to crack each of his knuckles. "We've known each other how long, pup? Fifteen years? Twenty? I asked no questions when I found you because I sensed I could trust you. And you proved yourself worthy of that trust. But you're no longer an urchin picking the pockets of the citizenry of London, and I can't allow my trust in you to supplant my need for the truth. I'm an officer of the Crown, Cain. 'Tis my sworn duty to bind you over for questioning."

"'Tis your duty to confine me to Newgate, you mean."

Gellicoe looked away. His face grew somber as he peered at the books lining his walls. "There are real felons running amok in the streets and alleys of London. There are men who would sell the Crown's secrets to the French for a groat. I think Henry Fielding would want me to address my efforts to these matters rather than concentrate my energies on prosecuting one of my best agents. But Fielding will allow me to dally only so long before he loses patience. He will expect answers, as will I. So I grant you four days headway. I can keep the girl's missive to myself for that long only. Do what you must to prove your innocence, and do it quickly. After four days I can promise you nothing. With a thousand pounds on your head, you may find yourself pursued by friend and foe alike. And the outcome may be not at all pretty."

Cain threw him a long look. "You do this for what reason?"

"Stupidity, no doubt. Friendship can do strange things to a man. Perhaps 'tis the reason that despite your coincidences and your silence, I find myself believing you."

Inwardly Cain smiled his relief. He nodded toward Lint then flung his cloak over his shoulders, securing the ties with purpose.

"Where do you head now, pup? Devon?"

"I look for a man who was too much the coward to assault me by himself. If he still lives, I will find him."

"We can cull no information from a dead man," said Lint, reacting to the venom in Cain's voice.

"I will cull my information before the wretch expires."

Lint shook his head. "You have nothing to go on. What can you—"

"I have a name." His voice was ugly. "Skagg. Someone called the name Skagg into the night. 'Tis this man I seek."

"You may already have killed him."

Cain's eyes blazed with something dark and menacing.

"If not already, then soon. One of the three who attacked me lived, but not for much longer."

Lint watched him stride to the door. "A whit of advice, pup. You would do well to avoid Maidenstowe."

Cain turned. "Do you think the girl's threats frighten me, Lint?"

"I did not read the end of her letter to you." Lifting the parchment before his face, he began to read. "'After the man who calls himself Cain is hanged, I want his heart cut out and sent to me. The man has proved by his actions that he has no heart. He therefore does not deserve to be buried with one.'"

The menace left Cain's eyes, to be replaced by a look uncommon among thief-takers or thieves. The hardness about his eyes grew soft; the grimness about his mouth grew sad. "Cut out my heart?" He laughed without humor. "You can't cut out what isn't there. The girl has no cause to request my heart, Lint. She already has it."

"Yours and Thomas Penmarck's. The girl must collect them."

"Penmarck?" Cain grew wary. "Why do you speak of Penmarck?"

"Because the lady adds a postscript informing me that after Wednesday a week, I should address future correspondence to her at the estate of Thomas Penmarck in Cornwall. I would guess she's about to wed the man."

Cain shook his head. "She told me there would be no wedding." It was why his plan was no longer feasible; why he had forced himself to leave her despite—

"Did she say she had cried off Penmarck? Apparently she's changed her mind."

The bed of tinder long dormant within Cain erupted into

a raging conflagration. So it was Penmarck who would reap the rewards from the old man's death. Penmarck who would gain the land, the wealth, the girl. Penmarck who would sample at his leisure what Cain had struggled not to covet, but failed.

In his youth he had done nothing while all that was his had been stripped from him. But he was no longer young, and what he wanted, he would allow no other man to strip from him.

"Godspeed to you, pup," bade Lint in farewell. "And I trust if this fellow Skagg is still abroad in Devon, you'll find him."

Cain nodded. He would go to Devon, but it was no longer Skagg he sought.

The scarlet pimpernel is in bloom, thought Elisabeth as she scanned a distant cornfield two days later. The petals dipped their tiny star-shaped heads, nodding into the wind. Elisabeth watched the flowers bend and sway as her mount set a walking pace back to Maidenstowe.

This was the first Wednesday she had visited the work-house since . . . she thought back . . . since she had broken her toe over a fortnight ago. Frith had been unwilling to let her ride to Bridestone Barrow on her own. He had been ready to call up the coach-and-four and a host of footmen to protect her, but she had been adamant. The ride to the village was a short one. There was no bogus thief lurking on the byway to accost her. And the day was too fine to be jostled about on the inside of a coach. She wanted to ride in the open, surrounded by blue sky and budding leaves. Before she had to leave it, she wanted to acquaint herself with the place she had never truly known. So she'd had a groomsman saddle the oldest horse in the stable for her, an aged hunter who would soon be turned out to pasture, and together they journeyed the village road for what might be the last time for each of them. It seemed appropriate to share this last experience with someone, even if the someone was an ancient hunter who could not appreciate the beauty of scarlet pimpernel.

In a week she would be married.

She touched the long-glass that hung round her neck, mindful of the change in Thomas since the tragedy. He had demonstrated a great capacity for kindness in her grief. He had been neither dour nor mirthless. Indeed, it was Thomas who had tried to inject levity into the conversations she'd conducted with her solicitors, with Reverend Fincham, with the tenants who had walked to Maidenstowe to offer their condolences. The levity helped. It was a side of Thomas she had never witnessed. Much like his sudden air of understanding. In deference to her period of mourning he had offered to postpone the wedding, something the old Thomas would never have suggested. The new Thomas seemed a gentler man, one with whom she thought she could live, and breed. She was ashamed of her earlier criticisms of him. It seemed she had no penchant at all for judging a man's true nature, though it appeared an impossible task to decide what was facade and what was not when a man presented so many sides for a woman's observation. That Thomas had changed so drastically in so short a time did not disturb her. She was not the same person either.

To her right she passed the stone cottage of one of the St. Mary tenants. The land was fronted by a fieldstone fence beneath whose shadow grew lily of the valley and yellow-horned poppies. She remembered that the last time she had passed by this cottage, Quintus had been sitting opposite her in the coach, expounding upon how he had never loved any of his wives.

And now he was dead.

Hatred so powerful surged within her that her lungs burned with the pressure. Thomas had been unable to remain for the funeral, so she had stood beside Quintus's coffin by herself, wishing that they had shared a few more days together, a few more weeks. Perhaps then he would have ventured to speak the words he had never spoken to her. *I love you, Elisabeth.* She would have treasured those words—words she knew would have found their way to his lips had his life not been wrenched so viciously from him. For those stolen moments of life she would never forgive the thief-taker. So it mattered little to her anymore whom she married, or when the wedding took place. It was unimportant what gown she wore or what piece of jewelry she donned. The only thing she remotely cared about now was hearing that the thief-taker had been captured and hanged. She lived for that moment. She burned for that moment.

The hunter's hooves clopped on the granite viaduct bridging the River Teign. His pace was weary, much different from the fiery gait that had once been his hallmark. Extending her hand, Elisabeth rubbed the glossy flesh of the animal's neck. Despite his age, his coat remained as black and lustrous as the satin of her petticoat, and so thinking, she bent her head to regard her attire.

She had frightened the children at the workhouse with her mourning garb. When she'd entered the building, they'd thought her a female highwayman, so they had huddled on their pallets, eyes wide and mouths open. Ned had shouted that there was nothing in a workhouse worth stealing, and Robert had been bold enough to ask to see her pistol, but when she'd thrown back her pug hood to reveal her face, they had laughed at themselves and at her, and she had joined them.

It was the first time she had laughed since the morning she'd found Quintus.

She'd left a sack of her medicines with Churchwarden Treacle and a sheet of parchment delineating the use of specific herbs and oils. And before she departed she amused the children with Thomas's long-glass. She'd paraded them outside, pointed the glass in the direction of Cornwall, and allowed each of them a look through the scope. She explained that after her marriage, Sir Thomas would take her to the farthest ends of England, to a place so far away that it could not even be seen with the aid of the long-glass. But she would not remain there forever. She would try to return to Maidenstowe every spring to check their health and progress, and, she thought silently, to place a spray of wildflowers before Quintus's crypt. She'd had to cradle her arms around one child who began to cry uncontrollably, and just when she thought her own emotions might shatter, Ned had shouted, "M'lady! M'lady! How did the church's steeple get inside this 'ere long-glass?" and they had all laughed again.

A blackbird cawed deep within the stand of alder and lime that forested the land beyond the bridge, and Elisabeth peered in that direction, wondering what had set the bird astir. It was a sound she had heard more than a thousand times in her life, but today it screeched along her spine to lift the hair on the back of her neck. She shot a look over her shoulder as if expecting to find another rider on the bridge behind her, but the way was deserted. Even so, she touched her riding whip to the hunter's flanks and quickened his pace to a slow trot. The trees seemed suddenly cold and oppressive, and she was anxious to be out of their shadow.

She heard it before she saw it. As she neared the cliff road leading to Maidenstowe, she heard a sound different from the creak of leather or the rattle of the stirrup iron, and she cocked her head to listen. It seemed to emanate from everywhere—a rumbling echo that grew steadily louder, as if someone were beating a staff against a hollow tree. Drawing back on the reins, she halted the black's advance then urged him to a quarter turn so she could peer down the road behind her.

The way was straighter here than any other section of the road, and in the distance, a mere speck on the horizon, she saw sudden movement. The shape was indistinguishable at first, a blur of darkness without form, but as seconds ticked by the blur gained definition—floating wings and massiveness, and she suffered a cold dread at the thing's approach. Digging out her long-glass from beneath her mantelet, she lifted it to her eye and extended the scope. What she had mistaken for wings was the fluid swirl of a man's cloak. And what she had seen as a mass of darkness was—

"Scylla." She whispered the word aloud, her tone disbelieving, and she felt her heart flutter as she lit on Cain's face, his smouldering blue eyes narrowed against the wind and trained far down the road on her.

"*'I will kill you!'*" she remembered his shouting. "*'You'll not escape me. I swear it!'*" And the pounding of Scylla's hooves bore testament to the truth of his vow. Releasing the long-glass, she laid her whip hard to the hunter's flank and with an urgent "Gidup!" bent over the animal's neck, as low as her sidesaddle would allow. The hunter stumbled in his gait, unaccustomed to the command to gallop, but sensing the urgency in Elisabeth's voice, he quickly found his stride, warming to the remembered rhythm of the chase, stretching out his neck and head as he had so many years before.

He flew. Like a young colt he ate up the road to evade pursuit. Past stone fences and greening hedgerows. Toward the stone cross that marked the fork in the road, the right trunk of which led to Maidenstowe. They rounded an impossible curve, to find the area around the stone cross clogged with dozens of black-faced sheep who possessed neither the swiftness nor the intelligence to move. With the entrance to the cliff road blocked off, Elisabeth jerked the hunter's reins to direct him down the only route open to her—the moor road.

Her pug hood blew back from her head as she and the hunter charged into the moorland. The wind ripped skeins of hair loose from her hair needles. It buffeted her head, causing her ears to ache. She struck the horse's flanks again, but already she knew the beast was tiring. His breath was coming in labored snorts. His flesh was growing moist with lather. She ranged an eye over the gray rock and bracken scarring the terrain and cursed the sheep who had blocked her path to safety. She fired a look over her shoulder.

Between strands of her hair she could see them closing the distance behind her. Like black wraiths from the netherworld they pursued her, less than an eighth of a mile behind. She could imagine a river of fire pouring from the nostrils of that beast. She could see the thief-taker's cape expand and stiffen in the wind. And she wondered if they were man and beast or Satan and his hound.

She used her riding whip again but the hunter paid it little heed. She knew if she could cross the clapper bridge into Postbridge, she could find protection, but the hunter's joints were so thick with lather that to push him farther would be to kill him. She slowed her pace, while behind her the sound of Scylla's hooves echoed louder and closer, *louder, closer,* until the earth shook with its intensity.

She drew rein by an outcropping of granite, threw her knee over the horn, and clambered from the saddle. Once her feet hit the stone she hiked up her petticoat and fled. There was no protection for her here, but she would not kill her horse and neither would she allow this man to kill *her* without a fight. With fingers clutched around her riding whip, she struck out across the uneven slopes of earth. Brambles tore at her booted legs. Hidden depressions caused her to stumble, but she ran without regard to safety or pain, across a granite trackway and down a stony incline where thornberry grew so thickly at the base that escape through the growth was impossible. She heard Scylla's hooves strike sparks on the granite trackway. She whipped round, mouth dry and heart racing, her hand pressed against a stab of pain in her side.

Cain peered down at her from the top of the incline, then with a touch of his knee, urged Scylla downward. She watched them descend, her hatred fanning courage she did not know she possessed. But it was there, burning her soul, and she tightened her fingers round her whip in response. She graced Cain with a frigid look as he drew rein before her.

"Do you come quietly, lady, or must I use force?"

She said nothing. She lowered her gaze to Scylla's prancing hooves and when Cain leaned sideways to wind his arm about her waist, she lashed upward with her riding whip.

"Jesus!" His hand flew to his cheek, and while he steadied Scylla, Elisabeth lifted her petticoat to her knees and ran in a path parallel to the growth of thornberry. Her heart pounded. Her chest heaved. Stone gave way to moor grass and moss. She heard the tramp of footsteps behind her and knew that Cain was giving chase on foot. Pain seared her lungs. Her right foot sank into a tract of spongy turf and as she struggled to maintain her balance, she felt something manacle itself around her ankle and flip her upward.

She fell like a hod of bricks. Her chin hit the ground. She bit the side of her tongue. Air rushed from her lungs in a flood of agony. For a long moment she lay prostrate, tears stinging her eyes, and when the pain subsided between her shoulder blades, she rolled onto her side, then her back.

Cain stood straddling her, a booted foot on either side of her hips. His eyes were stone cold. His cheekbone flamed where she had struck him. Undaunted, she raised the whip again, but Cain snatched the length of twisted bone from her hand and snapped it across his thigh. He flung both halves into the air before glaring down into her face.

"Never lift your hand to me again," he seethed. "I have killed men for less."

She tried to squirm from between his legs, but he braced his feet closer to her hips, wedging her solidly. Frustrated in her escape, she threw her head back and glowered up at him. "Will you kill me too? Or do you find 'tis more thrilling to use your blade on defenseless old men? Assassin!"

"I did not kill the old man."

"Liar! 'Twas your blade that pierced his heart. 'Twas the same blade I used to seal your wound. I wish I had slit your throat with it!"

"It was not my hand that drove the blade into his heart! Had I killed the man, would I have left the blade behind?"

Her eyes did not soften. "Murderers are cunning, like thieves and liars. What did you do with the dragon? Did you pluck the diamonds from its belly and the rubies from its eyes? Did some London pawnbroker line the pockets of your boots with gold sovereigns in exchange for that which you stole? Did you tell the broker 'tis my grandfather's blood that is responsible for your wealth? Coward! I hope you rot in the farthest corner of hell!"

His jaw bunched into knots that worked in an angry rhythm. "I tell you I did not harm your grandfather. Neither did I steal your trinket."

"Did you confect the same lie for the jailer who branded your hand?" She eyed his glove with loathing. "He did not believe you either. But he was wrong to stamp the felon's mark on your palm. He should have stamped it on your forehead."

He clenched his gloved hand and held it protectively to his breast. "Your tongue grows sharp and foolish, Elisabeth."

"Do not speak . . . my . . . name." She spat the words at him, and he, pushed beyond his limit of patience, clamped his hands around her upper arms and jerked her to her feet with such force that her teeth clacked.

"Where is the ring?"

She angled her head toward her shoulder to avoid looking at him, but he seized her chin in his hand and wrenched her face upward. His fingers bit into her cheeks. "Tell me!"

"'Tis somewhere you will never find it," she hissed. "I gave it to Thomas." She did not blink, did not allow her gaze to waver. And she felt no remorse for her lie. She had not returned the ring to Thomas. Preoccupied with Quintus's death, she had not even remembered to tell Thomas of its discovery. But if her lie made Cain uncomfortable, all the better. She wanted him to know fear. She wanted him to wonder if death awaited him beyond the next curve in the byway.

Cain slatted his eyes, looking as if he might strike her. But she did not feel cowed by him. She was too consumed by hatred to feel fear, so she squared her shoulders and returned his look measure for measure.

"Moreleigh," Cain said in a harsh whisper. "I warned you of the consequences should he ever look upon that ring."

She pushed against his wrist, trying to wrest her chin from his grip. "Exact what punishment you may, sir. I do not fear you. But I extend a warning of my own. Harm me, and Thomas will track you down like the animal you are."

"Vermin catching vermin?" Releasing her chin, he snorted with disdain. "Have you told Moreleigh that you found the dogs on Hound Tor less offensive than he?"

"Since your exodus from Maidenstowe, I have become privy to Thomas's finer qualities." She saw a muscle twitch beneath Cain's eye and felt his fingers tighten around her arms. She winced with pain.

"Indeed? I thought you considered the earl totally bereft of any finer qualities. You were willing to hawk your virtue to anyone who would spare you the man's advances. What has he done to change your stellar opinion of him? Why will you consent to marry him when there is no one alive to force your hand?"

She paused. Hatred glazed the blue of her eyes. "He does not murder old men."

Emotions so violent played across Cain's face that for a long, terrifying moment Elisabeth dared not breathe. "Tell me, lady, will you delight in rendering to Penmarck what you gladly would have rendered to me at the Saracen's Head? Will you pleasure to the touch of his hand in the same way that you did that morn in the stable block? Did you think I would allow another man to benefit so grandly from your misfortune?"

His words echoed across the moors, loud and belligerent, and he turned his head in the direction of the Cornish shore as if contemplating Thirlstane and all its splendor. He hardened his jaw, and narrowed his eyes, and in a gravelly voice said, "Not this time. Penmarck failed to account for one variable." He swung his head around, skewering her with a look more hellish than that of a gibbeted corpse. "I want you too."

"You will never have me," she said, her voice soft yet deadly.

"Brave words. But I told you before. I take what I want, and neither you nor Penmarck will stop me."

She almost smiled at him then, for her hatred gave her such strength of purpose that she felt as indestructible as she had once thought Cain. "Should you take by force what is none but a husband's right to take, you will wake on the morning after with one of your blades embedded in your gut. I will not do this with great pangs of conscience, sir. I will do it with joy."

The angry slopes of his face did not alter as he grabbed a fistful of her hair and pulled steadily backward, forcing her gaze to meet his. His face was so close that she could see the shadowed reflection of his lashes against the pale blue of his iris. She could feel his breath hot and moist against her cheek.

"Is this the same wench who tends the sick with so gentle a hand? The face is familiar, but the words give me pause. Perhaps 'tis the mouth that needs fixing."

" 'Tis your neck needs fixing, and none but the hangman to do it justice." She flinched as he wound her hair around his fist. His eyes were fierce.

"I've you to thank that every thief-taker in England will soon be on my scent. Are you pleased with the results of your meddling, lady?"

"The only thing that will please me is to know you will spend eternity feeding the fires of hell."

"But prior to that time, it seems I must go into hiding. And to lend a bit of sport to my isolation, I'm taking you with me."

Panic surged through her, but she disguised it with defiant words. "I'll go nowhere with you, thief. Now take your hands off me. Your London tarts might warm to your touch. I find it repugnant."

"Do you?" Pivoting his head slightly, he whistled to Scylla then scooped Elisabeth into his arms. "I suggest you accustom yourself to my touch, lady, because I intend to touch you a great deal in the days to come."

"I'd rather you kill me!" she screamed at him, scissoring her legs. "Why not cut my throat? 'Tis your style, is it not?" She swung her arm at him but he ducked out of range and banded his arms more tightly around her elbows and knees. "I'll not play your captive!" she spat, straining against his constraint.

Cain strode the few paces to Scylla. He swung Elisabeth high onto the animal's saddle, positioning her astride, then hoisted himself behind her. "You remain my captive only 'til this evening, when you become my wife."

"Your—!" He clamped his hand around her mouth. She clawed at his fingers, but he dug a handkerchief out of the pocket of his boot, slapped her hands away, and secured the linen over her mouth.

"Your prattle bores me." He tied the muslin at the back of her head then growled close to her ear, "Conserve your energy, lady. Be assured, you will need it later."

She hurtled her elbow into his rib, but the saddle was so big and she was so unaccustomed to sitting astride that the movement sent her sliding toward the ground. She let out a muffled scream. Cain caught her round her waist, setting her aright.

"'Tis a long way to the ground, lady. Be mindful how you vent your wrath. Next time I might be unwilling to catch you."

Curling her fingers around the edge of the saddle, Elisabeth leaned forward, trying to regain her balance. The soles of her feet tingled from her near fall. Her heart pounded with her fury. She would see he paid dearly for what he'd done to her grandfather, for what he was doing to her. She would wreak such havoc on his life that he would either have to let her go, or kill her.

Behind her, Cain leaned over the side of the horse. She

heard the rending of fabric as he wrestled with her under-petticoat. In the next moment he was blindfolding her with a length of black muslin. "If you have no notion where you go, there is little chance you will ever find your way back."

Immersed in sudden blackness she offered little struggle as he pulled her backward against him and girded his arm about her waist. But she was not the frightened girl he had kissed in the stable block. Perhaps he did not realize that. And perhaps that deception was her most powerful weapon. He might escape the hangman, but her wrath was something from which he would never escape.

Cain touched his spurs to the great black shire. As he did so, he threw Elisabeth's hood over her head, then struck out toward the south and west—where his life had once begun, and ended.

That same night, in the village of Meavy, twenty miles southwest of Maidenstowe, the Reverend Samuel Prawle was admiring the workmanship of his new pulpit when he heard the noise in the church's vestibule. Turning round, he held his candelabrum high and squinted toward the back of the church. "Is someone there?"

The door opened. Two figures appeared within the pocket of darkness that shaded the area beneath the choir loft. Reverend Prawle beckoned them with a wave of his hand. "Do you want something? Come closer. My eyesight fails me."

The sound of boot heels echoed in the shadowed emptiness of the church. One set was heavy, deliberate, the other shuffling and erratic, as if the person were hobbled. And there was another sound. Tinkling. Jingling, like a horseman's spurs. The two stopped beyond the fringe of light thrown out from the candelabrum. Reverend Prawle took a discreet step forward and held the candelabrum higher.

The man was tall and cloaked and beheld the reverend with eyes that seemed to burn with fever. The woman was small and garbed in widow's weeds. He could not make out her face, for her hood was pulled far forward, like a monk's cowl. The girl's arms were hidden beneath her mantelet, but the man had his hand vised firmly around what appeared to be her elbow. The reverend wondered if, without the man's support, the girl might collapse.

"We would have you marry us, priest," said Cain.

The reverend looked askance at Elisabeth, but Cain answered the man's inquiries even before he made them. "The girl can neither see nor speak." He did not mention that lengths of rope around her ankles and wrists likewise prevented her from running and scratching.

Prawle looked genuinely touched that so vital a man as this would take a blind mute to wife. However, there was a minor problem. "The hour is outside canonical hours, sir. I suggest you come back tomorrow."

"I suggest you do it now," Cain said in a quiet voice.

Taken aback by Cain's irreverence, Prawle fixed him with his most austere gaze. "Have your banns been called?"

"No banns."

"Then 'tis impossible. If your banns haven't been called, I can't marry you without a special license. Do you have a special license?"

Cain took a long step forward. He slid his hand beneath

his cloak then lashed out at the reverend's throat. "Will this do, priest?"

The Reverend Samuel Prawle blanched at the steel blade that flirted with his Adam's apple. "I have been known to make the occasional exception," he wheezed. "Shall we begin?"

chapter
twelve

It was impossible to know the hour, but they had been riding long enough to give Elisabeth a backache, so she gauged the time to be near dawn. Cain had not bothered to remove the bonds from her wrists and ankles after they had left the church last night, so she remained shackled, gagged, and blindfolded, and with each passing mile grew more livid with this man who dared call himself husband. She sat sideways on the saddle, his arms cradling her against his chest, *against his knives*. Those knives were her incentive to remain the compliant maiden, for if he thought her tamed, he would grow incautious. She waited for that moment of incaution, vowing it would be his downfall. She had wielded one of his blades before, and swore she would do so again, but this time, the end result would be painfully different.

They stopped after awhile in a place where she could hear the sounds of a swift running stream. Cain dismounted, then while she remained atop Scylla, he removed the rope from her wrists and ankles and lifted her to the ground. She swayed slightly. He grasped her shoulder to steady her, but she pushed his hand away.

"Would you rather fall?" he barked, unknotting her blindfold and gag.

She rubbed her eyes when the blindfold was off and squinted into the gray light of morning. They were in a clearing deep within a stand of alder that hid from view the landscape around them. She realized he would not be so foolish as to take her near civilization again. He had already risked much by dragging her to the church last night. She touched the back of her hand to her lips, finding them chapped from the abrasive rubbing of the gag. Her fingers prickled from the sudden rush of blood to their tips. She looked away from Cain, in the direction of the stream bank, but she knew there was little chance of escape for her amid forests and streams.

"Do not look so longingly at your surroundings, lady. You might convey the mistaken impression that you're about to take flight. Something which, I warn you, you would sorely regret."

She turned her back on him and rubbed her wrists while he removed his saddle pouch.

"Are you hungry?"

Hungry to see you swing on a gibbet, she thought.

"Thirsty?"

Thirsty to spill your blood as you spilled Quintus's.

"Answer me, wife, or would you prefer I trouble you with a diversion that will require no conversation at all?"

His threat muted her burgeoning courage. "Break your fast, thief-taker, but do not ask me to do so with you."

"Ah. She speaks. If you require no sustenance, I will not force it down your gullet, but I find that kidnapping renders my throat dry. Be an obedient wife and fetch a cup of water for me."

"Are there cups growing by the side of the stream, or did you manage to pilfer the St. Mary china in addition to the gold dragon?"

He was suddenly beside her, pressing a wooden cup into her hand. "I will have it in this cup, Elisabeth. Do you see this cup? 'Tis a simple piece, without frivolous markings. I will have a full cup of water, Elisabeth. I will have it now. And you will fetch it for me."

Placing his hand on the small of her back he gave her an emphatic shove in the direction of the stream. Elisabeth, realizing her thirst probably equaled his, allowed the liberty, but she dallied at the side of the stream and enjoyed four cups of cold water herself before returning to the clearing where Cain sat a fallen log.

She stood before him, holding his cup of water while he bit into the meat of a dried fig. The sight of the fruit made her stomach groan, but she was too proud to admit her hunger. She wanted nothing from this man, not his food, or his companionship, or his name. In point of fact she was even loath to hold his water. "You seem rather disinclined to drink what I've brought you, or have you forgotten the terrible thirst you professed?"

"In time, lady. A man's morning repast cannot be rushed."

She arched her brow as he bit into another fig. He seemed to be enjoying her enforced subservience. She watched him eat. She watched Scylla eat. And she sucked on the inside of her cheek when, after finishing two more figs, he still did not request the cup.

"Are you quite certain you do not feel some small

twinge of hunger?" he persisted, licking the stickiness from the tips of his fingers.

She heeded his glove, his hand—the same hand that had slain her grandfather. Bile rose in her throat. Cain extended his hand to her. "You're looking rather weary, wife. I'll have the cup now before you drop it."

"Your drink," she said, elevating the cup toward his face. "Would that it were hemlock."

The water hit his face with such force that it momentarily blinded him. His hands flew to his eyes and when he cleared his vision well enough to see again, he saw that Elisabeth stood in the same place, but in her hand she now brandished one of the daggers from his bandoleer. He dragged the back of his hand across his face to rid his flesh of moisture. He did this slowly, cautiously, for though she held his blade incorrectly, she seemed to have no qualms about using it. "Are you so impatient for my heart that you cannot await the executioner to cut it out? You need do it yourself?"

"Place your hands atop your head," she instructed, but he folded his forearms across his bent knees and leveled his pale blue eyes on her instead.

"What would you have done with my heart had the executioner sent it to you?"

"I would have fed it to the swine, but I begin to think that would be far too kind a fate for it. I tell you again, place your hands atop your head."

"And I tell you, lay the knife down before ill comes of it."

She held the knife stupidly in her hand, unsure what to do next. He was supposed to act frightened of the threat she posed. He was supposed to do as she bid. It vexed her that he considered her attempt at escape so inconsequential that he would not follow her directive. Too late she realized that she played *his* game when she wielded a knife. *Her* game would have to be executed with more subtlety. But still . . .

"Your bravado is to be commended, sir. But even cowards can mouth tenacious words when pitted against women and old men. Remove your knives and your sword, then show me what brave words you can utter."

He hung his head, as if he were contemplating her suggestion. "You disappoint me, Elisabeth."

"And you make me curse the woman who bore you." She addressed the words to his bent head, but it was his left arm that moved, shooting outward, slamming against her right wrist with such a powerful force that the knife flew from her hand. The blow sent a numbing shock up her arm, but before she had time to absorb the pain, Cain was on his feet. He manacled her wrists in his hands and wrestled them behind her back, then spoke close to her face in a voice that inspired fear.

"Damn my mother's name again and I will use one of these knives to relieve you of your vicious tongue. Do you understand?"

She pinched her eyes shut to avoid having to look at him.

"Do you?" His voice shook with anger and long-suppressed passion.

Drawing back her foot she drove it into his boot. It was in that instant that the tether of his control unraveled.

"A man detests insolence in a wife," he rasped. "Your manners are in sore need of improvement, Elisabeth, and you've put me in a mood to lesson you in your first duty as my wife."

He found her mouth with his own and kissed her with a harshness that made her mind scream in violation. She compressed her lips against the pressure of his mouth. She tried to jerk her head away from him, but he freed her left wrist to cup his palm around the back of her skull. He held her forcibly against him, smothering her with a kiss she no longer desired. He released her right wrist and shaped his hand round her buttocks, pressing her against his thighs so she could feel the hard shape of his desire. She knew then he wanted her in a way she no longer wanted him, and it filled her with a sense of power. His bandoleer pushed against the softness of her breast. She felt the massiveness of his arms and shoulders envelop her, urging her to respond, but still she resisted him. He tried to part her lips with his tongue.

She pursed her lips more tightly.

He traced the curve of her mouth with his tongue.

She wrenched her shoulders to and fro trying to loosen his embrace. To no avail. But when she felt the glide of her under-petticoat against her flesh and his hand on her bare thigh, she twisted her face away from him long enough to cry, "Shall I call you Thomas? You're no better! Hypocrite!"

She felt his muscles tense, his hand go slack at the back of her head, her petticoat glide back down her leg. She saw a wildness in his eyes as he thrust her away from him, and she suspected from the ominous look on his face that he would make her sorry she had dared cross him.

"Move from that spot, lady, and I will thrash you senseless."

So she stood motionless as he retrieved his dagger and cup from the ground. She obeyed him because she sensed her words had caused a fury in him that her resistance had not, and she dared not challenge him again so soon. She had escaped his advances. For the present she would have to be satisfied with that. But she wondered how much longer she could tempt fate with a man who called himself husband—with a man who was as ripe to steal her virginity as he'd been ripe to steal her grandfather's life.

She found herself bound and shackled again when they resumed their journey, but this time her bonds were tighter. Her hood fell back from her head sometime that morning. Cain did not bother to snug it back into place, but she was just as glad for later in the day the sun beat steadily on her face, warming the places hidden beneath her blindfold and gag, warming the crown of her head. She knew they headed west.

They headed for Cornwall.

"Fetter me again, thief-taker, and I will kill you." Elisabeth sat the ground in an unceremonious heap late that afternoon, in a place as alien to her as the man who had transported her here. Her eyes rebelled so vehemently to the reappearance of light that she had to shield her face in the crook of her elbow.

"You sound the fishwife," Cain reproved. He stood above her, her blindfold, gag, and wrist shackles in his hand. She angled her head in his direction and squinted at him through the spaces between her fingers.

"You haven't finished yet." She kicked her legs out from where she'd curled them beneath her and wishboned them on the ground, stretching the hemp that bound her ankles to its farthest limit. "Cut it."

Cain grinned at the position of her legs. "Should I consider this an invitation?"

"Your foul insinuations do not frighten me." Bright sunlight teared her eyes. She swiped the back of her hand across her cheeks to dry the moisture. "Cut the rope."

He hunkered down on one knee and braced his forearm across his thigh as he probed her face. "The words have been spoken over us, lady. The names have been entered in the parish register."

"You have no name."

"I am your husband."

"I *have* no husband!" And because he did not lower his hand to free her bonds, she wrenched on the rope herself. He made to grab her wrist, but she pulled away from him as if his touch were more lethal than the juice of deadly nightshade. She hugged her hand to her throat and skewered him with eyes that reflected her abhorrence.

Cain clenched his fist. "We are wed. Legal wed. Do not shrink from my touch."

"Wed? Think you a bogus ceremony conducted in a dark corner of some country church gives you the right to call me wife? You did not wed Elisabeth St. Mary. You forced yourself on a shackled female who had neither the ability nor the opportunity to voice her opposition to your farce. Could you find no tavern maid lackwitted enough to marry you? Could the mighty thief-taker do no better than to steal a bride who despises the very earth he walks on?"

The flesh strained at the corners of his mouth. The narrow wings of his nostrils flared dangerously. "Do not think to deny me what is my right to claim." Heaving himself to his feet, he took long strides away from her to fetch Scylla. She hurled silent epithets at his retreating back, then, red-faced with anger, seized the expanse of hemp between her ankles and shook it violently.

The knots would not give. The rope would not fray. Frustration made her clumsy, so she took a calming breath and compressed her lips. When she lent her bonds her full concentration, she stared dumbly. The rope was attached round her *boots,* not her ankles, which meant—

She looked askance at Cain to find him tending Scylla by a weather-worn shed some twenty feet to her left. When he turned his back to unstrap the animal's saddle girth, she clamped onto the heel and toe of her left riding boot and gave it one . . . two . . . three vicious tugs that loosened it enough to slide down her leg and off her foot. The right one came off with greater ease, so that by the time Cain was ready to carry the saddle into the shed, Elisabeth had already stowed the boots beneath her petticoat and was adjusting her eyes to the painful glare of light that washed her new surroundings.

The late afternoon sun, warm on her back, elongated her shadow on the scrubby earth upon which she sat. To the east, a sweep of flat, tawny moor stretched as far as the eye could see, hemmed in on the distant horizon by ribbons of mountains blurred by violet mist. The land was flat as an inland pond, cheered only by intermittent splotches of yellow and green on the vast, dull brown of its palette. Overhead, a flurry of gulls screeched and glided, prompting Elisabeth to visor her hands over her eyes and look up.

Awareness grew at the sight of the gulls—awareness of the undeniable moisture that hung in the air and the smell of something that pricked her nostrils with its earthy tang.

She twisted round to look behind her, and when she saw what lay beyond, she felt her breath catch and hover in suspension.

Less than a dozen paces away the land dropped off to nothingness, and beyond that—water. More water than she had ever seen in one place at one time. More water than she'd imagined existed in the entire world. Awed by the tableau, she gathered up her boots and shambled to her feet, then inched her way to the lip of the cliff.

She looked down, knowing instinctually where she was.

She was standing on the edge of the world.

With the bottoms of her feet prickling at the height, she took a cautious step backward. She was so high above the level of the sea that she imagined herself a swallow perched on the highest chimney pot of Maidenstowe. Far below her, a shingle of white sand curved between two great bulwarks of avalanched rock. Water lapped the beach with a soft, deep, rushing sound that seemed but an undertone of a restless wind. And in the shallow depths of the cove, amid a swirl of white-frothed waves and green ocean, stood a towering chimney stack of rock that time had sheered from the cliff face and toppled into the sea. She squinted at the shimmery reflections off the water's surface and thought that only a month ago she might have considered this a place of matchless beauty.

Now she saw it as little more than a prison, walled by sandstone cliffs and barred by the open sea. Again she heard the shrill cacophony of soaring gulls, and she searched out their forms, envying them their wings. But their freedom bolstered her resolve, for despite the water and the cliffs and the seemingly endless tract of hcath, she vowed to escape. She had lived the life of a prisoner for seventeen years and would abide such restraints no longer. She would find wings of her own, and given time, she would flee.

The crunch of loose stone announced Cain's presence behind her. In greeting she hugged her boots to her chest and snugged the tops beneath her chin.

"You may keep the boots so long as you try nothing untoward. Cross me again, lady, and shackles will become a more permanent part of your attire than pinner caps and stays."

He stood only inches behind her, so close that she angled her left shoulder forward to avoid contact with his chest. Ignoring his directive and the warning threat in his voice, she scanned the horizon, seemingly at ease. "Where is this place?"

"Your home," he answered without hesitation. "Granted, 'tis a more humble abode than Maidenstowe, but you shouldn't find it lacking for amenities. There is a fresh-water grotto at the base of the cliff for drink, a boundless ocean in which to bathe, and mussels, crabs, sea-beets, and rabbits to feast upon. What more could a bride want?"

"Your death," she remarked. "Promptly and painfully." Spine stiff, she circled around him, leaving the hand he had opened in silent entreaty as empty as his heart.

The cottage that Cain referred to as home reminded Elisabeth of a stray lamb. It was a small building of white-washed cob that she guessed would have fit into one small corner of her herb garden. The roof was solidly formed with neat bundles of thatching. A stone trough was located a half dozen paces from the front door, and affixed to the two shuttered windows on either side of the portal were rectangular flower boxes whose soil was dark and barren.

The presence of the boxes discomfited her. It seemed blasphemy to her that an assassin should ever look upon the beauty of a flower much less plant one.

Climbing the stone step that served as a stoop, she pushed open the door. With the windows shuttered, dimness reigned within, but she spied obvious shapes even within the shadows. A bed against the wall to her left. A long dining table set before the hearth. A bench beneath a window on the east wall. A trio of chairs placed without order. The smell within the cottage was close and dank, a testament to the hard-packed earth that served as a floor. It brought to mind the smell of the parish workhouse, though she knew she could expect no loving faces within to greet her.

The floor was smooth and cold beneath her stockinged feet. She threw open the shutters of one window, then another, and as she struggled with the latch of the third, she heard Cain's footfall on the stoop. He stopped at the threshold for a long moment before stepping inside.

"The mustiness will dissipate after awhile."

The shutters clattered open with a bang. Elisabeth locked them in place then turned around, saying nothing. Cain moved about the room, straightening chairs as he walked. He hung his cloak on a wall peg by the hearth.

"There are fresh linens in the bench behind you. Use them on the bed. And there should be cleaning rags buried near the bottom. I haven't been here for several weeks, so you'll have to rid the interior of the layers of grit that have accumulated in my absence." He bent down to open the lid of a wooden coffer, then, straightening, removed his rapier from the frog at his hip and set it inside. "The kettle may need rinsing before you use it. I have a modest supply of peat and some wood stored at the side of the cottage for fuel. I trust you know how to start a fire."

Elisabeth seated herself on the bench as Cain lifted his bandoleer over his head. He seemed relaxed in these surroundings. Almost genial. She had no doubt that at any moment he would start to hum. He dropped the bandoleer into the coffer, closed the lid, then hunkered down where Elisabeth could not see him plainly. It seemed he was reluctant to trust her near his knives again. She heard the rattle of a lock-plate, and then he was standing again, searching her face with eyes that still had the power to make her pulse quicken.

"There is a small garden at the back of the cottage. 'Tis suffering from gross neglect, but you should be able to find enough edible leaves and roots to satisfy even a hearty appetite."

When still she said nothing, he pulled a chair from beneath the table and straddled it, then braced his forearms atop the stay-rail. "Have you nothing to say?"

Her eyes knifed through him. "Did you murder the owner of the cottage before taking up residence yourself?"

His skin grew taut across the long bones of his face. "I have warned you before of your tongue."

"Mayhap I find it folly to heed the counsel of assassins. Why should I fear your threats? You can hurt me no more than you already have."

"If you think that, lady, you know little of what a man can do to a woman. Pray continue your harangue, and I will drill you in the meaning of the word."

The cold blue of her eyes masked her rising unease. "I will not squander my breath bandying idle words about with you."

"In that case the garden awaits you."

"Neither will I cook for you."

"Nay?"

She glared her hostility. "Nay."

A flick of his wrist and there appeared a glimmer of steel in his hand. He rotated the blade slowly with fingers that she knew to be deft and quick. "I have a gnawing hunger that grows in the pit of my stomach," he said in an even tone. "But I have an even more abiding hunger in my loins. So it matters little to me that you refuse to grub for roots. Stay. I should prefer to expend my energy in labors more pleasurable than eating." He skated his thumb along the edge of his blade. "And spare me any virginal protests of modesty. What you refuse to remove peaceably can be easily cut away. So," he said, tracing an imaginary path from her neck to her toes with the point of his blade, "do we start at the mantelet and work down?" Then reversing the motion, "Or would you prefer to start at the stockings and work up?"

Elisabeth looked from the knife, to Cain's eyes, to the portal. If the expression on his face could be trusted, he was prepared to finish what he had started this morning, and she was too weary to fight him. Momentary submission seemed her most prudent alternative. She stood up. "You said the garden was behind the cottage?"

Cain indicated the direction with a lazy flick of his blade. "That way."

Without another word she struck out toward the door, stopping when he called after her. "The boots remain here, lady. Shoe leather may provide too great a temptation for you at present, and I wouldn't want anything to distract you from your wifely duties. Just drop them by the door.

Ah, good wife. And do be advised that the moorland is both ruthless and unsparing on bare feet."

Thinking that the moorland would never be as ruthless as *she* intended to be, she waited at the door, stiff and angry and grinding her breath between her teeth. "Have you any more advice to impart before I leave?"

Several seconds passed before something came clattering along the floor at her. She turned and looked down to find a reed basket at her feet.

"Use that to collect your roots. And I suggest you find as much as you can. Given what I have planned for you, wife"—his voice dropped to a low, seductive tone— "you'll have little time for cooking in the days to come."

The backs of her knees went rubbery as she plucked the basket off the floor, but she did not betray her unease as she crossed the threshold. She would grant him claim to this one victory, but if the idea brewing in her head was successful he would never claim another.

He left her alone. While she combed through the strangled vines in the garden, he fetched fresh water from the grotto and, seeing the red valerian in bloom, gathered a tidy bunch and left them on the table for her. When she returned to the cottage, he remained outside to feed and groom Scylla. And when the sun began to set and he saw wisps of smoke curling from the chimney, he stripped off his shirt and glove and arm braces and headed for the stone trough.

He lathered a cloth with a sliver of soap from his saddle pouch, and in the coolness of pre-dusk, began to wash the fetor of London from his body. He scrubbed the arms that had embraced Elisabeth on their journey across the moors and the chest against which he'd cradled her head. He worked his way from breast to collarbone, and when he reached his throat, he slowed his hand, remembering how the wind had fingered her hair today, lifting it upward to stroke the naked curves of his flesh. He remembered how one pale white tendril had drifted upward to skim his unshaven cheek, then lower, cobwebbing the smooth inner flesh of his mouth. He closed his eyes at the memory, and with a thumb that was cold and slick traced a languid pattern through the moisture that drenched his throat.

He thought of the squalor of London—of the stink of unwashed bodies and rotting fish, and he wondered how this girl, who tasted of soap and strawberries, could exist in the same world that produced Londons and hanging Mondays. He ached to feel the press of her mouth against the pulse that thumped so passionate a rhythm beneath his thumb. He ached to have her tongue probe the secret places of his body, moistening what was dry, hardening what was soft.

And so thinking he felt himself stir and swell. He strained with his confinement, his discomfort only serving to thicken the desire that pressed full against his thigh. He had not lain with a woman for long months. He had never lain with a wife. And he could not ignore the manly need that fired his loins. His body thirsted for the touch of womanflesh.

His body thirsted for Elisabeth.

She was his wife.

He wanted her to give freely of herself, as she had seemed inclined to do when first they'd met. He wanted her to look upon him with laughter in her eyes and a smile bowing her lips. She possessed all the virtues he had shunned in his thirty-two years of life, virtues that had seemed unimportant until now. But he yearned for her to rekindle what was jaded and withered within him. He craved to share her goodness, her quietude. He craved softly spoken words that would heal his inner wounds. He was weary of bloodshed, and hangings, and death. He tired of having the earth for his bed and bitterness the only taste that filled his mouth. He longed to share his nights with someone soft and female. He ached to tell this woman who was his wife of the circumstances that had turned his heart to stone.

If she would consent to listen.

The wind, robbed of the sun's warmth, licked his bare back with a coolness that made him shiver. In response he set his hand in motion once again, smoothing his cloth over the bulk of his shoulder. The firmness of bone and joint that met his hand made him wonder how she would judge his body when he stood naked before her. Would she find his frame too big, his muscles too unyielding? Would his massiveness instill in her a fear that she might be crushed beneath his weight?

Nay, he reassured her mentally. *There is gentleness within me. Long neglected, but 'tis there. An ungentle hand could not pick valerian. Study the flowers, Elisabeth. As I did not bruise them, neither will I bruise you.*

His musings strengthened his purpose and bolstered his resolve. He rinsed his torso with sure, brisk swipes of the cloth, then dunked his hair in the trough and began to lather it with what was left of the soap. There seemed little sense in postponing the inevitable. He would tell her tonight. He would tell her what he had done and why he had done it—every sordid, wretched detail.

He plunged his head back into the trough and shot up again, shaking and sputtering. He fanned his fingers through the straggly wetness of his hair, shoving it back from his forehead, then caught the strands at the nape of his neck.

Tonight he would tell her the truth.

He trained his pale blue eyes on the cottage.

And then he would have her.

The cottage seemed wondrously transformed when he entered it some time later. The bed sported fresh linen. The furniture was ordered and dusted. The table was set with wooden bowls and spoons, and the aroma given off from the cook pot on the hearth masked the moldy earth smell of the floor with the scented sweetness of rosemary. Cain rubbed his jaw, wondering how she had accomplished so much in so little time.

She was bent over the cook pot, her petticoat gathered in one hand to guard her hem against the danger of burning embers. She'd tied her hair at the back of her head so that it hung to the base of her spine like rope waiting to be plaited. Against the black of her gown it looked the color of Bath stone, neither yellow nor white, but a soft hue that blended the muted tones of each. As she stirred the pot, he watched those unplaited strands shape themselves to the gentle contours of her back and waist. And seeing this, he stretched his hand in silent frustration and felt a tremor slice through his arm.

"You must have found a greater yield in the garden than

I'd thought possible," he finally said, taking measured strides across the room.

Elisabeth whipped round at the sound of his voice. Her cheeks were rosy red from the heat of the fire; the hair framing her face was frizzed into angelic wisps; and her eyes danced with such vibrant color that Cain stopped mid-stride, dazzled by the effect. His gaze drifted to the proper square of flesh exposed at her neckline, and he knew if he placed his hand atop that flesh right now, he would find it warm to the touch . . . and soft.

He expelled his breath slowly and flung his hand toward the cook pot. "It smells edible."

Elisabeth reached for one of the bowls on the table and ladled out enough broth to fill it near to overflowing. Setting it back on the table, she gestured for Cain to take his seat. "The test is in the eating." She filled the second bowl while Cain took his chair, and when she seated herself, he wondered if the interior of the cottage was the only thing that had changed this eventide. She seemed more docile tonight, as if she had come to accept the circumstances of her captivity and had softened her attitude in response. He smiled at the prospect, wondering if perhaps his bouquet of valerian had paved the way for his reentry into her good graces. He scanned the room for their whereabouts, frowning when he couldn't locate them.

"Did you find a suitable place for your flowers?"

"The fire," she said, lowering her spoon into the broth. "In future you would be wise not to waste your time. Such tawdry offerings will not gain you forgiveness."

He flinched inwardly, but he calmed himself, mindful that her anger was justified. "Tonight we will talk, Elisabeth." He plunged his spoon into the broth, unaware of the enigmatic smile that played across her lips.

The broth was greenish brown in color with unidentifiable chunks of herbage floating about the surface. It was bland to the palate, with a slightly bitter aftertaste, but Cain thought it a considerable improvement over dried figs. "Passable," he said after three mouthfuls. "Your Mrs. Pigeon has done well by you."

Elisabeth poked at the flotsam in her broth. "Mrs. Pigeon is allowed the use of a knife to prepare her food."

"And so will you . . . when I feel you can be trusted to limit its use to things that will not bleed when sliced." He downed two more spoonfuls. "I don't recognize the chunks of root you've added to the broth."

Elisabeth toyed with one of the morsels in question. "You did say you had little knowledge of herbs, didn't you?"

Cain swallowed what was in his mouth, thinking his throat about to close on him. *He* could not distinguish between parsley and hemlock, but Elisabeth could. Elisabeth knew the name of every plant, every herb, every flower. She knew which part of a plant could heal, and which part could kill. His fingers whitened around his spoon. He eyed her bowl.

She hadn't taken a single sip.

His heart slowed in its rhythm. "Eat, before your broth grows cold, lady."

With seeming disinterest she lifted her spoon to her mouth, parted her lips, then lowered it back to the bowl. "My appetite has apparently deserted me." Letting go the spoon, she folded her hands in her lap and graced him with a look of placid innocence. "But do finish your portion.

And after you finish yours, perhaps you could be persuaded to eat mine as well." She pushed the bowl toward him.

The bitter aftertaste of the broth grew stronger on his tongue. Gooseflesh welted his neck. He dropped his spoon into the bowl and stared at the handle. "What did you add to the brew that sours your appetite, Elisabeth?"

" 'Tis not the brew that sours my appetite."

He grabbed her wrist, squeezing so hard that her fingers numbed. "Did you find some pretty poison in the garden?" He squeezed harder, his voice tight and ugly. "Did you?"

Her answer was a look so laced with hatred that he seemed to be looking into his own eyes. A sudden spasm cramped his stomach. The bitterness on his tongue. The chill. The cramps. He had his answer.

"*Aaaaarr!*" He swept his forearm across the table catapulting his bowl off the edge. "Witch!" His chair crashed to the floor as he came to his feet, hauling Elisabeth upward with him. Fury ravaged the shapely lines of his face; madness blackened his eyes. He drew his forearm back as if he would strike her, then, marshaling the last threads of his sanity, shoved her away from him.

She fell against her chair, sending it toppling onto the floor with her. She bumped her head on the stay-rail and her elbow on the seat, and when she twisted round to peer through the legs of the table, she saw Cain's boots devouring the space to the door.

The sounds of his retching spilled into the cottage. She bowed her head, hating him, and despite her own convictions, hating herself. With a tug of weary limbs she picked herself and her chair off the floor then sat down, waiting for the sounds to stop. She told herself he deserved to be treated this way. She reassured herself that no punishment was too extreme considering the horror he'd wrought on her grandfather. But she expected to feel elated with the results. She hadn't intended that her stomach would be churning at the sounds of Cain's misery.

Reaching out her hand, she dragged her bowl to its proper place before her. She studied the green brown liquid, the curved handle of her wooden spoon, the open portal that framed the darkness into which Cain had fled. The sounds had stopped. Beyond the threshold there was naught but silence. She stirred the broth then lifted the spoon to her mouth. The liquid was hot, but not so hot that it would burn her tongue, so she swallowed one mouthful, and another, understanding then just how hungry she really was.

She was skimming the bottom of the bowl when she saw him appear in the doorway. He leaned his shoulder against the jamb and lifted the back of his hand to wipe his mouth. His face was ashen. Beneath his perusal she scooped out the last spoonful of broth and swallowed it. A dangerous emotion crossed his face as he watched her set her spoon down.

She eased back in her chair, her blue eyes boring into his. "I'm sorry you found the broth so distasteful. Except for being a trifle bitter, I thought it quite satisfying. Perhaps you'll find tomorrow's fare more to your liking." She smiled her enigmatic smile once again. He returned her look squarely, then pivoted round the door jamb and left.

She didn't move immediately. She sat in her chair and stared at the door, a little stunned by his reaction, a little ashamed. She thought her trickery would earn her a beating and that his further mistreatment of her would fuel her hatred. She was prepared to deal with those situations.

She was not prepared that he should look at her the way he had. But she was not totally unfamiliar with that look. She imagined she had looked the same way seventeen years ago, when she had stood at the edge of the ornamental pond, knowing the two people she had loved most in the world were lost to her . . . forever.

For more than a decade he had descended the path to the beach in rain and fog. His feet, therefore, did not falter in the darkness. He found a place for himself high above the strand line, where cliffstone met sand, and there he sat, awaiting the return of strength to his knees.

His head throbbed. His eyes ached. His insides were strung so tightly that he guessed if he moved too quickly, his body would snap, bringing death promptly and painfully. He thought he would retch again when he considered how delighted Elisabeth would be with that happenstance. Elisabeth, whose affection for him had burrowed in his heart, now wanted him dead. He had regarded her threat a hollow jest, but it seemed he had underestimated both her feelings and her mettle. She hadn't poisoned him tonight, but that did not mean she would not try in earnest tomorrow, or the next day. At this very moment she could be preparing something black and deadly for his unexpected consumption, but if he were confined in the same room with her right now, he would probably do something he would later regret. Jesus, he wanted to sire children with her, not give her the beating she so richly deserved.

Seated on a cold slip of rock, he bridged his forearms across his spread knees and canted his head against their support. The woman in the cottage was a stranger to him. She was a woman he did not know, did not like. He wanted the other Elisabeth back—the one who had spoken of the emotion that bound them one to the other, drawing them together despite who they were and what they felt. But he had hurt that Elisabeth, and now he could taste how she must have felt, for tonight she had returned the favor. It pained him, knowing how utterly she despised him. And the hurt reminded him of that other time, years ago, when his life had been reduced to pain and darkness. He had survived it once. He didn't know if he could do so again.

The pounding inside his skull increased until it roared like thunder. Compressing his head between his hands, he sagged forward then rolled onto the sand where he could lie flat. The unhurried glide of surf sang in his ears, and he knew if he listened long enough, the sounds would lull the deepest of pains within him. Even in those ugly days, the sound of the water had soothed his spirit. It always had. It probably always would.

It seemed he had closed his eyes for only a moment, but when he felt a sprinkle of windblown sand on his face sometime later, he cracked a lid to find the darkness gone. Startled, he shot upward, ruffling sand from his hair as he gained his feet. Dawn? Nay, he had closed his eyes only seconds before. But dawn it was. Jackdaws were already scavenging the strand line for food.

He climbed the path to the top of the cliff, anxiety quickening his step. Yet the clear morning air seemed to temper the oppression of the previous night's problems. Indeed, he and Elisabeth were facing problems of immense proportions, but nothing he could not address. Her grandfather's death, the brand on his palm, the white raven—he could explain all these things, if she would agree to refrain from poisoning him long enough to listen.

When he opened the door to the cottage, he discovered he had inherited another problem.

Like the darkness, Elisabeth was gone.

chapter thirteen

She had no notion where she was or where she'd been, but she hoped if she kept trudging eastward, she would stumble upon civilization, and eventually Maidenstowe ... *if I just keep placing one foot in front of the other.*

From the sun's position over her right shoulder, she judged the time to be nearing noon, which meant she had been walking for more than twelve hours. But much of that had been in darkness, so her progress had been halting at best, thwarted by furze bushes and treacherous stumps of moorstone. But she *had* escaped. Of that she was proud, even if her stomach was screaming from hunger and her throat from thirst. She told herself she could scarcely feel the places on her feet where her boot leather had rubbed her flesh raw. And she didn't mind that her legs felt leaden or that she was still wearing pieces of the furze bush that had attacked her last night. It didn't even bother her that she had no idea where she was, and that the land was flat and unfriendly and choked with spiky stalks of dog grass whose vines kept snaring her boots.

It didn't bother her.

It really didn't.

Through a hot bout of tears she spied a ledge of granite embedded in the soil ahead of her. Taking four hobbling steps, she sank down onto it, letting out a sigh of pain as she surrendered to exhaustion. She hadn't intended to become fodder for the great ravens who soared above the heath, but the slower her pace, the bolder the birds became, dipping lower in their flight, staking their next meal with impatient grace. The persistence of the creatures chilled her and made her question her decision to head east across the moors. She could have headed north, or south, but the coastal terrain had frightened her. It would be easy to step off the edge of a cliff in the darkness. Her greatest obstacle on the moors was walking into furze bushes, and escaping the heed of the carrion crows.

Three gathered above her. Then four. Their caws were hoarse and resonant as they caught the updrafts, black wings spread and plumage lush with a purplish green gloss. She blinked the unwanted moisture from her eyes, refusing to succumb to this new threat, then swiveled her head, combing the skies for more of the wedge-tailed predators. From the northwest she saw two motes of darkness winging toward the gathering circle, and from the west, against a backdrop of startling blue, she saw what appeared to be a blemish on the horizon—an inky stain that neither soared nor glided. And without lifting her long-glass to her eye, she divined what the image was and knew that her freedom would last only as long as it took a war-horse to cross a moor.

"You might have thought to steal the horse," said Cain

some minutes later. He regarded her from atop his saddle, making no move to dismount.

"I *did* think," she bristled, watching Scylla paw the earth with hooves that could split a man's skull with a glancing blow. "I couldn't hoist myself onto his back. The beast is too big."

"That was in your favor."

"Why? Had I stolen your horse, I might have reached a village where you never would have found me."

"Had you stolen my horse, your crushed bones would have fertilized the earth. The beast has little fondness for strangers."

Shoulders slumped in failure, Elisabeth bowed her head, but she would not admit defeat. She steadied the vibration in her throat and with fists clenched she choked out at him, "No matter how many times you drag me back, I will not stay. I will run from you, I swear it, again and again and again."

Cain urged Scylla closer to her—so close that if she extended her hand, she could stroke the feathering on the animal's leg. Uncomfortable with the beast's nearness, she scooted backward a space, then hurled a contemptible look at Cain whose gaze froze her where she sat.

"And no matter how many times you run, I swear I will find you, again and again and again." His voice slashed through the silence like a thrust of steel.

"I'll not share the same saddle with you," she spat.

"I don't recall offering."

The implications of that remark sent shock waves to her toes, where her blisters had sprouted blisters of their own.

"You made your way here by foot, lady. You'll return the same way." He swung Scylla away from her and with a wide gesture of his hand directed her toward the western horizon. "You have a long walk ahead of you so I suggest you get started. I'd like to arrive home before dark. Rumors abound that the devil himself roams the moorland at night. On horseback no less. It surprises me you didn't come eye to eye with him in your wanderings."

"I did." She struggled to her feet, sucking in her breath as her blisters suffered the full weight of her limbs. "His eyes are blue. *Pale* blue." Making a painful moue with her mouth, she trudged past him, her step more lame than lithesome.

"The ravens seem disappointed I found you," Cain said once he'd set a steady pace behind her.

Elisabeth glanced upward to find the birds dispersing. She was relieved not to be the source of their next feast, but the alternative was no less agonizing. A broken toe was sheer bliss compared to the constant chafing of leather against raw flesh. She altered her gait in an attempt to shift pressure to other parts of her foot, but the pain was everywhere, gnawing at the back of her heels, rasping against the knuckles of her toes.

"Have you caught a stone in your boots?" he continued. "You've developed something of a limp."

"I'll manage," she flung over her shoulder at him. But she didn't know if she could. Either her boots had shrunk or her feet had grown, but one no longer fit the other. Her bones felt as if they were being ground to stubs. She took another step and smothered a whimper in her throat. When she removed her stockings, she knew all she would find would be pulp. She could feel the textured silk sticking to her fresh ulcers and pulling away, sticking and pulling away, aggravating what was already sore and bleeding. Her eyes rimmed with tears.

Another step, and her ankles buckled with the pain. She fell to her knees in a swirl of black satin, then sank onto her left thigh and buttock, like a bird with a broken wing.

"Are you of a mind to share my saddle now?" Cain asked from somewhere above her, but she lashed out blindly with her arm, laying claim to the space around her.

"I don't *want* your help!" she cried at him, swinging her fist in a vicious arc. "And I d-don't want to be your wife. I—" She pinched her eyes shut, but she could feel the wall she'd built around her emotions cracking at the seams, disintegrating with the flood of despair, anger, and pain that surged within her. She bunched her fists against her eyes, hiding her humiliation from him, but to no avail. Her tears slid beneath the heels of her palms and floated onto her cheeks and wrists. They were hot tears. Scalding tears. And they had no end.

Cain dismounted, but she did not see him. She cocooned herself against her knees and sobbed great wracking sobs that threatened to choke her. Her shoulders shook. Her back shook. Images assailed her, reminding her of all she had hoped for that would never be. "You . . . you killed him before he . . . before he could say he loved me!" she wailed. "He loved me . . . I n-know he did. But he never said the words. I wanted to . . . to hear him say the words." Her voice broke on a high, keening note that ravaged her throat with its intensity. Cain dropped to one knee. He reached out a hesitant hand to caress her blond head, then drew back on it.

"I love you, Elisabeth," he whispered.

"I miss him," she sobbed, despising what her hatred and

anger were doing to her. She felt sick inside, worm-eaten with loathing, with bitterness. She ached to be the person she used to be, to feel whole again, to . . .

A sob died in her throat. Cain's words fluttered softly against her eardrums.

Her choking wails quieted. Her breathing calmed. She dragged her palm across her cheek, across her nose. Her whimpers softened to sniffs. She inched her head upward and squinted at him through the burning sting of her tears. "What . . . *sniff* . . . what did you say?" She saw a twinned image of his bowed head and a ruffle of hair that was black as the plumage of a great raven. She stared at him, waiting for him to lift his face, waiting for him to speak, but he did neither. He gathered his right arm close to him, slipped his left thumb beneath his glove, and peeled the wool off his hand. She rubbed her eyes to dry the moisture from her lashes, and when she looked back, his hand was extended toward her, palm up, openly, freely, in a gesture that one friend might offer another.

For a stunned moment she eyed his uplifted palm, thinking it obscene that a killer should pretend to know anything of friendship. But then she saw how vividly the sun highlighted the stark white of his scar—a scar so abhorrent to him that to hide his shame he cloaked its existence—and she wondered what it had cost him to bare to her what he bared to no one.

She looked up at him, her eyes red with her tears. "You offer your hand to me, but if . . . if I accept it, will you take me home? I want to go home."

He held her gaze to his with the seductive power of a tame but terrible beast. "This is your home. Here, or wherever else I choose to lay my head. If you could suffer its homeliness for a space, perhaps I could make you feel welcome. I want you to be at your ease with me, Elisabeth. It does not please me what you do to yourself to escape me." He focused on her feet. "Do you find me so vile a creature that you choose such violent pain above my company?"

She averted her eyes, unable to bear his scrutiny.

"Elisabeth?"

Tiny folds of skin puckered her brows. "How can you ask me to stay with you? How can I ever accept you knowing what you did?"

"I did nothing. *Nothing*. Listen to me. On the night I returned to the Saracen's Head for your long-glass, there were three men in the common room who left before I did. An unholy threesome as I recall. No doubt the same three men who attacked me on the road. I dispatched two of them with my sword, but the third man was more cunning. He knocked my sword from my hand. I speared him with a dagger, but the man still found the strength to retaliate quite convincingly, as you may well remember."

Elisabeth nodded. Yes. She remembered only too well.

"He left me neither the capability nor the presence of mind to withdraw my blade from his flesh. But I would guess the man survived his wound, as I survived mine. I would also guess he sought my presence at Maidenstowe to finish what he had started, but what he found instead was your grandfather and a dazzling gold dragon that presaged greater worth than a thief-taker's blood. I would maintain, lady, that my presence in your grandfather's house may have contributed to his death. I admit that I provided the weapon, albeit unknowingly. But I did not kill him. You call me thief and liar. Perhaps 'tis so. Even my flesh attests to my sins. But I do not butcher old men. Judge me if you must, but judge me on the truth. I did not kill Quintus St. Mary. I could slay no one you cherished so much."

She listened to his explanation, but when he finished all she could say was, "Why?"

"Because I love you, Elisabeth. Because I am not afraid to speak the words your grandfather could not."

She shook her head, disbelieving. "If you loved me, you would not have kidnapped me."

"Indeed. I would have allowed you to remain at Maidenstowe where you would have become wife to another."

"If you loved me, you would grant me my freedom!"

"Freedom to escape across the moors where you could fall prey to the carrion crows?"

His reasoning unsettled her. His words of love still fluttered in her head. Could she believe them?

She dwelled on his outstretched hand. She remembered this hand as it had searched out her hair needles in the stable. It was the same hand that had slain the mongrels on Hound Tor and bound her injured toe. He might have thrashed her with that hand for what she'd done to him last night, but he hadn't. Thomas, she knew, would have thrashed her for much less.

But did he love her?

He had never fawned over her or filled her head with petty flattery. Perhaps a man whose hands were strong and finely formed showed his affection in quiet ways, without need for flamboyance. What others sought to express with lavish gifts and flowery speech, this man might express by binding broken toes and searching out hair needles in the straw of a stable floor.

Perhaps his was a quiet love, as he was a quiet man.

She recalled the night on Hound Tor. He had slain one of the mongrels with his dagger, but he'd retrieved the blade from the carcass even before he had helped her off the ledge. Did it follow that a man so conscientious of his weapons would leave his dagger at the scene of a murder so that blame could be immediately assessed to him?

It made no sense. Only a stupid man would do such a thing, and Cain was not a stupid man.

"I want to believe you," she whispered.

"Come back with me, Elisabeth. I want to show you I'm not the ogre you think me. I want to win back the place in your heart. It was a good place. A safe place. I miss it."

Her eyes lingered on his hand a moment longer. The symbolism of his gesture appealed to a part of her that had not yet eroded with distrust, to a part of her, within her heart, that began to thaw . . . and quietly smile. She elevated a shy hand to allow her fingertips to hover above his palm and then her hand greeted his flesh in gentle harmony—a touch that spoke of willingness and belief—a touch that, in its silence, answered his question as surely as he had asked it.

They rode back to the cottage in silence, but Elisabeth's mind was not at rest. If she closed her eyes she could see a faceless man enter Maidenstowe's withdrawing room through the unlocked doors from the terrace. She saw Quintus lift his head and open his mouth to cry an alarm. And then she saw a blade descend to quiet an old man whose life meant nothing to this stranger. Quintus's killer was a man totally lacking in mercy and conscience; a man who would have little time for hair needles and broken toes. A man who would have little compassion for offering a hand in friendship, or love. She would write Henry

Fielding. She would tell him when they found Quintus's killer, he would not have Cain's face. She was sure of it.

And it filled her heart with joy.

But the fact that Cain loved her filled her with another emotion. He was her husband. He would expect her to fulfill her marital duty. And that thought suddenly frightened her. At the Saracen's Head she had offered herself to Cain in order to escape Thomas. The actual thought of coupling with either man had not loomed vividly in her mind. But now, with the vows recited, all that was left was the consummation. She remembered Emma's talk of broad axes and pain, and though she suspected Cain would treat her gently, she could not help but feel her flesh shrink with dread.

It was dark when they sat down to supper that night.

When they'd arrived back at the cottage earlier that afternoon, Cain had had to cut Elisabeth's hose and boots from her feet. The raw and inflamed flesh beneath the black silk was so revolting that she might have cried aloud had she not been so overridden with disgust at the loss of another pair of riding boots. She'd soaked her feet in a bucket of fresh water, and Cain applied bruised tansy leaves to the worst of her blisters, then wrapped clean rags around her feet. She still wore the rags, but they'd had to burn her boots and hose for there was little left of them worth wearing. The only thing that redeemed her dejection now was the aromatic smell bubbling in the cookpot.

She didn't know what Cain had cooked while she napped. She didn't ask. It was not unlike what she had prepared the night before, except that it tasted of fennel. She smiled. "Quintus had a special liking for fennel."

"And women with enough flesh on their bones to insure him a comfortable ride, if my memory serves me correctly."

"Your memory serves you too correctly." She studied the bowl of her spoon in embarrassment. "I should not have made so cheeky a remark in your presence. You might have done me the courtesy of forgetting."

"Forgetting?" A rare smile tugged at his lips. "I have lain awake many a night wondering how so diminutive a man as your grandfather avoided being crushed beneath the weight of his many brides."

Elisabeth set her spoon down and elevated her eyes, the expression on her face deadly serious. "Beneath?" She formed a picture in her head of a stallion mounting a mare —how the stallion covered the mare from behind and balanced his front legs against the mare's flanks to support himself while he thrusted. Her eyes went blank as she tried to conceive how the stallion might do this while beneath the mare. Would he be on his back?

She shook her head at the picture her mind constructed, which prompted Cain to ask, "Did anyone in that great house of yours ever bother explaining to you how things are between a man and a woman? Between a husband and a wife?"

"Of course they did," she lied, not wanting to appear ridiculously naive in his eyes. "Emma was quite specific in her . . . discourse about the matter."

But Cain wondered how accurate the old woman's information had been, and why Elisabeth was holding her head so stiffly upright, as if trying to avoid looking at his fingers. He would almost guess that his new bride was completely untutored in the details of the marriage bed, and though that did not displease him, he wondered if consummating their vows would cause her such trauma that she would run from him again. The first time for a woman, he knew, could often be unpleasant, especially if the woman had no idea what to expect. He assumed he had convinced her of his innocence in Quintus's death. He had no wish to lose her over this. "Elisabeth, when a man and woman have . . . when they couple, a man's body—"

"I know what happens to a man's body." She was familiar with the sight of a stallion's erect member, but she was still unsure how he could put it to use while marooned on his back.

Cain nodded, somehow relieved that she knew. Massaging the unfamiliar warmth at his throat, he continued. "While a man undergoes his changes, a woman . . . a woman's body—"

"I know what happens to a woman's body," she said, remembering what had happened to her own body on occasion.

Cain nodded again, thankful to be spared another explanation. It could be he had underestimated the extent of her knowledge. "The meeting ground for these two people is . . . well, it can be anywhere. The woman—" He coughed. He thought to use his forefingers to demonstrate, but knew he would be more comfortable performing the act than talking about it. "The man faces the woman and—"

"They face each other?" Elisabeth felt herself pale. If the stallion and mare in her mind faced each other to couple, the mare would be most uncomfortable and the stallion, by the time they finished, would be dead.

Cain saw her eyes grow owlish with her thoughts, alerting him to the fact that his original assessment had been correct. She knew nothing. Hoping to allay her vexation, he leaned across the table and hooked his hand around her neck. He lazed his thumb in the hollow of her throat, and as he spoke he smoothed it in a gentle arc, up and down, up and down, learning the wondrous feel of her flesh.

"It was no doubt an oversight on Mrs. Pigeon's part, but I suspect she meant to tell you that unlike animals, people face each other when coupling." He stroked upward with his thumb, sketching its tip along the underside of her jaw, paralyzing her with the gentleness of his touch. "A man enjoys seeing evidence of the pleasure he imparts." But Elisabeth didn't look as if she was anticipating pleasure. She looked as though she was anticipating unimaginable pain.

Seeing her dread, he silently cursed it. He feathered his knuckles down her cheeks, then withdrew his hand and sighed. "I won't press you, Elisabeth," he conceded, hating the noble streak she aroused in him.

His reassurance seemed to quell her fear, for her eyes gradually returned to a size better suited to fit her face. He could not remember a time when he had denied himself womanly pleasures when the need was upon him, but it seemed more important now that he wait for Elisabeth's scars to heal. Perhaps then she would come to him willingly, without fear or reservation. And so thinking he extended another olive branch to her. It was not a tangible thing, but he knew it would heal as well as any poultice. Its curative powers were undeniable, yet he had shunned its application for the better part of his life and had lived to regret it. He did not want to see the same thing happen to Elisabeth. If she would talk, he would listen. It was the greatest gift he could offer her.

"Tell me of your grandfather," he said after awhile. "Entertain me, lady. We have the night ahead of us yet."

And so she did, haltingly at first, then with more fervor, laughing at some stories, grinning at others. The minutes stretched into hours, and in that time he saw the softness return to her eyes. He heard the lilt return to her voice. And it made him smile. The journey was a long one, but she had taken her first step. She was healing. Though she might not know it yet, she was becoming whole again.

The noise woke her from a sound sleep. *An injured animal,* she thought, turning over on the pallet Cain had prepared for her and straining her ears to listen. The fire had burned to embers that washed the darkness with a reddish glow. She slanted a look through the shadows, and when the whine sounded again she boosted herself upward and peered across the room where Cain was lying abed. She had heard the sound before. Not an injured animal. It was Cain.

A chill in the night air caressed her bare arms as she threw off her blanket. While she'd slept, her chemise had inched its way around her hips. She yanked it back round her knees as she clambered to her feet, standing cold and unsure on the earthen floor. His sobs were the sobs of a child and they seduced her in the same way that a call to war would seduce a man. Shivering, arms folded across her chest, she padded across the floor, an unearthly wraith draped in black cotton, a shadow floating among shadows.

She stood above him, remembering how he had listened to her so patiently that evening, never interrupting, always attentive. She had expected him to force himself on her, but he hadn't. She could see movement within the darkness, could hear him thrashing. She listened to his anguished moans, and though she could not see a clear definition of his face, she knew if she touched his cheek, she would find it moist with tears. And it pained her. This man had told her he loved her. It was inhumane to prolong his suffering when she could end it by waking him.

"Leave her!" he sobbed, at which point Elisabeth reached out her hand to wake him.

"Cain."

No sooner had the word left her mouth than the shadows seized her. Her arm. Her waist. The blackness swirled about her for a dizzying moment and when the motion stopped, she found herself pressed beneath the long length of his body, lumpy ticking at her back, his dagger at her earlobe ready to decapitate her.

"Nay!" she cried. She felt the power of naked muscle, then a quick surge of restraint as he recognized her voice. He stayed his dagger below her earlobe and in the next instant sent it hurtling across the room.

"I could have killed you!" he hissed, the gruffness in his voice belying the sudden tremor in his hand. "Little *fool*." His muscles were strung tight as bowstrings, and as he lay atop her, she could feel them begin to tremble with the slow release of tension. His heart thundered against her breast. He bowed his head against her forehead, and when he did his hair winged forward, newly washed and fragrant, veiling them both with its blackness. "Jesus." His breath was hot and smelled sweetly of fennel. His hair grazed her temples, touching her with a softness like mist. And then he turned his head, pressing his cheek to her brow, and she felt the warm flow of his tears upon her flesh.

"Your dreams make you cry," she whispered, struggling to tame the vibration in her voice. She wrested her hand from beneath him and with a gentleness she'd thought lost to her, shaped her palm to the curve of his skull. "Tell me why."

He said nothing, but she could hear something catch in his throat, so she drew his hair away from his face and smoothed it against his head with long, backward strokes. "Share this with me," she pleaded with him. "You forget. I am your wife." Feeling a sudden possessiveness she let her hand stray from his head to the bulk of his naked shoulder, and there she allowed her fingertips to sample flesh whose solidness she had only guessed at. His contours were smooth and hard and male. His flesh warmed her fingers and tempted her with mysteries she was not yet bold enough to probe. A hollow here. A rise there. She molded her hand to the back of his arm and felt the sudden flex of sinew so powerful that it reminded her how dangerous this man was, and that he was now her husband.

Without warning he rolled off her, propping himself on her left side. He captured her hand in his and lifted it to his mouth, whispering against her knuckles, "I'll not soon forget I call thee wife." His lips brushed each of her fingers then traveled to her wrist to linger at the pulse that fluttered beneath her flesh. The touch of his mouth quickened that pulse and kindled other pulses—in her throat, in her breast, in that place deep within her whose warmth was created to embrace a man's flesh. He circled the pulse beat at her wrist with the tip of his tongue, and when her hand went slack he pinned it against his chest, to the left of his breastbone, so she could know that his pulse beat as rapidly as her own. He manifested his desire in this way, without stale sentiment, and Elisabeth, knowing it was she who caused the explosive rhythms in his chest, felt herself stir.

Cain glided his palm from her wrist to her elbow, then higher, to a place of such incredible softness that he bent his head to touch it with his mouth. Her flesh was so cool against his lips that he feared she might take a chill, so he angled his torso closer over hers, thinking the massiveness of his body might warm her.

And so it did. Though his weight was something to be reckoned with, it was more blessing than burden, and she found herself warming to the feel of his bulk atop her. She could see little within the deep shadows of the cottage, but the darkness heightened her awareness of other things—of touch, of sound. She felt the press of his ribs against her own and in a wondrous rush of sensation felt the heavy fullness of her breasts crushed beneath the hard steel of his chest. Her chemise skewed across her bosom, trapping awkward folds of cotton between his flesh and hers. She felt his heart pound an unyielding knot of ribbon into her breastbone. She flinched as embroidery and lace scraped the sensitive flesh of her nipple, and in that moment she wanted nothing more than to be rid of the barrier that lay between them, to feel her husband's nakedness full and unashamed atop her.

She knew such heated desire then that her head grew light with sensations that began to spin behind her eyes. In the darkness she imagined a glimmering of lights, a thickness in her ears, and when she felt Cain's mouth at her shoulder cap she shuddered with emotion that spiraled to her loins. He lifted his head, worried he had hurt her. "Elisabeth?" But she responded by tangling her fingers in the dark mane of his hair and urging his face close to hers.

Near breathless, she whispered against the shadow of his face, "If I am to be wife to you, I would know thee now." She could feel his body stiffen with hesitation. She could feel the questioning probe of his eyes even through the darkness, and then he was touching her lips in the gentlest of kisses, erasing from her mind all fear of the pain Emma had talked about. His mouth was warm like an oven is warm; his need so urgent that he seemed unable to catch his breath. His mouth played over her, hot and masterful, savoring all that had been forbidden him. And when it seemed her lips were too raw to endure further pleasure, he cupped his hand behind her head and parted her lips with his tongue, then kissed her so deeply that her breath hovered in quiet suspension. His shoulders formed a great dark cowl around her face. His tongue drifted over the shy length of hers, caressing her with moist, lithe strokes that made her breasts throb. She bent as he advanced, twined as he retreated. She grazed the inside of his cheek with the edge of her tongue, sketching an errant pattern over flesh that was smooth as the skin of an apple and teeth that were strong and hard.

"'Lisbeth," he whispered into her mouth, communicating with that one word all the passion he had lived with and suppressed. She wreathed strands of his hair around her fingers as he turned her head in his palm, nuzzling the soft angle where her jaw blended into the long curve of her throat. She felt the dewy touch of his tongue on the lobe of her ear then tightened her grasp on his hair as he bathed her neck with warm kisses and hot whispers of breath, from her ear, to her collarbone, to the wide strap of her chemise.

He kissed the strap off her shoulder and sampled the flesh with his teeth. His loins tightened as he traced the upper edge of her chemise with soft lips and a tongue that dipped below the black cotton, probing the gentle swell of her woman's flesh. He lingered at her breastbone, leaving her skin damp with the touches of his mouth, and then he slid his hand from beneath her head and rested it at the place where the chemise was fashioned with a ribbon bow that joined right side to left.

The bow came loose with a tug. He tamed the loops with a deft finger, and while Elisabeth's breath grew shallow he folded the material back, exposing much of her breastbone, but little else. Growling his frustration he molded his hand to the flattened shape of her breast then cupped it into fullness. It strained against the cotton, rising into a provocative shape that sent hot blood searing through his veins. Lust eclipsed restraint. With his thumb he found the stone-hard peak of her breast through the cotton, and dipping his head, drew it into the heat of his mouth.

Elisabeth's head reeled with the sensation. Her eyes rolled back in their sockets as the relentless sucking motion of his lips hardened what she thought could be hardened no further. She panted and held her breath and panted again while the beaded crest of her nipple grew as hot and damp as the inside of his mouth. She dug her fingers into his scalp. She held his head steady and arched her back to offer more of her breast to his roving tongue. A groan of pleasure rasped in her throat, and when she felt his tongue press the moist cotton of her chemise against the sensitive spike of her nipple, she let out a cry that rang of entreaty rather than pain.

Without lifting his mouth Cain straddled her. He unbuttoned the falls of his knee breeches with his free hand then flattened his palm against the indentation of her waist. After a moment he released her breast and elevated his face so that his mouth was but a hairbreadth above hers. "Know that I love you, Elisabeth."

Seized by a terrible thirst, with tears welling in her eyes, she locked his head in the bowl of her palms and urged his mouth against the pliant curve of her own. Soft and inviting, she opened her mouth beneath his, so he kissed her long and deeply, and in so doing, gave succor to her thirst.

He drugged her with his touch. He shifted his shoulders, his hips, then balancing himself on his shins, inched her chemise upward. She felt her hemline glide above her knees, where ribbon and lace normally gartered her thighs, then higher, where the flesh was lean and firm and virginal. She tensed as he shaped his hands around her naked hipbones. He felt the change in her body, so he eased his mouth away from hers and shinnied backward, stopping when he felt the press of her knees against the inside of his thighs.

"Cain?" She reached out her hand to him in the darkness, extending her fingers toward the shadow of his face, desperate for the touch of his mouth. And she was rewarded. As he parted her thighs and angled himself between the vee of her legs, he found one of her fingers, then another, and sucked the tips gently into his mouth. Waves of sensation danced up her arm, lifting every filament of down on her forearm. She felt the broadness of his palm circling her upper thigh, the brush of his fingertips against her buttocks, and then she felt the gentle press of his thumb as he found a soft, shapely place buried within her maidenhair. He stroked upward once, twice, and suddenly what lay beneath his thumb became as thirsty for his touch as the rest of her body. Another stroke and sensation burst hot and fluid within her.

She writhed beneath him, but he did not stop his labors: sucking deeply on her fingers, stroking the tiny bud of sensation beneath his thumb. Up and down. Up and down until he felt a spasm riffle through the length of her body. And she was wet. As wet with her desire as he was hard with his.

With a gentle finger he found her opening. She bore a virgin's tightness, and as he touched the head of his phallus to her flesh, he worried what harm his considerable size might cause her. But his experience told him that a woman's flesh was resilient. He prayed it would be so for Elisabeth. He slid his hands beneath her buttocks and lifted her to meet his probing length.

He thrust gently.

She felt her flesh yield at the intrusion of his body. He was thick and silken and though his entry caused discomfort, it was nothing she could not bear. Slowly, delicately, he probed deeper into her being, and like a flower she opened to his penetration, wrapping him in the tight sheath of her flesh, giving succor to his thirst as he had given succor to hers. And when he could probe no deeper, he slanted his body over hers, braced an arm on either side of her head, and showed her with the power of his flesh how much he wanted her.

His rhythm was flawless, her response instinctual. She circled her hands around his arms and rose to meet his driving thrusts. Sinew flexed against her palms. Flesh met flesh, blending, chafing, quickening. Her loins throbbed as he plunged deeper, deeper. Harder. Faster. He stretched and strained and then he was piercing a hidden core of sensation that burst like an overripe berry in the pit of her stomach. Her muscles contracted as if singed by flames. Her buttocks squeezed tight. The backs of her legs seemed weighted by a hot flow of sand that prickled from her calves to the arches of her feet. She felt heat—white, glowing heat—and when Cain touched her inner core again and shuddered with his own release, Elisabeth St. Mary, wife to Cain in all things, dug her fingers into his elbows and expressed her rapture in the only way that seemed humanly possible.

She screamed.

chapter
fourteen

She woke to find herself against her husband's side, her nose burrowed in the angle of his shoulder, her arm flung across the width of his chest. She had no idea what time of day or night it was, so blinking the sleep from her eyes, she craned her neck to peer at the window embrasure.

Light filtered through the cracks in the shutters. Morning light, she guessed from the intensity of the beams. Yawning, she lowered her head again and stretched quietly against Cain's long flanks. Her knee scraped his naked thigh, making her wonder at what point in time he had rid himself of his breeches. After they had made love?

She blushed as she remembered her conduct of the previous night. She had comported herself with the dignity of a London doxy. Great ladies endured the marriage act as a necessary evil in order to beget heirs. It was a conjugal debt to be paid to their husbands. Great ladies, she was quite certain, did not scream their delight while in the throes of passion. What must he think of her?

Reluctant to find out, she eased herself from the bed

with such great stealth that Cain did not stir—an extraordinary feat considering how quickly he'd reacted last night to the threat of her presence. She touched her hand to her throat in memory of what might have happened and chased away the chill that accompanied the thought. It would be maudlin to dwell on anything this morning except the pleasure she had shared with her husband, on that bed, in the darkness, face-to-face.

She smiled at that.

He had been unable to see what pleasure he imparted, but he had no doubt heard. The residents of the nearest fishing village had probably heard. Mortified, she smoothed her chemise over her hips and readjusted the rags that were still wrapped around her feet. Amazingly enough, the bandages had survived the vigors of their lovemaking in fine fashion. Perhaps more so than she. She pressed her fingers into the tender flesh of her abdomen as she retrieved a cake of soap. She wanted to wash the mingled sweat of their bodies from her flesh. Not because she wanted to cleanse herself of Cain's scent, but because she harbored a need to be pure and fresh for him. Indeed, a saltwater bath might even heal the blisters on her feet.

"Mmmmm." The sound rumbled in Cain's throat as he drifted toward consciousness. Rotating his head he bellowed out a yawn and squinted an eye open.

The bed was empty.

"Elisabeth?"

He heaved himself to an elbow, instantly awake, and scanned the dim corners of the room.

Nothing.

A long, icy finger coiled itself around his vitals. He

shoved his covers to the foot of the bed and flung his legs over the side, sustaining a cold shock when his feet met the earthen floor. He strode to the door and threw it open.

He ducked his head against the sunlight and splayed his fingers over his eyes. Barefoot and naked, he staggered beyond the door stoop. Visoring his hands against his brow, he tossed a look at the shed.

Scylla was housed safely inside.

Five fingers now clutched his vitals.

He spun in a slow circle, eyes searching, ears pricked. "Elisabeth?"

Nothing.

He jogged beyond the shed, beyond the cottage, where the moorland impressed its flatness on the earth. He raked the horizon. Nothing moved among the wind-pruned shrubs.

The fingers around his vitals began to squeeze.

In his mind he heard her scream ring out as it had last night—at the moment when he had filled her with his seed. He had hurt her. He should have warned her what to expect from their initial coupling. He shouldn't have foisted himself on her when he was still unsure of her feelings. But instead he had driven her from him, and she had run again. Just as she had threatened. And he had no one to blame but himself.

Fists clenched, eyes wild, he raced toward the edge of the cliff. The beach was deserted. His eyes darted over the surface of the water. The tide had receded as far as the chimney stack of rock that bisected the cove, but he could see no head bobbing in the surf. Would she be so foolhardy to hazard an escape by water? Could she swim? Had she been caught in the undertow?

The fingers became a fist that twisted mercilessly in his gut. He took the footpath at a run. Sand geysered beneath his feet as he pelted down the strand and across the shallow arcs of water that washed the tidal plane. He charged toward the far side of the chimney stack, heart hammering, lungs burning.

He stopped, stared.

Deserted.

She wasn't behind the chimney stack. She wasn't in the water. She was gone.

Gone.

She didn't love him. To think she ever could was madness. How could anyone ever love what he was?

The finality of her rejection washed over him like the waves lapping his feet. It sapped his will. It drained him of emotion, of hope. "Elisabeth!" he choked out, his voice still gravelly from sleep. Bile rose in his throat. Strength bled from his legs. He sank to his knees and fell back onto his haunches. "*Eliiiiisabeeeth!*" he wailed, in a cry so despairing that even the guillemots nested on the stack-top took flight to escape the sound. Face raised skyward, cords swelling in his neck, he gritted his teeth with the pain, then hung his head against his chest. He smacked his palms against the surf. Dug his fingers into the underlying sand. "'Lisabeth," he whispered, his great broad shoulders slumped in exhaustion. He was a score and twelve years, but at this moment in his life he felt an old man—very old, very broken, and too tired to continue.

"I'm here," came Elisabeth's voice.

He snapped his head up. As if in a dream, she stood before him, her hair falling loose and tangled over her shoulders, her white blond strands dark with water. She was wet, and naked, and she shivered as she clutched the black cotton of her chemise to her breast. "I was there." She nodded breathlessly toward the landslip on her right. "Behind that boulder. Out of the wind. I was rewrapping the cloth 'round my feet." She saw the tears starring the blue of his eyes. A stitch caught in her throat. "The rock was . . . it was kinder on my blisters than the sand would have been."

He lifted his hand from the water and cupped it round the back of her knee, reassuring himself that she was flesh and blood, not some apparition he had conjured out of desperation. She shivered at the cold touch of his hand, proving that she was indeed real.

"I thought you had left me." His voice cracked as he said it, and when it did, she reached out her thumb to skew a tear that escaped the corner of his eye. She shook her head, her eyes soft and dewy.

"I will never leave thee," she whispered, shaping her palm to the slope of his cheek. "I love thee, husband. I will always love thee." Her chemise dropped between them as she opened her arms to him, and Cain, dazed by her admission, dazzled by her nakedness, could do little but touch with his eyes what the darkness had cloaked the night before.

Her flesh was pale as her hair. Her bones were formed into angles so fine and fragile that he wondered how she could bend without shattering like a teacup. Water dropped from the ends of her hair onto her hipbone, beading there for a moment before flattening into rivulets that streamed down her thigh. Water pearled the ridge of her collarbone, the cleft between her breasts. With an unsteady hand Cain traced a finger down her breastbone, dissolving the droplets with a touch. He outlined the contour of her breast with his fingertips then cupped its fullness in the curve of his palm. She was young and firm, and her breast filled his hand with its weight. Her nipple was puckered with cold and stood out like the tip of his finger, proud and erect. The protruding nub was dark as wine, a color so rich and erotic that it put him in mind of that other part of her body that was equally rich, equally erotic.

Arousal came so hard upon him that as she inched closer to him, he rose up on his knees, steeled his hands around the spheres of her buttocks, and pulled her flush against him. The swell of her breasts flattened softly against him yet their rigid peaks rasped provocatively against his hair-roughened chest, taunting him with memories of the way his tongue had played over her last night, stiffening what was soft, warming what was cold. She circled her arms around her neck and when she touched her mouth to the curve of his ear, he thought he would go mad.

He came to his feet in a single motion, lifting her with him. She clung more tightly to his neck, and twined her legs around his hips. "Stay with me, Elisabeth," he pleaded against her cheek. "Never leave me." He turned so that his back was braced against the stone of the chimney stack. Cold and straining, he angled her away from his belly. With a single, silken thrust he parted her flesh with his own, and then he took her—hard and quick and wholly—in the cool light of dawn, with the Atlantic swirling about his ankles.

He carried her back to the cottage that morning, all the while planting kisses in the hollow of her throat. They broke their fast by dipping stale bread in water, and then, because Cain was unwilling to be parted from her, he escorted his bride to his bed. With his back propped against the wall, he cradled her against him. Bundling herself in a blanket, Elisabeth pressed her cheek to his chest and snugged his hand beneath her chin.

"I'm sorry you had to go looking for me," she said, opening his palm to her mouth. "But I am not sorry you found me." Warm, sated, she traced the scar on his palm with moist strokes of her tongue then retraced it with her thumb. "Tell me the story, Cain. Tell me why I have seen such hatred in your eyes. Is it because of this?"

The nearness of her body gave him courage. The promise of her love gave him hope. Sighing, he regarded the communion of their intertwined hands. "I was a young boy once, Elisabeth. Perhaps a thousand years ago, it seems so long. I had father, mother, a bed made of finer stuff than matted straw." He tilted his head against the wall and pondered the rough grid of rafters below the thatching. "My father was lost at sea while crossing the Channel over two decades ago. I was eight at the time, and devastated. The ship's master told us that rough seas had swept him off the deck. 'An accident,' says he. And we believed him. For a while we believed him.

"My father's brother was an officer in the military, but after my father's death, he returned home to assume a caretaker's interest in my father's enterprises, supposedly maintaining them 'til I reached my majority. He craved the taste of spirits though, and when he was deep in his cups his tongue would flap without cease. I heard him on one such night. He was having merry discourse with a man whose voice was unfamiliar to me, but their words were clear enough. They were boasting how easy it had been to do away with my father." He gathered up a handful of her hair and rubbed it gently between his fingers. "I went to my mother with the knowledge. She was terrified. And then she explained to me that if my uncle could plot the death of his own brother, he could likewise plot the death of his nephew and claim for himself all that was rightfully mine."

Elisabeth shook her head. "What brand of demon would consort to murder his own family?"

For a short space Cain was silent, then he said, "In a week you would have called him husband."

The words paralyzed her, but slowly she pushed away from his chest so she could look him square in the face. "Thomas?" Her voice was a croak of disbelief.

"Thomas Penmarck. Earl of Moreleigh. Lord of Thirlstane. My uncle."

Elisabeth blinked numbly while bits of the puzzle Cain presented sifted through her brain and fell into place. "'Tis why you looked familiar to him," she breathed with sudden understanding. "'Tis how you knew of Thirlstane and its great stone steps. But . . . in all the many years I have known him, he has not once mentioned a nephew, deceased or otherwise. He has spoken of Cicely and Justin, but—"

"Why mention something of such little import? Had you ventured to Thirlstane, you no doubt would have seen a marker atop my grave, and perhaps Thomas would have deigned to tell you of the nephew who fell from his bedchamber window to the rocks below when he was but a lad of eight. What he would not tell you is that the grave lies empty."

Intrigued, Elisabeth settled herself against his bent knee and nodded at him. "Go on." And quietly, he continued.

"My mother kept the family seal locked in her jewelry

coffin, but on the night I went to her, she placed it in my hand and charged me to hide it somewhere where Thomas would never find it. 'He can legalize no document without the seal,' she told me. 'Whosoever retains the signet ring holds the power of Thirlstane.' So I secreted it away." A vertical crease split his brow as the memory filled his consciousness. Elisabeth squeezed his hand in support.

"They woke me the next night with their arguing—my mother and my uncle. They were on the landing outside my mother's chambers, at the top of the staircase. 'Where have you hidden it?' Thomas was barking at her. I started running toward them, yelling at Thomas to leave her alone. She threw up her hand to strike him. He fended off the blow, and the next thing I knew she was falling." The blue of his eyes darkened with emotion and Elisabeth suddenly understood what rendered his dreams so intolerable. "She didn't stop until she reached the bottom of the stairs."

"I'm sorry," Elisabeth murmured against his knuckles.

"I tried to run down the stairs after her—she was so very still—but Thomas caught my arms and began to shake me. 'She gave it to you!' he screamed at me, and I knew then he'd been drinking. 'Where is it? Give me the ring!' I swore I didn't have it, but he didn't believe me. I begged him to let me go to my mother, but he dragged me back to my room and told me that perhaps I needed a dose of solitude to improve my memory. He removed my tinderbox from the mantel then locked me within the walls of my chambers."

Elisabeth shook her head, puzzled. "Why remove your tinderbox? Did he fear you might set your room aflame while you were locked inside?"

"Quite the opposite. Thomas was not so kind as that.

You once accused me of not understanding the meaning of fear, of never having suffered a moment's trepidation. You were mistaken, Elisabeth. As a child there was something I feared more than death itself. I feared the darkness. To greet the night without a lighted candle in my hand, to sleep without a flame burning by my bed was to invite terror. And Thomas was well aware of that fact. A cunning man, my uncle. He assumed I would rather sell my soul than spend one night in the company of shadows."

"But you proved him wrong."

"I surprised him. Angered him. He visited me once a day after that, sometimes with food, sometimes not. He kept badgering me about the ring's whereabouts. 'Has your memory improved yet?' he would ask. ''Tis November, boy. Your room will only grow colder without a fire to warm it. Your nights will only grow blacker.' I asked him where my mother was. He told me she had taken up residence in the family plot and it was most regrettable I'd been unable to attend her funeral, but everyone understood it was best for a fever-stricken boy to remain abed 'til he had fully recuperated."

"Oh, Cain. How could he confect such lies? How could he treat your feelings so brutally?"

"Greed, my love. Greed makes all manner of brutality acceptable."

"But couldn't you scream for help? Were there no servants who would question your outcries?"

He caressed the angle of her jaw with a long stroke of his thumb. "I heard no servants on the landing. Whatever Thomas told them to keep them away from my room worked. During the week I was locked in my room, I would guess there wasn't a single servant who ventured into that wing of the manse."

Elisabeth remembered the edict she had issued to avoid the east wing of Maidenstowe and realized it took little effort to have one's orders obeyed. Indeed, if Thomas had bade his servants stay away from an entire wing of Thirlstane, they would have obeyed without question. "How did you fare after a week?"

"I was hungry. I was cold. I was frightened. But I vowed that whatever he did to me, I wouldn't give up the ring. It was mine now. I was lord of Thirlstane. But Thomas had a different opinion. He came to me late in the night after a week had passed, in a drunken rage. He'd actually brought wood for the hearth, but after he lit the fire, I saw he'd brought with him something more than fuel and my tinderbox. In his hand he carried a branding iron with the letter 'T' affixed to the end."

Elisabeth's stomach churned for what must follow.

"I'm sure he'd come by the thing quite by accident. When the first Penmarcks were responsible for meting out justice in the parish, they practiced the custom of branding the hands of felons. The sheriff eventually assumed responsibility for justice, but the Penmarcks kept the brand, and Thomas unearthed it. He thrust the cold iron at me that night; backed me into a corner with it. 'If you don't give up the ring, I'll brand you for the thief that you are,' shouts he. He stabbed the iron into the fire and then he began to ransack my room. He cleared my bookshelves and overturned my bed. He checked for loose stones in the fireplace and loose boards in the floor, but he found nothing."

"Was it hidden in your room?"

"Beneath his nose, but in a place so obvious he couldn't

fathom its being there. My Bible lay open on its reading stand close to the hearth. Thomas flipped a single page and read a passage aloud to me. '. . . And the Lord set a mark upon Cain, lest any finding him should kill him.' He closed the book then. He snatched the iron from the fire, and then he did exactly what he said he would do."

Elisabeth pinched her eyes shut and bowed her head with imagined pain. She could understand his hatred now, could understand why he found more comfort in a steel blade than in human compassion. And it made her heart ache from wanting to shield him from any more harm, any more suffering. "How could you bear it?"

"I couldn't. I fainted. And when I regained consciousness, Thomas was gone and the room was dark again. And my hand . . ." He made a fist that corded the muscles in his forearm. "I'd never thought to feel such pain."

"You've felt it twice," she commiserated. "Once with Thomas and once with me." She kissed the center of his palm. "I thank God you've been blessed with such powers of endurance."

"I felt less than enduring that night. I felt . . . if I remained in that room for one more night, Thomas would find a more creative form of punishment for me, and I didn't think I could withstand anymore of his torture. Despite the dark, despite my fear, I knew I had to flee."

"But the door was locked."

"The window wasn't locked. It overlooked a cliff that dropped a hundred feet to the sea, but it wasn't locked. There was a way out that window, if I could summon the courage to use it. You look skeptical, Elisabeth. Do you think it absurd that a child with an injured right hand, a child terrified of darkness, would try to crawl out into the night to scale a hundred-foot cliff to safety?"

"Absurd? Not absurd. I think it impossible."

"It *was* impossible, at least it would have been had I been forced to scale all hundred feet." A sudden calmness tempered the sharp planes of his face. "Do you know the meaning of the word 'thirl,' Elisabeth?" And when she shook her head, he continued. "It means an opening, a hole. Thomas had lectured me on the subject once, Thomas being given to bookish pursuits because of his game leg. 'Thirlstane' meant 'a hole in stone' and Thomas surmised it derived its name from the network of caves tunneled into the coastal rock. I was never allowed to explore any of the caverns, but I discovered one of my own some months before my father died.

"If you stood at my bedchamber window and looked down, you could see five shallow ledges, like steps, leading downward. I sometimes saw choughs disappear beneath the fourth ledge and not appear again for hours, so one morning, while I was supposedly doing my lessons, I decided to explore. Out my window I went, climbing backward over each of the ledges, and when I reached the fourth, I discovered a three-foot-wide opening in the cliff face."

"Occupied by a family of incensed choughs no doubt."

Cain grinned. "Among other things. I crawled in as far as I dared, which wasn't very far because of the lack of light, but from what I could tell, it was a natural cave that channeled much farther back into the rock than I dared explore at that juncture in time. But it didn't prevent me from going back. It became an obsession. I collected a supply of candles and stored them in the cave, then went back every day, exploring deeper every time. It was high in some places and so low in others that I had to crawl on hands and knees. At the lowest point the natural cave ended, but it was connected with a man-made shaft, much like the tinners might construct. The manor house was built during Cromwell's reign, so 'tis my guess that my ancestors hired local tinners to finish tunneling through the cave to provide a means of escape should Cromwell go on one of his rampages. When Cromwell was no longer a threat, I suspect the occupants of the house forgot about the existence of the thirl."

"Did you ever find your way to the end?"

Cain shook his head. "Not while I was exploring. I was always too frightened of what I might find at the end of the shaft to venture too far into its depths. I thought I would be more courageous when I was nine. But nine came unexpectedly." He inhaled a sober breath. The calmness left his face as he relived that November night. "I climbed out into the darkness, but my hand caused me such pain that I lost my handhold and my footing and fell down the face of two ledges before I caught myself." He smoothed his forefinger down the slope of his nose. "'Tis how I broke my nose—escaping from my uncle down the rocks of Thirlstane. I found the cave entrance after I stopped shaking long enough to claw my way into it, but my nose was bleeding, my hand was burning, and the blackness was so absolute that it felt as if a living thing were crawling over me. There were candles in the cave, but I had no flint to strike a flame. Bats were swooping above my head. I didn't know if an exit lay at the end of the tunnel. And I was alone, Elisabeth." He looped his wrist around her neck and drew her against his chest, bending his head to bury his lips in her hair. "I never want to be that alone again."

"You won't be, my love. I promise you." She spread her fingers over the taut flesh of his back and held him tight.

"Sometimes we hold an image in our minds of the most terrifying thing that could ever befall us, and if we live through it, we know we've lived through the worst that life can offer, and nothing else will ever have the power to frighten us again."

Elisabeth nodded, knowing exactly what he meant.

"I survived the tunnel and the blackness, and I knew if I could survive that, I could survive anything. Crawling inside that cave was like crawling inside a mother's womb and being born again. I entered fearing darkness. I emerged knowing I would never fear the dark again. Darkness became my friend, not my enemy. And there was nothing in the world that would ever again be worthy of my fear."

"You found your way to the end of the tunnel?"

"All the way. And upward through a false crypt in the graveyard."

Elisabeth smoothed her palm over the finely hewn muscles of his chest while she listened to the sound of his heartbeat thrumming against her ear. "Where did you go?"

"North. I stole food in Sithney, and clothes in Camborne. And on the fringes of Bodmin Moor I found a band of Romanies who were not averse to accepting as one of their number a young pauper who already bore the mark of a thief. They taught me skills beyond one's imagination, Elisabeth. And I became the very thing that Thomas had accused me of being. A thief. A gypsy thief. There was a woman among them who called herself Black Nell. She wore knives across her chest like a man, but she could wield a knife better than any man. I once saw her cleave a gnat lengthwise while it was still in flight."

"And she taught you."

"She was a widow. I was alone. She shared her mastery with me in exchange for my company."

Elisabeth wondered if the woman's sharing of expertise had stopped at knife throwing, but she bit back her words.

"She asked me only one question in the years I knew her. She wanted to know my name. I remembered the Bible passage Thomas had bellowed at me, and I told her, 'Cain.' 'A good name,' she said. 'It means spear.' Then she opened my hand and nodded at my palm. 'A spear could prevent this from ever happening again.' So I became Cain. Gypsy. Vagabond. Thief."

"And what of the white raven?" Elisabeth prodded. "Where had you hidden it that it was so well concealed from Thomas?"

Cain laughed aloud. "The fool. Had he opened the Bible halfway it would have been his for the taking. I'd cut a deep hole in the pages of the book and stowed the ring there. He was no more than five hundred pages from what he sought most in the world."

Elisabeth touched her mouth to his breastbone. "You emerged from the cave as Cain. Who did you go in as?"

He paused. "Stephen," he said quietly, as if he had not spoken the word for a very long time. "My parents called me Stephen. But Stephen died in the cave, Elisabeth. It was Cain who learned of horseflesh and knives from the gypsies. It was Cain who lost his way in the streets of London, never to be reunited with the Romanies who had carted him there."

"And it was Cain who rode into Maidenstowe on the twenty-eighth day of April some two decades later. I'm still not sure I understand why."

His voice became an undertone. "In those years after Thirlstane I survived any way I could find. I lied. I cheated. But I survived mostly on my hatred. It fed me when there was no food. It strengthened me when I was too weary to draw another breath. I lived for the day when I would make Thomas Penmarck suffer as I had suffered."

"But why did you come to Maidenstowe?" she persisted.

"For you. You were to be my revenge. I wanted to deny Thomas what he craved above all else—a wife who would bring him more wealth, more land, more power than even Thirlstane had offered him. I intended to abduct you from Maidenstowe before your wedding, and when I was sure that I had driven Thomas sufficiently insane with worry, I would have sent him word of your whereabouts. He would have found you, but he also would have found me. I would have seen to it that he died a slow and painful death that night, but not before he had watched me rape the woman he had hoped to take to wife."

She eased herself away from his embrace and drilled him with a look that made his tongue want to shrivel in his head. "You would have done that?"

He nodded, albeit reluctantly. "I would, had I not fallen in love with you."

"How kind of you to claim my hand before you decided to claim my maidenhead."

"Elisabeth—"

She waved off any explanation and with a determined nod of her head announced, "You're mistaken if you think you could have raped me."

"You think not?"

"I know not." She smiled at him then, with a blend of love and affection that was as pure as sunlight. "I would have been much too willing a participant to be your victim. Whether to my shame or my delight, I was willing from the moment you walked into the drawing room of Maidenstowe. Be you Stephen or Cain, fugitive or vagabond, you are husband to Elisabeth"—she pressed her palm to his inner thigh and worked upward from there—"who loves you more than life itself."

chapter fifteen

In the days that followed they talked unremittingly, ate sparingly, and reconsummated their marriage vows in daylight, moonlight, and fleeting moments in between.

"Who is this Lint fellow you speak of?" This, while they were attempting to assign some order to the plot of earth Cain so optimistically called a garden.

"Gellicoe Lint. I picked his pocket when I was twelve and was so grateful he didn't have me flogged and pilloried that I began to follow him around like a lost puppy. We struck up a kind of guarded friendship, and when he was commissioned to organize his secret force, he invited me to join ranks with him. Where do we start assigning this order you're prattling about?"

Elisabeth shook her head at the herbage before her. "My darling husband, these two plants belong nowhere near each other. This one delights in morning sun. That one prefers afternoon. You should have planted them the other way round."

"I did not plant the garden, Elisabeth."

She arched an eyebrow, not at all convinced, and directed him to the southwest corner. "Nettles need to be weeded from the tansy." So while he busied himself with nettles, and she sat cross-legged pulling up couch grass, she asked, "How did a vagabond acquire a cottage?"

"From a thief," he called back. "Lint once sent me to St. Merryn to capture an infamous highwayman."

"Lint has information on everyone, does he?"

"Everyone in Mother England. He has yet to start on the Continent."

"So did you capture your highwayman?"

"I did that. But my highwayman turned out to be female, and none other than Black Nell herself. She'd tired of her roving ways and decided to try respectability for awhile. She married a carter who built the cottage for her, but when the fellow died she decided she was bored with respectability and began taking to the high road at night. After I caught her, I couldn't very well deliver her to the constable for gibbeting, so I dragged her back here and threatened to seize her horses if I heard anything more about the St. Merryn highwayman."

"Did you hear anything more?"

"The brigand vanished from the face of the earth."

"And Nell?"

"Spent the rest of her days breeding the most spectacular shires in the land. When she passed on, she left me all she claimed as her own—her cottage, her knives, and Scylla."

Elisabeth brushed wisps of hair from her face with the back of her hand. She studied the disarray of vines and greenery around her. "So this is Nell's garden. Pity she didn't think to plant lavender."

Cain crossed the garden and with weeds overflowing his

hands, sat on the ground beside her. "Why lavender? In memory of your mother?"

"Because lavender—" Her eyes locked on the greenery in his hands. "What have you done?"

He lifted the weeds for her perusal. "Picked nettles."

She shook her head, laughter brightening her eyes. Cain surmised his mistake from her mirth.

"Not nettles, eh?" He frowned at the clump of vines. "They were the only things growing around the tansy. Hell, Elisabeth, I'm not a bloody farmer. What in the devil did I pick?"

She freed one of the plants from its tangled clump and held it up. "Goat's beard, my love. You picked goat's beard. You are most definitely not a bloody farmer."

With a wicked glint in his eye he tossed the plants over his shoulder and grabbed Elisabeth's foot, upending her.

"Cain!"

Straightening her leg, he elevated it to his mouth. "A farmer I may not be, but my planting techniques have been extolled by more than one wench who was well lessoned in the art of cultivation."

Elisabeth chimed her laughter as he feathered kisses above her ankle. She swatted the goat's beard at him, missing badly. "We have no time for this!" she giggled. "Not if you want to eat."

"I want to eat, lady." He glided his hand toward her knee, whispering as his mouth followed, "I very much want to eat."

Her giggles turned to gasps, her gasps to groans. And that night for supper, to Elisabeth's dismay and delight, they feasted on goat's beard root, and little else.

* * *

"Was that bit of creativity something else Black Nell taught you?" They lay on the beach, the sun warming Elisabeth's spine, the sand warming Cain's.

He rolled her onto her back and kissed the sweat from her temple. "*That* was something an orange-headed tart on Mincing Lane taught me."

"When you were a boy of twelve no doubt."

He nuzzled the corner of her eye. "Thirteen."

Playfully indignant, she thrust him off her. "I was wrong to place a price on your *head*. 'Tis obviously not the part of your body which inspires the most recognition. Had I placed my reward on a more noteworthy appendage, you probably would have been caught by now."

He laughed full and heartily at her jest before lacing his fingers behind his head. "There is still time for that, Elisabeth." And as he watched the winged flight of a jackdaw above him, his voice grew sober. "Lint gave me four days headway before making the contents of your letter public knowledge. By now the country should be swarming with thief-takers anxious to retire on the bounty my head will bring them."

Elisabeth's breathing slowed at the consequences her error in judgment might wreak. "But I was wrong, Cain. I don't want men tracking you down. I don't want you punished for a crime someone else committed." Then, in a burst of sudden decision she said, "I shall pen a letter to this Gellicoe Lint person and tell him I retract my reward."

"And how will he circulate that information to the men already sniffing out my whereabouts? No matter how thorough his network, there is little chance he will reach everyone. Should I be found, I doubt my captor will be deterred by the fact that my wife has retracted her reward. And more to the point, Elisabeth, Nell could neither read nor write, which means I have neither ink nor parchment in my possession."

She studied the configuration of his ribs and lightly touched one long spur. "I have as much as condemned you." And because her voice was so disconsolate, Cain boosted himself upward and enfolded her within the security of his arms. He pressed his cheek to her ear and rocked her gently back and forth, loving her as he had loved no other being who'd touched his existence.

"Cornwall is a great distance from London, Elisabeth. At the ends of the earth. No one will find me here."

"But how long will you be content to hide? You are the Earl of Moreleigh. Will it sit well with you to bequeath a cob cottage to your firstborn son rather than your rightful home? Will it not grate upon your pride that your wife has neither shoes for her feet nor brush for her hair? Will ignoring Thomas's sins free you from your nightmares?"

He buried his face in the soft curve of her neck, refusing to allow her doubts to thwart his newfound happiness. "That was another lifetime. I no longer wish to taste the bitterness of those years. Thomas and Thirlstane be damned. You are my life now. 'Tis enough."

But as he scooped her into his arms and carried her into the surf with him, she wondered how long it would be enough.

On May twenty-fifth, the day when Elisabeth would have exchanged vows with Thomas Penmarck, Cain saddled Scylla before dawn and headed across the moor to Padstow. He professed disenchantment with a constant diet of bird's eggs and flowers, and promised to return with more appetizing fare to tantalize their palates. He told her that Padstow was a ride of two leagues or more, so it therefore surprised her when, at mid-morning, she heard a bell jingling on the moor. Setting down the costmary leaves she was strewing about the floor, she tucked loose wisps of hair behind her ears and hurried out into the open, wondering how Cain expected to make use of a bell.

But the bell did not belong to Cain. It was attached to a two-wheeled cart that was being drawn by a man whose gait was more uneven than the bounce of his cart. As he drew near, Elisabeth saw why. *He has only one leg*, she thought, amazed that he would brave the terrain thusly handicapped. And it left her somewhat shamefaced that he could manage on one leg what she'd been unable to manage on two.

He rattled past the shed and with a tip of his tricorne hailed a greeting. "Mornin', mum. Thickpenny's the name." He halted several paces from her, disconnected himself from the harness he'd rigged to fit around his shoulders, and lowered the shaft to the ground. He was pleasant faced and stout and not unlike any of the score of peddlers who had wiled away an afternoon at Maidenstowe while she and Emma perused their wares. "Can I be temptin' you with some fancy trinkets today, mum? I have hollow kettles, bodkins, porringers, snuff rasps, and a pair of fine gloves made at Somerset." And when he unhinged the side of the cart and flipped it up, she saw what else he had. Spitalfields silk. Black calamanco from Norwich. Stoney Stratford lace. Great Marlow edgings. Worsted stockings. Cut glass buckles. A pair of low-heeled shoes made of fine black leather...

She curled her naked toes beneath her feet as she eyed

the shoes. What she wouldn't give to slide her feet into leather once again! But the prospect was quite dim. She had no coin. She could purchase neither the black leather shoes, nor the parchment and ink lying in the far corner of the cart, but she kept shifting her gaze between the two. Despite what Cain said, she felt obliged to tell *someone* in London that her reward was no longer valid. Was it not her duty to inform Gellicoe Lint that it was not Cain who had committed the crime she'd accused him of committing? Armed with that information would he then not call off some of his henchmen? That would reduce the chances of Cain's being captured, wouldn't it?

Her tongue made a slow sweep of her lips as her gaze lingered on the parchment. It seemed divine intervention that the peddlar had happened by with all the necessities she required. But which did she need more—the shoes or the parchment and ink? And even if she could choose between the two, how would she pay for them?

Waving her hand toward the cottage, she favored the peddler with the same smile that, weeks earlier, had thawed Cain's heart. "Would you care to come inside, Mr. Thickpenny? I have little in the way of confections to offer you, but I could brew a pot of Woodruff tea and we might chat awhile. What news in the rest of England?"

And because Thickpenny was a gregarious fellow who would never refuse an offer of tea in the company of a pretty girl, he followed Elisabeth into the cottage and seated himself at the table.

"Have you been through Somerset of late, sir? Your gloves look of the finest quality."

"Somerset. Devon. Been through them all, mum."

Her ears perked up at the mention of Devon. "Do you

ever pass through Underdown . . . or Bridestone Barrow?"
She poured water into the kettle to heat and splashed a
goodly amount onto herself in anticipation of news from
home, but Thickpenny shook his head.

"I steers clear of Dartmoor, mum. It's no good that's
ever come to a bloke peddlin' through that godforsaken
bog."

"Oh," she said, disappointed that she would learn nothing of Maidenstowe from him. Setting the kettle on its
hook, she turned back to him, deciding it would behoove
her to come directly to the point. "If a lady were low on
coin, Mr. Thickpenny, how would she go about making a
purchase from your cart?"

The peddler bobbed his head from side to side, not at all
shocked by the question. "I've been known to barter on
occasion, mum."

Barter, she thought, her eyes searching the room for
anything of value. But there was nothing. Nothing except—

Her eyes lit on the mantel, causing her to smile, for
indeed she had found the very thing.

Cain returned before sunset that night with a sack of
goods the peddler would have envied. He brought with him
a sugar loaf, a flitch of bacon, flour, a skin of wine, black
puddings, a wheel of cheese, and, to Elisabeth's jubilation,
a pair of kid slippers for her feet and a brush for her hair.
Once out of the sack the brush became a permanent fixture
in her hand as she tried to remove a week's worth of knots
and tangles from the white blond strands. Cain reclined on
the bed supping idly on black pudding sausage and cheese
as he watched her. He cringed as the brush caught time and
again on a hidden snarl, wresting tiny yelps of pain from

her. He flinched as she located the snarl with her fingers and separated individual hairs from around the knotted mass, working it down the length of her hair. When, after an hour, she was only halfway through the project, Cain swigged a final mouthful of wine and swung his legs over the bed.

"I can no longer bear your suffering. Come over here, Elisabeth." When she turned her head, he saw such tears welling in her eyes that he sighed. "The gift was meant to evoke pleasure, not pain. Let me try, love. Mayhap I have a kinder hand."

And indeed, he did. While Elisabeth knelt between his legs, he set about plucking every snarl from her hair, patiently, painlessly, until he could glide a finger through its length without finding a single obstruction. That done, he took up her brush and with long, deft strokes, brushed the pale strands till they were so glossy and flyaway they looked to be spun by angels. He reveled in the intimacy of this most private of rituals, usually enacted by a lady and her maid in the privacy of the lady's bedchamber. In his years of wenching he had done many things to a woman's body, but he had never brushed her hair. Doing so now filled him with such a sense of goodness that he could feel a warm glow kindling inside him. To be a part of someone, to belong—these things were a source of far greater joy to him than a quest for stolen riches and depraved murderers.

He set the brush aside but continued stroking her hair with his hand. In the quiet of the cottage, with the fire crackling in the hearth, he stroked her hair, and was content.

"Shall I model my slippers for you?"

Reluctant to let her go, he nonetheless gave in to her

enthusiasm and lifted his hand from her head. "If that would please you."

"Will you close your eyes?"

He laughed as she crossed the floor to fetch the shoes. "Why so secretive? I have had occasion to see your feet many times over, Elisabeth."

"Perhaps. But on the last occasion you saw very little of my feet and very much of my—" She bit her lip, unable to say the word aloud. Cain fixed her with a slow smile.

"My memory needs no assistance recalling what I saw, lady." Then, in a voice husky with remembered passion he said, "Or what I tasted."

Elisabeth turned her back on him, blushing to her toenails. "Your eyes," she persisted.

So he obliged her, and when next he opened them, she was standing before him wearing the slippers, and nothing else. Blood sluiced to his groin rendering his breeches more insufferable than a stone lodged in too tight boots.

Elisabeth pointed her toe and pivoted her ankle for him. "Do they not look comely?"

Cain couldn't look at her feet. Her hair mantled her body like a veil of palest gossamer, yet where her hair shaded her breasts the veil was parted, exposing the wine-dark thrust of flesh that was peaked with wanting him.

"Jesus," he rasped, pulling her near. He smoothed her hair behind her shoulders, then with his hands riding her hips dipped his head to kiss one of the ribs that underlaid her flesh. "I should not come to you with the dust and sweat of travel still clinging to my body."

Elisabeth loosed the ribbon from his queue and with loving hands ruffled dust from his unbound hair. "You bathe overmuch. A bath, a purge, and a bloodletting in the spring is sufficient for any man." Her eyelids fluttered shut as he traced the curve of her rib to her side. "Look at poor Sir Edmund. Agreed to a bath last year and"—she moistened her lips with a languid motion—"dropped dead afterward."

Cain pressed his mouth to the underside of her breast, lingering there as he murmured, "Nay, lady. He slipped on a cake of soap and broke his neck. At Lady Vain's in London." His hand fumbled with the buttons of his breeches as his mouth rained a circle of kisses about the place on her breast where white flesh fused with wine. "He'd just spent a rousing hour with a saucy chit who sent him off in proper style."

Elisabeth bowed her head against his, luxuriating in the warmth of his mouth, the sleek touch of his desire against her inner leg. "How do you know that?" Her words were nearly slurred with languor.

"Because." Cain lifted her atop him. "I was occupying the room next door." When she made to protest, he found her mouth, and, after awhile, he found something else.

It was dark before Elisabeth cut a slab of bacon to fry for supper that night. Cain sat at the table, oiling the blade of his rapier, and nodded his thanks when Elisabeth poured him another cup of wine.

"I did not tell you earlier." She stoppered the wineskin. "I entertained today."

Cain felt himself grinning. "Rather grandly, I might add."

She rolled her eyes. "I wasn't referring to that. I was referring to earlier. A peddler came by this morning. I served him tea."

He set the blade down and impaled her with a look of horror and alarm, as if she had just told him that Thomas

Penmarck had paid her a neighborly visit. "What did he want?"

She laughed at his reaction. "What does any peddler want? He wanted me to purchase any bit of finery that caught my fancy."

"'Tis unsafe talking to strangers. Need I remind you we are in hiding?"

"He appeared a pleasant enough fellow."

"Thomas Penmarck may appear pleasant, but that doesn't make him any the less dangerous!" Anxiety made his voice loud. Elisabeth responded in kind.

"And what of dangerous-looking men? If looks are so deceiving, should dangerous men not be fairly *bursting* with pleasantry?" She eyed him with cool disdain. "I see none of your seams bulging with the strain." She spun round to tend the bacon. "I have spoken to none other but yourself for a week now. I have no cause for complaint, but perhaps you should tell me if this is how you intend I should spend the remainder of my life." She looked over her shoulder at him, spearing him with her eyes. "Do you expect that I should never again speak to another living being save you? Because if that is what you intend, husband, it would appear I remain in the same prison Quintus built around me. The only thing changed is the face of my jailer."

He returned her stare but could say nothing. For the first time since leaving Thirlstane he could not see the future. What he had always envisioned as his future was a reckoning with Thomas, but now. . .

He could see the moment, but not beyond. He knew he could secrete Elisabeth away in this cottage, but for how long, he did not know. *For the rest of her life?* He could not project that far and the uncertainty filled him with disquiet. She trespassed into areas he was guarding against intrusion. She asked him questions he cared not to think about . . . not now. Not ever. So, thinking to avert further questions in this vein, he tried a different tack. "You accuse me of bathing overmuch. Perhaps I worry overmuch as well. Should I beg your forgiveness for caring more than a tinker's damn about your well-being?"

Elisabeth bowed her head, pondering his words, then came to her feet, sheepish and contrite. She crooked her mouth in apology. "I misspoke. Forgive me. Should you choose to remain here for two score years, I would remain with you, but—"

"Did the peddler succeed in capturing your fancy with any of his wares?" The question further diverted her, for he saw the malaise that clouded her eyes dissolve into something that resembled suppressed excitement. A smile flirted with the corners of her mouth.

"He did. He left me dazzled with the grandness of his sundries. He also left me rather in a quandary over which of two items I should purchase."

"Which were . . . ?"

"Shoes to replace the ones we burned or writing materials with which I might plead your case to Gellicoe Lint."

Cain nodded thoughtfully. "A choice between the future condition of your feet or my neck. An apt reason to find yourself in so great a quandary, but I would hazard the shoes would be the more logical choice."

"Why do you say that?"

"Because as I already told you, lady, your writing to Lint will not necessarily prevent some overzealous thief-taker from finding me."

Scowling darkly, she marched to the bench beneath the window, threw up the seat, and removed her purchases. "*You* may not be interested in saving that mulish head of yours," she said, brandishing parchment and ink at him, "but *I* have acquired quite an inexplicable affection for ragged hair and crooked noses and have no wish to have them snatched from my presence. I expect you to live as long as Quintus, which means you owe me at least a half century more of wedded bliss. So if writing to Gellicoe Lint might gain you pardon, then write to Gellicoe Lint I shall!"

Cain arched a brow at her tirade before lifting a hand to touch his skull. "Ragged hair?"

"Well, not ragged exactly . . . but it could do with a bit of trimming."

He was touched that she had placed his welfare above her own comfort but nonetheless shook his head at her honesty. "You had no coin, Elisabeth. How could you make a purchase without tender?"

"I tendered something other than coin."

He laughed. "Your hand and your virginity have already been spoken for. What more of value was there to offer the man?"

"I offered him something quite expendable."

Cain scanned the contents of the room while Elisabeth packed her acquisitions away. "I see nothing missing."

She shrugged her innocence as she returned to the fire. "Then surely you will never miss it."

Still curious, he continued a mental and visual accounting of their scant possessions. "I trust in future I should afford you coin for these unexpected purchases. One never knows how many pleasant peddlers might happen by."

"He'd been through Somerset recently. And Devon. I asked him if he'd had occasion to pass through Bridestone Barrow, but he hadn't." Her voice turned wistful. "I thought he might carry news from Maidenstowe."

Cain studied her back as she knelt by the fire, her cheerless tone disturbing him. "Do you miss Maidenstowe so much, Elisabeth?"

She grew very still then cocked her head to gaze at the overhead thatching. "Not the place so much. But I miss Frith, and Emma, and I worry that they may think me dead. They have no idea what befell me. I know if I write them, Thomas could become privy to the information, so I hesitate doing that. But I wish they knew I was well, and happy. I wish I could go back to see them, if only for a little while."

But Cain knew they couldn't go back. With a price on his head and thief-takers scouring the byways for him, they could never go back. They could never go anywhere.

He stared into the fire, of a sudden feeling as trapped as he'd been in his bedchamber at Thirlstane. Only this time, he knew of no escape, except perhaps one. "Write your letter, Elisabeth," he said in resignation. "I will post it for you in Padstow." And as he stared, he felt the delicate fabric of his contentment fray at the edges and begin to rend.

May stole silently into June. On the western coast, waves of red valerian blended their colors with the flesh pink of thrift and the whiteness of campion. On the southern coast, the cold gray stone that was Thirlstane sat like an ancient bird of prey atop a lonely precipice. It was during the third full week of June that the doors of the mansion were thrown open to commerce. It was in the late hours of a Thursday afternoon that Thomas Penmarck, beset by a sudden craving for syllabub, made his way into the kitchen to find the cook seemingly bewitched by a man garbed in peddler's smock.

"I have hollow kettles, bodkins, porringers, snuff rasps, and a fine pair of gloves made at Somerset."

"And this," said the cook, pointing to another object. "What is this?"

The peddler lifted the object into his hand and extended the scope. "Long-glass, mum. Pretty thing, ain't it? Don't look to've been used as more than a fancy piece on a mantel."

Thomas's eyes riveted on the piece. His feet stopped cold, and then he was storming toward the man who was enticing his cook with the long-glass *he* had given Elisabeth. Without preamble he snatched it from Thickpenny's hand. "Where did you get this?"

The peddler blinked at the man's rudeness, but rudeness among the aristocracy was something with which Thickpenny was both accustomed and well equipped to handle. "Got that about a month ago, yer lordship."

"I didn't ask how long it has been in your possession," Thomas snapped. "I asked you where you got it."

And because the peddler remembered a cup of morning tea and hair as pale as sliced lemons, he was reluctant to disclose anything that might do the girl ill. "Beggin' yer pardon, yer lordship. But why do you want to know?"

Only with great restraint did Thomas control his temper. "I gave this to the woman who was to be my wife. A yellow-haired woman with blue eyes. She disappeared nearly six weeks ago. Perhaps you can understand how distraught we have been over her disappearance, not knowing whether she has been brutalized, or kidnapped, or worse."

Thickpenny shook his head. "Not been brutalized, yer lordship. If it's the same yellow-haired woman, she's right as rain and pretty as a mornin' glory."

"You've seen her? You've seen Elisabeth?"

"If that's the lady's name. She served me tea and we chatted a bit. Seemed comfortable enough to be where she was, though. Never would have suspected she was there against her will."

"Was there anyone there with her?"

Again, Thickpenny shook his head. "All by herself, she was. But I do remember she asked me if I had news from away. Underdown, she asked about. And Bridestone Barrow."

Thomas shot the scope back into the cylinder with a sharp click. "Did she? Well, it seems we've found our little daffodil, and once you tell me where she is we can return her to the bosom of the family who loves her."

Thickpenny smiled, pleased he had found some way to repay the girl her kind offering of tea.

It was only minutes later that Thomas entered his study, long-glass in hand. He strode toward the chair where a man sat polishing the stock of a military pistol. He slammed the long-glass onto a side table.

The man looked up. He rubbed the scar tissue of his missing ear as he eyed the scope. "You cracked the glass."

"I know where the girl is," Thomas seethed. "Bring her to me. And this time you'd better not disappoint me."

chapter sixteen

"Can you not see that?" Cain pointed to an object that he claimed was floating at the mouth of the cove. "Your eyesight is failing you, Elisabeth. Fetch your long-glass." When she made no attempt to move, he threw her a long look. "Have you suddenly been struck lazy as well as blind?"

"There is little sense fetching what is not there, husband." And to his look of vexation she replied, "'Twas the long-glass I gave to the peddler in exchange for the parchment and ink."

He said nothing, but in the pale blue depths of his eyes she saw something crack like pond ice, making her feel as if she had committed a terrible crime. "'Twas only a gift from Thomas," she said in her defense. "It bore little sentiment."

"It was my mother's," he whispered.

Every functioning organ within her ground to a halt. Of *course* it was his mother's. Thomas had told her on the day he'd given it to her that it had belonged to Cicely Penmarck. But on that morning a month ago, she hadn't made the connection. The only thought in her head had been to obtain the writing materials at any cost. "I'm sorry, Cain. I . . ."

He plucked a stone from the ground and hurled it far over the side of the cliff. " 'Tis done. Think no more of it."

But she couldn't help thinking of it. And judging from the rigid set of Cain's jaw, she imagined he would rather be hurling *her* over the side of the cliff than the stone he had settled for. "We could try to find the peddler. Buy it back from him."

Cain hefted another stone into his hand, drew back his arm, and let it fly. He nodded in response to her suggestion, but he did not look at her.

She sighed inwardly. Ever since the day she had written her letter, she had noticed an almost imperceptible change in her husband. Small things. His moods more quiet. His eyes more brooding. They still talked, and laughed, and loved, but in those moments when he sat alone, she noticed a troubled look about him, as if he were bearing the weight of the world on his shoulders. She understood he had much to resolve in his own mind, so she did not torment him with endless questions. But she hoped that after tomorrow night, he might feel compelled to smile with a trifle more ease.

Cain had added a note to her letter requesting a meeting with Miles Loveland on the night of Friday, twenty-four June, at a place on Bodmin Moor that was familiar to them both. If Loveland showed, he would bring news with him of London, and news of how Gellicoe Lint might assist in extricating Cain from the difficulties her accusation had caused him. But she somehow sensed there was more to

Cain's withdrawal than anxiety about what news Miles Loveland would impart on the morrow.

She cast a glance seaward, following the direction of Cain's gaze. " 'Tis no longer enough, is it." Her words were more statement of fact than question—words she knew he would be unable to deny. She heard his breath sough through his mouth.

"I thought it would be, Elisabeth, but . . ." His tone became strained, irritated. "I think of Thomas Penmarck giving away the treasures that belonged to my mother. I think of him flaunting ill-gotten riches and freedom while I rot in a gypsy's cottage. I think how I must deny you your family home, the people you love. I think of the man who killed your grandfather walking the earth freely in his guilt while we wallow here in innocence. I think of these things, and it eats away at my soul until I think, Nay. 'Tis no longer enough. I don't love you any the less, Elisabeth, but I suppose I somehow thought that by loving you I could blind myself to the reality of that other part of my life. I can't. I thought I could, but I can't."

"Thank God," breathed Elisabeth, and when Cain swung his head round she favored him with a look that bespoke much more than understanding. "I did not expect our love to obliterate the truth, my love. And the truth is that Thomas Penmarck is guilty of terrible misdeeds and must be brought to justice. But not by you. He must be tried by his peers in the Court of the King's Bench. He has only lies and half-truths to support him. We have the white raven and the riches of Maidenstowe. So it pleases me you are tiring of Paradise. There is a new season upon us. 'Tis a time to heal; a time to cast away stones; a time to gather stones together. We will see the wrong done you righted, Cain. Perhaps then, loving me will be enough."

He drew her hand into his and held it tightly, and in his silence she felt his gratitude.

He left early the next day, for the place where he was to meet Loveland was a ride of many leagues.

"Are you sure I cannot come with you?" she wheedled.

He smiled down at her from his saddle, then leaning far over the side, braced his arm around her waist and lifted her high off the ground to meet his waiting mouth. He kissed her long and hungrily and against her throat murmured, "'Tis still unsafe, 'Lisbeth. But after tonight I hope we will no longer have need to hide. Pray that Loveland will be the bearer of good tidings."

She watched him go, and as she stared after him, watching his silhouette fade into the darkness of the moor, she felt as if she were reliving another moment in her life, and it chilled her to the bone. When she could no longer see him, she touched a finger to the lips that were still warm with his kiss, and turned away. But in her mind's eye all she could see was the top of a frizzed periwig poking above a sofa back, and all she could hear was the terrible silence that had echoed her grandfather's death. She had never questioned Cain's abilities to defend himself, but as she walked back to the cottage she found herself in sudden fear of his life.

The feeling persisted throughout the morning. It was with her as she collected mussels and weeded the garden. It deepened as she washed bed linens and laid them out to dry. But it was when she was cutting a slice of black pudding for her supper and looked up to see a man standing in the doorway, sword drawn, that she knew her fear had been real, but unfortunately, misplaced.

The night was black as a hangman's hood. On Bodmin Moor a low peat fire devoured a small slice of the darkness and threw scant illumination on the faces of the two men who kept company around it.

"Lint didn't make public the contents of Elisabeth's letter?"

Miles Loveland gaped at Cain. "Letter? The only thing Lint has been doing these past weeks is burying people. I gather you didn't hear about the outbreak of jail fever at Newgate. When the prisoners came to trial at the Bailey, they spread the fever to just about everyone in attendance. Judges, jurymen. Between finding replacement judges and personally overseeing vinegar baths for the prisoners who aren't sick, Lint had no time for letter reading, except for the one he received from your lady a month ago. The man's always had a soft spot for you, hasn't he? And damned if I know why."

"So there's no price on my head?"

"On your head? Not that I'm aware of. But there's a buxom wench of your acquaintance in Whitechapel who's been asking about your—"

"Have you come this long way to tell me of naught but jail fever?"

"I told you you're not sporting a price on your head. That seemed a scrap of welcome news. And I've two more messages for you. Lint tells me there can be no suspicion of guilt where there are no accusations. I assume you can derive some meaning from that?"

Cain nodded. Lint was not blaming him for Quintus's

murder. He would thus be free to come out of hiding without endangering Elisabeth's safety. "And the second message?"

"Before the outbreak of the fever he set some men about snooping for you. The name Skagg was familiar to one of them. Said it belonged to some tough who'd lost an ear in the military. Works as a toady now for gentlemen of quality. He hasn't been seen in the city for some weeks, but someone recognized him as one of two men who were occupying a table at the Horn on the Hoop at the beginning of May."

"And the other man?"

"An acquaintance of yours. Thomas Penmarck."

Cain had been staring into the fire. His head shot up at the mention of Thomas's name. "Penmarck? This Skagg is Penmarck's lackey?"

"One would think. Our informant tells us that coin exchanged hands at the meeting."

Cain's mind became a whir. He remembered the morning in the stable block when he had dispatched Thomas like a naughty child and Thomas had vowed revenge for the insult. It made sense now. He had not been struck down outside the Saracen's Head by a legion of enemies. He had been struck down by a man exacting retribution for Thomas Penmarck. "And still he tries to kill me," he rasped. His uncle had tried to harm him in two lifetimes, once as Stephen and once as Cain. He had tried twice, and failed twice, and the frightening look on Cain's face attested to the fact that the man would never be allowed another opportunity. Elisabeth wanted to see Thomas tried before his peers, but Cain knew it was too late for that. He would have his final reckoning with his uncle, but *he* would act the part of judge, and his blade would be the jury.

"Does the information help?" Loveland asked as Cain rose to his full height.

"It helps me a great deal," said Cain. "It helps Thomas Penmarck not at all."

He rode through the night, pushed by a sense of urgency he could not explain. He decided that when he arrived back at the cottage, he would gather together Elisabeth's belongings and take her to an inn in Padstow where she would be safe until he settled matters with his uncle. She would object, he suspected, but it did not sit well with him to leave her alone for more than a day. There was safety in numbers. More safety than an isolated cottage could afford.

By noontime the following day he could smell the salt air. By three he was ducking his head beneath the lintel of the cottage door, but what he found upon crossing the threshold made him think he had just crossed the threshold to hell.

The table was lying on its side. Mussels lay scattered and smashed on the floor. A chair was overturned, its stay-rail and spindles broken off. The reed basket was upended, its bottom ruptured, as if someone had driven a fist through it.

Beads of perspiration prickled his hairline as he circled the table.

The black pudding lay by the hearth. Beside it rested the dagger he had left Elisabeth for her use about the cottage.

He hunkered down. Lifted the dagger.

A veneer not unlike rust befouled the steel. Blood. Dried blood.

But whose?

If it was Elisabeth's . . .

His heart hammered so violently that for a moment he could not breathe. "Thomas," he choked out, knowing without a doubt where she was and who had taken her. *"You baaastarrrd!"* He gripped the dagger so tightly that his hand numbed. If it was Elisabeth's blood glazing his knife, it would be Thomas's heart that sheathed the blade for all eternity.

With eyes blazing like a madman he mounted Scylla and spurred him toward the south—toward Thirlstane—where the child known as Stephen Penmarck had once lived, and died.

The buzzing in Elisabeth's head diminished to a drone and then an irritating hum. The pain in her jaw, however, did not diminish. In fact it seemed to increase as she drifted unwillingly into consciousness. She groaned and lifted a comforting hand to her face.

"You should have been more cooperative, Elisabeth."

She inched her eyelids open to find Thomas standing over her.

"I instructed my associate to treat you with a gentle hand, but really, my dear, breaking a chair over his back? And the cut on his arm is quite nasty. One can hardly find the man blameworthy for having to resort to such drastic measures. Though the bruise on your cheek *is* rather colorful. Perhaps he should have restrained himself a bit."

The intrusion of light stung her eyes, causing them to water. She made a blindfold of her hand.

"You missed the wedding, Elisabeth. It might have been rather a festive affair had the bride deigned to make an appearance, but you obviously had more pressing affairs to distract you. Your steward told me you disappeared without a trace, that your horse was found wandering the moors. The poor man feared you'd been carried off by thieves. I would guess you'd been carried off by someone. How else would you explain your arrival on the coast of Cornwall? You surely didn't make the journey on foot. And you seem in so glowing a state of health. How does a woman, alone, find the means to survive in the middle of nowhere?"

Elisabeth squinted her eyes open again. She was in a room—a bedchamber—but it was not a grand salon. It was small and modest and smelled as if it had not been aired for a very long time. "Where am I?"

"Can there be any doubt in your mind about where you are? You are where you belong, Elisabeth. You're at Thirlstane. And if you don't object, I think I should be the person asking the questions. I am, after all, the one who has suffered the most embarrassment from this unfortunate situation." Hands clasped behind his back, he began to pace. "You lied to me. You told me you wanted to see the thief-taker hanged from the highest gallows in England. A fortnight later you run off with the man. Can you explain that happenstance to me, Elisabeth?"

"I didn't—"

"*Don't* tell me you didn't run off with him!" His eyes burned like coals in his head as he thrust an accusing finger at her. "You were slicing black pudding sausage with his dagger! Don't play me for a fool!" Tiny cracks scored his cosmetic as his face contorted with his rage. "You have been *living* with the man, haven't you! What else have you been doing with him? Or do I even need ask?"

She returned his look glare for glare, for the first time seeing that Thomas was not so much dour and mirthless as he was diabolical, without conscience, and she felt suddenly compelled to hurt him as much as he had hurt Cain. "I suspect your imaginings wouldn't do justice to half what I've been doing, Thomas. But a lady should never divulge to anyone the details of the intimacies she shares with her husband."

He shook his head, skeptical yet . . . "You could not—"

"I could. We did. Cain is husband to me in every sense that the word implies."

He stared at her, disbelieving. "You did this to me, Elisabeth? You did this knowing how long I have waited to make you my wife?" He strode to a chair and seated himself, as if her declaration were too great a burden for him to bear. "So where was your illustrious husband when my associate found you? Reckless of him to leave you unattended. But I imagine his absence saved him his throat. Otherwise my associate might have felt constrained to finish what he started so many weeks ago. He does so hate leaving loose ends dangling about."

"Loose ends?" She narrowed her eyes, unsure of his meaning, until she recalled Cain's description of the trio of men at the Saracen's Head—the same three men he suspected of attacking him on the road. He had referred to them as "unholy" looking. The man she had fought with at the cottage was nothing if not unholy looking. "Your associate, the man who dragged me here, he was the one responsible for ambushing Cain, wasn't he? *Your* man. You wanted Cain dead as far back as May. Dear God, why?"

Thomas lifted a painted eyebrow. "He insulted me. Or had you forgotten?"

"You wanted him dead because of what happened in the stable block? You *deserved* to be insulted that morning! How far would you have gone if he hadn't stopped you?"

"Are you implying I would have compromised your virtue?" Indignation made his voice shrill. "I wanted a simple kiss! One small sign of affection. Nothing more. Do you deem that so unreasonable a request after a year's betrothal and a lifetime's acquaintance? Do you think me a sybarite? A voluptuary? I am *none* of those things! I have never so much as *lain* with a woman! Does that surprise you? Do you find it impossible to believe that a man would so love you that he could deny himself the pleasures of woman-flesh until the day he made you his wife? Can your thief-taker lay claim to so self-sacrificing a feat? Despite what you may think, I love you, Elisabeth. I have always loved you."

"You love me? You expect me to believe that a man who thinks death a fitting punishment for insult knows anything of love? You sanctioned your henchman to slay Cain. Did you sanction that same henchman to bury the dagger in my grandfather's heart?"

Thomas shook his bewigged head. "The man was much too indisposed to do anything of the kind. But as you've already witnessed, his condition is greatly improved. So much improved, in fact, that I think another visit to the western coast might be in order. And yes, my dear, you have every reason to look concerned. But as you well know, a lady is allowed only one husband, and I intend to be the sole bearer of the title. As for your present spouse, I think an unfortunate accident awaits him. Thief-takers are so susceptible to accidents these days."

"An accident?" Elisabeth mocked. "Like the accident your brother suffered?"

He forced a smile that did not quite reach his eyes. "You spout nonsense, Elisabeth. Apparently Skagg's blow damaged more than just your lovely jaw." He came easily to his feet. "You were unconscious for an infinitely long time. Perhaps you need more rest to fully regain control of your faculties."

"Leaving the room won't enable you to alter the truth!" she flung at his retreating back.

He paused at the door and bowed his head toward the chamber's lone window embrasure, ignoring her comment as he had ignored anything she'd said over the years. "'Tis quite a long drop to the sea from this height. Your lunatic ravings necessitate my having to lock you inside, but I might warn you to consider the hazards of escape. Someone disappeared through that window once, with disastrous results."

Elisabeth's gaze flitted about the room, from the diamond-paned windows, to the bookshelves, to the book stand and Bible in the corner. It struck her then whose room she was occupying and why it smelled so close. "It was your nephew who disappeared, wasn't it?" This, as Thomas had the door halfway open. He peered back over his shoulder at her.

"I don't recall telling you of my nephew, Elisabeth. Perhaps because he didn't live long enough to warrant telling about. But you're quite correct. This was his room. Poor lad fell to his death quite some time ago. My only living relative. I was understandably heartbroken over the incident."

"You disgusting creature," she spat. "Do you paint yourself with ceruse because 'tis the height of fashion or because you cannot bear seeing your reflection in the mirror? I *know* of Stephen. I know what you did to him in this room, and I know you suffered not one moment's heartache over his disappearance."

Thomas closed the door and turned back to her, an odd expression on his face. "Where did you hear the name Stephen spoken?"

"From the lips of a man who once knew him."

He took slow steps toward the bed, his eyes never leaving her face. "Everyone who knew the boy is dead. The servants were old. They passed on only a few years after the boy's death."

"The boy did not die," corrected Elisabeth. And when she saw further confusion creep into his eyes, she added, "He is my husband."

The sounds of Thomas's laughter exploded within the confines of the room. He threw back his head and held his side then grabbed the stay-rail of the nearest chair for support. "What a clever jest," he howled before dissolving into another round of mirth.

"'And the Lord set a mark upon Cain,'" Elisabeth shouted above the sound of his laughter, "'lest any finding him should kill him.'"

His laughter ceased abruptly. His face grew sober, as if he remembered having recited that same passage in this room years before. Her jest seemed suddenly no jest at all.

"Do you not think the name appropriate?" she taunted him. "Cain. You thought his face familiar. You simply assigned his ancestry to the wrong family. He is *your* ancestor, not mine. And the name—why, you placed that seed in his head when you placed the mark upon his palm. You do remember branding him with the felon's mark? Why else do you think he wears the glove on his hand?"

He opened his mouth, but no words were forthcoming.

"He will see you brought to justice for the murder of his father," she continued, "and then he will delight in stripping you of everything you have gained wrongfully from him."

Thomas gripped the back of the chair. His eyes leaped with agitation. "There is no proof that Justin's death was anything more than an accident. He deludes you with fantasies."

"He *heard* you boast of the plot!"

"And who do you think would believe the babblings of an eight-year-old? An eight-year-old who died twenty-four years ago!"

"There is no body! When the constable digs up Stephen Penmarck's grave, he will find it empty. How can you verify the boy's death without his body? You can't. It will prove that Stephen lives."

A smug look replaced Thomas's earlier agitation. He smiled. "There never was a body, Elisabeth. Stephen's gravesite is only a memorial. 'Tis common knowledge his body washed out to sea. So the constable can exhume anything he wishes from the family cemetery, but none of it will aid your thief-taker in proving his identity as Stephen Penmarck. I fear the only thing your husband can prove is that he bears the mark of a thief on his palm."

Elisabeth foundered, until she remembered the one thing that would substantiate Cain's identity beyond a doubt. "He has the ring," she announced. "He has the white raven. How will you explain the existence of two signet rings when there should be but one?"

This, indeed, gave him pause. His eyes darted left and right, as if he were ferreting out an answer in the corners of the room. "He can't have the ring. He died with the ring in his possession. It lies at the bottom of the sea with his wretched bones. 'Tis why I had another fashioned."

Elisabeth pressed her advantage. "If it becomes apparent that the raven did not wash out to sea, perhaps you will have difficulty sustaining the belief that your nephew did too. Cain may have to expend little effort convincing the members of the King's Bench that he is who he says he is. And then, my dear Thomas, you will have much to answer for."

His eyes began to glow with a maniacal kind of fire. His breathing grew erratic. He began to pace again, taking short, choppy steps, and as he paced Elisabeth watched him slowly unravel. "I won't let them take anything away from me. I won't! 'Tis mine now. Everything is mine. The land, the power. Without power a man is nothing. A second son is nothing! He's an . . . an inconvenience who must be shepherded out to the military to justify his existence. Without the land I'm nothing more than a . . . a cripple who must depend on the generosity of relatives for his livelihood, who must endure their piteous looks as I hobble past them. 'Poor Thomas. Sad thing about his birth.' I endured those looks for years, but I will never endure them again. Thomas Penmarck, cripple, evokes pity. The Earl of Moreleigh commands respect *despite* his infirmity. I will allow no one to strip that from me! I will not be embarrassed by my condition ever again. I will not be laughed at!"

Elisabeth was awestruck. "Is that your rationale for plotting other peoples' deaths? That someone once laughed at you?"

"It was more than once!" he bellowed. "My leg made me different. Everyone takes great pleasure in laughing at those of us who are different. I remember the face of every person who ever laughed, and I will never forgive them. Just as I will never forgive your grandfather for what he tried to do to me."

"Quintus?" A sick feeling settled in the pit of her stomach. "What did Quintus try to do to you?" But she knew. Even before he answered, she knew what he would say.

"He intended to make them laugh again. Do you know what he called me? He called me a self-righteous prig. He told me he had changed his mind about the betrothal. That you no longer wished to marry me. What kind of laughing-stock would that make me? It would make me an object of ridicule throughout the realm. I couldn't countenance that. It was unspeakable."

"So you killed him," Elisabeth said softly. "Your hench-man was indisposed, so you killed him yourself."

"I had no other choice! It wasn't my original intent when I rode to Maidenstowe that night, but the old man was in the room and started yammering at me as soon as I was through the door. I'd ridden to Maidenstowe with only one purpose in mind. To see if Skagg had inflicted a mortal wound on the thief-taker."

"But you never made it to the second floor. You killed Quintus, and stole the dragon, then left Cain's dagger behind to cast all suspicion on him."

"What else was I to do?"

"He was a defenseless old man!" she screamed at him.

"He was going to deny me the right to make you my wife! He didn't care that I love you, just as you seem not to care. But what I feel for you is real, Elisabeth. And neither your grandfather nor my nephew will ever stand in the way of my laying claim to your hand."

"My hand? You care not one whit about my hand. You want Maidenstowe. You want *more* land, *more* wealth, *more* power. Why else would you want to bind yourself in marriage to a woman who has lain with another? To a woman who may already be quickening with another man's seed?"

He glowered at her, but in that look she divined an emotion that engendered something other than hatred. Something she could not fathom. "Be not mistaken, Elisabeth. You will never lie with him again. Where is the ring? Does he carry it with him?"

"He does not have the ring. 'Tis hidden. At Maidenstowe."

"Where?"

It was in her jewelry coffer, but she could not tell that to Thomas. She had to find some way to escape this room, to escape this place. "I buried it in the garden," she lied. "In the area where I usually plant sundew."

Her answer confounded him. He frowned. "And how am I to know where you usually plant sundew?"

"'Tis beside the gromwell. I assume you know gromwell."

This precipitated further confusion. He had never heard of gromwell much less seen it. And she was being much too biddable. "Never mind telling me where it is. I will take you with me. Then you can simply show me. That seems the most timely thing to do, doesn't it? You and I will see to the ring, and Skagg will see to your husband. But I think it will be unnecessary to send my associate all the way back to the coast. Your husband will no doubt come looking for you. When he does, Skagg will be waiting. Do not relax. We'll be leaving shortly."

He closed the door behind him and turned the key in the lock. Elisabeth searched the room with her eyes, hoping she had done the right thing. Her chances for escape would be greater on the moors than they would be in this room. Here, she was in Thomas's stronghold, at his mercy. Out there, at least, they would be on relatively equal footing. She could delay him, stall for time in the hopes that Cain might come after her. Would he know where to look for her?

How can he possibly know? she thought. But as she recalled how intertwined their lives were with Thomas Penmarck and Thirlstane, she thought, *How can he not?*

They left the manse before two hours had passed. Thomas was in such a state of frenzy that he never thought to ask how Cain had escaped twenty-four years ago, and Elisabeth, having unlatched the windows in her room, never offered to tell him.

chapter
seventeen

Cain entered Thirlstane the same way he had escaped. In the darkness. Down the false crypt in the graveyard. Through the underground shaft and tunnel. Up the stone ledges. Through the windows of the room that had once served as his prison.

He withdrew his sword.

The house was filled with shadows, with silence. He stole across the second-floor landing and down the main staircase. A riser creaked beneath his feet.

"I know you're out there," came the man's voice. Cain spun to his left. The voice emanated from the room that had served as his father's study. A faint, flickering light gilded the doorway. "Come in, thief-taker. We have a score that needs settling."

Cain circled round the base of the staircase. He peered into the room.

The man sat a chair facing the portal. In each hand he brandished a pistol at half-cock. He motioned to Cain with the barrel of one weapon. "I've been expecting you. I won't ask how you got in. I'll only ask you to lay down your sword and remove your bandoleer." A flick of his thumbs brought the pistols to full-cock. "Now."

Cain stepped into the room.

"On the floor," said Skagg, indicating the place where Cain should deposit his weapons. "Quickly, boy, quickly. I'm anxious to repay the kindness you dealt my shoulder. And your uncle is anxious to be rid of your pretty face."

Cain tossed his sword onto the floor in front of him. "Where is Elisabeth?"

"Ah yes. Your wife. Strange what an ill effect a woman can have on a man. They can drive you nearly insane, can't they? They can make you feel powerful. Invincible. They can make you feel as if you can rescue them from the enemy and actually escape with all your body parts still attached to the right places. The world would be better off without the little chits flitting about, but you're not going to be well off at all unless your bandoleer joins your sword before I draw another breath."

Cain dropped his bandoleer beside his sword. Skagg nodded his approval.

"I see you're not entirely stupid. But I saw that a long time ago. It's one of the reasons why I suggested getting rid of you. In fact if I had been the one wielding a hot iron those many years ago, I guarantee you would have stayed dead, and I wouldn't have to be bothering myself with you tonight."

Cain narrowed his eyes at the comment. Skagg sneered his delight.

"Do I detect confusion in the mighty thief-taker's eyes? Perhaps if I tell you where your wife is you'll be less confused. She and your uncle raced off to Maidenstowe to dig up a bird—a white raven to be exact. But you already know about the ring, don't you? Once the bird is caged I imagine your uncle will take great pleasure sampling what you've already tasted. I've never had a wife, but I've seen what Thomas does to women. I should warn you, it's not a pretty sight."

Cain's fury spilled into his eyes. As he made to lunge forward, Skagg steadied his pistol at his groin. "Far enough. I'm not quite ready to blow you into oblivion. That's a good fellow. Just stand there awhile and think about your bride in Penmarck's arms. Think about the places where a man could have his way with a woman at Maidenstowe and never be found." He laughed at a private jest. "I wasn't so lucky. I got careless. But it was the woman's fault. They always make you feel so invincible. And she wanted me. She was hot after me from the minute I set foot on the grounds. But no one would believe ill of the Lady Constance. So the old man threw me out in a trice when he found out what we'd been up to. He didn't wait for explanations. He didn't want to hear anything from a man who was nothing more than a stable master."

"You?" Cain rasped, remembering Elisabeth's preoccupation with her Aunt Constance and Maidenstowe's stable master.

"Me. So you see, if it hadn't been for Quintus St. Mary, I might never have met Thomas Penmarck. You have the old man to thank for your forthcoming demise."

Cain eyed the man's pistols. *Military issue*. He recalled Loveland's information. And he suddenly knew the one denominator that had allied Skagg and his uncle. "You and Thomas were in the military together."

Skagg bowed his head. "A common ground that brings

together wandering stable masters and second sons alike. But if you knew anything of His Majesty's service, you'd know that the officers are treated like royalty and the recruits like dogs."

"A title that well suits you," Cain derided. "You should have fit in admirably."

Skagg drew his mouth into a sneer. "I didn't fit in at all. I despised every detail of his supreme majesty's service. So I left."

"You deserted."

Skagg laughed. "I deserted. And it was Captain Thomas Penmarck who came after me. He was all of twenty years old and his chest was so bloated with his newfound power that he was an easy mark indeed. 'What one thing would you give up your sword hand to own?' I asked him. 'You let me go, and I promise you, that one thing will become yours.'"

Cain felt a wave of bile rising in his throat. "He wanted what was my father's," he said in a strangulated voice. "He wanted what would one day belong to me."

"He did indeed. And I was the one who gave it to him. But he couldn't very well just take me at my word, could he?" He tossed his head back, clearing hair from the place where his ear had once rested. He bared the scar for Cain's perusal. "He told me if I didn't keep my part of the bargain, he'd find me and lop off the other one. He enjoyed wielding that sword. It made him feel so important. He was so brave when he sat his horse with his pistol in one hand and sword in the other. Too bad he's such a sniveling coward under all that bravado. I bartered my soul to a milksop and there's not a day that goes by that I don't despise him for it."

"You became what you wanted to become."

"No!" Skagg yelled. "I was forced into it! First with your father, now with you, and one day I'll kill Penmarck himself."

Blood began to pound in Cain's temples. It was Skagg who had killed his father. Skagg whose voice he'd heard in conversation with his uncle so many years ago. "You murdering bastard. You ugly son of a—"

"Ugly? You see this face? There was a time when the ladies called this face handsome. But not anymore. Do you know why? Because hatred has taken its toll. It's eaten lines into my flesh. Hatred for that slut Constance, and Quintus St. Mary, and Thomas Penmarck. I can see the same hatred in your eyes, thief-taker, but you're not going to live long enough to let it distort your pretty face."

Cain saw the change in the man's eyes—that sudden glint that augered the break between saying and doing. And in that half second, as he imagined Skagg's finger squeezing the trigger, he let fly the blade that was sheathed at his wrist.

Skagg cried out as the blade plunged deep into his throat. Cain dropped to his stomach. One pistol fired. Cain seized his rapier and rolled to his feet. Skagg doubled over in the chair and slumped to the floor. His pistols skated out of his reach.

Cain strode to the chair. With the toe of his boot he rolled the body onto its back. Skagg's eyes were open and lucid. There was a bubbling sound in his throat. "Kill . . . Penmarck," he gasped in a gurgling breath. "For me."

With the mercy Cain might render any animal, he picked up the unfired pistol. "The knife," he said as he leveled the gun at Skagg's head, "was for my father. This," he squeezed the trigger, "is for me."

Having ridden for two days and nights, stopping only long enough to rest and water the horses, Elisabeth realized she should have been exhausted. But she wasn't. Her nerves were riding a razor's edge. She could no more surrender to fatigue than she could surrender to Thomas's deranged will. She rode beside and slightly behind him, tethered to him by a lead line on her mount's bridle. It was the one precaution he had taken to check any idea she might entertain of escape. So far, it had been successful. So far, she had played the docile captive. But she suspected Thomas was not aware that docility could cloak stouter fabric.

For two days, as they made their way north and east, she had had the opportunity to study the leg that Thomas claimed had been the source of such derision for him. She had lent no thought to the leg in the years she had known him, most probably because his elevated sole allowed him to walk without so much as a limp. But she wondered if, even without the boot, he had ever limped so much as to provoke peoples' laughter. Had they actually laughed, or had the mimicry taken place solely in Thomas's mind? She thought of the peddler, Thickpenny, who traveled the byways on a wooden stump. He had no doubt been made fun of in his lifetime, but she questioned if he sought redress by murdering his tormentors. She would guess not. Strange how some men could be presented with the same set of circumstances and react so differently to them. Perhaps Thomas would have found life more palatable had he been born a peddler rather than a second son.

It was nearing late afternoon. They were deep within the interior wilds of Dartmoor, skirting the Forest of Bellever in their journey toward Maidenstowe. Elisabeth worked her head back and forth, wondering when they would stop again to water the horses. She'd been able to delay Thomas only a few short minutes each time they had stopped, but she hoped those precious seconds had worked to Cain's benefit. He would keep up a merciless pace until he found her. She knew he would. And so thinking, she shot a look behind her, hoping, praying she would see a horseman in the distance.

"He's not coming," said Thomas. She pivoted her head back, crossing glances with him. "Skagg is quite thorough, and you, my dear, are quite alone. But it grieves me that you appear so forlorn. I suppose the anguish of losing a grandfather *and* a husband in so short a time has left its mark on you."

She would not believe Cain dead. He had outwitted Skagg once. He would do so again.

But a niggling fear began to gnaw at her. What if Skagg had gained the upper hand? What if Cain would not be coming after her?

She eyed Thomas's back. He had killed before. What would happen when he discovered that the signet ring was not buried in the garden—that she had lied about its whereabouts? Would he become so angry as to harm Frith or Emma or anyone else at Maidenstowe? Dare she set foot on the grounds of the estate if there was a possibility of that happening?

She was the mistress of Maidenstowe. It was her duty to protect those who devoted their lives to the St. Mary name.

She could not allow Thomas near Maidenstowe to harm anyone else she loved.

She would not allow it.

"The East Dart is just ahead," warned Thomas. "We'll water the horses there."

She saw the massive slabs of granite that spanned the river, and beyond that, like the teeth in an angry maw, the hulking shapes of the moorland's many tors. She knew that one of those shapes was Bowerman's Nose, and another, farther still, was a spired tower that was as malignant as a cancer. She had nearly lost her life on that tower. If she led Thomas there, she could very well die on the summit, but so too could Thomas. They would be free of him then. Safe. And never again would he be able to hurt another being.

She remembered what Cain had said about the darkness in the tunnel at Thirlstane. He had lived through it—lived through the worst fear life could offer him—and he had emerged unscathed. She had lived through fear of a different kind, fear of condemnation, but she too had emerged unscathed, unscathed and stronger. Her weakness had become her strength. So there seemed little left to warrant her fear, neither man, nor storm, nor rabid hounds, for she had already lived through the worst. She had lived through it once and did not cower from doing so again. She was no longer ruled by her fear, so she could face the danger of Hound Tor unafraid. The risk to herself would be enormous, but she understood now that there were times when you had to be courageous enough to risk everything to achieve your purpose.

This was one of those instances. And Hound Tor, once her enemy, was about to become her friend.

On the near side of the clapper bridge, Thomas guided her down the shallow embankment to the river's edge and dismounted. With the tether to her horse still secure in his hand, he led the animals to water, but as Elisabeth's mount dipped his head to drink, Elisabeth spoke with some distress.

"The horses are not the only creatures on the moor with bodily needs, Thomas."

"You wish a drink?"

"I drank some time ago. 'Tis another need I must relieve now."

Reluctantly, he dropped the reins of his own horse and clucked at Elisabeth's to swing round so he could assist her from her sidesaddle. "Don't even think of leaving my sight," he cautioned as he raised his arms toward her waist. "There is nowhere here you can—"

She drove her foot into his chest and with every ounce of strength within her, shoved. He stumbled backward, hands flying outward to balance himself. She ripped the tether from his hand and as he tottered on the lip of the riverbank, she swung her mount sharply left, forcing him off solid ground and into—

Splat!

Amid a backdrop of shouts and splashes she wheeled her horse around and pounded up the embankment, uprooting every sprig of greenery in her path. She charged across the clapper bridge. By the time Thomas could remount his horse, she would have a substantial lead on him—near enough for him to still see her, but far enough so he would be unable to catch her.

With eyes focused on a distant peak she raced toward the southeast.

Toward a place that would spell her salvation or her doom.

Toward Hound Tor.

Cain didn't know how far he was behind them. He might have gained two hours, four hours. He might have gained no time at all. He had crossed into Dartmoor at its southwest tip, following the course of the River Plym. From here he could chart a path along the River Swincombe to the confluence of the East and West Dart, cross the clapper bridge at Dartmeet, and from there, head directly north. It was late afternoon. He still had a ride of several hours ahead of him, and with each passing hour, the images that haunted him became more unbearable.

What would he find when he arrived at Maidenstowe?

He dug his spurs into Scylla's flanks and pushed relentlessly forward.

At the base of Hound Tor's eastern slope, where a break in the vegetation allowed for entry to higher ground, Elisabeth clambered off her horse. The animal was one of the fine St. Mary blacks Thomas had purchased from their stables. She recalled the fate of the cob she had ridden to this place in May, so having no wish that this animal suffer the same fate, she sent him on his way with a rousing slap on his rump. That done, she hiked up her petticoat and waded through the first wave of brambles that obstructed her path. Beyond, the tor rose dark and ominous before her. She fought her way out of the brambles, then swallowing her fear, began her ascent.

Halfway up the incline she looked back. Thomas stood at the base of the tor peering up at her. She watched him tie

his horse to a bramble and remove his pistol and powder
flask from his saddle pouch, and then, to her satisfaction
and terror, she watched him begin the climb after her.

Twilight. On the northern horizon Cain could make out
the spires of Hameldown, Hookney, and King Tors, but in
the foreground, he spied something else, and he spurred
Scylla toward it.

A riderless horse.

But not just any horse. This one was a St. Mary black—
alone, strapped with a sidesaddle, and grazing on a sparse
patch of clover. Thomas bred St. Mary blacks. It had to be
Thomas's horse, Elisabeth's mount. But where was Elisabeth?

He combed the horizon from west to east. He was surrounded by a veritable mountain range of tors, from Hameldown in the north, to Hound in the east, to Hay in the
south. Thomas might have grown impatient. He might
have decided that the isolation of the moors provided him
an ideal place to force himself on Elisabeth . . . if he hadn't
done so already.

With rage flaming in his eyes Cain searched the moor.

They were out there somewhere. But where?

It was then he heard the echoing fire of the pistol.

Darkness. Elisabeth touched the pile of stones she had
gathered, assuring herself they were still there. She had
thought to hurl them at Thomas if he charged the summit,
but he had not yet made his move. So she waited, perched
behind one of the saw-toothed spires that impaled the tor's
crown, her ears pricked, her palms cold and clammy. She

poked her head out from behind the spire and peered down the face of the incline.

Earlier, just before dusk, she had seen him moving among the rocks, but then she had lost sight of him. She'd heard his pistol discharge but had no idea whether the firing was accidental or a deliberate ploy. Was this one of the tactics he had employed to apprehend deserters while in the military? She thought she'd outwitted him by gaining higher ground, but now, with darkness surrounding them, she wondered who had outwitted whom. She heard faint skittering noises somewhere below her. Thomas? Or wild dogs? Could she even be sure that Thomas was still alive? Had he fatally wounded himself when his gun discharged? If he was alive, where was he? Dear God, what was he waiting for?

With her nerves threatening to shatter she grabbed one of her stones. "Thomas!" she screamed into the night, then springing to her feet, hurtled the stone down the face of the tor. Her voice reverberated across the moorland. The stone thwacked onto the bedrock and ricocheted sharply. "What are you waiting for?" she shrieked.

No answer.

She seized another stone and just as she drew her arm back to fling it, she heard a noise close behind her. She whipped around.

A hand clamped itself over her mouth, yanked her against a chest that was firm and broad. "Do not cry out," a voice instructed against her ear. "Can you do that for me?" And she nodded breathless compliance, for the voice was not Thomas's. It was Cain's.

His fingers slackened. He turned her in his arms and then she felt the hot pressure of his mouth against her own, kissing her with a passion born of his fear. He bruised her lips with his frenzy. He filled her mouth with his ragged breath. He tasted and touched her, and only when she pushed against his chest did he seem ready to let her go.

"It was Thomas who killed Quintus," Elisabeth gasped out, safe within the circle of his arms. "He's insane and he's out there somewhere, but I don't know—"

"Did he hurt you?"

She braced her forehead against his chin. "Nay." Relief flooded her voice. "He did not hurt me." She squinted up at him through the darkness. He cupped his hands around her head and kissed her again, fiercely and thoroughly, allowing his hunger for her to dull the edge of his caution.

Elisabeth felt something jab into the small of her back.

"Ease away from the girl, thief-taker, or the next sound you hear will be that of my finger squeezing the trigger." Thomas's voice. Thomas's gun pressing into her back.

Cain slowly dropped his hand from her head.

"And raise your arms high in the air. Higher!" He grabbed Elisabeth and twisted her arm behind her back. He trained his pistol on Cain. "Now very slowly, and very carefully, I want you to walk down into the crater. I say carefully because I'll have my pistol aimed at your wife and it's already misfired once today."

"Our conflict has nothing to do with her, Penmarck. Let her go."

"Nothing to do with her? It has *everything* to do with her. Start walking. And remember, carefully. Very carefully."

When they reached the floor of the crater, Thomas threw an object at Cain's feet. "Your tinderbox, Stephen. I return it to you. But it appears you've outgrown your fear of the dark. Even so, take off your cloak and set fire to it. I shouldn't want you to miss the evening's festivities because of darkness. And remember. My gun is still leveled at the back of your wife's skull."

With no other choice available to him, Cain did as he was told, and when the cloak was aflame he looked back toward Thomas who stood with his forearm braced across Elisabeth's neck.

"Now the bandoleer and boots. I imagine burning jackboots will provide light for quite a lengthy amount of time."

Off came one boot, then the other. When the bandoleer joined the fire, Thomas smiled his satisfaction. "You don't look so brave without your knives. You'll look even less brave without your sword." He nodded toward Cain's hip. "Leave it in its scabbard and slide it this way."

Cain unfastened it from the frog at his left hip and shot it across the floor of the crater toward Thomas. "Do we meet in hand-to-hand combat now," he sneered, "or are you too comfortable hiding behind a woman to face me like a man? You wanted me dead. But you were too much the coward to kill me yourself. You wanted my father dead, but you were too spineless to do your own dirty work then too. It was much easier to hire someone to be brave for you. Well, your thrall is dead, uncle, so it appears you'll have to sully your own hands tonight. Will you face me, man to man? Or does your bravery come to the fore at no other time except when you confront feeble old men?"

Thomas's dunking in the East Dart had robbed him of his wig and wreaked havoc on his face paint, eroding it into grotesque splotches that likened him to the leper of biblical lore. With the glow from the fire highlighting the freakish placement of his cosmetic, he looked quite mad. "You think me less than a man?" he fired at Cain, voice shaking. "You're all the same, aren't you—you people with your flawless limbs and brawny backs. You're so haughty with your perfection. You have no right to be! Below the waist we all function the same, don't we, nephew? Below the waist there *is* no superiority. Do you think your wife will be able to note the difference between uncle and nephew when I mount her? Have you taught her well of the marriage bed?" He shifted his hand from her throat to her breast. Elisabeth bit her lip in disgust. "I should thank you in advance for the use of your wife, Stephen. It does seem rather ironic that whatever is yours eventually finds its way into my hands. You can be assured I will delight in using these hands to uncover all the secrets she has hidden from me these many years."

Cain looked beyond him, toward the crest of the tor. His lips curled with loathing but his eyes reflected another emotion. "Behind you," he cautioned.

Thomas laughed. "Do you think me so much the fool as to turn around? Caution all you like, nephew, but I will not be duped by your trickery."

Cain's eyes did not waver from the crest of the tor. "We stand on the summit of Hound Tor. If you have a care to know how it came by its name, I suggest you turn around. But not too quickly, Uncle. I'm told that wild dogs are drawn by swift movements."

Indecision restructured Thomas's face. He narrowed his eyes at Cain as if searching for the truth, then, unable to contain his curiosity, he leveled his forearm once more across Elisabeth's throat. With his gun poised at her right temple, he shot a look behind his shoulder.

Elisabeth chose that moment to act. Twisting her head to the right, she found his wrist with her teeth and bit down hard into his flesh. He screamed, and as he tried to wrest his hand from her mouth she pushed upward on his gun arm. Cain lunged forward. He caught Thomas's right wrist within the vise of his mighty fist and began to squeeze.

Thomas's hand numbed. He cried out. The gun fell to the ground. Elisabeth ducked beneath his arm and spun away from him. She riveted her eyes on the crown of the tor.

There was nothing there. It was deserted. Cain had deceived him.

Berserk with rage Cain ground his fingers into the back of Thomas's neck and propelled him against a boulder. Thomas hit the rock full force with his chest and knees. He staggered backward, ready to collapse, but Cain caught his shoulder, spun him around, and drove his fist into his face, catapulting him back against the boulder.

"Tell me again how you would have used my wife!" Cain roared, closing in on him.

Blood spurted from Thomas's nose, from his cheekbone. He angled his arms upward to protect his face, but Cain wasn't interested in his face.

"Tell me!" Bunching the brocade of Thomas's waist-vest in his fists, Cain lifted him against the boulder, then drove his knee upward between his legs.

Thomas howled insanely. Cain flung him to the ground then stood over the writhing heap he made. "I await your answer, Uncle. Speak!" He whipped Thomas's sword from its sheath and trained the point at his throat. "What would you have done to my wife?" His voice was calm, deadly.

Thomas nudged his head upward from where he was

doubled over, broken and bloody. "Nothing," he whimpered. "I would have done nothing!" And then his whimpers turned to tears that glistened on the perverted planes of his face. "Damn you to hell!" he choked, shoulders quaking. "I *can't* do anything. Does that p-please you? I've *never* been able to do anything! Damn you!"

Cain stared at him, stunned, but he held the blade steady while Thomas strangled on his sobs.

"I didn't want Maidenstowe. I didn't care about the girl's wealth. I wanted *her*. Can't you understand? She caused me to stir! I could look at her and feel what a man is supposed to feel! No one had ever made me feel that way before. No whore. No lady. Only Elisabeth. I thought with her . . . it would be different for me. I have to find out. Don't you see? I want to feel what every man has felt. I want Elisabeth. She can help me sustain the feeling. I know she can. Please, Stephen. Help me with this one thing. I'll give everything back to you. I swear it. Just don't take her from me!"

Cain peered down at the pitiful creature who was his uncle—this man who had been the primary driving force in his life for twenty-four years—this man he had vowed to kill with his bare hands. Hatred for the man had been his lifeblood. But he saw now he hadn't hated a man; he'd hated an image. Skagg had lied to him. Thomas had never used a woman. Thomas was incapable of using a woman. This man he had loathed for twenty-four years was not a man at all.

He tightened his fist around the hilt of the sword, but as he prepared to thrust the point into Thomas's neck he heard Skagg's dying plea again, and he hesitated. He saw again the terrible lines of hatred that had been etched into Skagg's face, and he suddenly knew that if he followed the man's directive to kill Thomas, he would be as good as etching that first line of hatred into his own face, into his own soul. Two months ago he would have driven the blade home without a twinge of conscience. But now, there was Elisabeth. She had shown him how to live without bitterness and hatred and he cherished those lessons too much to destroy them now. The life he had come to share with her was more precious than anything he had ever known. He would not throw it all away now to avenge something that God had avenged for him.

He hurled Thomas's sword toward the crest of the tor. "You pathetic, mincing little creature," he spurned. "You're not worth killing."

He left him there, without a backward glance, and strode to where Elisabeth stood. She held his scabbard out to him. He cupped his hand beneath her chin. "Your jaw," he said, marking the bruise. "He hurt you."

She shook her head in denial. "I'm fine. Relieved, thankful, and most anxious to be off this mountaintop."

Cain scanned their surroundings then nodded toward the west. "This way." But as they started to climb, Elisabeth turned back to the place where the fire was still burning.

"Your knives."

Cain cast a final look at the burning mass. "Knives are the weapons of hunters. I no longer need them, Elisabeth. I've found what I've been hunting for."

And so it was that as husband and wife reached the bottom of the tor and mounted the husband's war-horse, the man who still remained on the summit of the tor came slowly to his senses. He struggled to his feet and in the waning firelight began to climb toward the crown of the tor. He reached the crest and, scaling over the ridge, descended into blackness.

He heard the sounds quite suddenly. Below him. To his right. Scratching. Skittering. "Stephen?" he shouted.

He saw their iridescent eyes then, and heard their growls, and as he reached for the rapier that wasn't there, they were suddenly upon him.

A half mile to the north Elisabeth heard the howl—an agonized, inhuman howl—while on the slopes of Hound Tor, the wild dogs who prowled among the crags were providing a source of undefiled pleasure for the carrion birds who would greet the dawn.

epilogue

In the great house of Maidenstowe Lady Elisabeth Penmarck lent a discriminating eye to the portraits she'd ordered removed from the walls of the drawing room. In the year since her marriage, she had divided her time between Thirlstane and Maidenstowe, but for the past six months, during her confinement at Maidenstowe, she'd had precious little time to devote to such domestic pursuits as portrait rearrangement. Today, with Cain busy in Quintus's study and the twins asleep, she decided she would plot out exactly where the portraits would be re-hung.

The drawing room had a new look about it. The screaming red wallcover had been stripped and re-covered with silver green japanned paper. And the St. Mary barons, viscounts, and earls now kept company with the portraits of Quintus's six wives. Elisabeth decided the women had served enough years in the obscurity of the withdrawing room. It was time to reacquaint them with the rest of the family.

The most recent addition to the portrait gallery was the oil that had been completed only last week. She walked toward the fireplace, where the eight-foot painting leaned against the wall, and smiled at the faces whose likenesses had been set to canvas.

Cain had refused to sit for a portrait without Elisabeth and the babies, so she decided to part with tradition and had commissioned a group portrait. She was delighted with the outcome. She looked very much herself seated in a chair with Stephen in her lap. And Cain, standing behind her chair with Cicely in his arm, looked—she eyed him with wifely appreciation—magnificent. He was quite fetching in his ruffled shirt and black velvet waistcoat, with his hair long, and trimmed, and tied at his nape. He no longer looked a thief-taker, but neither did he look entirely a gentleman for there was still that about him which lent itself more to danger than drawing rooms. It was the danger she still saw lurking in the pale blue of his eyes, even in the portrait. She had once guessed his hunger for passion would be incessant. In that she had been correct, but she thrived on that passion. She could quicken at the very thought of his hands on her flesh, of his mouth on her—

"Might I interest my lady in some gentle sport while the babes entertain themselves with sleep?"

She jumped at the touch of his hand on her throat then welcomed his caress as he kissed her hard on the mouth. He tasted of morning chocolate and manly lust, and she slipped her fingers beneath his waistcoat to hold him near while he brushed his knuckles the length of her cheek, then her throat. "The babes will no doubt awaken within the quarter hour," she whispered against his lips.

Cain shot a look at the two cradles that sat near the hearth. "Then we'll have a need to hurry."

She stayed the hand that sought the ribbon tie at her waist. "Do you forget, m'lord, that I have contented you once this morning already?"

"I have not forgotten, lady. 'Tis the reason I seek you out. The memory lingers and craves to be repeated." He found her mouth again, but remembering her duties, Elisabeth flattened her palms on his chest and pushed him gently yet firmly away.

"The walls have been bare long enough, Cain. Allow me to finish what I'm about and then"—she graced him with a wicked smile—"you may finish what you are about."

He returned her smile. The glow kindling in his eyes turned hot. "Be quick, lady. Remember, I am not a patient man."

But Elisabeth knew that to be untrue. In the past twelve months he had demonstrated patience and gentleness in abundance, not only with her, but also with the twins, the servants, the children in the workhouse. He had proven himself to be everything Thomas never could have been, and as the weeks and months passed, she discovered more about him to cherish, to love. "Perhaps if you helped with the rearrangement, we might put a quick end to this business."

"If I were to help with the rearrangement, I fear your noble barons and viscounts would find themselves hanging from places other than the drawing room wall. Must you re-hang them, lady? I have seen pleasanter things decaying in the Thames."

"These people are your children's forebears," she chastised him.

"Do you think it absolutely necessary that we tell them?"

Elisabeth shook her head. "The St. Mary men may not have been endowed with the exceptional looks of the Penmarcks, but that is no reason for you to act so smug, husband. Artists' renderings can sometimes be inaccurate. *Your* portrait, for instance."

"*My* portrait?" He eyed the eight-foot canvas before him. "What do you find amiss with my portrait?"

"The thumbs."

"The thumbs?" He held his hands up before his face and rotated them slowly so he could scrutinize the aforementioned digits. "What is wrong with my thumbs?"

"Nothing is wrong with them, my love, but the artist should have made them . . . bigger. Much bigger."

Cain frowned. Elisabeth laughed at his confusion. "Do not ask. I fear you would not believe me, but trust me when I tell you that Emma is privy to much more than one might think." Her gaze drifted to a nearby chair where she spied a wooden writing case. "Is that Quintus's writing case?" She hadn't seen it since last year. She assumed Frith had placed it in her grandfather's study, but she had lacked the fortitude to sort through his papers and personal effects in the past months. Cain had volunteered to begin the process today.

Cain spun round. "I'd nearly forgotten. I believe I have a pleasant surprise for you, Elisabeth. Something I found in your grandfather's study." He strode to the chair, opened the case, and removed a sheet of parchment. Elisabeth watched him without moving. Quintus remained a painful area in her life, but she was learning to cope with her feelings, just as she knew Cain was learning to cope with his.

"I think it would be best if you sat down while you read this."

Something cold settled in her bones. "What is it, Cain? You're frightening me."

He smiled his reassurance as he escorted her to a chair. "You've nothing to fear, love. Just sit"—he pressed her into a chair—"and read." He handed her the parchment.

Unsure, she cast a furtive glance at the parchment. The words were penned in Quintus's script and addressed to her, and seeing this, she allowed her gaze to linger. She lit on the date. "He wrote this on the fourth of May. That was the night—" She didn't finish her sentence. They both knew what had happened that night.

"Read it aloud, Elisabeth."

Inhaling a calming breath, she did as she was bade. "'My Dear Elisabeth, Now that I've decided to start celebrating life, I feel as if I owe you a confession. You once asked me if I loved any of my six wives, and I told you most certainly not. That, I regret, was a bald-faced lie. I loved them in my own way, but a man is not at his ease discussing such matters in the open. These things are better left to the privacy and silence of quill and ink. I write you of this matter now because I have just finished penning a missive to Moreleigh, and in it, I inform him of something I have never been at my ease to tell you. I'"—her voice faltered as she saw the words—"'I love you, young woman. It might not be important for you to hear the words, but it's important for me to say them. I wish I had said them long before now, but sometimes it takes a man eighty-four years to unhitch his tongue. I know I said I was going to start celebrating life, and I intend to do that, but with this said, I can die with a clear conscience. Not that that event will take place anytime soon, mind you. I fully expect to be walking the halls of Maidenstowe for another eighty-four years.'"

A teardrop trickled off her chin and splashed onto the parchment, blurring the ink. Cain had not moved from her side. Bending down, he kissed the crown of her head. "You always had a place in his heart, Elisabeth. I spent little time with the man, but to me his feelings were apparent. He loved you deeply, as do I."

Elisabeth scattered her tears across her cheeks. "He did love me," she sniffed, her heart swelling with emotion.

"And you have more than a memory of his spoken word. You have something that will be a reminder of that love . . . forever."

Nodding silently, she cradled Cain's hand against her cheek, and when she heard a whimper from one of the cradles, she waited for a moment to regain her self-possession then stood up and made her way to the babies.

They both still slept soundly so she smoothed their coverlets over their backs and touched her hand to Cicely's tiny head. "Three months old tomorrow," she mused, her voice still trembling. "Emma says they resemble my father. Frith says they look like Quintus." She dragged her hand across her eyes then looked to the place where the portraits from the withdrawing room were lined against the wall. "I

rather think Cicely looks like Quintus's second wife. Or
. . . or perhaps his third. What do you think, Cain?"

He walked up behind her. He loosed the ribbon tie at her
waist, parted the fabric over her milk-swollen breasts, and
then with slowness and mastery, he showed her what he
thought.